THE SHEIKH'S CONVENIENT PRINCESS

BY
LIZ FIELDING

MILLS & BOON

First Published in Great Britain 2017
By Mills & Boon, an imprint of HarperCollins*Publishers*
1 London Bridge Street, London, SE1 9GF

© 2017 Liz Fielding

ISBN: 978-0-263-92272-1

23-0217

Our policy is to use papers that are natural, renewable and recyclable products and made from wood grown in sustainable forests. The logging and manufacturing processes conform to the legal environmental regulations of the country of origin.

Printed and bound in Spain
by CPI, Barcelona

Romantic Getaways
Escape to Paradise!

This Valentine's Day escape to four of the world's most romantic destinations with these sparkling books from Mills & Boon Romance!

From the awe-inspiring desert to vibrant Barcelona, and from the stunning coral reefs of Australia to heart-stoppingly romantic Venice—get swept away by these wonderful romances!

The Sheikh's Convenient Princess
by Liz Fielding

The Unforgettable Spanish Tycoon
by Christy McKellen

The Billionaire of Coral Bay
by Nikki Logan

Her First-Date Honeymoon
by Katrina Cudmore

Liz Fielding was born with itchy feet. She made it to Zambia before her twenty-first birthday and, gathering her own special hero and a couple of children on the way, lived in Botswana, Kenya and Bahrain—with pauses for sightseeing pretty much everywhere in between. She now lives in the west of England, close to the Regency grandeur of Bath and the ancient mystery of Stonehenge, and these days leaves her pen to do the travelling.

For news of upcoming books visit Liz's website: www.lizfielding.com.

I'm dedicating this, my 65th title, to my wonderful readers—some of whom have been with me from the first Friday in December 1992, when my first book, *An Image of You*, was published. You are my inspiration.

CHAPTER ONE

'Bram...'

Bram Ansari had answered the phone without looking up from a document that had just arrived by courier. 'Hamad... I was about to call you.'

'Then you've received the summons to Father's birthday *majlis*.'

'It arrived ten minutes ago. I imagine I have you to thank for that.'

'No. It's his wish. He's sick, Bram. It's a significant birthday. You need to be home.'

His brother did not sound particularly happy at the prospect.

'I doubt everyone thinks that.'

'It's covered. The old man has negotiated a secret deal with the Khadri family.'

'A deal?' Bram frowned. 'What kind of deal?' The last time he'd seen Ahmed Khadri the man had threatened to cut his throat if he ever stepped foot in Umm al Basr. 'Tell me.'

As his brother explained the secret deal his father had negotiated to enable Bram to return home the colour leached out of the day until the sky, the sea, the flowers overflowing the tower turned grey.

'No...'

'I'm sorry, Bram, but at least you're prepared. If Bibi

hadn't managed to smuggle a note to her sister you would have been presented with a *fait accompli*.'

'You think I can go through with this?'

'It's the price that must be paid.'

'But I won't be the one paying it!' He took a breath. 'How is your family?' he asked, cutting Hamad short when he would have argued. 'The new baby?'

'*In sh'Allah*, all my precious girls are thriving. Safia sends her fondest wishes and thanks for the gifts.' He hesitated. 'She said to say that you are always in her prayers.'

Bram ended the call then swept the invitation from the table in impotent fury. The longed-for chance to kneel at his father's feet and beg his forgiveness had come attached to a tangle of string that would take more than prayers to unravel. It would need a miracle.

The phone beeped, warning him that he had a missed call. He glanced at the screen and ignored it. His aide was spending a long weekend with friends in the Alps and the last thing he needed right now was a joyous description of the snow conditions.

Qa'lat al Mina'a, perched high on its rocky promontory, shimmered like a mirage in the soft pink haze of the setting sun.

Far below, beyond a perfect curve of white sand, a dhow was drifting slowly along the coast under a dark red sail and for a brief moment Ruby felt as if she might have been transported back into some *Arabian Nights* fantasy, flying in on a magic carpet rather than a gleaming black helicopter.

The illusion was swiftly shattered as they circled to land.

The fortress might appear, at first glance, to be a picturesque ruin, a reminder of a bygone age, but behind the mass of purple bougainvillaea billowing against its walls was a satellite dish, antennae—all the trappings of the communications age, powered by an impressive range of solar panels facing south where the *jebel* fell away to the desert.

And the tower did not stand alone. Below it she glimpsed courtyards, arches, gardens surrounding an extensive complex that spread down to the shore where a very twenty-first century gunmetal-grey military-style launch was sheltered in a harbour hewn from the rock. And they were descending to a purpose-built helipad. This was not some romantically crumbling stronghold out of a fantasy; the exterior might be battered by weather and time but it contained the headquarters of a very modern man.

As they touched down, a middle-aged man in a grey robe and skullcap approached the helicopter at a crouching run. He opened the door, glanced at her with astonishment and then shouted something she couldn't hear to the pilot.

He returned a don't-ask-me shrug from his seat. Sensing a problem, Ruby didn't wait but unclipped her safety belt, swung open the door and jumped down.

'*As-salaam aleykum. Ismee*, Ruby Dance,' she said, raising her voice above the noise of the engine. 'Sheikh Ibrahim is expecting me.'

She didn't wait for a response but shouldered the neat satchel that contained everything she needed for work, nodded her thanks to the pilot and, leaving the man to follow with her wheelie suitcase, she crossed to steps that led down to the shelter of the courtyard below.

The air coming off the sea was soft and moist—bliss after hours cooped up in the dry air of even the most luxurious private jet—while below her were tantalising glimpses of terraces cut into the hill, each shaded by ancient walls and vine-covered pergolas. There was a glint of water running through rills and at her feet clove-scented dianthus and thyme billowed over onto the steps.

It was beautiful, exotic, unexpected. Not so far from the fantasy after all.

Behind her the pilot, keen to get home, was already winding up the engine and she lifted her head to watch the helicopter take off, bracing herself against buffeting from the down force of the blades. As it wheeled away back towards the capital of Ras al Kawi, leaving her cut off from the outside world, she half lifted a hand as if to snatch it back.

'*Madaam...*'

Despite her confident assertion that she was expected, it was clear that her arrival had come as a surprise but, before she could respond to the agitated man who was following her down the steps, a disembodied voice rang out from below, calling out something she did not understand.

Before she could move, think, the owner of the voice was at the foot of the steps, looking up at her, and she forgot to breathe.

Sheikh Ibrahim al-Ansari was no longer the golden prince, heir to the throne of Umm al Basr, society magazine cover favourite—a carefree young man with nothing on his mind but celebrating his sporting triumphs in some fashionable nightclub.

Disgraced, disinherited and exiled from his father's court when his arrest for a naked romp in a London fountain had made front page news, his face was harder, the bones more defined, the natural lines cut a little deeper. And not just lines. Running through the edge of his left brow, slicing through his cheekbone before disappearing into a short-clipped beard was a thin scar—the kind left by the slash of a razor-sharp knife—and dragging at the corner of his eye and his lip so that his face was not quite in balance. The effect was brutal, chilling, mesmerising.

He was never going to be the beast—his bone structure beneath the silky golden skin was too perfect, the tawny eyes commanding and holding all her attention, but he was no longer the beautiful young man who had appeared in society magazines alongside European aristocrats, millionaires, princes. Whose photograph, trophy in hand, had regularly graced the covers of the glossier lifestyle magazines.

She was momentarily distracted by a flash of pink as a droplet of water, caught in the sun's dying rays, slid down one of the dark, wet curls that clung to his neck.

She was standing with her back to the setting sun and he raised a hand to shade his eyes. 'What the devil?'

Mouth dry, brain freewheeling and with no connection between them, her lips parted but her breath stuck in her throat as a second drop of water joined the first, hung there until the force of gravity overcame it and it dropped to a wide shoulder, slid into the hollow of his collarbone.

She watched, mesmerised, as it spilled over, trickled down his broad chest, imagining how it would feel against her hand if she reached out to capture it.

The thought was so intense that she could feel the tickle of chest hair against her palm, the wet, sun-kissed skin, and instinctively closed her hand.

She hadn't expected him to be wearing a pin-striped suit or the formal flowing robes of a desert prince, but it was her first encounter with an employer wearing nothing but a towel—a man whose masculinity was underlined by the scars left by his chosen sports.

'Who are you?' he demanded.

Not some empty-headed ninny to stand there gawping at the kind of male body more usually seen in moody adverts for aftershave, that was for sure, and, sending an urgent message to her feet, she stepped down to his level.

'Not the devil, Sheikh.' She uncurled her clenched hand and offered it to him as she introduced herself. 'Ruby

Dance. I've been sent by the Garland Agency to hold the fort while Peter Hammond recovers from his injuries.'

Sheikh Ibrahim stared at her hand for what felt like forever, then, ignoring it, he looked up.

'Injuries?' Dark brows were pulled down in a confused frown. 'What injuries?'

She lowered her hand. Well, that explained the confusion at her arrival. Obviously the message about his aide's accident had failed to reach him.

'I understand that Mr Hammond crashed off his snow-board early this morning,' she replied, putting his lapse of manners down to shock. 'I was told that he'd spoken to you.'

'Then you were misinformed,' he said. 'How bad is it?'

'The last I heard was that he'd been airlifted to hospital. I'll see if I can get an update.' She took her phone from her bag. 'Will I get a signal?' He didn't bother to answer but she got five strong bars—those antennae weren't just for show—and hit the first number on her contact list.

There were endless seconds of waiting for the international connection—endless seconds in which he continued to stare at her. It was the look of someone who was sure he'd seen her before but couldn't think where.

'Ruby? Is everything okay?' Amanda Garland, the founder of the Garland Agency, had called her first thing, asking her to drop whatever she was doing, fly out to Qa'lat al Mina'a and hold the fort until other arrangements could be made.

'Yes…'

'Tell me.' There was no fooling Amanda.

Ruby swallowed, took a breath. She was imagining it, she knew. It had been years since her photograph had been all over the media, but his sculptured chest, the smattering of hair arrowing down beneath the towel—far too reminiscent of that scene in the fountain—was wrecking her concentration.

In an attempt to get a grip, she turned away, focusing on the sea, the misted shape of the dhow far below, dropping its sails as it turned to edge up the creek.

'Ruby!'

'Everything's fine,' Ruby said quickly. 'The flight went without a hitch but my arrival has come as something of a surprise. It seems that Sheikh Ibrahim did not get the message about Peter's accident.'

'What?' Amanda was clearly shocked. 'I'm so sorry, Ruby. Is there anything I can do? Do you want me to speak to the Sheikh?'

'All I need is an update on Mr Hammond's condition.' Amanda gave her the details. 'And which hospital…? Thanks—that will be perfect. I'll speak to you later.' She disconnected.

'Well?' he demanded as she turned to him, keeping her gaze fixed on his face. Tawny eyes, a hawkish nose, a mouth with a one-sided tug that gave it a cruelly sensuous droop—

'Peter has broken his left leg in two places, torn a ligament in his wrist and cracked some ribs,' she said, blotting out the thoughts that had no place in a business environment—thoughts that she didn't want in her head. 'They've pinned him back together and he'll be flown home in a day or two. Amanda is going to text me contact details.'

'Who is Amanda?'

Hello, good to meet you and thank you for rushing to fill the gap would have been polite. *Thank you for putting my mind at rest* was pretty much a minimum in the circumstances. But Ruby had long ago learned to keep her expression neutral, to never show what she was thinking or feeling, and she focused on the question rather than his lack of manners.

'Amanda Garland.' The name would normally be enough but Sheikh Ibrahim did not work in London, where it was shorthand for the best in business and domestic staff. There was no smile of recognition, no gratitude for the fact that his injured aide's first thought had been to summon a replacement. 'The Garland Agency supplies temps, nannies and domestic staff to an international clientele. Amanda is also Peter's godmother.' She returned her phone to her bag and took out the heavy white envelope that she'd sent with the driver who'd picked her up. 'When he sent an SOS for someone to hold the fort, she called me. I have her letter of introduction.'

She'd already had her hand ignored once and did not make the mistake of offering it to him so that he could ignore the letter too, but waited for him to reach for it.

'A letter of introduction from someone I don't know?'

'Perhaps Mr Hammond thought you would trust his judgement.'

'How good would your judgement be if you were lying in the snow with a broken leg?' he demanded.

'Since that's never going to happen, I couldn't say.' Her voice was deadpan, disguising an uncharacteristic urge to scream. She'd been travelling for hours and right now she could do with a little of the famous regional hospitality and a minute or two to gather her wits. 'All I know is that his first concern was to ensure that you weren't left without assistance.'

His only response was an irritated grunt.

Okay, enough…

'Your cousin, His Highness the Emir of Ras al Kawi, will vouch for her bona fides,' she assured him, as if she was used to casually bandying about the names of the local royals. 'Her Highness Princess Violet entrusted Amanda with the task of finding her a nanny.'

'I don't need a nanny.'

'That's fortunate because I've never changed a nappy in my life.' Her reputation for calm under pressure was being put to the test and there had been an uncharacteristic snap to her response that earned her the fractional lift of an insolent brow. 'Miss Garland's note contains the names of some of the people I've worked for, should you require reassurance regarding my own capabilities,' she continued, calling on previously untested depths of calm.

'Will I have heard of them?' he asked, with heavy emphasis on *them*.

Since she had no way of knowing who he'd heard of, she assumed the question was not only sarcastic but rhetorical. Choosing not to risk another demonstration of the power of that eyebrow, she made no comment.

In the face of her silence he finally held out his hand for the letter, ripping open the flap with the broad tip of his thumb.

His face gave nothing away as he scanned the contents but he turned to the man holding her suitcase, spoke to him in Arabic before, with a last thoughtful look at her, he said, 'I'll see you in my office in fifteen minutes, Miss Dance.'

With that, he turned away, his leather flip-flops slapping irritably as he crossed the stone terrace before disappearing down steps that led to a lower level.

Shakily, Ruby let out her breath.

Whew. Double *whew*, with knobs on. Forget the grateful thanks for dropping everything and flying here at a moment's notice—that had been tense. On the other hand, now that he'd taken his naked torso out of sight and she could think clearly, she could understand his reluctance to take her at face value.

It wasn't personal.

Doubtless, there had been attempts to breach his security in the past, although whether for photographs of his isolated hideout, gossip on who he was sharing it with, or

insider information on who was about to get the golden
touch of Ansari financial backing was anyone's guess.

Any one of them would be worth serious money and
an unexpected visitor was always going to get the hard
stare and third degree. She, more than anyone, could understand that.

Easy to say—as she followed the servant through an
ancient archway and down a short flight of steps, her skin
was goosebumped, her breath catching in her throat—but
it felt very personal.

At the bottom of the steps, sheltered from the sea by
stone walls and from the heat of the summer by pergolas
dripping with blue racemes of wisteria, scented with the
tiny white stars of jasmine, was a terrace garden.

She stopped, entranced, her irritation melting away.

'*Madaam?*' the servant prompted, bringing her back to
the reason she was there, and she turned to him.

'*Sho Ismak?*' She asked his name.

He smiled, bowed. '*Ismi* Khal, *madaam.*'

She placed her hand against her chest and said, '*Ismi*,
Ruby.' Then, with a gesture at the garden, 'This is lovely.
Jameel,' she said, calling on the little Arabic she'd learned
during working trips to Dubai and Bahrain and topped up
on the long flight from London.

'*Nam.* It is beautiful,' he said carefully, demonstrating his own English with a broad smile, before turning to
open the door to a cool tiled lobby, slipping his feet from
his sandals as he stepped inside.

She had no time to linger, admire the exquisite tiles
decorating the walls, but, familiar with the customs of the
region, she followed his example and slipped off her heels
before padding after him.

He opened the door to a large, comfortably furnished
sitting room, crossed the room to draw back shutters and
open a pair of doors that led onto a small shaded area over-

looking the sea. There was a rush of air, the scent of the sea mingled with jasmine and, despite the less than enthusiastic welcome and her own misgivings about coming here, she sighed with pleasure.

When Amanda had explained that Sheikh Ibrahim was sitting out his exile in a fort in Ras al Kawi, his maternal grandmother's native home, she had imagined something rugged, austere. It was all that, but below the ancient fortress a home, a garden, had been carved from the shelter of the hillside.

The man might be a grouch but this place was magical.

Khal was all set to give her the full guided tour of the suite, starting with the tiny kitchen, but she had just a few minutes to freshen up and get her head straight before she had to report to Sheikh Ibrahim.

'*Shukran*, Khal.' She tapped her watch to indicate that she was short of time. 'Where… *Ayn…?*' She mimed typing and he smiled, then took her to the door, pointed at the steps leading down.

'*Marra,*' he said, and held up one finger, then, '*Marrataan.*' Two fingers.

Once, twice?

'*Etnaan?* Two floors?'

He nodded, then rattled something off that she had no chance of understanding, before heading off down them.

Bram had showered on the beach when he came out of the sea but he stood in his wet room with cold water pouring off him while he caught his breath, recovered from that moment when he'd looked up and seen the dark, foreshortened silhouette of Ruby Dance against the sky and his heart had stopped.

In that split second he'd imagined every possible drama that would have brought Safia flying north to Ras al Kawi. To him. When Ruby Dance, and not Safia, had stepped out of the shadow, the complex rush of disappointment, guilt had hit him like a punch in the gut.

Her hair was the same dark silk as Safia's but it had been cut in short, feathery layers. Her eyes were not the rare blue-green that was the legacy of Iskandar's army, who'd fought and scattered their seed every inch of the way along the Gulf to India, but the cool blue-grey of a silver fox. She was a little taller and, while her voice had the same soft, low musical tones that wrapped around a man's heart, when she spoke it was with that clear precision—as English as a rainy day—of the privileged aristocratic women he'd known in Europe.

What she did have in common with Safia was a rare stillness, a face that gave no hint of what she was thinking or feeling.

Schooled to obedience—accepting without question a marriage arranged to keep the peace between their warring families when they were children—Safia would have played the role of perfect wife, borne his children, never by so much as a breath betraying her love for another man.

The arrival of a courier that morning bearing the summons home, and the difficult call from his brother, had stirred up long-buried memories, bringing Safia's image so vividly to mind that it had taken time for his brain to catch up with what his eyes were telling him. A seemingly endless moment when everything dead within him had stirred, quickened and he'd come close to taking her hand to draw her close. To step back five years and, if only for a moment, be the man he was meant to be. Husband, father, heir to his father's throne.

He shook his head, grabbed a towel and scrubbed at his face to erase the treacherous thought and concentrate on what Ruby Dance had said about Peter.

A badly broken leg, a wrist that would be out of action for weeks, the agony of cracked ribs; the timing couldn't be worse. There were a number of projects requiring his undivided attention and, after five long years of exile, the longed-for call home with a sting in the tail…

He glanced at the letter of introduction, picked up his phone and keyed Amanda Garland into the search engine.

Her reputation—clients who were prepared to publicly laud her to the skies, a Businesswoman of the Year award, an honour from Queen Elizabeth—was as impressive as the list of people she'd offered as a reference.

He'd asked the Dance woman if he would have heard of any of them and the fact was that he'd met all of them. If she was used to working at this level she must be seriously good at her job and, unlike Peter, she wouldn't be itching to disappear into the desert for days at a time with a camera.

Ruby wasted no time in stripping off and stepping into the walk-in shower. She let the hard needles of water stream over her for one long minute, stimulating, refreshing, bringing her body back to life.

It was warmer here than in London, than on the air conditioned jet, and she abandoned her dark grey trouser suit in favour of a lightweight knee-length skirt and linen top. And, having already experienced the ancient steps, she slipped on a pair of black ballet flats.

She still had a few minutes and used them to check her phone for Amanda's text, copying the details of the hospital onto one of the index cards she carried with her before going in search of Sheikh Ibrahim's office.

The evening was closing in. The sea was flat calm, the sky ranging from deep purple in the east to pale pinks and mauves in the west while, in the shadows, tiny solar lights twined around the pergolas and set amongst the casual planting, were blinking on, shining through leaves, glinting on a ripple of water trickling down through rocks.

The garden had a quiet magic and she could have stood

there for hours letting the peace seep into her bones. She took one last look then, out of time, she walked down to the next level where, in a corner, a few shrivelled fruits still clung to a pomegranate tree.

She found another flight of steps half hidden behind the thick stems of the bougainvillaea that softened the tower wall. These were narrower, skirting the cliff face with only a wall that did not reach the height of her shoulder to protect her from a nerve-tingling drop onto the rocks below. She did not linger and, precisely fifteen minutes later, as instructed by the Sheikh, she stepped down into a courtyard where concealed lights washed the walls, turning it into an outside room.

Sheikh Ibrahim, wet hair slicked back and now wearing shorts and a loose-fitting T-shirt that hung from those wide shoulders, was sitting, legs stretched out, ankles crossed on the footrest of an old-fashioned cane planters' chair, smartphone in hand.

There was a matching chair on the other side of the low table.

She placed the card with the hospital details in front of him, slid back the footrest on the empty chair, removed her phone, tablet, notepad and pen from her satchel and, tidily tucking her skirt beneath her, sat down.

He looked at her for what seemed like endless minutes, a slight frown buckling the space between his eyes.

Ruby had learned the habit of stillness long ago. It was her survival technique; she'd schooled herself not to blink, blanking even the most penetrating of stares with a bland look that had unnerved both the disapproving, pitying adults who didn't know what to say to her and the jeering classmates who knew only too well.

Perhaps she'd become complacent. It was a long time since anyone had bothered to look beyond the image of the professional peripatetic PA that she presented to the world. Now, sitting in front of Sheikh Ibrahim, waiting for him to say something, say anything, it took every ounce of concentration to maintain her composure.

Maybe it was the memory of water dripping onto his bare shoulder, running down his chest, the certainty that he'd been naked beneath that towel that was messing with her head.

Or that his thighs, calves, ankles honed to perfection on horseback, on the blackest of black ski runs, were everything hinted at beneath the jodhpurs he'd been wearing on the *Celebrity* cover she'd downloaded to the file she'd created as soon as Amanda had called her. Confirmed in the photograph of him cavorting naked in a London fountain, one arm around a girl in transparently wet underwear as he'd poured a bottle of champagne over them both. The photograph that had cost him a throne.

Or maybe it was that she recognised the darkness in his eyes, an all-consuming hunger for redemption. It crossed the space between them and a shiver rippled through her as if he'd reached out and touched her.

'Jude Radcliffe tells me that he offered you a permanent position in his organisation,' he said at last. 'Why didn't you take it?'

'You talked to Jude?' Amanda hadn't held back when it came to references.

'Is that a problem?' He spoke softly, inviting her confidence. She was not fooled. His voice might be seductively velvet but it cloaked steel.

'No, but it is Sunday. I didn't think he'd be at the office.'

'He wasn't. I know him well enough to call him at home.' His response was casual enough, but she didn't miss the underlying warning; someone he knew on a personal basis would be totally frank.

'Did he tell you that his wife was once a Garland temp?' she asked, demonstrating her own familiarity with the family. 'It's how they met. She was expecting her second baby the last time I worked at Radcliffe Tower.' She picked up her phone and checked her diary. 'It's due next month.'

'You keep files on the people you work for?'

She looked up. 'The way they like their coffee, their favoured airlines, the name of their hairdresser, shirt collar size, the brand of make-up they use, important birthdays. They're the small details that make me the person they call when their secretaries are sick,' she said. 'They're the reason why their PAs check whether I'll be available before they make their holiday bookings.'

'You don't undersell yourself. I'm surprised you were free to fly here at such short notice.'

'I'd taken a week's holiday to do some decorating.'

'Decorating?' he repeated, bemused.

'Paint, wallpaper?'

'You do it yourself?'

'Most people do.' Obviously not multimillionaire sheikhs.

'And at the end of the week?'

Was he suggesting a longer stay? The thought both excited and unsettled her. 'Shall we see how it goes?'

His eyes narrowed. 'Are you suggesting that I am on some kind of probationary period, Ruby Dance?'

Yes... At least, no...

For a moment there was no sound. A cicada that had been tuning up intermittently fell silent, the waves lapping at the rocks below them stilled in that moment when the tide, suspended on the turn, paused to catch its breath.

She hadn't meant... Or maybe she had.

Deep breath, Ruby.

'My role is to provide emergency cover for as long as needed. A day, a week... I had assumed you would have someone to call on to stand in for Peter? Although...'

'Although?'

'If there had been anyone available to step into his shoes at a moment's notice I doubt he would have called his godmother.'

He gave her a thoughtful look but neither confirmed nor denied it, which suggested she was right.

'Do you have a file on me?' he asked.

Back on firmer ground, she flicked to the file she'd been compiling. 'It's missing a few details. I don't know your collar size,' she replied, looking up and inviting him to fill the gap in her records.

He shook his head. 'You are bluffing, Ruby Dance.'

'You like your coffee black with half a spoonful of Greek honey,' she replied. 'You have your own jet and helicopter—the livery is black with an A in Arabic script in gold on the tail—but, since you only travel once or twice a month, they are available for charter through Ansari Air, the company you set up for the purpose. The demand for this service apparently exceeded supply because you've since added two more executive jets and a second helicopter to your fleet. Should you need to travel when they are all busy you use Ramal Hamrah Airways, the airline owned by Sheikh Zahir al-Khatib, a cousin on your mother's side of the family. Your birthday is August the third, your father's birthday is…'

He held up a hand to stop her.

'The day after tomorrow.'

Amanda had passed on everything she knew about the man and the cabin crew on his private jet had been more than willing to share his likes and dislikes—anything, in fact, that would help her serve their boss. Like the entrepreneurs whose companies he had financed with start-up loans, they appeared to believe the sun shone out of the Sheikh's backside.

Perhaps he improved with acquaintance.

'You've made your point,' he admitted, 'but you haven't answered my question.'

'Jude offered me a very generous package as PA to his finance director,' she said, 'but I enjoy the variety offered by temping.'

Again there was that long, thoughtful look and for a moment she was sure he was going to challenge her on a response so ingrained, repeated so often, that she had almost come to believe it. His perceptiveness did not surprise her. A man who'd made a fortune in a few short years as a venture capitalist would need to read more than a business plan; he would have to be fluent in body language.

Under the circumstances, a man looking for a hidden agenda might well read her give-nothing-away stillness as a red flag and, since he wasn't about to divulge his collar size, she leaned forward and put the phone down.

'Radcliffe urged me to make other arrangements before the end of May,' Sheikh Ibrahim continued after a moment. 'He mentioned a wedding.' His glance dropped to her hand.

'Not mine.'

'No, I can see that you already wear a wedding ring. Your husband does not object to you working away from home?'

Her fingers tightened protectively against the plain gold band she wore on her right hand, the hand on which she knew they wore wedding rings—if they wore them at all— in this part of the world.

'It's a family ring,' she said. 'My grandmother wore it. And my mother. If I were married I would wear it on my left hand.' She looked up but he said nothing and she knew that he could not have cared less whether or not she was married or what her husband thought about her absences. That was the reason she temped. She was here today, gone tomorrow and no one, not even the person she was working for, had the time or inclination to concern themselves with her personal life. 'I'm booked to cover Jude's PA,' she said. 'She's getting married at the beginning of June. Hopefully, Peter Hammond's leg will be up to all these steps by then.'

Sheikh Ibrahim was saved from answering by the appearance of Khal, carrying a tray, which he placed in front of her.

'*Shaay, madaam,*' he said, indicating a small silver teapot.

'*Shukran*, Khal.' She indicated a second pot. 'And this?'

'That is mint tea,' Sheikh Ibrahim said before he could answer. 'I'm surprised you don't have a note of my preference in your file.'

'My files are always a work in progress, but I do have a note that, unusually, you take it without sugar. Would you like some now, Sheikh?'

'We're on first name terms here.' If her knowledge irritated him he kept the fact well hidden. 'Everyone calls me Bram.'

She was on first name terms with most of the men and women she temped for on a regular basis, but she hadn't seen any of them half naked.

It shouldn't matter, but somehow it did.

She glanced up at the sky, the stars beginning to blink on as the hood of darkness moved swiftly over them from the east, and took a steadying breath. When she looked back it occurred to her that she wasn't the only one struggling to hold onto at least the appearance of relaxation. She was pretty fluent in body language herself and, despite the way he was stretched out in that chair, he was, like her, coiled as tight as a spring.

'Would you like tea, Bram?' she managed, hoping that the slight wobble was just in her head.

Their gazes met and for a moment she felt dizzy. It wasn't his powerful thighs, shapely calves, those long sinewy feet stretched out in front of her like temptation. It was his eyes, although surely that dark glowing amber had to be a trick of the light? Or maybe she was hallucinating in the scent-laden air?

CHAPTER TWO

A PING FROM her phone warning her of an incoming text broke the tension. Bram nodded and, miraculously, Ruby managed to pour mint tea into a tall glass set in a silver holder and place it in front of him without incident.

As if he too needed a distraction, he reached for the card on which she'd written the hospital details, murmured something.

'I'm sorry?'

He shook his head. 'He's in Gstaad. I broke my ankle there years ago.'

'Remind me never to go there. It's clearly a dangerous place,' she added when he gave her a blank look.

Her Internet search for information had thrown up dozens of photographs of him in skin-hugging Lycra, hurtling down vertiginous ski runs, and with the resulting medals around his neck.

'Maybe,' he said, his eyes distant, no doubt thinking of a different life when he'd been a champion, a media darling, a future king.

'I'm sorry.'

He didn't ask her what she was sorry for and in truth she didn't know. If he wanted to ski, play polo, there was nothing to stop him, other than shame for having disgraced his family. Was giving it all up, leaving his A-list social life in Europe to live in this isolated place, atonement for scandalising the country he had been born to serve?

Or did he want the throne of Umm al Basr more than the rush of competition, the prizes and the glamorous women who hung around the kind of men who attracted photographers?

Was the hunger at the back of his eyes the need for forgiveness or determination to regain all he had lost?

He dropped the card back on the table.

'Call the hospital. Make sure they have all the details of Peter's medical insurance and tell them that whatever he needs above and beyond that he is to have. Talk to his mother,' he continued as she made a note on her pad. 'Liaise with her about flying him back to England as soon as he's able to travel. Make sure that there is a plane at their disposal and arrange for a private ambulance to pick him up and take him wherever he needs to go.'

She made another note. 'Is there any message?'

'You're a clumsy oaf?' he suggested, but without the smile that should have accompanied his suggestion.

She looked up. 'Will there be flowers with that?'

'What do you think?'

What she thought was that Peter Hammond hadn't crashed his snowboard for the sole purpose of annoying his boss although, if she'd been him, she might have been tempted to take a dive into the snow rather than spend one more day working for Bram Ansari.

What she said was, 'Get well soon is more traditional under the circumstances, but it's undoubtedly a man thing. I'm sure he'll get the message.'

She certainly did but, despite the cool reception, she had some sympathy. It was bad enough to have your routine disrupted by the drama of outside events without having a total stranger thrust into your life and, in Bram Ansari's case, his home.

He might be an arrogant jerk but she was there to en-sure that Peter's absence did not disturb his life more than absolutely necessary and she was professional enough to make that happen, with or without his co-operation. Not that she'd waste her breath saying so. The first few hours were show-not-tell time.

'No doubt he'll be as anxious to be back on his feet as you are for his return,' she said as she picked up the card and tucked it into her notebook. 'Unfortunately, bones can't be hurried.'

'I'm aware of that but Peter manages the day-to-day running of Qa'lat al Mina'a. Without him we don't eat.'

'Everything is flown in from the city, I imagine.' She could handle that. It wouldn't be the first time that run-ning a house had come within the remit of an assignment. 'What did people do here before?'

'Before?'

'Before there was a city with an air-conditioned mall selling luxuries flown in from around the world. Before there were helicopters to deliver your heart's desire to places such as this.'

He shrugged. 'They fished, kept livestock and there were camels to bring rice, spices, everything else.' He gave her another of those thoughtful looks. 'Have you ever wrung a chicken's neck, Ruby? Or slaughtered a goat?'

'Why?' she asked, not about to make his day with girl-ish squealing. 'Is that included in the job description?'

'There is no job description. Peter has an open-ended brief encompassing whatever is necessary.'

He was challenging her, she realised. Demanding to know if she was up to the job.

Clearly the quiet diligence she usually found most help-ful when dealing with a difficult employer wasn't going to work here, but they were stuck with each other until one of them cracked and summoned the helicopter.

'You're saying you make it up as you go along?' she asked, lobbing it right back because it wasn't ever going to be her. She couldn't afford the luxury.

'Is there a better way?'

'Personally, I'm working to a five-year plan,' she said, 'but, for the record, exactly how many goats has Peter Hammond slaughtered?'

A glint appeared in those amber eyes and a crease deepened at the corner of Bram Ansari's mouth. Not a smile, nothing like a smile; more a warning that she was living dangerously. Not that she needed it. She'd been aware of the danger from the moment she'd first set eyes on him.

'One?' she suggested. Then, when he didn't answer, 'Two?' Still nothing. 'More than two?'

'So far,' he admitted, 'he's managed to dodge that bullet by ensuring that the freezer is always fully stocked.'

'Much less messy,' she agreed briskly, 'and I'm sure the goats are grateful for his efficiency. If you'll point me in the direction of his office I'll attempt to follow his example.' Apparently she'd won that round because his only response was to wave a hand in the direction of a pair of open glazed doors leading from the terrace. 'And your office?'

'My office is wherever I happen to be.'

Having dished out the if-you're-so-damned-good-get-on-with-it treatment, he leaned back in the chair and closed his eyes.

She wasn't entirely convinced by his relaxed dismissal—she had won that round on points—but she picked up her glass, crossed the terrace, flipped on the light and kicked off her shoes as she entered Peter Hammond's office. She half expected to find a man cave but it was uncluttered, austere in its simplicity.

A huge rug, jewel-coloured and silky beneath her feet, covered the flagstone floor. The walls were bare ancient stone, hung with huge blow-ups of stunning black and white photographs: weathered rock formations; the spray of a waterfall frozen in a moment in time and so real that if she put a hand out she might feel it splashing through her fingers; a close-up of the suspicious eye of a desert oryx.

The only furniture was a battle-scarred desk and a good chair. The only item on the desk was a slender state-of-the-art laptop which, no doubt, had the protection of an equally state-of-the-art password.

She put her cup and bag on the desk, opened up the laptop and, sure enough, she got the prompt.

It wasn't the first time she'd been faced with this situation and she reached for the pull-out ledge under the desk top—the classic place to jot down passwords.

Nothing. While she approved of Peter Hammond's security savvy, on this occasion she would have welcomed a little carelessness. No doubt Bram Ansari was, at that moment, lying back in his recliner amusing himself by counting down the seconds until she called for help.

She sat down, checked the drawers.

They were not locked, but contained nothing more revealing than the fact that he had a weakness for liquorice allsorts and excellent taste in pens and notebooks.

A walk-in cupboard at the rear of the office contained shelves holding a supply of stationery on one wall and a neat array of box files. Against the other wall was a table containing a printer and a scanner.

She took down the file labelled 'Medical Insurance', carried it to the desk and, having found the relevant paperwork, discovered that there wasn't a phone. Of course not. There was no landline here—Bram had been holding the latest in smartphones, the same model as her own—and Peter would have his mobile phone with him.

Not a problem. She took her own phone from her bag—the cost of her calls would be added to his account—and saw the waiting text. Number unknown.

She clicked on it and read.

Amanda gave me your number, Ruby, so that I could give you the password for Peter's laptop. It's pOntefr@c! Can you let me have the details of his medical insurance when you have a moment? Good luck! Elizabeth Hammond.

She grinned. Pontefract—where the liquorice came from. She tried it and was in.

'Bless the man!' she said and called Elizabeth Hammond to pass on the insurance details, along with the rest of Bram Ansari's instructions.

'Heaven's, that was quick, Ruby. You're clearly as hot as Amanda said.'

If only the rest of the 'open-ended brief' was as simple…

'If there's any other information you need just call me on this number,' she said. 'How is Peter?'

'Sore but the breaks were clean and should heal without any permanent damage.'

'That is good news. Sheikh Ibrahim said to tell him that he's a clumsy oaf, which I assume is man-speak for get well soon.'

'It's going to be weeks, I'm afraid.'

'Weeks?'

'Can you manage that? Bram Ansari is…' She paused, called out to someone that she was coming, then said, 'I'm sorry, Ruby, but I ordered room service and it has just arrived. Thanks again for all your help.'

Ruby, phone at her cheek, wondered what Elizabeth Hammond had been about to say when she'd been interrupted.

Bram Ansari is difficult to work for? Bram Ansari is a pain in the butt? Bram Ansari is very easy on the eye?— a fact which did not cancel out the first two. She knew, no one better, that attractiveness, charm, in a man could hide a multitude of sins.

Obviously, she had no concerns on the charm front.

Bram watched from beneath hooded lids as Ruby Dance picked up her glass and disappeared into Peter's office.

Something about her bothered him and it wasn't just that first shocking moment when he'd thought she was Safia. It was nothing that he could put his finger on. She was clearly good at her job if a little waspish. No doubt she was simply responding to his own mood; Jude Radcliffe, not a man to bestow praise lightly, had said that he was very lucky that she'd been free. Apparently she had a memory like an elephant, was cool-headed in a crisis and was as tight-lipped as a clam. She certainly hadn't been fazed by his clumsy attempt to unsettle her, to get a feeling for the woman hiding behind that cool mask.

On the contrary, he felt as if he'd been in a fencing match and was lucky to have got away with a draw.

Only once he'd caught a momentary flash of irritation in those cool grey eyes. Such control was rare, a learned skill. That she'd taken the trouble to master it suggested that she had something to hide.

He thumbed her name into a search engine but all he came up with was a dance studio. That, too, was unusual. His curiosity aroused, he called up the security program he used when he ran an initial check on someone who was looking for financial backing. Again nothing.

No social media presence, no borrowing, not even a credit rating, which implied that she didn't have a credit card. Or maybe not one in that name. It was definitely time to go and check what she was up to in Peter's office.

He'd just swung his feet to the floor when his phone rang.

'Bram?'

The voice was sleepy, a bit slurred, but unmistakable.

'Peter…' No point in asking how he was; he would be floating on the residue of anaesthesia. 'I suppose you were trying to impress some leggy chalet maid?'

'You've got me,' he said, a soft chuckle abruptly shortened into an expletive as his ribs gave him a sharp reminder that it was no laughing matter. 'Next time I'll stay in bed and let her impress me.'

'Good decision. What's the prognosis?'

'Boredom, physio, boredom, physio. Repeat until done… What's the Garland Girl like?'

'Garland Girl?'

'That's what they were called before it became politically incorrect to call anyone over the age of ten a girl. She did turn up, didn't she? I told Amanda that it was urgent. Tried to tell you but your phone was busy and then…' He hesitated, clearly trying to remember what had happened next.

'Don't worry about it. She's here and right now staring at your laptop wondering where you hid your password. I was on my way to rescue her when you rang.'

'She won't need you to rescue her,' he said. 'Garland temps are the keyboard queens, the crème de la crème of the business world. Her job is to rescue you. Ask m'father,' he said. 'M'mother was one…' He coughed, swore again. 'She sends her love, by the way.'

'Please give her my best wishes. Is your father there?' he asked.

'He's at the UN until next week. Why?' he said, suddenly sharper. 'Is there a problem?' When he was too slow to deny it Peter said, 'What's happened?'

'Well, the good news is that I have received an invitation to my father's birthday *majlis*.'

'And the bad news is that Ahmed Khadri will gut you the moment he sets eyes on you.'

'Apparently not. Hamad phoned to warn me that my father has done a secret deal with Khadri. Safia hasn't given my brother a son and they're impatient for an heir with Khadri blood. The price of my return is marriage to Bibi Khadri, Safia's youngest sister.'

Peter's soft expletive said it all. 'There's more than one way to gut a man…'

'He wins, whichever way I jump. If I go, he has more influence in court as well as the eye-watering dowry he will demand from me. If I stay away, my father will take it as a personal insult and any chance of a reconciliation will be lost. I doubt Khadri can make up his mind which outcome would please him most.'

'Who knows about this?'

'No one. Hamad only found out because Bibi managed to smuggle a note to her sister.'

He was not the only one to be horrified by such a match.

'Okay… So if you turned up with a wife in tow—'

'You're rambling, Peter. Go to sleep.'

'Not a real wife. A temp,' he said. 'And, by happy co-incidence, you happen to have one handy… Ask the Garland Girl.'

Ruby put the phone down, turned to the laptop and began to go through Peter's diary, printing off each entry for the following week. She had collected the sheets from the printer, sorted them and clipped them into a folder when a shadow across the door warned her that she was no longer alone.

'I realised that you didn't have the password to Peter's laptop but I see that you've found it. Did he have it written down somewhere obvious?' he asked.

She counted to three before she looked up. Bram Ansari was leaning against the doorjamb, arms folded, but there was an intense watchfulness in his eyes that belied the casual stance.

'No,' she said.

'No, not obvious?'

'No, he didn't have it written down.'

'And yet you are in. Should I be worried?'

Ruby was seriously tempted to leave it at that and let him wonder how she'd done it. She resisted. He'd taken his time about it but he had eventually turned up and playing mind games was not the way to build a working relationship. She took pride in the fact that when she had worked for someone she always got a call back.

'I'm good, Bram, but I'm not that good. Peter asked his mother to text it to me.'

'I was just talking to him. He didn't mention it.'

'Maybe he forgot. Or maybe he wanted to make me look amazingly efficient. How is he?'

'High on the lingering remains of anaesthetic. Talking too much when he should be resting.'

'Did you rest?' she asked. 'When you broke your ankle?'

His shoulders moved in the merest suggestion of a shrug. 'Boredom is the mother of invention.'

His smile was little more than a tug on the corner of his mouth, deepening the droop, but it felt as if he had included her in a private joke and her own lips responded all by themselves. And not just her lips. Little pings of recognition lit up in parts of her body that had lain dormant, unused, not wanted in this life. Definitely not wanted here.

'He rang to make sure that you'd arrived safely and to tell me how lucky I am to have you.'

'What a nice man,' she said. 'I'll send him a box of liquorice allsorts.'

'It didn't take you long to discover his weakness.'

'One I confess that I share.' He didn't respond and, feeling rather foolish, she said, 'I've spoken to Mrs Hammond and passed on all the information she needed.' He nodded. 'It's going to be weeks before Peter will be able to manage all these steps.'

'He won't be coming back.' She frowned. 'His father was Ambassador to Umm al Basr when Peter was a boy. He loves the desert and when he dropped out of university, didn't know what to do with himself, I asked him if he wanted to come here and give me a hand. I'd given financial backing to a friend who wanted to go into commercial production with winter sports equipment—'

'Maxim de Groote.'

'Is that in your file too?' he asked.

'It's all over the Internet.'

'I don't use social media.' He shook his head, as if the interest of other people in his life bewildered him.

She wasn't convinced. This was a man whose naked romp in a fountain, caught on someone's phone, had gone viral on social media networks before the police arrived to arrest him.

'When he publicly floated his company Maxim told a journalist that he owed everything to you,' she said. 'Did he?'

'No, he owed it to his own vision and hard work.'

'And the fact that you had the faith to invest in him.'

'I knew him,' he said, 'but I was immediately inundated with would-be entrepreneurs looking for capital. Peter was going to stay for a few weeks and do the thanks-but-no-thanks replies while he thought about his future.'

'But that didn't happen.'

'He would insist on reading the crazier ideas out loud and one of them caught my interest. The rest, as they say, is history.' He shrugged as if his ability to pick winners was nothing. 'Peter stayed because it suited him at the time.' He gestured towards the photographs. 'These days he spends more time out in the desert with his camera than at his desk.'

'Peter is the photographer? He's very talented.'

'And it's time he got serious about it. If I hadn't been so busy I would have kicked him out a year ago. The fact that he had Amanda Garland's number to hand suggests that he'd been working on an exit strategy of his own.' He nodded at the folder she was holding. 'What have you got there?'

She glanced at it. 'It's your detailed diary for tomorrow and a summary for the week. I wasn't sure how Peter handled it. I usually print out a list.'

'Run me through it,' he said, finally leaving the doorway and crossing to her desk.

'You have a conference call booked with Roger Pei in Hong Kong tomorrow morning and there's a reminder that you should call Susan Graham in New York before Wall Street opens.' She went through a list of other calls he was both expecting and planned to make. 'The times and numbers are all there.'

'And the rest of the week?'

'You have video conferences booked every day this week, you're flying to Dubai on Wednesday and there's a charity dinner here in Ras al Kawi hosted by His Highness Sheikh Fayad and Princess Violet tomorrow evening.'

'I can't miss that,' he said, taking the folder from her and checking the entry. 'Have you got anything to wear?'

'Wear?'

'Something suitable for a formal dinner.'

She felt her carefully controlled air of calm—which hadn't buckled under the suggestion that she might have to slaughter a goat—slip a notch. But then she hadn't taken that threat seriously.

'You want me to go with you?' Meetings, conferences, receptions were all grist to her mill, but she'd never been asked to accompany any of the men she'd worked for to a black tie dinner. They had partners for that. Partners with designer wardrobes, accessories costing four figures, jewellery…

Perhaps sensing her reluctance, he looked up from the diary page. 'It comes under the "whatever is necessary" brief. You were serious about that, Ruby?' he asked, regarding her with a quiet intensity that sent a ripple of apprehension coursing through her veins.

'Whatever is necessary within the parameters of legal, honest and decent,' she said, hoping that the smile made it through to her face.

He handed back the diary. 'Call Princess Violet's office and ask her assistant to send you some dresses from her latest collection.'

'I have a dress,' she said quickly. Even the simplest of Princess Violet al Kuwani's designer gowns would cost more than she earned in a month.

'Let me guess,' he said. 'It's black.'

Black was practical and her capsule wardrobe had been created to cover all eventualities, although she hadn't anticipated wearing anything so formal on this assignment.

'A simple black dress will take you anywhere,' she told him. 'It's the female equivalent of a dinner jacket.'

'So it's a boring black dress.'

'I'll be working, not flirting.'

'I'm glad you understand that.' He held her gaze for a moment then said, 'There has been a development that will involve rescheduling some of those appointments, but first we will eat.'

No, no, no…

No socialising in the workplace. No getting into situations where people would ask where she came from, about her family, all the conversational gambits used to probe who you were and where you would fit into the social layers of their lives.

She didn't do 'social'.

'Come,' he said, extending a hand towards her, and for the first time since she'd arrived she saw not the A-list pin-up, the sportsman, the venture capitalist, but a man born to command, a prince. 'Bring the diary with you.'

The diary. Right. It was a working dinner. Of course it was. He only wanted her with him to keep track of who he spoke to, the appointments he made. That she could handle and, fortifying herself with a steadying breath, she gathered her things and headed for the door and that outstretched hand.

She was sure he was going to place it at her back, maybe take her arm as they descended the worn, uneven steps. He waited until she passed him, closed the door behind them and, having held herself rigid, knowing that no matter how much she tried to relax she would still jump at his touch, she felt a weird jolt of disappointment when he simply paused beside her.

Disappointment was bad.

She looked up, anywhere but at him.

During the short time she had been working, every trace of light had left the sky. Above them stars were glittering diamond-bright in a clear black sky, but she was too strung up to look for the constellations; all her senses were focused on the man beside her. The warmth of his body so close to hers. The scent of the sea air clinging to his skin overlaid with the tiny flowers that had fallen on his shoulders as he brushed past a jasmine vine.

No...

The word clanged in her brain so loudly that when Bram glanced at her she thought he must have heard.

It wasn't as if she even liked the man but it was pointless to pretend that she was immune to the magnetic quality that had once made him a *Celebrity* cover favourite.

Work, she reminded herself. She was here to work.

Concentrate on the job.

'What's your routine?' she asked in her briskly efficient PA voice as he led the way down to a lower level, determined to blot out emergency signals from synapses that hadn't been this excited in years.

'Routine?' He frowned, as if it was a word alien to his vocabulary.

'What time are you normally at your desk? I imagine it's earlier than London.'

'Peter usually goes for a run or swim at first light, has breakfast and if he's not chasing the light with his camera he deals with overnight emails.' He glanced down at her. 'Do you run, Ruby?'

'Only for a bus.' She'd hoped to raise a smile, lessen the tension, but there was no noticeable reaction.

'Swim?'

She glanced across the tumble of walls, courtyards, to the dark water sucking at the foot of the fort. 'Not in the sea.'

'There is a pool.' If he'd noticed her involuntary shiver, he made no comment. 'There's also a fully equipped gym if you prefer.'

'No, thanks.' She'd already seen him wet from the sea and she wasn't about to risk walking in on him slicked with sweat. 'I keep in shape by walking to work when I can, using the stairs instead of the lift and taking a weekly tap dancing class.' He gave her another of those looks. Assessing, unnerving... 'It's cheaper than a gym membership and the shoes are prettier,' she said quickly.

'There's no shortage of steps here.' His smile, unexpected as the sun on a winter morning—he knew how to smile?—took her by surprise. For a moment her foot hung in mid-air and then, as she missed the step, she flung out her hands, grabbing for something—anything—to hang onto and found herself face first in Bram Ansari's washed soft T-shirt, nestled against the hard-muscled shoulder it concealed. Drowning in the scent of sun-dried laundry and warm skin as he caught her, held her.

'Sorry,' she mumbled in a rush of embarrassed heat, jerking back from the intimacy of the contact. 'Apparently I can't walk and talk at the same time.'

'The steps are old, uneven.' Her head might have made a bid to escape the mortifying closeness but the rest of her was pressed against hard thighs, a washboard-flat stomach, her breasts pinioned against the broad chest that she was picturing all too vividly. 'Maybe you should stick to swimming while you're here,' he said, moving his hands to her shoulders and, still holding her steady, taking a step back. 'If you didn't bring a costume then send for one. You'll be glad of it when the weather heats up.'

Forget the weather. Bram Ansari was creating all the heat she could handle.

'It seems hardly worth it for a week.'

They had reached a point where the steps narrowed and he'd taken the lead so that when he stopped, turned, he was looking directly into her eyes.

'And if I need more than a week?'

Ruby had been a temp for a long time and she knew that there were people you had to flatter, those you had to mother and those rare and wonderful individuals who just got on with it and required nothing from you except your ability to keep things running smoothly in a crisis. Then there were the ones you had face down, never showing the slightest hint of weakness, never showing by as much as the flicker of an eyelash what you were feeling.

It had been clear from the moment that she'd set eyes on him that Sheikh Ibrahim al-Ansari fitted the latter description. Ignoring the battalion of butterflies battering against her breastbone, she looked right back at him and said, 'At this rate I'll be surprised if I'm here for more than twenty-four hours.'

They continued to stare at one another for the longest ten seconds in her life and then he said, 'Is that it or have you run out of smart answers?'

'I wouldn't count on it.'

This time his smile was no more than a tiny contraction of the lines fanning out from eyes that said nothing but it softened his face and had much the same effect on her knees.

'No...' For a moment he seemed lost for words. 'Shall we eat?'

'Good idea. With my mouth full I'll be less likely to put my foot in it.'

His smile deepened and it was probably a good thing that he placed his hand beneath her elbow, keeping her safe as they continued down the steps. *Probably.* She wouldn't fall, but her skin shimmered with the intimacy of his touch and she didn't let out her breath until they stepped down onto a terrace from which wide steps led down to the beach and he finally let go.

A table had been laid with a white cloth, flowers, candles sheltered within glass globes, sleek modern silver cutlery. The only sound was the lulling ripple of the sea, the shushing of the sand moving as the tide began to recede.

The scene was seductively exotic, a long way from the usual end to her working day. Khal gave her a wide smile as he held out a chair for her then, when she was settled, he turned to Bram and asked him a question.

For a moment the conversation went back and forth until finally Bram said, 'Antares.'

'Ruby?' Khal asked, turning to her and evidently expecting her to understand what he'd said.

'Khal is asking if you wish to ride in the morning.'

'Ride?'

The soft, fizzing intimacy of the moment shattered and in an instant she was in the past, hugging the fat little Shetland pony that had arrived on her fourth birthday, the feel of his thick, shaggy mane beneath her fingers, the smell of new leather.

'Do you ride?' Bram prompted when she took too long to answer.

Ruby forced a smile. 'Not for years and, in view of what happened to Peter, I promised Amanda that I wouldn't take part in any dangerous sports while I was here.'

'Life is a dangerous sport, Ruby.' He held her gaze for a moment, a questioning kink to his brow, but when she said nothing he turned back to Khal, said a few words in Arabic.

The man bowed, wished them both goodnight and left them to their supper.

'Antares?' she asked as she picked up her napkin and laid it on her lap, determined to keep the conversation impersonal. 'You name your horses after the stars?'

'Only the brightest ones. Antares, Rigel, Vega, Hadar, Altair, Adhara. They were my polo string.' He shook his head. 'I should have sold them when I left England. They're getting fat and lazy.'

'It's hard. They become an extension of you,' she said. 'Part of the family.' Her mother had wanted to sell her ponies as she grew out of them but she'd pleaded with her father and they had all stayed, eating their heads off and costing a fortune in vet's bills.

His look was thoughtful—so much for keeping it impersonal—but a woman appeared with a tray and he said, 'Ruby, this is Mina. She is an extraordinary cook but she only has a few words of English. Her husband, son and daughter-in-law take care of the fort for me.'

'*As-salaam alaykum*, Mina.'

Mina responded with a rush of Arabic and a broad smile. 'She's very happy to meet you,' Bram said, filling their glasses from a jug of juice. 'You have some Arabic?'

'I've worked in Bahrain and Dubai so I picked up a few words. Amanda assured me that you worked in English but I assumed all the staff would be Arabic speaking so I downloaded a basic course to my tablet. It was a long flight.'

'The legend is true then.'

'Legend?'

'Peter suggested that to have a Garland Girl as a personal assistant or nanny is considered something of a status symbol.'

She rolled her eyes. 'A newspaper did a profile on Amanda's agency years ago and came up with that ghastly name. They made us sound like the office equivalent of the Playboy Bunny.'

His jaw tightened as he fought a grin.

'It's okay,' she said, 'you can laugh. I'm twenty-seven. No one's idea of a girl,' she said. 'Or a bunny.'

'There is no right answer to that,' he said, offering her a plate. 'Have one of these.'

She took one of the hot, crispy little pastries without comment. It was filled with goat's cheese and as she bit into it Ruby almost groaned with pleasure. They had to be about a million calories each, but she told herself that she'd work them off walking up and down all those steps.

'You approve?'

'They are scrumptious.'

'That's a word I haven't heard in a while. If I had to make a guess, I'd say you went to one of those exclusive boarding schools where the British upper classes park their children.'

The kind of women whose social calendar would include afternoons at Smith's Lawn watching as princes whacked a ball with a polo stick, and après-ski parties in Gstaad...

'What is this? Tit for tat?' she asked, with a smile to disguise the fact that she'd changed the subject. 'I know how you like your coffee so you checked me out online?'

'And if I had, Ruby Dance,' he replied, his voice softer than a Dartmoor mist and twice as dangerous, that almost-smile a trap for the unwary, 'what would I have found?'

Her skin prickled, her mouth dried.

He had...

Despite Jude's reference, despite the fact that Peter Hammond was Amanda's godson, he'd put her name into a search engine and knew exactly what he would find.

'Not very much,' she admitted.

'Not very much suggests that there would be something,' he pointed out, 'but there was no social media, no credit history and no Ruby Dance who was born twenty-seven years ago.' He sat back in his chair. 'I could dig deeper and unearth your secrets, but why don't you save me the bother and tell me who you really are?'

Protected by the reputation of the Garland Agency, her anonymity as a temp, this was the first time anyone had ever bothered to question Ruby's bona fides and the air rang with the silence as she tried to marshal her thoughts.

She wasn't fooled by the casual way he'd asked the question.

She'd been joking when she'd suggested that she'd last no more than twenty-four hours. Apparently the joke was on her because she wasn't going to be able to brush this aside, laugh it off as an aversion to the rush to tell everyone what she had for breakfast, of sharing pictures of cute kittens, as an excuse for her low profile.

He'd already gone far deeper than social media, was

certain that she had not been born Ruby Dance, and the less he found the more suspicious he would become.

She unstuck her tongue from the roof of her mouth and said, 'I changed my name for family reasons.'

'A clause in a will? Your mother remarried?' he suggested.

She shook her head. He was dangling easy answers before her. Testing her. 'There was a scandal involving my father. Newspaper headlines. Reporters digging around in dustbins and paying the neighbours for gossip.'

He raised an eyebrow, inviting her to continue.

'Amanda Garland knows my history,' she said, 'and her reputation stands on trust.'

'Trust her, trust you—is that the deal?'

Her throat was dry and the juice gleamed enticingly but she resisted the urge to grab for it, swallow a mouthful. 'That's the deal.'

'And that's why you continue to temp rather than accept a permanent job? For the anonymity?'

'Yes…' The word stuck like a lump of wood in her throat.

'Where is your father now, Ruby?'

'He's dead. He and my mother died when I was seventeen.'

'Do you have any other family?'

'No.' She shook her head. 'I was the only child of only children.' At least as far as she knew. Her father might have had a dozen children…

'Can I ask if you are in any kind of relationship?' he persisted.

'Relationship?'

'You are on your own—you have no ties?'

He was beginning to spook her and must have realised it because he said, 'I have a proposition for you, Ruby, but if you have personal commitments...' He shook his head as if he wasn't sure what he was doing.

'If you're going to offer me a package too good to refuse after a couple of hours I should warn you that it took Jude Radcliffe the best part of a year to get to that point and I still turned him down.'

'I don't have the luxury of time,' he said, 'and the position I'm offering is made for a temp.'

'I'm listening.'

'Since you have done your research, you know that I was disinherited five years ago.'

She nodded. She thought it rather harsh for a one-off incident but the media loved the fall of a hero and had gone into a bit of a feeding frenzy.

'This morning I received a summons from my father to present myself at his birthday *majlis*.'

'You can go home?'

'If only it were that simple. A situation exists which means that I can only return to Umm al Basr if I'm accompanied by a wife.'

She ignored the slight sinking feeling in her stomach. Obviously a multimillionaire who looked like the statue of a Greek god—albeit one who'd suffered a bit of wear and tear—would have someone ready and willing to step up to the plate.

'That's rather short notice. Obviously, I'll do whatever I can to arrange things, but I don't know a lot about the law in—'

'The marriage can take place tomorrow. My question is, under the terms of your open-ended brief encompassing "whatever is necessary", are you prepared to take on the role?'

CHAPTER THREE

'ME?'

Bram let go of the breath he'd been holding as Ruby reached for the glass of juice. Her hand was shaking but, rather than throwing it at him, she lifted it to her lips. She was taking a moment to gather her thoughts and he did not interrupt them.

'You're suggesting that I pretend to be your wife.'

'No.' He was a fairly shrewd judge of character and everything she'd done and said suggested she would appreciate straight talking, but there was no way of knowing how she'd take such an outrageous suggestion. 'What I'm suggesting is a temporary marriage of convenience with the divorce, at a mutually convenient moment, as easily arranged as the wedding.'

The dark arch of Ruby's brow hit her hairline. 'But you don't know me...'

'I don't have to know you. That's the deal with a temp and, as you've been at pains to stress, you are a temp with the highest references.'

'As a temporary PA!'

'I still need one of those.'

'But the marriage would be real?'

'There will have to be a contract witnessed by someone my father trusts but, to be quite clear, this will be a simple business arrangement with a title upgrade from temporary personal assistant to temporary princess. While the pay grade is on a scale to match the new position, there would be no additional duties.'

'By *additional duties* you mean sex?' she said. 'To be absolutely clear.'

She was direct; he'd give her that. 'No sex,' he assured her. If this was to work it had to be a business arrangement. No complications.

'You simply want to convince your father that you're married.' She sat back in her chair, sitting holding the juice 'Are you gay, Bram?'

Direct? That was direct...

'I realise that in some parts of the world it's difficult,' she continued. Her face might be made for poker but he could imagine the thoughts racing through her brain. The real nature of his relationship with Peter...

'No!' He stopped as Mina appeared. She spoke little English but she understood the word no, and thought he was telling her to wait, but he quickly reassured her and when she had removed their empty plates he said, 'No, Ruby, I'm not gay but if I was I wouldn't hide the fact behind a paper marriage.'

'So what are you hiding?'

'There are pressing reasons, Ruby.'

'No doubt.' Those wide silver eyes were fixed on him and the drop in temperature of her voice was like a cold draught. 'I'm sorry, Sheikh, but I can't be party to such a deception.' A draught cold enough to be coming off the Russian Steppes in January.

The fact that she'd turned him down flat was no more than he had expected and only served to prove everything that Jude and Peter had told him about her.

'My father had heart bypass surgery last year, Ruby.'

Her eyes softened. 'I didn't know. I'm sorry—'

'He refuses to step down, rest. I have to be there to kneel at his feet, receive his forgiveness.'

'And he will want you there.' She paused as Mina returned with plates, more food, urging them to eat. 'I don't understand what the problem is,' she said, as she spooned spiced chicken and rice onto his plate and then hers. 'He's the Emir. His word is law.'

'A ruler has to put aside personal feelings for the good of his people. Umm al Basr was once torn apart by tribal infighting and no one cared until oil was found. The prospect of wealth focused everyone's minds and a meeting of the tribal elders chose the Ansari family as their leader. The Khadri family were soothed with a marriage contract, a political alliance between the oldest daughter of the Khadri family and the future Emir of Umm al Basr, joining the bloodline in a pact to end decades of discord.'

'The medieval solution. Seal a peace deal with the sacrifice of a daughter.'

'I was ten years old and Safia Khadri was four at the time the contract was written. When I dishonoured Safia with my escapade in the fountain, Ahmed Khadri threatened to kill me if I ever set foot in Umm al Basr.'

'A bit excessive?' She was toying with her food now. 'Presumably he was seizing a handy excuse to cause trouble and stir up feelings against your family?'

He smiled. 'You are very quick, Ruby. I do not place my life at so great a value, but my death would have had to be avenged and that would have meant a return to the kind of tribal conflict that tore my country apart in the past, with the possibility of the Khadri family seizing power.'

'So your father disinherited you to keep the peace,' she said, leaning forward to put her glass on the table, propped her elbows on the table and rested her chin on her hands.

The frost had melted but her sympathies were with his father, with Safia. He would have expected nothing else.

'He flew to London and disinherited me because he was furious. I'd been given an international education to prepare me for my duties as a modern ruler, given freedom to enjoy the sports I loved because it brought honour to our country, and I'd repaid him by behaving like a dissolute playboy and was not fit to rule.' His father's words were carved into his heart. 'He banished me to keep the peace.'

She nodded, clearly understanding the difference. 'So what's this deal, Bram?'

'The price of my return to Umm al Basr is marriage to Ahmed Khadri's youngest daughter, Bibi.'

Only the movement of her throat as she swallowed, drawing attention to the glow of candlelight on the cream silk of her neck, betrayed her shock.

'I'm sorry, Bram, but I don't understand your problem.'

'You are remarkably sanguine,' he said. 'I was sure your western sensibilities would be outraged.'

'By an arranged marriage? It's the cultural norm in this part of the world,' she said, 'and at a much earlier age than the average western marriage.' His surprise must have telegraphed itself. 'This is a return to the status quo,' she added. 'A second chance.' Then she frowned. 'What happened to Safia?'

'The contract was for the marriage of the oldest daughter of the Khadri family to the heir to Umm al Basr. When I was disinherited,' he said, 'my brother took my place. He married Safia Khadri.'

Like Ruby telling him that she had changed her name because of a scandal, that her parents were dead, he kept his voice expressionless, shrugged as if it was no big deal. As if he hadn't given a damn about being disinherited, banished…

'I'd ask how she felt about that,' Ruby replied, 'but I don't suppose she had any choice.'

'Feelings did not come into it. They did their duty.'

'Right…' Ruby eased a finger around the neckline of her top, not quite as laid-back about the situation as she would like him to believe. Which suited him perfectly. She took a sip of juice, set the glass down. 'So what has changed?' she asked.

'Changed?'

'Why is Ahmed Khadri, the man who threatened to kill you on sight, willing to give you his youngest daughter?'

'Safia has given my brother three daughters in five years. With the last pregnancy there were complications. Pre-eclampsia. Hamad has been warned to wait a full two years before trying again for a son.'

'So now her father is prepared to forgive you and sacrifice another daughter to the baby factory?' she demanded, her natural instincts as a liberated woman clearly outraged.

'This has nothing to do with forgiveness; this is politics.'

'To think that when I said medieval I was being flippant. Does Bibi have a choice?'

'In theory. In practice, she will obey her father.'

She shook her head in disbelief. 'Do you know her?'

'Her mother died when she was born and both Safia and Bibi were educated with my sisters at the palace. The last time I saw Bibi Khadri she was a brainy twelve-year-old with her heart set on becoming a doctor. She took her university entrance exams a year early and the last I heard she was going to begin her training in September.'

'*What?* When I said sacrifice—'

'You had no idea how close to the truth you were. Being forced to give up her heart's desire and marry a scarred old man to provide her father with a grandson, her country with an heir, has to be as appalling a prospect to her as bedding a seventeen-year-old virgin is to me.'

'Seventeen? But she's a child,' she said, clearly horrified. 'Not that you're old,' she added quickly.

'You are not a teenager, Ruby. I'm twice her age,' he said, amused by her attempt to save his feelings but determined to press the point home.

She looked thoughtful. 'You do know that it's the man who decides the sex of the infant? If girls run in your family her sacrifice will have been in vain.'

'Good point. I have four older sisters.'

'Four?' Those expressive brows did a little dance. 'Ahmed Khadri might have a long wait to see a grandson.'

'The seas will run dry before I give him one,' he assured her. 'Bibi is going to be part of a modern Umm al Basr where women have rights, are valued as equals, not traded at the whim of men.'

'So you're doing this for her?'

'No, Ruby, I'm doing it for me. Have you any idea what living with an unwilling teenage bride would be like?'

She sat back and as she looked at him he could see the cogs turning in her brain.

'Are you certain that she's unwilling?'

'What are you suggesting?'

'That while she might have wanted to be a doctor at twelve, at seventeen being the wife of the Emir's son might be a lot more appealing. And if she produces a boy in nine months from now I imagine Ahmed Khadri would be applying pressure for you to be restored to the succession.'

'No doubt,' he said. 'Thankfully, Bibi, who is already in pre-wedding seclusion, managed to smuggle a note to her sister. A plea for help. Until that moment no one but my father and Ahmed Khadri knew of the plan.'

'Your brother warned you?' He nodded. 'But if you arrive with a wife surely it will be back to square one?'

'A secret works two ways. On the one hand I return home to be presented with a *fait accompli* in which the consequences of my refusal to accept Bibi as my bride would be catastrophic. On the other I arrive, totally unaware of what has been planned, with a brand-new wife to present to my family. What can anyone say?'

'Quite a lot, I imagine.'

'No doubt, but none of it out loud. My father is a politician. He will hide his pleasure at besting an old enemy. As for Ahmed Khadri, he has nothing to gain from creating a crisis. No doubt he extracted an eye-watering dowry from my father in return for giving his youngest daughter to a disgraced son. More than enough to cover the expense of setting up and running a house for Bibi in England while she studies medicine.'

'So everyone will be satisfied.'

'You don't sound convinced.'

With the slightest movement of her head she said, 'I was wondering what will happen a few weeks down the line when you announce the marriage is over.'

'Everyone will think I've been a fool?' he suggested. 'Nothing new there.'

'Everyone will think it was very convenient.'

'Point taken.' He hadn't thought much beyond the immediate problem. Beyond this week. 'What is the longest you've ever temped for anyone?'

'Six months. To cover maternity leave.' She lifted elegant shoulders in the briefest of shrugs. 'It was my first temporary job. A one-man office.'

Six months... What would it be like to have Ruby Dance at his side for six months? Sparky, smart-mouthed. Those extraordinary grey eyes full of questions...

'Did you enjoy it?' he asked.

'He was patient, very kind at a bad time for me. I still temp for him when he needs someone.' The implication being that while she was now in demand from those at the top of the business tree, she did not forget those who'd helped her.

'I'm neither patient nor kind,' he said, 'but if you will give me six months of your time I will make it worth your while.'

'Is there no one else you could ask?' she said. 'A friend?'

'Time is short, you are here and a straightforward business arrangement will be simpler.' He met her direct gaze head-on. 'How much is six months of your life worth, Ruby?' he asked. 'Name your price.'

Ruby froze. Until this moment his proposition had felt rhetorical but suddenly it was very real and her first reaction was *No way*. Deception of any kind was abhorrent to her but this was different. She would be hurting no one. On the contrary, she would be reuniting Bram with his father, saving a very young woman from a forced marriage—both noble aims.

And he'd asked her to name her price. It wasn't an idle offer. He was a billionaire and the sum in her head would be peanuts to him while to her it would mean a new start, a chance to clear the last of her father's debts, wipe the slate clean, be free...

'I need to think,' she said. 'I need to walk. Is the beach safe?' she said, standing up.

'Walking at night by yourself is not wise,' he said, rising to join her, apparently able to read her mind. 'I go to the stables when I need to think through a difficult decision. Horses make great listeners.'

She swallowed down the sudden lump in her throat, remembering the hours she'd spent talking to her horses as she'd brushed their coats. The confidences she'd shared with them. Her ambitions, her first crush, her first kiss...

'Would you like to come and meet them?' he asked.

No... Yes... She looked at her barely touched plate. 'Will you apologise to Mina for me?'

'Of course.'

He paused to speak to Mina and then led the way across the terrace and down more steps that led to a large courtyard sheltered by the rear of the fort.

Concealed lighting, activated by movement, flickered

on around the yard and for a moment she paused to breathe in the familiar scent of hay and warm horseflesh as Bram disappeared into the tack room and returned with a handful of carrots.

There was a soft whicker from the first horsebox and then the pale grey head of a magnificent horse appeared over the half door and reached towards Bram.

He murmured soft words in Arabic as he rubbed his hand down the dished face before turning to her. 'This is Vega. The brightest of my stars.'

'*Salaam*, Vega.' She approached him carefully, as she would any unknown animal, offering her hand to be sniffed at and, when that was approved, offering him the carrot that Bram handed to her.

The horse lipped it from her palm, allowing her to rub his nose as he crunched it.

Bram led the way around the yard, introducing her to his beautiful horses, saying nothing as she greeted each one, was accepted, allowed to run a hand down a warm neck, fondle an ear, stroke a cheek.

'They are all so beautiful, Bram,' she said with a sigh.

'Who do you think would make the best listener?'

'Rigel,' she said, without hesitation. A silky chestnut with a black mane and a white blaze on his forehead who had pushed his head towards her, laying his forehead against her shoulder.

Without another word, Bram fetched a body brush from the tack room, handed it to her and opened the door to Rigel's stable. 'Get to know one another. Take as long as you need. I'll be with my hawks.'

Bram was smiling as he walked across to the mews. He'd seen her hesitation when he'd invited her to ride, the longing in her eyes even as she'd shaken her head, made a joke about keeping out of danger.

Any doubts he might have had were banished the moment Rigel, the most intuitive of his horses, had pushed his head into her shoulder. From across the yard he could hear her voice, silky soft, as she brushed him down, coming to her decision.

Ruby did not need time. She had seen the man with his horses, the way they reached to him, almost purred at his touch, and her decision was made. But this closeness with a horse, once so much part of her life, this was a pleasure she would not surrender. She laid her hand against Rigel's neck and he turned to look at her, gave her a nudge as if to say, *What are you waiting for?*

Half an hour later, having returned the brush to the tack room and washed her hands, Ruby found Bram in his mews.

He returned the hawk on his fist to its perch, removed his glove. 'All done?' he said, joining her in the yard.

'I have a question,' she said.

'Just one?'

'Just one.'

'Go ahead.'

'If I said no, what would you do?'

The moon had risen, silvering her hair...

'Bram?'

He shook off the thought. A straightforward business transaction. It had to be that.

'I wish to see my father, receive his blessing more than anything in the world, Ruby, but not at any price. If you say no, then I will send my father my good wishes for his birthday, as I do every year, and my regret that I cannot be there to celebrate the day with him.'

He saw her throat move as she swallowed, took a breath. 'Six months?'

'It's a great deal to ask.'

'It's just a job,' she reminded him.

'Yes.' Silvering her hair, her cheek, her mouth—

'I don't know anything about marriage laws in this part of the world,' she said, cutting off the thought before he could put it into words. 'Can it be arranged in the time?'

'Practical as ever.'

'And?'

The simple answer, the practical answer, was yes. Right at that moment, standing in the moonlight, he was feeling anything but practical.

'Under normal circumstances there would be months of negotiation over the dowry.'

'Months?'

'A man's sons are his future but his daughters are his wealth. That's why they're so carefully protected.'

'Oh, I see. Well, we don't have months to haggle but that's not a problem. What I'm asking for is not up for negotiation.'

'I'm listening.'

'One—you will pay Amanda for my services as your temp while I'm here. I will need something to do, you will still need a PA and she's going to have to reschedule all my bookings so she's entitled to her fee.'

'That is eminently reasonable.'

'Two—you will pay a lump sum, clear of tax, to my lawyer at the end of this engagement as a bonus.' The amount she named was not a round sum, but down to the last odd pence.

He would have gladly given her four times that, but clearly there was a reason for that odd amount and now was not the time to argue. 'Consider it done. Go on.'

'Go on?'

'Three?'

'There isn't a three.' She gave him an odd little smile. Bright on the surface but suspiciously close to tears underneath. 'So,' she said, as they returned to the terrace and their abandoned supper. 'That's the dowry taken care of. What comes next?'

Mina arrived, clucking and worrying. He'd explained that Ruby was feeling tired after her journey and now she'd brought mint tea, dates, nuts, little sweet pastries.

He assured her that he would see she ate something and, reluctantly, she left them to it.

'Next,' he said, pouring the tea, 'you eat something or I'll be in trouble with Mina.'

'What comes next in the wedding arrangements?' she asked, taking a date.

'Next, you would go into seclusion for weeks, seeing no one outside the women in your immediate family until the *maksar*. That's a gathering where the entire Ansari tribe come to check out the dowry and eat themselves sick for days. No one will expect that with a disinherited son and a western bride.'

The corner of her mouth tilted up, revealing a dimple. 'Shame. It sounds like quite a party.'

'But not one that the bride takes part in. She stays hidden away until her groom fights his way through her family to claim her.'

'He has to fight his way through?' she asked. 'Despite the dowry?'

He found himself hesitating as an old image flooded his mind. The anticipation of the mock battle as he fought his way past her brothers. Safia swathed in veils that he would remove one by one...

He shook his head. 'All of which is irrelevant in our case. I'll call my cousin and ask him to draw up a contract. I could do it myself but the seal of the Emir of Ras al Kawi will lend it legitimacy. We will formalise the arrangement tomorrow before the charity dinner.'

'I hate to break this to you, Bram, but you're going to

need more than a contract to convince your family that this is a genuine marriage.'

'A contract is hard to ignore,' Bram pointed out.

'I agree, but this isn't an arranged marriage with every detail hammered out by families who have known one another for generations. I can't speak for the men, but the women in your family will want all the details. The when, where and how we met. How we got from there to here. We're going to need a story.'

Bram rubbed a hand over his face. 'I thought this was going to be simple.'

'It will be,' she assured him. 'All it requires is a little preparation so that we get the basics straight.' She took another date. 'Let's start with how we met. London seems the most likely place.'

He shrugged. 'I was there for a week last December.'

She shook her head. 'That's too recent. How often do you go to London?'

'It varies. About once a month, more often when a new project is kicking off.'

'Do you take Peter with you?'

'He usually takes advantage of my absence to go into the desert with his camera.' Then, catching her meaning, 'I suppose, if I needed someone, he could ask his god-mother to provide a PA.'

'That seems likely and, naturally, she would have sent her very best.'

'Naturally.'

'And you were so impressed—'

'—that I always asked for you when I was in London.'

'Anyone would,' she assured him and he rewarded her with a smile for her cheek. 'Obviously, when Peter called asking her to send someone to cover for him, she would have asked me to drop everything and fly to Ras al Kawi.'

'Obviously.' His grin faded. 'And that first moment, when I saw you—'

'—you realised that you couldn't live without me.'

For a moment they just stared at one another as the whisper of a breeze caught the flame of the candle and sent it dancing, throwing shadows up the walls.

'Well, that's a great start but we're going to need more than that.'

'Are we?'

Ruby firmly suppressed a little shiver that ran up her spine. It was getting chilly.

'Me,' she said. 'I'm going to need more. You'll probably just get a blokeish slap on the back, but the women in your family—your mother, your sisters—will give me the full who-the-heck-are-you-and-what-makes-you-think-you're-good-enough-for-our-boy? interrogation.'

Amused, he said, 'I didn't realise you'd met them.'

'Mothers, sisters, are the same the world over, Bram, and once they've sorted out the how and where they'll want every detail of how we got from personal assistant to personal.'

His smile faded.

He clearly hadn't thought this through before he'd asked for her help. He'd been solely focused on protecting Bibi Khadri from her father's machinations and was only now beginning to realise the extent of what he'd taken on. Or, more realistically, what she'd taken on, because men didn't do personal stuff. She was the one who would be facing the in-depth interrogation.

'Will you be able to handle that?' he asked.

'Yes,' she said, 'but we will need to have our stories straight.'

Neither of them spoke for a moment, then Bram said, 'Okay, keeping it real... I could have kept you late one night and then insisted on taking you out to dinner.'

'To thank me for all my hard work?'

'Maybe I was being selfish,' he said, a smile tugging at the corner of his lip. 'I didn't want to eat alone and you are an intelligent and attractive woman.'

It was ridiculous to blush. He said attractive, not beautiful, and they were creating a legend, a story. A lie.

'You eat alone?' she asked, ignoring the little cold spot at her core. The realisation that she was inventing a history, just as her father had done a hundred times or more. And so easily…

In a good cause, she told herself. In a good cause.

'My life has changed,' Bram said, distracting her. 'I no longer move in the same circles as I did when I lived in Europe.'

He was lonely?

No, no…

Stick to the details. Working late. Dinner… It could have happened exactly like that. She'd had the invitations, but had always said no…

'Right, well, that's real enough,' she said briskly. 'So, where did you take me?'

He thought about it for a moment before naming a selection of the most exclusive and expensive restaurants currently fashionable in the city.

'Bram Ansari, you are the kind of boss I've always dreamed of,' she said, 'but I would have been working for ten hours and would have needed a shower and change of clothes for anywhere that special.'

'The shower I could arrange…' He cleared his throat. 'Perhaps not. Besides, it was late and there was no way I could have got a table. My gratitude would have had to wait until the following evening.'

'You were leaving the following day,' she reminded him.

'I was?'

'Your plane was waiting at London City Airport, the flight plan filed. And neither of us had eaten since I shared my packed lunch with you at lunchtime.'

He looked at her for a moment and then, unexpectedly, he laughed. 'You're really getting into this.'

Of course she was. She was a con man's daughter and the apple didn't fall far from the tree but she wasn't hurting anyone, cheating anyone...

'I'm the go-to woman for detail,' she said.

'Okay, so it's late, we're tired and hungry. What do you suggest?'

'A quick trip to the nearest fast food outlet?' she offered, mentally waving goodbye to the Michelin stars. 'Or we could have ordered in a Chinese. Where would we have been? You don't have an office in London.'

'I have a service flat at the Savoy,' he said. 'I work from there.'

Okaaay... 'Well, no problem. Obviously, you called up room service. I would have been happy with scrambled egg and a pot of tea but you insisted on a proper meal and champagne because one of the ventures you'd financed had just been launched on the Stock Exchange...' She snapped out of her story. 'Do you drink champagne?'

'It has been known,' he said wryly.

'Oh, yes...' Colour rose to her cheeks as she recalled the photographs of him in that fountain, naked, his arm around a girl who had stripped down to transparently wet underwear, his mouth open as he'd poured champagne over them both. She cleared her throat. 'So let's say this happened about eighteen months ago. That would have been about the time of the Maxim Sports flotation.'

'How would you know that?' he asked, losing the smile.

'It's not a secret.'

'I'm not suggesting that it is. I'm asking how you know

that off the top of your head,' he persisted. 'Please don't tell me that you read up on it on your way here.'

She swallowed, wishing she'd kept her smart mouth shut instead of getting carried away with their story. Too late and now he'd gone all suspicious on her. She would never tell him the truth—that she'd hoped to recoup a large amount, at least large enough to finally settle her father's debt. She wouldn't have seen a penny of that money for herself.

'I know,' she said, 'because I invested some of my hard-earned in the launch shares.'

'You play the market?' he asked with an edge in his voice sharp enough to cut steel.

'I don't play at anything.' She had done nothing wrong and yet all her instincts had instantly gone on the defensive. As had his. There was no smile now, none of the warmth that a moment ago had fed their game, only suspicion as she was forced onto the back foot, having to justify what she did. 'That six-month maternity cover was for a stock-broker. I've learned a lot from him over the years, including the advice to follow a smart venture capitalist by the name of Bram Ansari.'

'No doubt. And I imagine that as you go from company to company you pick up a great deal of privileged infor-mation,' he said, ignoring her last comment, 'which you feed back to him.'

On the word of a friend, the assurance of a young man who'd never met her, he had confided in her, laid himself bare, hostage to her discretion. With one careless remark she had shattered that trust. She didn't answer but reached into her bag for her tablet, calling on every ounce of self-control to keep her hands steady as she pulled up a folder.

'That's my portfolio. If you check it against my work diary you'll see that I've never invested in any of the companies I've worked for.' She stood up, placed it in front of him and turned to leave but he caught her hand.

'Ruby...'

'It's all there. Dates, amounts, profits...'

'Sit down.'

When she didn't move he looked up, his golden eyes gleaming in the light of the candles.

'Will you please sit down, Ruby?'

She lowered herself to the edge of the chair but he still kept his hand lightly wrapped around hers as he flicked through her trading history. He wasn't restraining her, simply holding her hand. She could have pulled away. She should have pulled away—

'You had funds from the sale of the Maxim shares but you didn't invest in Oliver Brent's venture,' he said after a while.

'No.'

He looked up. 'Was there any special reason for that?'

'Nothing that would make sense to you.'

'Try me.'

'It was nothing.' Bram Ansari simply waited. 'He had a smile that could sell false teeth to a shark.' She lifted her shoulders a millimetre or two. 'I'm sure Oliver Brent is solid as a rock. Shares in his company have gone through the roof in the last twelve months. My mistake,' she added.

'No.' He released her hand, sat back in his chair, putting a little distance between them so that she could breathe again. 'You have to trust your instincts. If your gut tells you to walk away, no matter how good it looks, then that's the right decision.'

He looked up, met her gaze then closed her tablet and handed it back to her.

'An interesting portfolio but you take your profit too soon.'

'I have expenses.'

He nodded. 'Take a look at the pitches in my pending file when you have time. I'd be interested to know if anything catches your eye.'

He hadn't apologised for jumping to the wrong conclusion, accusing her of insider trading, but she had been given something infinitely more precious. His trust.

'So tell me, Ruby, what did we eat that first night?'

She blinked at the abrupt change of subject, taking a moment to catch up. 'Eat? I don't know. I'll have to check the Savoy's menu online.'

'They will prepare anything at the Grill but there is a great seafood bar.' He glanced up and his eyes glowed amber in the candlelight. 'Do you enjoy shellfish?'

'Yes,' she said quickly. 'Yes, I love it.'

'Then maybe we'd have started with a shared platter. Oysters, lobster tails, smoked salmon?'

The night was still, black and warm around them. The only sounds were the soft swoosh of the sea lapping against the sand in the cove below them, a cicada warming up in fits and starts. They were alone in the small circle of candlelight and for a moment the beginning of this make-believe love affair felt real. She could imagine them sitting over supper, talking, just like they were tonight.

'D-delicious,' she said, her voice thick.

'What next? Will you stay with fish or they do a very fine burger?'

'We were talking,' she said. 'I didn't notice what we had next except there was something out of this world made of chocolate for dessert and the richest coffee I've ever tasted.'

'Oh?' He propped his elbows on the table and rested his chin on his hands, smiling now. 'What were we talking about that was so distracting?'

'I asked you about the company you were about to invest in, why them…'

'Eighteen months ago?' He thought about it for a moment. 'That would have to be Shadbrook. It's still early days.'

'I read something about them last week,' she said. 'Eco-energy?' And, just like that, they were off and talking about the company, the passion of the people involved, and she didn't notice that she'd demolished the dish of fruit and sweets that Mina had brought them.

Eventually she ran out of questions and they fell silent.

'And then, Ruby?' he said softly, looking at her intently. 'When we stopped talking what did we do then?'

'I...' For a moment it had been so real, almost as if they were back in London eighteen months ago, eating fabulous food, talking about something that fascinated them both. 'It was late,' she said. 'You called for your car and sent me home in style.'

'And immediately cancelled my flight to New York so that I could see you the next day.'

'No... I wouldn't have been free. You were lucky to have had me for a day.'

'Ruby, Ruby...' He laughed softly. 'Okay, so I had to leave the next day but my driver had your address,' he said, his voice like silk velvet against her skin. 'I would have been on your doorstep as the sun rose with coffee and warm *pain au chocolat* so that we could have breakfast together.'

The image he'd painted was so real that she could see herself rushing to the door in her bathrobe, imagining her elderly neighbour had some problem. Opening it to find Bram Ansari filling her doorway, a glossy paper carrier from some smart bakery in his hand, his tawny eyes hungry for more than pastry.

'Yes...' The word was little more than a breath.

For a moment neither of them moved.

'You've had a long day,' Bram said, abruptly pushing his chair back and standing up. 'We'll continue this in the morning.'

She swallowed, forced herself to focus on the reality not the dream.

'Long and unusual,' she agreed as he held her chair so that she could get to her feet. From doubting that Bram Ansari would accept her as his PA, she was now going to be his wife. It might be no more than a paper marriage but she still needed to process the situation, make a plan, think herself into the role and become a woman his family would believe he loved.

There were a dozen details they needed to hammer out but she needed a little space to think it through and, slipping her tablet back into her bag, she rose to her feet.

She was tall but he was half a head taller. As she turned from the table she found herself staring at the scar beneath his left eye and, without thinking, she reached up, her fingers a hair's breadth from touching him.

'I dishonoured Safia Khadri. Someone who loved her thought I should have a permanent reminder.'

'You could have lost an eye.'

'He was too angry to care,' he said, reaching up, taking the hand hovering over the scar and, still holding it, headed for the steps, walking her up to her suite as if they were really that couple who, lost to reality, had shared breakfast in bed in her tiny flat before he'd flown away. Who had snatched precious moments whenever he'd passed through London.

Who had looked at one another this evening and re-alised that they could no longer live without one another.

They were creating a legend but that was not enough. They were going to have to put on a convincing performance as newlyweds, appear to all the world as if they couldn't keep their hands off one another.

It was just part of the job, she told herself as he glanced back to make sure she was managing the oldest, narrowest and most uneven part of the steps. The place where she'd stumbled on the way down and he'd held her and for a moment she'd forgotten everything she'd learned about the danger of getting close to someone. The risk of hurting not just herself, because that didn't matter, but some innocent who deserved more.

Briefly forgotten and just as quickly recovered.

This was a business arrangement first, last and everything in between. Bram couldn't have asked her to go through with a paper marriage if it had been anything more.

She could not have accepted.

'Have you thought about a gift for your father?' she asked, retrieving her hand as they reached her level, determined to focus on her job.

'I've been training a young falcon.' He was looking to the south, to Umm al Basr, and for a moment his guard was down and the longing to be home was painfully exposed.

'I'm sure he'll appreciate the personal nature of such a gift,' she said.

'I hope so.'

'He made a deal with an old enemy because he wants you near him,' she said softly. 'He won't send you away again.'

He turned to look at her and for a moment it took all her willpower not to put her arms around him, hold him. Then he shook his head and all trace of vulnerability vanished.

'Give me your phone. I need your number. And the name of your lawyer.'

'Do you need it now?'

'Please.'

'I'll text their details to you.'

'What about Amanda?' he asked as he sent the numbers to his own phone.

'She'll invoice you.'

'Will you tell her why you're staying on?'

'Oh, yes, I suppose so. There's bound to be publicity. Errant son arrives home with unsuitable bride is a story made for *Celebrity*.'

'Not in Umm al Basr. Family matters are private. Wives are very private.'

'In this day and age? You were an internationally famous sportsman. Front cover material.'

'No one who values the good opinion of the Emir will be phoning in this story,' he assured her. 'Despite all the publicity when I was disinherited, Safia's name was never mentioned.'

'Well, good.' She managed a grin. 'It will make returning to work when this is all over a great deal easier.'

She'd changed her name and the chances of anyone seeing her photograph and connecting it with a slightly tubby sixteen-year-old astride a horse were vanishingly small but even so his confidence was reassuring.

'In fact, the fewer people who know the better. I'll simply tell her you've asked me to stay until Peter returns.' She nodded towards the phone he was holding. 'I should have your number too.'

'It's done,' he said, handing it back to her. 'You'll be getting a call from Princess Violet's assistant, Leila Darwish, within the hour. She'll want your measurements, shoe size.'

'Oh, but—'

'You will need more than a boring black dress if you're going to convince anyone that you're my wife.'

'Really?' she replied, back in PA mode. 'I fly in out of the blue, we fall into one another's arms and twenty-four hours later you present me to your father as your new wife.

Do you really think we'd have wasted much time worrying about what I was going to wear, let alone going on a major shopping spree?'

'I...' He shook his head, clearly not prepared to go there. 'No.'

'And your sisters will have less time to cross-question me if they're distracted by the task of helping me shop for a wardrobe fit for a princess.'

'They are going to love you, Ruby.'

'But not too much. You'll want their sympathy, not their blame when it's over. I may have to let being a princess go to my head. Become a bit of a diva.'

He shook his head. 'Peter was right. You are very good.'

CHAPTER FOUR

RUBY CLOSED THE door and leaned back against it, heart pounding, mouth dry. A princessy diva? She'd spent the last ten years living below the radar, being invisible. How on earth was she going to pull that off?

It had seemed so simple when Bram had put the proposition to her. No more than a little extra twist on the job. But it wasn't going to be that easy. His family would be suspicious—any family would be suspicious—and there were a dozen questions she should have asked.

Where would they stay in Umm al Basr? And if it was in the palace, how would they handle the sleeping arrangements?

And that was before she got into the whole major wardrobe makeover. Her limited wardrobe of classics in a grey/black palette wouldn't take her past day one and, much as she hated the idea of having clothes bought for her, it was obvious that she'd need clothes to support the story.

Princess Violet's mouth-watering designs had made a big impact when they'd been launched at London Fashion Week and she was woman enough to want to appear at the palace wearing something stunning, if only to give her the poise she'd need to carry this off.

And if she blasted into the palace full of confidence and with a knock-out wardrobe, his female relatives would take an instant dislike to her. Uncomfortable, but for the best.

* * *

Bram was not about to embarrass his cousin by asking him to collude in this paper marriage and was relieved to find that his quick sketch of the story Ruby had woven around their 'romance' had been accepted without the least suspicion.

'This is wonderful news, my friend. You've been alone for too long,' Fayad said, clearly delighted. 'Does Ruby have family to negotiate for her?'

'No, she is quite alone. Will you stand for her in the question of the contract?'

'It will be my pleasure. There's not much time so we should begin.'

Fayad was as meticulous as if he'd been negotiating for his own daughter but finally it was done and arrangements made for the signing ceremony before the charity dinner the following evening.

Ask the Garland Girl, Peter had said and, in desperation, he'd asked the impossible of Ruby Dance. He could hardly believe that she'd said yes. He should have insisted that she sleep on her decision. He should call her now and tell her that she must do that.

He picked up his phone but, with his thumb poised over the call button, he pulled back. She'd do that anyway and he wouldn't have to ask her on which side her decision had landed when he saw her tomorrow morning. She might have a face made for poker but he'd know the moment he set eyes on her if she'd changed her mind.

Meanwhile, there were things he needed to do, to have in place, in case she was prepared to go ahead.

Ruby knew that she would not sleep until she had her head straight around all the questions that seemed to spring into her mind the moment she was alone. She explored the little kitchen and made herself a cup of tea before settling down with a notebook and pen and began making a list.

She wasn't clear whether he had been completely cut off from his family. He appeared to be in touch with his brother, but what about the rest of the family? Did he meet them in London? Did they visit him here in Ras al Kawi? Would he have talked to her about them, or would such a relationship have been off the conversational agenda? And how should she address his mother, for instance? And his father, assuming things went well enough for her to meet him.

And there were a hundred other things.

What was his favourite food? What music did he enjoy? What would he have shared with her about his childhood? Those were the details that would help her convince a sceptical mother or sister that their relationship was real.

And the really big one, the elephant in the room, where were they going to sleep?

There wasn't going to be a lot of time tomorrow and she texted him her questions so that he would have time to think about it and have his answers ready.

That done, she laid out the clothes she would wear to travel in, checked over the dress and bolero jacket she would wear for the dinner at the palace in Ras al Kawi and then ran a bath. She was about to step into it when her phone pinged.

She picked it up and smiled as she saw that Bram had responded.

My sisters are Almira, Hasna, Fathia and Nadiya. I'll give you a list of their children and their accomplishments in the morning. Music? A mixed bag from rock to classical. Where do you live, Ruby?

She sank into the bath and texted back.

Good point. Camden.

She added the address.

Up the first flight of stairs and on the right. Tiny hall, sitting room on the left, bedroom on the right, bathroom, minute kitchen. 'Stairway to Heaven'?

She added a smiley and clicked 'send'.

A moment or two later the guitar solo at the opening of the track rippled softly from an unseen speaker and she sank lower into the bath, closing her eyes as the song built and the lyrics filled her head. There was a line in there somewhere about looking to the west. Was he torn, she wondered, between his longing for home and his old life in Europe? The rush of downhill racing, the polo matches, the aristocratic groupies...

A beep recalled her to their conversation.

What do you drive?

In London? Are you kidding? A bike.

With a basket on the front?

Is there any other kind? she replied, smiling now. What's your comfort food?

Comfort food?

The only thing you want when you've been dumped...

Although she doubted that had ever happened to him.

Or have man flu, or your team lost the big match.

Her thumbs were flying over the letters.

Tinned tomato soup? A fried egg sandwich? A cheese-burger?

I'll go with the burger.

With pickles?

With extra pickles. What's your favourite colour? No, don't tell me—dark ruby-red.

Before she could reply, the phone rang.

'Whoah!' she said.

'Did I startle you?'

'I nearly dropped the phone in the bath.'

There was silence from the other end of the phone and she bit her lower lip. Stupid thing to say...

'Do you have speakers in every room in the house?' she asked quickly.

'Each apartment is individually Internet enabled. You can download anything your mood dictates.'

'Impressive. What are you listening to?'

'You,' he said. 'I'm listening to you. No, I'm talking to you. Are you quite sure about this, Ruby?'

'Quite sure,' she said, touched that he was concerned about her when this meant so much to him. He could have no idea how much it meant to her. Freedom... 'This is a temporary assignment like any other but there are a few details we have to sort out.'

'Be certain,' he warned, 'because the moment the contract is signed you will be Princess Ruby of Umm al Basr.'

She swallowed. She was kidding herself; this wasn't like any other temp placement she'd had. Not at all.

'That will be weird.'

'It's just a form of address. Like Miss. Or Mrs.'

Of course it was…

'I'll try and remember that.' Back to the list. 'Do you see any of your family?'

'Occasionally. When my mother and sisters are in London.'

'Your brother?'

'We keep in touch. I saw him when my father had his heart bypass operation in London last year.'

About to ask if he had seen his father then, she thought better of it. He would have said he'd seen his brother when he was visiting his father. Clearly, banishment meant more than exile from his country.

The water was tepid when she finally climbed out of the bath, wrapped herself in the fluffy robe hanging behind the door and curled up with her notebook, writing down everything he'd told her about his family, his life.

It was barely light when Bram mounted Antares and rode him hard into the dawn. Last night everything had seemed so simple but in the light of dawn he knew that where emotions ran high nothing was certain.

He paused at the top of a low promontory looking down the Gulf towards the Indian Ocean and, for just a moment, wondered what it would be like to have Ruby beside him astride Rigel, witnessing the sunrise, watching the shadows shrink…

He headed for the kitchen, planning to grab a cup of coffee, take a shower then find Ruby and offer her a last chance to change her mind. Ruby was ahead of him.

She was sitting at the breakfast counter, long legs twined around the stool, a fork halfway to her lips, laughing at something that Mina was saying more with actions than words.

He leaned over and helped himself to a piece of the pineapple she was eating. She turned and looked up at him, her lips a startled O, gleaming with sweet juice…

'*Aasif,*' he apologised as Mina muttered disapprovingly. 'I've brought the smell of the stables into her kitchen.'

'It's a good smell. It takes me back…'

She broke off, but she didn't need to explain. Scent was the most evocative of the senses and it was obvious last night that she had spent a great deal of time around horses before whatever scandal had blighted her family. Before the death of her parents.

No ties.

Like him, she was not so much unattached as detached.

'I saw last night how good you were with the horses. Rigel would never let just anyone take a brush to him.' He poured himself a glass of juice. 'You were one of those horse-mad little girls,' he said, resisting the temptation to lay his hand on her shoulder so that she would know she was not alone. 'A member of the Pony Club. Bouncing around on a little pony.'

She didn't say anything but the answer was in her eyes. The painful glow of a passion that could never be entirely extinguished. The memory of horses that had become a part of her.

'When we return to the fort we'll ride together.'

She shook her head, stiff now. 'No. I told you. I don't ride. Thank you.'

'Did you have a fall?' he asked.

'No…' She pulled a face, made an effort to smile that was painful to watch. 'Well, yes, obviously, dozens of them, but it's not that.'

Ruby's mouth was dry. She would have picked up the glass of juice Mina had poured for her but her hand would shake so much she'd spill it.

Last night she'd felt the soft lips of a horse taking a carrot from her hand, she'd run a hand over its neck, remembered the exhilaration as half a ton of the most beautiful animal on earth lifted her over a fence. Riding was something that had happened in another life—one that she'd lost on the day when her world had fallen apart.

She could ride here on one of Bram's fine horses—was already half in love with Rigel. But when she returned to London, to reality, she would lose it all over again.

Aware that he was waiting for some explanation, she fell back on her original excuse. 'You'll recall that I'm under strict orders from Amanda not to take part in any dangerous sports while I'm here.'

'And yet you agreed to marry me.'

'Marriage isn't a sport.' The heat coming off him might be warming her, the scent of fresh sweat, horse flesh, warm leather making her feel slightly dizzy, but they had laid down the ground rules and any danger was entirely in her head. 'In this case it's not even a marriage.'

'Just an extension of your role as my personal assistant.' He didn't say the words that they were thinking—no sex— but his smile was little more than a twist of his lips. 'With the fewer people who know about it the better.'

Confused by his irritation—surely he must want the same thing—she said, 'What about Khal? He knows that you hadn't met me before today.'

'Khal will keep his thoughts to himself.'

'And Mina? How will she take the news?'

'Shall we find out?' he asked as she returned with his coffee.

Her response was to let out a scream, put her hands to her face as she poured forth a stream of joyful congratulations. Then she flung her arms around him, kissed him on both cheeks before grabbing Ruby and repeating the performance, almost bouncing on the spot before rushing off to share the news with the rest of her family.

'Does that answer your question?' he asked with a wry

smile, clearly expecting her to be amused. He couldn't have been more wrong.

'She thinks you're happy,' she said, horrified. As would his mother, his sisters…

'I am,' he assured her. 'Tomorrow, thanks to you, I will be home for the first time in five years.' He picked up his cup and made a move. 'Eat your breakfast, Ruby. It's going to be a long day.'

'It's going to be a long day for both of us but Mina will think it odd if you rush away.' She offered him a piece of pineapple on a fork. 'We need to talk.'

'Those details you wanted to sort out?' He ignored the pineapple but slid onto the stool beside her. 'I imagine you're concerned about sleeping arrangements.'

She felt her cheeks heat up. Which was ridiculous.

'We'll take the boat down to Umm al Basr and stay on board while we're there,' he said, cutting her off before she could get the wrong idea. 'It has a communications centre—there are those video conferences, phone calls—and we'll have our own living space and staff, which will cut out the palace gossip,' he added, lifting his head as he heard the helicopter approaching. 'How soon can you be ready to leave?'

Ruby had just zipped up her case when her phone rang. She looked at the caller ID and said, 'Hi, Amanda.'

'Is this a good time?'

'Not really. We're leaving for the capital very shortly. Princess Violet is holding a charity dinner this evening.'

'Then I won't keep you. I just need to know how long you'll be staying. If it's more than a week I'll need to re-arrange your schedule.'

'Bram wants me to stay until Peter is well enough to return,' she replied, fudging it.

'Bram? When you called yesterday I had the feeling things were not going that well.'

Oh...sherbet dabs.

'My arrival came as a complete surprise. Communication failure,' she said. 'Once he'd spoken to Jude Radcliffe and Peter he was fine.'

'First name terms, fine?'

'Everyone is on first name terms here.'

'Oh, right. Are you happy to stay that long? According to Elizabeth, it's likely to be a few months before Peter's back on his feet.'

'If it's not a problem?' She hated letting down people who were expecting her but, while there were plenty of well qualified staff on Amanda's books to cover for her, there was no one else who could be the temp that Bram needed right now.

'Yes, but it's mine, not yours. I knew the situation when I sent you to Ras al Kawi. I'll keep an eye on your flat while you're away. Do you want me to forward your mail?'

'Don't bother. It will be nothing but junk mail and bills and they're paid by direct debit. I have to go, Amanda. I'll give you a call later in the week.'

Ruby and Bram were met at the helipad by a car that took them into the heart of the palace complex. When it came to a halt, Bram helped her out but left the car door open.

'You're not staying?' she asked as he made a move to get back in the car.

'Fayad is expecting me. Go and enjoy yourself.'

'Enjoy myself?'

He smiled. 'I'll come and fetch you when everything is ready.' With that, he climbed back into the car and she watched as he was driven away.

For all her outward confidence, all her experience at the high end of business, nothing had prepared her for this. It was one thing to agree to be a pretend bride but, despite the easy banter as they'd built the story of their meeting, the comfortable way they'd shared breakfast with Mina fussing around them, she was about to marry a total stranger and she was a bundle of nerves. As she'd lain awake in the unaccustomed darkness, silence—missing the background sound of a great city to lull her to sleep—her mind had conjured up a dozen reasons why it was not going to work.

'Miss Dance?' She turned to find an elegant young woman walking towards her, hand outstretched. 'Welcome to the palace, Miss Dance. I'm Leila Darwish, Princess Violet's assistant.'

She took her hand. 'Please, call me Ruby.'

'If you'll come this way?'

Ruby followed her through the ornately decorated arch, across a courtyard where water burbled softly over smooth rocks, cooling the air, and on into the interior of a reception room large enough to throw a serious party.

Waiting there was a woman of about her own height, dark hair falling nearly to her waist. She was wearing a soft silk *salwar kameez* in a stunning mix of violet and a rare turquoise green that exactly matched the colour of her eyes.

With a wide smile she took her hands, kissed both her cheeks and said, 'Welcome, Ruby. I'm so glad that Bram has found someone to share his life.' Despite a serious nose that betrayed the Arab genes handed down from her great-grandmother, Princess Violet retained a touch of the streets of London in her accent. 'I've always thought how lonely he must be out at the fort.'

'Th-thank you, Princess—' she managed, stunned that the Ruler's wife had taken time to meet her when she had to be busy putting the finishing touches to her charity dinner. Or maybe a princess had people to do that for her.

'Violet,' she urged. 'By this evening we will be cousins. Fayad and I are so happy that the Emir has called Bram home. It's such an important moment and made even more special by the fact that he can take the woman he loves home with him.'

'I…' Speechless, she fell back on the only thing she could say. 'Thank you.'

'Let's have tea while we talk clothes.'

'Clothes?'

'Bram spoke to Fayad last night and asked if I'd help you sort out your trousseau. His mother and sisters will want to see everything and his instructions were to ensure that they drool with envy.'

'Oh, but…' He'd totally ignored her suggestion that his sister should have that pleasure. Or maybe he'd listened when she'd said that they shouldn't love her. 'That's what he meant when he said to enjoy myself?' she asked.

Violet laughed. 'Undoubtedly, and we will, but first we have to find something for you to wear for the ceremony. I don't imagine you packed a just-in-case wedding dress?' she teased.

'Um, no… Just my work wardrobe. I'm a bit shell-shocked at the speed of this, to be honest,' Ruby said, making an effort to get with the narrative.

'I know the feeling. Fayad took me by surprise too. If I hadn't had Leila to guide me through the minefield of palace etiquette I don't know what I would have done. She is the sister of my soul.'

The two women exchanged a look of such fondness that Ruby felt a pang of loneliness. She was close to Amanda but this was clearly something very special.

'I envy you,' she said. 'I longed for a sister.' And then, when her world imploded, had been glad that there was no one else to be hurt.

'Bram said you have no family.'

Clearly he'd done everything he could to make this easy for her and she shook her head. 'No.'

'Neither had I.' Violet reached for her hand. 'Fayad's family took me to their heart and Bram's mother and sisters will do the same for you.'

Ruby swallowed and, realising that she was too full up to speak, Violet became brisk.

'The dress… There isn't much time. I've brought across some of my own collection but we'll measure you up, have a chat about what you like. Once we have an idea of your style Leila will have a selection of clothes sent up from the boutiques in the mall.'

Violet ushered her through to a less daunting room where comfortable sofas, piled with huge soft cushions, invited her to kick off her shoes and curl up. Rails of exotic clothes in glowing jewel colours had been lined up but, before she could look at them, Leila ran a tape measure over her and checked her shoe size. That done, the two of them flicked through the clothes, transferring those they thought would suit her to an empty rail.

Shot silks with Violet's trademark appliquéd designs, swirls of chiffon, deep reds to match her name, embroidered and beaded creations, each one costing more than she would earn in months.

'No…'

Violet turned. 'A bit over-the-top for your taste?'

'They are gorgeous,' she said, afraid that she'd offended the Princess. 'It's just that I usually wear black. Or grey. And I have a dress for this evening. It's designer,' she added a little desperately.

'Show me.'

'I don't know what's happened to my bag.'

'Noor is unpacking it for you,' Leila said.

Violet led the way through another, smaller, sitting room and then into a dressing room where a young woman had an ironing board set up, pressing each item as she unpacked it and then hung it in the cupboards that lined the room.

'This is Noor,' she said. 'You will need a companion, someone who knows her way around, to look after you. She speaks some English and she has family in Umm al Basr.'

She dropped a quick curtsey. 'Welcome, *sitti*.'

'Thank you, Noor,' Ruby said, trying not to show that she was totally overwhelmed.

Violet, meanwhile, had taken her little black dress from the wardrobe and was holding it up for a better look. 'This is it?'

'Yes. There's a bolero with long sleeves,' she added, showing her the little jacket with its stand away collar. Then, feeling something more was required, 'It's my go-anywhere dress.'

'And absolutely perfect,' she said, as she flicked through the rest of her clothes. 'As you said, this is a working wardrobe but you have a distinctive style. Classic, a touch retro.' She smiled. 'A little bit Audrey Hepburn?'

'You've got me,' Ruby admitted. 'I do the books for a woman who owns a high-end worn-once boutique. In return she keeps her eye out for anything that she thinks will suit me.'

'She's done you proud,' she said with a smile, 'but, even though it's just a simple signing ceremony, we'll do everything we can to make it special.' She turned to Leila to show her the dress. 'What do you think?'

'Elegant, perfect for Bram's personal assistant, but His Highness Sheikh Ibrahim will expect his bride to be wearing something a little more decorative for the ceremony.' She thought for a moment. 'There's a dress in the new collection…'

Violet smiled. 'Two minds…' She turned to Noor and asked her to fetch it. 'And if you'll make those calls, Leila?'

Leila nodded, leaving them alone. 'Let's go and have some tea while we're waiting.'

'I'm so sorry to put you to so much trouble.'

'It's no trouble,' she said, grinning broadly. 'I think the whole thing is utterly romantic. I want to know everything. How long have you known one another? How did you meet…?'

Hours later, Ruby stood in front of a mirror in the vast luxurious bedroom. She had been bathed, had her hair, nails, make-up done by what felt like an army of maids and now she was wearing a whisper of the finest silver-grey silk and lace underwear that a billionaire Sheikh, in desperate need of a wife, could buy. But she'd seen neither hide nor hair of him since he'd driven away and left her to the tender ministrations of his cousin's wife.

She reminded herself that if she'd been his real intended bride he wouldn't have seen her for much longer than five hours, so it wasn't such a stretch.

'Ready?' Violet asked.

She took another look at her reflection, her legs stretched by the four-inch heels she was wearing—one of a hundred or more pairs that had arrived that afternoon. Four-inch heels and clever strips of the softest pale grey suede.

She'd had little say in the choice. Violet and Leila had gone through everything and chosen for her, leaving her with little to do but nod her approval because this kind of dressing was way above her pay grade.

'Ready,' she confirmed, her voice little more than a whisper.

A seamstress had stood by while Leila and Violet had nipped and tucked and now the dress slid over her body like a lover's sigh—a drift of silk and chiffon sparkling with thousands of crystals clustered thickly over the bodice, falling in sprays over her hips, glittering amongst the gathers as it fell to the floor.

Noor spent long minutes closing the tiny fastenings at the side until the dress fitted like a second skin. There were no sleeves but a cape of chiffon sparkled and flowed unlined from her shoulders to cover her arms in front and fall into a short train behind, a miracle of cut and design.

That done, all three stood back, waiting for her reaction.

It was simple, it was breathtaking and, just for a moment, Ruby wondered what it would be like to be Bram's Princess, not on paper, but for real…

'I don't know what to say.'

'That is always the effect we aim for,' Violet said before kissing her cheek, taking her hand and leading her out through a sitting room that was now stacked with boxes and bags filled with clothes, shoes, underwear, and into the vast reception room.

They stopped in the centre of the room. Leila adjusted the fall of the skirt. Violet arranged the train then stood back and took a photograph of her using her phone.

'Stunning,' she said. 'Absolutely stunning. I wish I could be here to see Bram's face…' Then, having kissed her again, they left her standing alone to await the arrival of her groom.

Her heart was racing and, in an attempt to slow it, reclaim control of her body if not her life, she closed her eyes. When she opened them again Bram was standing in front of her and her heart rate shot through the roof.

She had only seen in him in the most casual of clothes— a towel, a pair of shorts and a T-shirt, dusty riding clothes, the chinos he'd worn with a loose collarless shirt to travel into the city. Now he was wearing traditional robes.

Everything was simple, understated. A plain white *thaub* over which had been thrown the finest camel hair *bisht*, a fine white *keffiyeh* held in place by a plain black *egal* and at his waist he carried a traditional curved knife in a black and silver filigree scabbard. Simple, understated, regal, he was every inch the desert prince, but it was his face that held her—his golden eyes, a jaw strong enough to slay dragons, the seductive curve of a lower lip that she wanted to suck into her mouth.

No, no, no—

'Wow…' she said, all faux brightness. 'Look at us.'

'Rabi…' his voice was unexpectedly soft '…you are every inch a princess.'

Rabi… She blinked. 'You do know that when we're married I'll expect you to remember my name.'

'Fayad thought an Arabic name would be more suitable for the contract. That it would please my father. Rabi was the nearest to your own. It means harvest.'

All afternoon Violet and Leila had talked about weddings. Their own, those of their friends. They'd shown her photographs of their children, assuming that she would soon be a mother, and she'd had to play along, smile as if she couldn't wait.

The name Bram had given her implied fertility, fecundity and the lie was like a cold hand squeezing her womb.

'Your father will like that,' she said as he put down the leather case he was carrying. He glanced up, frowning, clearly catching something in her tone. 'Good choice,' she added with the smile she'd once practised in the mirror. The smile she used to cover hurt, pain, the spiteful remarks of others. It had been so long since she'd used it that her cheeks creaked a bit, but it seemed to reassure him and, as he opened the case, she didn't have to pretend to catch her breath as he revealed the jewels within.

Her gasp was totally real.

'Oh, my…' she said, staring at the Art Deco parure of diamonds and rubies.

At one point, feeling that she had to add something to

the dress, shoe, underwear debate, she'd suggested that perhaps she needed some colour to offset the silver-grey but Leila had it covered with ruby polish for her nails and colour for her mouth.

'You like it?' he asked.

'It's perfect... How did you know?'

He smiled. 'Violet sent me a photograph of the dress, although I have to say it looks a lot better on you than a tailor's dummy.'

She felt her cheeks warm as he continued to look at her and she said, 'You owe her, Bram. She must have had a thousand things to do today but she and Leila have overseen every detail.'

'I'll repay her when I donate to her charity tonight.' He turned to the case and picked up one of a pair of bracelets that nestled against the silk. 'Shall we begin?'

She raised her hand without a word and he fastened the wide cuff of diamonds and rubies over her left wrist. Was he taking care not to actually touch her or was that her imagination?

He repeated the performance with her right wrist and no, it was not her imagination. When the clasp proved awkward she saw that his hands were shaking, no doubt at the cost of this temporary arrangement, but the jewels, at least, could be returned when it was all over.

She held out her hands to look at the result. Hers were shaking too, she realised, and he caught them and held them, held her gaze. If he thought that was going to steady her he couldn't have been more wrong.

'Are you going to be all right, Ruby?' he asked.

'Fine,' she managed through a throat that felt as if it had been stuffed with boulders. 'It's just that I've never worn anything quite so...sparkly.'

He laughed. 'Shall we try the collar?'

She nodded and he released her hands to pick up a neck-

lace that was a simple V-shaped geometric collar of diamonds and rubies, with clusters of rubies forming hearts
down the centre of the V.

It was set dressing, she told herself. Just set dressing.
Like the dress, the shoes, the contract. All to convince his
father that this was real.

'You seem taller,' he said as he lifted the collar to her
throat.

'It's the shoes.' She lifted the skirt an inch to reveal a
barely-there sandal, her ruby-painted toenails.

He glanced down and it seemed half a lifetime before
he finally looked up. 'Very pretty,' he said, his face expressionless, 'but I'm going to have to ask you to bend
forward a little.'

She dipped her head and as his fingers brushed against
the back of her neck she struggled to control the shiver
that rippled through her body, tightened her nipples into
hard buds against the lace that he would see the moment
she straightened.

After what seemed like an age with his arms around
her, drowning in the scent of clean laundry, warm skin,
something that might have been sandalwood, the clasp
finally clicked into place. He stepped back and she could
breathe again. Too soon…

The backs of his fingers brushed against her skin as he
lifted the collar and eased it into place so that the row of
hearts was perfectly vertical and the necklace echoed the
neckline of the dress where it dipped between her breasts.

'How does that feel?' he asked.

'Heavy…' There was a heaviness in her breasts and
low in her belly. An ache between her thighs. It had been
a long time since she'd shared a bed with a man but with
every touch the heat, the need, was building.

'It will soon be over,' he said, reaching for one of the
earrings—long falls of diamonds and rubies.

'Shall I...?' she asked shakily. She was unravelling and if he touched her again...

'Your hands aren't steady enough.'

'Believe me, if you were wearing this many diamonds you'd be feeling a bit wobbly,' she said.

'You'll get used to it,' he assured her.

'Not in a million years and you wouldn't do this for Bibi,' she said desperately, her knees, hips melting as women's bodies had melted since the morning Eve woke up and discovered Adam staring down at her.

'No, she would come ready gift-wrapped,' he agreed as he carefully fitted the earrings in place.

And it would be his duty to unwrap her. In her case he was doing the wrapping but it wasn't going to be Christmas for either of them.

'Are they comfortable?' he asked. 'Not too heavy?'

She shook her head and they brushed against her neck.

Finally he took the last item from the case, a curious piece of white gold, scattered with diamonds and rubies arranged in flower shapes.

'What is that?' she asked.

'Give me your left hand.'

She raised it and he took it in his, held it for a moment before sliding the confection onto her hand so that the gems sparkled along her thumb and index finger. 'A double ring,' he said, continuing to hold it.

'Did I say wow?' she asked.

'I think that's my line. No one is going to lift an eyebrow when I tell them that when you appeared at the fort yesterday morning I knew that I could never let you go. They'll only wonder why on earth it took me so long to figure it out.'

'A fabulous dress and a king's ransom in jewels will work wonders.'

'It takes more than that.' For a moment he just stood there looking at her, then seemed to catch himself. 'Ready?'

She nodded. 'I might need a hand in these heels.'

'Not a problem.'

He took her right hand, turned and tucked her arm beneath his and slowly, giving her time to become accustomed to the height of the heels, the length of the dress, the tug of the train, he led her across the courtyard to a limousine that was waiting to take them to the Emir's audience room.

Noor was waiting to arrange her dress and the train so that she could sit without crushing it, then she climbed into the front seat beside the driver so that she could make any final adjustments when they arrived.

Bram joined her, reached for her hand. It was all show from here on in...

He glanced at her. 'Are you still trembling?'

'It's just a touch of stage fright. I've never been married before.'

'That makes two of us,' he said with a smile that only made the butterflies worse. 'The trick is to remember that this is all make-believe.'

'Yes.' None of this was real so being nervous was just plain silly and she was about to say so but the car came to a halt and the door was opened by whatever passed for a footman in this part of the world. It was like a scene from the evening news where one of the royals was arriving at a gala, even down to the red carpet.

Bram stepped out and turned to offer her a hand, tightening his grip as she steadied herself on the heels. He waited for a moment while Noor adjusted the folds of her skirt, her train, tweaked a curl into place and then loosely draped a scarf made from the same material as her dress, sparkling with crystals, over her hair.

Ruby stared up at the splendour of the floodlit dome at

the centre of the palace complex as she took her time arranging the ends so that they trailed behind her to the floor.

'It looks like a picture in a book of fairy tales I had as a child,' she said. 'Scheherazade telling cliff-hanger stories so that she would live for one more day…' A shiver ran through her. 'Is your home like this?' she asked.

'Similar in layout. I have—had—a house there.'

'It's going to be very dusty after five years,' she said, making a feeble joke to cover her nerves. And then, as his eyes clouded, wished she hadn't. 'Don't worry; I'm familiar with the working end of a vacuum cleaner.'

He grinned. 'You Garland Girls are such good value,' he said as he led her along the red carpet that had been laid not for them but in preparation for the arrival of guests for the banquet later that evening.

'Have you told your brother?' she asked as they entered a great central hall glittering with chandeliers. 'About this.'

'No.'

'You were afraid I'd change my mind?'

'It seemed wise to ensure that he was as shocked as everyone else.' He paused, turned to look down at her. 'You can still change your mind, Ruby. It's not too late.'

'I would never have let it go this far.'

'Even so.'

'We're keeping their Highnesses waiting,' she said and after a moment he moved on, leading her by the hand to a smaller, less intimidating room.

Ruby had imagined a host of people gathered to witness the occasion but there were only four people present: Princess Violet, Sheikh Fayad al Kuwani, Leila and another man who was presumably the Emir's aide.

On the table between them was an exquisitely modern floral arrangement—three perfect dark red roses progressing from a bud at the top to a fully open bloom at the bottom. There were three leather folders, presumably holding the marriage contracts—she wondered what they actually said—a gold pen and a seal. Two chairs had been placed facing the table.

She had been briefed by Leila and dropped a brief curtsey to the Emir and his Princess and, having received warm smiles from both of them, began to relax.

The formalities did not take long. First there were photographs, the two of them alone and then with the Emir and Princess Violet, taken by the aide.

Once they were all seated, he opened the leather folders, took more photographs of Bram signing the contracts and of his cousin signing on her behalf. He then applied the Emir's official seal to the documents and returned them to their folders.

Once that was done, Bram reached for her right hand, inviting her to stand before turning to his cousin. The Emir, smiling broadly, produced a ring, a circle of oval diamonds that blazed like fire in the light of the chandelier above them as he handed it to Bram.

A ring? That wasn't a tradition in this part of the world. A simple ceremony, the signing of a contract, was just business. A ring made it a wedding…

Bram held it for a moment between his thumb and forefinger and then, never taking his eyes from hers, spoke in Arabic as he placed the ring on the third finger of her right hand. Then, in English, he said, 'Rabi al-Dance, you have honoured me by consenting to be my wife and I give you this ring as a sign that we are joined for ever.'

For ever…

She stared at it, then up at him, but before the question could form in her head Violet held out her hand and lying on her palm was a plain silver wedding band.

Bram's fingers tightened over hers and she saw that he had not anticipated this. However, there was nothing to be done but to take the ring and, having drawn in a steadying breath, place it on the third finger of his right hand. That done, she looked up.

'Ibrahim bin Tariq al-Ansari, you do me great honour by taking me as your wife,' she said. Then, repeating his pledge back to him, 'Wear this ring as a sign that we are joined for ever.'

And it was not a lie. They would be linked for ever by the secret they shared.

There was a moment of total silence and then there was a spontaneous burst of applause from their small audience before Violet, smiling from ear to ear, said, 'You have married an Englishwoman, Bram. Where we come from, it's traditional to kiss the bride.'

CHAPTER FIVE

BRAM FELT THE startled tremor ripple from Ruby's hand to his as Violet demanded a kiss for his bride but she lifted her face, not betraying by as much as a blink that this was an intimacy over and above what she'd signed up for.

Or maybe, once the rings had been produced, she had anticipated where this had been leading. The ceremony itself had been more than he'd bargained for when he'd asked his cousin to draw up the marriage contract but Fayad's English-born wife had been determined to make the moment special for her countrywoman and this was part of the show.

It was nothing. A formality. They were on a stage, acting out the story they had devised, and if the audience insisted on joining in it simply proved how successful they had been.

All that was required was the briefest touch of his lips but he instinctively lifted his hand to her face, cradling the soft curve of her cheek as he shielded her in this moment of intimacy. He felt the warmth of her breath as her mouth, red as the rubies he'd placed at her throat, parted on an intake of breath and sweet, soft lips trembled against his.

Or maybe it was him because he couldn't have been more wrong about this kiss.

This was that moment when he'd looked up and seen her silhouette against the lowering sun, the moment when she'd stumbled on the steps and he'd held her close, felt her curves fit him as if they were one and knew the scent of her hair, her skin. In that moment the heat of possession surged through him and he became the groom he was supposed to be—primed to fight his way through the throng of her family, overcome his bride's reluctance to surrender her honour and claim her as his own and his kiss became a brand.

The flash as someone took a photograph, a smattering of applause, brought him to his senses. As he raised his head Ruby opened eyes that were more black than grey; her cheeks were flushed, her bee-stung lips slightly parted as if on a breath that was stuck in her throat.

'The official photographs are for your father,' Violet said, apparently noticing nothing amiss in the reaction of two people who had supposedly been lovers for more than a year and had now chosen to make a lifelong commitment. This was a life-changing moment: stunned was the perfect response. 'For the family album. I'll have copies printed to put with the contracts but this one,' she said, grinning as she thumbed something into her phone, 'is just for you.'

And then Fayad was hugging him, shaking his hand, and Violet and Leila were kissing Ruby.

'I'm so sorry that we cannot raise a toast to you both at dinner this evening,' Violet said, 'but Fayad has explained that Bram wishes to keep the news under wraps until he has told his father.'

'We'll celebrate properly when you return,' Fayad said as they walked back through the vast audience chamber and out into a courtyard that was now lit with thousands of white fairy lights in preparation for the evening. 'Or will you be staying in Umm al Basr?'

'If all goes well I hope to spend time there but the fort is my home,' he said. Behind him, Violet—walking with Ruby—gave a little cough, reminding him of his changed status and, feeling exactly like the awkward, new-to-this groom he was supposed to be, he looked back. 'Our home.' And he reached back for Ruby's hand, enfolding it in his as he gave it a squeeze of reassurance. 'Give me a minute, *ya habibati*, this is all very new.'

'Yes.' The word came on a little gasp that exactly echoed the way he was feeling and he wanted to tell her that she'd been amazing, tell her...

Tell her nothing.

This was a business arrangement. Six months' salary. Plus the fee to pay her lawyer. And the financial settlement due to the wife of the Sheikh in the event of divorce that Fayad had negotiated on her behalf. They had been writing prenuptial agreements in this part of the world long before the Californians thought of them.

'I'm sorry for rushing you away, but I have to check the last-minute details for tonight's banquet.' Violet's apology as they reached their car was no more than a formality— from her very un-princess-like grin it was clear she believed they couldn't wait to get back to their apartment.

Instead they were sitting an arm's width apart in the rear of the limousine taking them back to their apartment with that kiss sizzling between them. They might be playing newlyweds on a strictly business basis, but all he could think about was the silk of her cheek beneath his hand. The heated welcome of her mouth. What it would be like if this were real...

Ruby cleared her throat. '*Ya hab...?*' She struggled for the word.

'*Ya habibati*,' he said, keeping his eyes straight ahead. 'A woman would say *ya habibi*.'

'Only if she knew what it meant. It's not a word I've come across in my *Arabic for Beginners*.'

'Beloved.' He turned and looked at her. 'It means *my beloved*.'

'Oh.' The diamonds he'd placed at her throat sparkled as she swallowed.

'We tend to be extravagant in our endearments.'

Making a determined effort to get them back on a businesslike footing, but keeping her eyes on the back of the driver's head, she said, 'Perhaps you should teach me some…' She faltered. 'I should know them.'

'We are not in the west,' he replied, hanging onto his self-control by a thread. 'Here, intimacy is a private thing.'

He had been sharp and she did not reply. Maybe she understood—she seemed to have a rare, instinctive understanding of most things—that he'd been caught without a defence against a kiss that he hadn't anticipated, for which he had not been prepared.

He'd had more freedom than his brother—he'd been indulged, given time to enjoy the sports he'd loved, because there would come a time when he'd have to assume the mantle of responsibility, put his people before his own pleasures—but he'd always known that marriage was a rare and precious thing, an alliance of honour between a man and woman whose future had been written for the benefit of family and state.

Right now he was in the grip of a physical response to an age-old need but this was not a flirtation with a chalet maid or one of the snow bunnies who followed the sport. This was… This was strictly business.

After what seemed a lifetime of silence the car stopped, the door opened and he was able to step out, draw in a lungful of the cool evening air before turning to offer Ruby his hand.

He sensed her reluctance to take it; he wasn't the only one who'd been swept away by that kiss. Hampered by the dress and the height of her heels, however, she had no choice but to lay her hand against his as she stepped from the car. Aware that they were still on show, that unseen eyes would follow their every move, he continued to hold her hand as he escorted her into their apartment.

Once there, she couldn't wait to let go of his hand as she kicked off her shoes and headed for the bedroom with an abrupt, 'I have to get out of this dress.'

Bram had kissed her. Neither of them had anticipated it. The ceremony was supposed to be a formal signing of the contracts, but clearly Violet had other ideas. The dress, the jewels, the perfectly fitting rings…

He had placed a circle of diamonds on her finger, made a public vow with a private meaning and then he'd kissed her. It should have been little more than a formal touch of his lips but she could still feel his hand against her cheek, the heat of his mouth…

She needed a moment, time on her own to put the pieces back together but, as she reached the bedroom door, she stopped in her tracks.

While they'd been plighting their troth, Noor had dressed it for the arrival of the bride and groom.

There were roses. Dark red roses that filled the air with a heavy scent.

On the long, low table that stood at the foot of the bed a silver bowl had been filled with sugar-frosted fruit. Beside it was a tray of sweets—Turkish Delight, truffles, tiny pastries and nuts. A silver-lidded glass jug filled with some dark red juice, another of water, stood in a casket of ice. Everything to refresh them, sustain them, as they consummated their marriage.

And the white damask spread that covered the bed had been scattered with ruby-red rose petals…

Her mouth opened but nothing emerged.

Noor, waiting to help her out of the dress, take it back to Violet's workshop, dropped a shy little curtsey and said, 'Congratulations, *sitti, sidi.*'

Sitti…

'It means Lady.' Bram, at her shoulder, eased her into the room.'

'Yes… I know…' She'd heard Violet addressed that way by the staff bringing deliveries from the boutiques in the mall. '*Shukran*, Noor.'

Bram dismissed the girl with a word as he unfastened his belt and tossed the *khanjar* he was wearing onto a sofa. A sweep of his hand and his *keffiyeh* followed it and the girl ducked her head, giggling, as she scurried to the door.

He kicked it shut behind her.

'Bram!' she protested.

'She will tell Leila that I was impatient,' he said. 'Leila will tell Violet and tonight Fayad will give her a son, a cousin to grow up as a companion for our firstborn.'

The image was so vivid that her legs buckled and her protest was no more than a small noise at the back of her throat and, without warning, his arm was around her, steadying her. 'And so the legend grows,' he said with a wry twist of his mouth.

'Well, that's great,' she said, horribly conscious of the blush heating her cheeks, his body keeping her upright, his mouth just inches from her own. 'Unfortunately, it leaves me in a dress that I can't get out of without help.'

'An impatient groom would tear it off you. Maybe, in the pursuit of reality…?'

'Don't even think it, Bram Ansari!' she said, finding the strength to pull away. 'Violet loaned me this dress to please you. It's to be the centrepiece of her new collection and it took weeks to make.'

'Then it's a good thing that I can handle a zip.' He turned to the table, poured juice into a glass, glanced at her but she shook her head.

'I don't doubt your familiarity with the zip fastening,' she snapped. She'd seen that photograph in the fountain.

Which was none of her business, she told herself. 'Unfortunately, this isn't a dress I picked up in a high street boutique. It is hand-made couture, made to look as if it was created on my body.'

His sipped the glowing red juice, his gaze an almost physical touch as it lingered on the way it clung to her breasts, her waist, how it flared at the hips.

'There are tiny hidden hooks and eyes,' she said, before he said something outrageous. 'Little stitches where Noor fitted it to me.'

'We have an hour to kill. Hunting for invisible fastenings will pass the time.' He replaced the glass on the tray, his eyes dark, his lids hooded and she shivered, not with fear but anticipation. Her head might have signed up for the no-sex deal but her body appeared to be on another planet. 'If you'll give me a clue where to start?'

'Don't worry about it. I'll manage somehow,' she said, unhooking the earrings and laying them carefully on the table beside the tray of sweets. The bracelets caused her more trouble and he made a move to help but she fended him off with a look that must have summed up all the frustration she was feeling because he raised his hands in a gesture of surrender, took a step back. She should be happy about that but she was not supposed to be feeling anything. Certainly not disappointment.

The ruby and diamond cuff on her left wrist slipped off after a bit of a tussle with the safety catch. The one on her right wrist defeated her and she let out a little puff of frustration.

'I'm sorry,' he said, but he didn't look it. He looked as if he was struggling not to laugh.

'It's not funny, Bram.'

'No.' He straightened his face. 'You were right, *sitti*. I should not have sent away your maid.'

'Then call her back.'

'And have the entire palace know that my bride cared more about a dress than satisfying her husband?'

'Damn it, Bram!' She shook her head. 'I'm sorry. It's just that I've spent most of the day being carried along on the current of Violet's excitement. I was going to wear my black dress but no one was listening to me.'

'I'm sorry.' They looked at one another and then, because it was so ridiculous, they both laughed.

'Shall we stop apologising to one another, Bram? We knew this wasn't going to be easy.'

'When I spoke to Fayad last night it never occurred to me that there would be any kind of ceremony but Violet wanted to make the day memorable for you.'

'She succeeded beyond her wildest dreams but I should been have been firmer. At least about the dress.'

'Remember that when you meet my sisters,' he said. 'Given free rein with my credit cards, they will be unstoppable.'

'I don't need any more clothes,' she said.

'Don't tell them that. They'll think you're crazy.'

'I think I'm crazy,' she replied.

'Undoubtedly, but in the meantime if you don't let me help you we are never going to make the banquet this evening.'

'Do we have to go?' she asked. 'The thought of an entire evening pretending one thing to Violet and Fayad—' she wouldn't have the least trouble blushing '—and something else to everyone else…' She swallowed. It shouldn't be a problem. She'd spent all her adult life pretending… 'Do *I* have to go?' she added quickly.

He smiled, shaking his head. 'Ruby, Ruby, Ruby…'

'Forget I said that,' she said, realising just too late how that would look. She held out her wrist. 'Just concentrate on the bracelet.'

He took her hand but seemed to find it no easier than

when he'd fastened it. 'The safety catch on this one is tougher to crack than Fort Knox.'

'You wouldn't want anything flimsy on something so valuable,' she said, doing her best to ignore the cool touch of his fingers, the delicious slide of his dark hair over his forehead as he bent over her wrist, the waft of pheromones that had her hormones whizzing around in a frenzy.

She had met many attractive men as she'd moved from company to company and there had been invitations to carry the day over into the evening but she'd never once been tempted to mix business with pleasure. She knew, as they did not, that there would have been no future in it.

There was a big difference between the boardroom and the bedroom, however. The arrangement with Bram involved the kind of intimacy that she'd never encountered in the office. The only way she could see this through was by being totally professional. And taking a cold shower the minute she was out of this dress.

The cuff finally parted and he tossed the bracelet beside its pair as if it was no more than a trinket from the market.

'The necklace?' he prompted.

She half turned so that he could reach the fastening. 'Don't step on the train!' she warned.

He scooped it up and dumped it in her arms. 'Just keep still while I try and figure this out. I've had more practice putting jewels on a woman than taking them off and they're a lot trickier than a zip.'

A little dart of something sharp, something green, shot through her at the thought of him dressing other women in precious stones and her hands tightened into little fists all by themselves. Realising that she was creasing the material, she forced herself to relax. It was ridiculous to feel jealous of the women who'd passed through his life.

She was the one wearing the diamond and ruby collar that was causing him so much trouble. It was her neck his fingers were touching, sending a charge as if she'd touched a live wire rippling through her.

She was the one he'd turned to, trusted not to betray him.

'Ruby,' he protested as she twitched nervously.

About to apologise, she caught her lip and lowered her head to his shoulder to make it easier for him to gain access to the clasp, her face in the snowy white of his robes, breathing in the scent of fresh linen, soap, warm skin. It would be so easy to let the train fall, reach for him, hold him...

He muttered something as the clasp finally parted and he stepped back. 'I think I broke it.'

'The jeweller will repair it when you return it,' she said, taking it from him, laying it carefully beside the cuffs.

He looked as if he was going to say something but when she waited he shook his head. 'Can you manage the rest?'

'Of course,' she said, sliding off the double ring he'd placed on her hand with little regret. It was pretty, but would catch on her clothes, her stockings. 'I know how Cinderella felt when the clock struck twelve,' she said, making a joke of it as she slipped off the diamond wedding band.

'Your clock has months to run before midnight strikes but your coach won't turn into a pumpkin. You will keep the ring and the title that goes with it.'

She looked up, startled. 'I can't do that,' she protested.

'Complain to Fayad. It's in the contract he negotiated on your behalf.'

'And you agreed?' Stupid. Of course he did. He was supposed to be in love. 'I won't use it. And I can't keep the ring either.'

'You are giving me back my family, Ruby. Six months of your life. That is worth a lot more than a few diamonds.'

'Six months?' They hadn't got around to discussing

how long they would have to keep up the pretence. 'You want me to stay until September?'

'Even the most hasty and ill-conceived marriage needs time to fall apart.'

'You think? I've seen celebrity marriages that have lasted less than six days.'

He shrugged. 'No doubt, but I'd like to put off the break-up until I'm sure that Bibi is safely settled in Cambridge.'

'You're suggesting that if it's too soon there might be pressure to revert to Plan A?'

'That's one reason,' he agreed, with one of those rare smiles that seemed to light her up from the inside.

'And the other?' she asked, her voice not quite steady.

'It will take time to replace Peter.'

'Oh. Yes…' What on earth had she expected him to say? Six days, six months—it was just a job. She'd made a commitment and once she was wearing her own sensible clothes, away from the heady scent of roses, the sparkle of diamonds, the need to pretend, she would be fine.

'Will you call Jude Radcliffe and break the news?' she asked, cranking up a smile to let him know that she was okay with his plan, 'or will I?'

'Leave it to me,' he said, the creases in his face deepening into a smile. 'It's the least I can do, under the circumstances.'

She nodded, her smile fading as she looked down at the circle of diamonds lying in the palm of her hand. 'This is the most beautiful ring I've ever seen but I'll forever be worrying about losing it in a washroom. An old-fashioned plain gold wedding band that you never take off is a lot more practical.'

'A princess does not have to think of practicalities.'

She rolled her eyes and got another smile for her effort.

'On the subject of practicalities,' she said. 'As your personal assistant, I'd advise you to remove your own ring before you forget.'

'Do you think anyone would notice it?' he asked, looking at the plain silver band she'd placed on his finger.

She arched a brow at him. 'Hello… Single, sexy billionaire, undoubtedly the most eligible man in the room? Allegedly.'

'Most of the women there will be with husbands or partners,' he reminded her.

'You think that will deter them? You must have been leading a more sheltered life than you'd have me believe.'

'Are you suggesting that I'll be propositioned?'

'Isn't that why you need your PA with you?' she asked. 'To ensure there's an orderly queue. That is if I ever get out of this dress. It will do your image no good if Noor returns to help me dress for this evening and I'm still wearing it,' she pointed out and, certain that she had everything under control, she lifted her arm so that he could reach the tiny hooks holding the dress together.

She was wrong.

It started well enough but the combination of the cool air and the touch of his fingers skimming her skin as the dress slowly parted from breast to hip sent a shiver rippling through her and she grabbed his shoulder for support.

'It's done,' he said at last.

'Thank you.' She was forced to clear her throat. 'If you'll just help me get it over my head.'

'*Tawaqqal!* Enough.' He took a step back and her hand slid from his shoulder. 'The dress is yours. No one else will wear it.'

She clamped her lips shut against a protest. If she was trembling from the intimacy of the moment, how much worse must it be for Bram?

'I'm sorry,' he said. 'I did not mean to shout at you.'

'Don't… I wasn't thinking…' She drew in a slow breath, gathered herself. 'For me this is just a job. For you…'

For him it was a chance to return home, but at what cost?

He was a man who'd been born to lead and he'd done that all his life. On the ski slopes, on horseback, in the financial market. Now, when he could have had it all—a good political marriage that would restore him to the succession—he'd turned his back on the prize because… Because the girl chosen as his bride wanted to be a doctor?

Really?

How likely was that?

She didn't doubt Bibi Khadri's ambitions; she'd had ambitions of her own but there was a world of difference between a dream and reality. And what girl would rather be a doctor than the wife of the Emir? To be Umm al Basr's first lady? With jewels, clothes—everything she desired.

Had she really begged her sister for help or had Bram's brother, aware that the crown was slipping from his grasp, invented the smuggled note to keep him away? And, if so, why on earth did he imagine that Bram would care?

She took a step back. 'I'll manage,' she said quickly, picking up her skirt and heading for the privacy of the dressing room so that she could think.

Bram stared for a moment at the closed door. He should never have allowed that to happen. He'd made Ruby a promise and he should have been able to help her out of a dress without making a fool of himself, but sending that girl away—as if he had been a real groom and Ruby had been his bride—had been an instinctive reaction. Not exactly fighting his way through her male relations to claim her, but it was right out of that tradition and he retreated to his own dressing room, shed his robes and took a cold shower.

* * *

Ruby wriggled carefully out of the dress and placed it on a padded hanger. If Noor was disappointed that he hadn't torn it off her in a fit of passion… Well, it wasn't as if she was his new bride, seen for the first time, claimed…

She stopped the thought, stripped off and stepped under a cool shower.

Five minutes later, having forcefully reminded herself why she was here, she wrapped herself in a soft towelling robe, opened her tablet and logged into Bram's email account, made a note of who needed to be responded to as a matter of urgency. Then, having restored herself to PA mode, she began to get ready for the charity dinner.

Noor had laid out her dress for the evening, along with a set of filmy black lace underwear. Realising that it would look odd if she discarded it in favour of her own rather more functional underclothes, she slipped them on and then covered them with her black dress and the matching long-sleeved bolero that covered her arms.

There was a new pair of delicious black suede peep-toe shoes parked neatly side by side that Noor had chosen for her to wear. They were utterly gorgeous and she could not resist slipping her feet into them, checking them out in the mirror. She was seriously tempted to keep them on but the heels were ridiculously high and a hard-working PA needed to be quick on her feet and, reluctantly, she changed into her own black ballet flats. Finally she fastened the single strand of pearls and matching pearl ear studs that her mother had been given on her eighteenth birthday, slipped on the ruby ring that had been in her family for over a hundred years and checked her reflection.

It was reassuringly familiar. She was Ruby Dance, in-demand temporary personal assistant, and she had a job to do. Speaking of which…

She straightened her back, opened the door to the bedroom and, relieved to see that it was empty—she really did not want a witness for this—wasted no time in messing up the bed.

Rose petals scattered across the floor as she pulled back the cover, tugged loose the sheet, punched the pillows to look as if they had been used, knocking one onto the floor in the process.

Heart pounding, she stepped back to check the effect. It would do, she decided, and turned her back on the mess, only to discover that Bram, immaculate in a dinner jacket, was watching her from the doorway of his own dressing room on the far side of the room.

'I just…' She made an attempt at a shrug, aware that she was blushing. Which was ridiculous.

'I saw.' He crossed to the table at the foot of the bed, poured some water into a glass, taking a sip as he walked around the bed examining her handy work.

Work. Concentrate on that. She cleared her throat. 'You've had a couple of urgent…'

Her voice trailed away as he stretched his arm out over the bed and tilted the glass, spilling a little of the water onto the centre of the rumpled sheet.

A completely involuntary sound escaped her lips and he said, 'For future reference, Ruby, if you're going to fake a scene you have to pay attention to the details.' When she didn't answer he glanced back. 'A couple of urgent what?'

'Emails…' Her mouth made all the right moves but no sound emerged and she cleared her throat again. 'Emails. One from Michael Shadbrook about setting up a meeting on Friday in London. One from Jimmy Rose in Hong Kong. He's been trying to call you.'

'I've spoken to him,' he said, his tone brisk and businesslike, as if he hadn't just left a damp patch on the bed… 'We can fly on to London from Dubai on Thursday morning. I'll leave you to organise a time, sort out the details and let Shadbrook know. Is there anything else?'

Clearly her boring little black dress was doing the job.

'Will you want to return here to Ras al Kawi or Umm al Basr before going to Mumbai?' she asked.

'Let's see how it goes tomorrow,' he said briskly. 'Is that it?'

'Yes. Have I got time to do it now?'

He glanced at his wristwatch. 'You have fifteen minutes.'

She retreated to the sitting room, sat at a small desk and, keeping an eye on the time, swiftly organised the flight, warned the Savoy that he would be in residence at his service flat on Thursday and possibly Friday night—she would stay in her own flat—changed his booking in Dubai for a suite with two bedrooms and emailed Michael Shadbrook to let him know that Bram Ansari would be available to meet him at eleven o'clock on Friday morning.

She finished with a minute spare and she used that to go and change into those pretty suede shoes that Noor had left out for her.

The dinner was over. Bram, waiting while Ruby received a farewell hug from Violet, paused to have a word with Nigel and Lorraine Grieg, the British Ambassador and his wife, who were waiting for their car.

He turned as she re-joined him but, before he could introduce her, Lorraine said, 'Jools? Jools Howard, Future World Champion?' She laughed. 'What on earth are you doing here?'

Jools?

Ruby who, despite her earlier reservations, had sailed through the evening completely at ease in whatever company she found herself, lost every scrap of colour from her face.

She'd told him that she'd changed her name after some scandal but not just her family name, it seemed. Ruby was not her real first name…

'My wife answers to Princess Rabi these days,' he said when the silence went on for too long.

'Princess…?' Lorraine Grieg looked from Ruby to him and back again but this time it was Nigel who leapt diplomatically into the breach.

'Congratulations, Bram,' he said, offering his hand. 'I had no idea you'd finally given up the bachelor life.'

'It's a recent development,' he said. 'There has been no public announcement.'

Nigel met his eye. He knew the situation with his father and instantly got the message. 'I understand,' he said, and turned to Ruby. 'My best wishes, Princess Rabi.'

'Thank you.' Given a moment's breathing space, Ruby had swiftly recovered her poise if not her colour, painted on a smile. 'I'm sorry, Lori—' She went through the air kiss ritual and anyone who didn't know Ruby would have thought she was delighted at having found an old friend. It was an impressive performance but he'd seen her smile when she meant it and realised that he'd seen this smile too. It wouldn't fool him again. 'Seeing you was so unexpected. It quite took my breath away. How long has it been?'

'Not since school…' Lorraine faltered, clearly remembering something unpleasant, and turned to her husband. 'You should have seen her on horseback, darling. Such a star. We were all convinced that she would come away from the London Olympics with a handful of gold medals. Do you still ride?'

'No.' Ruby's smile slipped and, without thinking, he reached for her hand.

'These days she's my star.'

'So sweet.' Lorraine smiled indulgently. 'Perhaps we

could get together for lunch soon, Jools? Catch up on all the news?'

He didn't need the tremor in her hand to know how little she relished the prospect and he tightened his grip. 'We'll be away for a week or two, but why don't you both come out to Qa'lat al Mina'a when we return?' he suggested as their car, flying the Union flag, pulled up alongside them. 'I'll give you a call, Nigel.'

They waited while they boarded, returning a wave as they were borne away down the hill and out of sight.

'Bram—'

'Not here,' he said, tucking her arm under his so that she could lean on him as they headed away from the central dome of the palace and through the palace gardens.

'Bram, I'm so sorry. I n-never imagined...' She had hung onto her composure but now reaction was setting in. Her teeth were chattering and she was struggling to catch her breath. 'I c-c-can't...'

She buckled against him and, with a muttered curse, he caught her and, arm about her waist, supported her to a seat set in the privacy of a jasmine-covered arbour. She was shivering, more with shock than cold, but he took off his jacket, slipped it around her shoulders and then put his arm around her and held her close.

CHAPTER SIX

BRAM'S JACKET WAS warm from his body, his arm was around her and Ruby's cheek was pressed against fresh linen, the steady beat of his heart. This was the hug she'd been dreaming about, yearning for ever since her world fell apart and for a moment she soaked it up, knowing that, like so much of these few days, it would be a treasured memory. But he hadn't signed up for this. He wanted an uncomplicated, no-strings temporary wife not a baggage-laden emotional wreck.

'Th-thank you,' she said, summoning every scrap of inner strength to ease away, sit up. 'Thank you for rescuing me back there.'

'I thought you were going to faint,' he said, his hand still at her back.

'I thought I was,' she admitted. 'But I meant when Lori said my name.'

'So did I, but it was a great recovery. She had no idea.'

'You knew,' she said.

'Our relationship has been short but intense,' he said, 'and I wasn't distracted with the problem of who I was going to text the minute the car arrived.'

'No.' She managed some sort of smile. 'You read her pretty well too.'

'I've met her before.' He glanced at her. 'Jools?'

'It's what I was called at school. It's short for Juliet.'

She risked a glance in his direction. His profile was lit by the soft lighting hidden amongst the branches and she couldn't read his expression but it wasn't that which was making her shiver. It was being forced to confront memories that she'd buried deep, locked away. Memories that she'd been hiding from for years. 'I'm sorry, Bram.'

'I thought we'd banned the word *sorry*?'

'But I should have told you before all this...' She made a gesture that took in the palace, the gardens, everything that had happened that day.

'Tell me now,' he said.

'Yes...' And, doing her best to ignore the cold, sick feeling in the pit of her stomach, she said, 'I was born Juliet Dorothea Howard.' There was no response but there was no reason for him to remember a sordid story that had filled the headlines ten years ago. 'My home was a small manor house that had been in my mother's family for ever and, until I was sixteen, I had the kind of life that most people dream about.'

She let her eyes flicker in his direction. His arm was still a comforting support but, although he'd turned to look down at her, his face remained impassive, giving no clue as to what he might be thinking.

'A week after my sixteenth birthday my father was exposed as a con man who preyed on vulnerable, older women. He wooed them, seduced them and when they were putty in his hands, ready to sign anything he put in front of them, he robbed them.'

She opened the elegant little shoulder bag that contained her phone, tapped her father's name into the search engine, clicked on a link and handed it to him.

'It's all there.'

She fixed her eyes on the glowing dome of the palace as he skimmed through the newspaper story that had brought her world crashing down.

After a few minutes he handed the phone back to her. 'You were sixteen years old, Ruby. None of this has anything to do with you.'

'Tell that to the photographers who camped outside my school gates, the reporters who rang my mobile phone day and night, wanting a comment, an interview, anything… According to them, I was a pampered princess living a lifestyle that most people could only dream about.'

'They hounded you?' He didn't sound surprised.

'Of course they hounded me. I didn't rob those poor women of their savings, their pension funds, their self-worth, Bram, but my little ponies were the real thing and I was having the most expensive, most privileged education that the money my father stole from them could buy.'

'But the school protected you?'

'They kept the gates locked, refused to comment, but they couldn't stop the long-range lenses, keep out the photographers who climbed the walls,' she said, wrapping her arms about herself as if she could hold in the pain. 'Stop the girls who used their phones to send in photographs that they'd snapped during the year, of me fooling around in the pool, giggling at impromptu birthday parties, on prize-giving day with my father. I was desperate to go home, to be with my mother, but the house, the village, was besieged by the media and the head smuggled me out of school and I was in Scotland before anyone realised I'd gone.'

'Scotland?'

'My mother's old nanny had retired there.'

'You had no other family to turn to?'

She shook her head. 'My grandmother died very young and my mother stayed at home to care for her increasingly frail father. When he died she inherited a house that had been in her family for centuries, what was left of the original estate, a couple of cottages and a London flat. She was in her mid-thirties and alone in the world, apart from a few distant ageing cousins she had only met at funerals.'

'The perfect mark for a man who preyed on vulnerable women.'

'The death notices, obituaries, the publication of wills are meat and drink to a con man.' Restless, unable to sit there a moment longer, she said, 'Can we walk?'

He stood up and, his arm still around her, they walked back through the gardens towards their apartment. The palace was built on the highest point of the city and far out in the Gulf she could see the lights of a ship heading out towards the Indian Ocean.

'It's so peaceful here,' she said, pausing to watch its stately progress. 'You could hear a star fall.'

'They don't make much of a splash.'

She glanced at him. Was that humour? Sarcasm? There was nothing in his voice to give her a clue and his face was all shadows.

'Your mother was the perfect mark but, instead of robbing her, he married her,' he prompted after a while. 'Did he fall in love with her?'

'Making people believe he loved them was just something he did to get what he wanted, Bram.'

'So?'

'He fell in love with the image.' His lack of emotion made it easier. 'He saw a lovely old manor house with a couple of cottages and a hundred acres of grazing land bringing in a tidy income. There were ancient wax jackets hanging in the mud room, good-looking Labradors in front of a log fire and a perfect chocolate box Cotswold village. He didn't steal my mother's inheritance, Bram; he moved into it. He became part of the community, always ready with a generous donation for repairs to the church hall or the cricket club pavilion. Always good company in the pub with his fund of stories about adventures hunting down new oil fields for his clients.'

'That was his cover for his absences?'

She nodded. 'He used to bring me little souvenirs. A perfect desert rose, a fossil, an amethyst geode from some-where in Africa. A little meteorite that he'd picked up in the Arctic.'

Precious, precious things that she had cherished, clung to through his long absences. All bought from specialist shops. All lies.

'Did you ever doubt that he loved you?'

'No.' The word stuck in her throat. 'No, I never doubted that he loved me but I was just part of his picture-perfect family. His English rose wife whose family tree made the upstart Tudors look like newcomers. His little girl on her pony at the local gymkhana. It was a fairy tale with him as the handsome stranger who'd arrived out of nowhere to woo the lonely princess.'

'But without the happily ever after.'

'No.' She fought down the lump in her throat, want-ing this over. 'I was taking part in the show-jumping at the county show and the friend of a woman he'd relieved of her savings spotted him with me in the collecting ring. His hair was a different colour, he'd shaved off the beard he'd grown for the con but she saw him smile up at me…'

She faltered. He would remember what she'd said about Oliver Brent, know where the expression had come from, and she felt naked, exposed…

'What did she do, Ruby?'

'She went to the local police, certain he was running one of his scams. They assured her that she was mistaken. Mr Howard was a well-known and respected member of the community.' She rushed on, wanting this over. 'Real-ising that she wasn't going to get anywhere with the po-lice, she took her story to one of the tabloids. They ran the standard background checks and discovered that no one in the oil industry had heard of Jack Howard and there was no trace of him before he met my mother.'

'If he'd had any idea it was going to be a permanent identity he'd have taken more care but I imagine after so many years he thought he was safe. Did they ever discover his real name?'

She shook her head. She had no idea who her father really was. He had denied everything and, despite all the publicity, no one had ever come forward to claim him as a son, brother, father...

'They watched, waited and when he moved in on a new mark they told her what he was up to and asked her to play along. They installed hidden cameras, recorded all his phone calls and when they had it all they ran a big exposure piece before handing everything over to the police.'

'They wanted their story before reporting restrictions were imposed.'

'They wanted other victims to come forward. Some did but who knows how many were too embarrassed to admit to their family, friends what had happened to them?'

'You said they were both dead, Ruby?'

She looked up at him. 'You think I lied about that? That he's in jail?' She didn't wait for him to answer. 'My father was sent to the Crown Court for trial but cases like that take an age to prepare and he had a good lawyer. He was granted bail on the condition that he surrendered his passport, stayed at his home address and reported regularly to the local police station. When he missed his appointment they went to the house and discovered them both. The autopsy found horse tranquilliser.'

'A suicide pact?'

'That was the coroner's verdict but my father was a sociopath, Bram. He had no conscience.' Holding onto her emotions by a thread, she said, 'It was my mother who was suffering. She'd been cut dead by friends, neighbours, people she'd known all her life.'

'He had fooled them all. They would have been angry, embarrassed.'

'Yes…' The word caught in her throat.

'I was wrong when I said he hadn't stolen from her. He stole her life and now he's stealing yours.' He muttered something under his breath. 'That's why you asked about publicity. You didn't want to risk being recognised.'

She shrugged. 'At least you have the perfect excuse to divorce me.'

'I wouldn't use this.'

He looked almost angry at the suggestion. 'No one would blame you,' she said, 'but it's all academic now. Lori will already be texting gossipy messages to her old school chums and the story is too good not to pass on. Sooner or later it will leak.' He wouldn't use the story, but he wouldn't have to. It had all worked out perfectly.

She eased away from his arm, pulled his jacket around her. 'Thank you, Bram.'

'For what?'

For not judging her. For understanding. 'For listening.' She hunched her shoulders. 'That's all. Just listening.'

'You thought I would be angry?'

'You have every right. I told you I'd changed my name because of a family scandal and you accepted that.'

'If I'd known the whole story,' he said, 'I would have still gone ahead.'

She nodded. Of course he would. He'd wanted an unsuitable wife and he'd got one with capital letters.

'Come,' he said. 'You've had a shock. What you need is a cup of tea.'

'Tea?' Despite everything, she laughed. 'How long did you live in England, Bram?'

'Too long, apparently,' he said as, with a wry smile, he put his arm around her, encouraging her to lean against him.

'No,' she said, her head against his shoulder. 'Just long enough.'

They walked back to the apartment where Noor, working on an exquisite piece of embroidery, was waiting to help her undress.

'There's no need to stay, Noor. I can manage.'

Bram added something in Arabic and she bobbed a curtsey, said goodnight and left.

Ruby slipped off his jacket, placed it over the back of a chair while he crossed to a table where a kettle and a tray of tea things had been left.

'Let me do that,' she protested.

'Sit,' he said, filling the kettle from a bottle of water and switching it on. 'Tell me what happened to you.' He turned and glanced at her. 'Afterwards.'

'Nothing. I stayed with my mother's nanny in Scotland while the lawyers dealt with the fallout.' She shrugged. 'She was getting frail, needed looking after more than I did, so I signed up for a business course at a local college, using her name.'

'And your home?'

'Sold. I could never go back there.'

'No... And I imagine the victims' lawyers lined up with compensation claims.'

'There wasn't as much as they'd hoped. The house and its contents, the cottages, the family jewellery, the London flat had all been inherited by my mother and on her death passed to me. Since I was a minor, the proceeds from the sale of the house and the rest of her estate went into a trust until I was twenty-one.'

'As was right.'

'My father hadn't been tried, found guilty, but lawyers representing my interests agreed that his estate should be liquidised and the funds split between anyone who could prove that he'd stolen from them. His bank accounts, his cars, personal possessions.' She lifted her hand to her chest to relieve what was still a physical pain. 'The horses he'd bought for me.'

'Your horses? That's why you stopped riding?'

'I'm sure the lawyers would have released money to keep me riding, Bram, but can you imagine sitting up there, taking part in competitions with everyone looking at me, knowing what had happened? Can you imagine what the newspapers would have done with that?'

'I have a very good idea.' His face was expressionless but she knew he was remembering what had happened to him.

'I just wanted to disappear.'

'Yes…' For a moment their eyes met. After his disgrace he'd disappeared from the ski circuit, stopped playing polo, vanished from the society pages. 'In my case the damage was self-inflicted.'

'Why?' The question slipped out before she could stop it. He frowned. 'Why?'

'It was out of character.' He raised an eyebrow. 'You appeared in the society magazines, lined up with other aristocrats and dignitaries at charity functions. All very staid and proper. The rest was all about your sporting triumphs. The romp in the fountain was a one-off.'

He looked away. 'Once was enough.' He dropped a couple of tea bags into cups and poured on the freshly boiled water. 'You disappeared. What then?'

She continued looking at him for a moment but he concentrated on the tea, avoiding her gaze, and she knew there was a lot more to the story than that but he wanted her story, all of it, so that there would be no more surprises.

'When I was twenty-one and had control of my inheritance I sold the family jewellery, added it to the money from the sale of the house and put it all into a fund for the women my father had robbed.'

'I don't imagine your lawyers were happy about that.' He didn't sound surprised. 'Did they try and stop you?'

'Yes, but I wanted an end to it, Bram. I kept the London flat because I needed somewhere to live, the family wedding ring that I wear, the pearls my mother was given on her eighteenth birthday,' she said, touching the single strand at her neck, 'and my great-great-great-grandmother's engagement ring. I got a job and got on with my life.'

'It was that easy?'

'Actually, yes. People go through the motions, ask the standard questions, but all they really want to talk about is themselves.' She looked up as he placed two cups of pale straw-colour liquid on the table in front of her. 'I appear to have overestimated the living-in-England effect.'

'It's camomile. It will help you sleep.'

He had more confidence in the calming power of herbal tea than she had, but she thanked him.

'There was no one close?' he asked.

'A relationship, you mean?' She pushed away the bitter memory of betrayal and shook her head. If she couldn't trust someone with her life then it wasn't a relationship. 'This is the first time I've talked to anyone about this.'

'I thought Amanda Garland knew every detail,' he said, joining her on the sofa.

'She does, but not from me.' *Everything*. She had to tell him everything… 'I'd been at my first job for nearly a year when a girl I'd been at school with came to work in the same company. There was that same astonished, "*Jools?*" Within twenty-four hours everyone knew who I was.' She hadn't been sure which was worse, the faux pity or the prurient interest, but there had been worse to come.

'Ruby…' He sounded, looked so concerned that, without thinking, she reached out and put a reassuring hand on his arm.

'The man I worked for said that I'd done nothing to be ashamed of, that it would be a nine-day wonder and I should just keep my head down and ignore any comments.'

'You were that good, even then?'

'Attention to detail,' she said and then, remembering what had happened earlier, blushed. 'I imagine I get that from my father.'

'I'm guessing that didn't happen,' he said.

'No. Jeff…' She stopped. That part of the story had no relevance to what she was telling him. 'Someone I worked with phoned in the story and the following morning I was on the front page of the paper that had run the original exposé. It must have been a slow news day because they reran the whole story, updating it with the cost of everything I was wearing, the salary I was earning, how much the London flat was worth. How I was still living a life of luxury, unlike my father's victims.'

'I don't suppose they mentioned that you had given up most of your inheritance to repay them?'

'The Trustees complained to the PCC and they placed a small statement to that effect on page thirteen of the paper about two months later.' She held her finger and thumb a few centimetres apart to indicate the size of their retraction.

He let slip a word—clearly he had no love for the press—and then said, 'You were a victim too.'

'Not in the eyes of most people. I owned a valuable piece of real estate, had a decent job, good clothes… It was school all over again. I was a prisoner in my own flat, with the press camped out on the pavement, my phone ringing non-stop with hacks wanting my "story", photographs of me on horseback to demonstrate my privileged lifestyle all over the Net.'

'As if once in a lifetime wasn't enough.'

'Maybe if my father had been tried, gone to jail, but there was no closure...' She shook her head. 'I managed to slip out, took the train to the coast, walked along the pier—'

'No!' He took her hand from his arm and held it tightly, as if he would save her all over again.

'No!' She shook her head. 'No,' she repeated, wanting to reassure him. 'But for the first time I understood why my mother had chosen that way out. Her life, as she knew it, was finished and at that moment so had mine.'

'You shouldn't have been on your own.'

'I wasn't. A fisherman saw me looking into the depths and brought me a cup of tea from his flask. He didn't say anything, just stayed with me until I was ready to leave, then walked back along the pier with me and when he'd seen me safely back to solid ground went back to his rod.'

'Where did you go?'

'To Amanda. Her agency had placed me in my first job and she called me, left a message to get in touch. She found me somewhere to stay, helped me find a new home, coaxed me into a new look, a new identity and then found me a temp job in a one-man office.'

'That would be the very helpful stockbroker whose secretary was on maternity leave?'

'Yes.' She smiled, remembering how kind he'd been. Obviously he'd seen the papers, knew who she was, but he'd never said a word. 'I've worked for her agency ever since.'

'So where did Ruby Dance come from?' he asked.

'My great-great-great-grandmother,' she said, spreading her hand so that the half-hoop of rubies glowed with hidden fire in the soft light. 'She was a chorus girl back in the days when foolish young men drank champagne from their slippers.' She looked up, smiled at what was a happy memory. 'The foolish young man who married her was my great-great-great-grandfather.'

'And this is the ring he gave her, the one that you kept,' he said, taking her hand.

'She was wearing this ring in a portrait that hung in the gallery at home.'

'Do you look like her?'

'She was fair, but my mother said that I have her eyes.'

'Then I understand why your many times great-grand-father was prepared to defy convention and make her his wife.'

'I...' She swallowed, conscious that he was still holding her hand. 'You said you wanted an unsuitable wife, Bram, and you've got the real deal,' she said. 'No one will blame you for wanting to be rid of a woman who kept her past a secret. If Sheikh Fayad knew I'd kept this from you he'd tear up the marriage contract right now without a second's thought.'

'That is not going to happen. I still need a wife, Ruby. I still need you.'

She sat back, the niggle that had been poking around at the back of her brain all evening finally coming to the fore.

'Are you sure about that?'

Bram instinctively tightened his grasp on Ruby's hand, sensing that she was about to slip away, disappear from his life as not once, but twice she'd disappeared from her own.

'It's a bit late to suggest another candidate.'

'Is it?' Her expression was grave, thoughtful. 'This is a foot in the mouth question, Bram, but I won't be doing my job as your PA if I don't ask it.'

His PA...

At some point during this extraordinary day he had stopped thinking of her as his personal assistant, stopped thinking about this as a business transaction and he tried to pin the moment down.

Had it been when Fayad, negotiating her dowry, had tackled the question of settlements for the children they would have? When, having placed a ring on her finger with the vow that they would be joined for ever, he'd touched his lips to hers and felt her lips tremble beneath his own?

Or was it that moment when he'd seen the blood drain from her face and, without a moment's thought, had said, 'My wife…'?

Her words brought him back to reality with a jolt but Ruby had never lost sight of reality. Having spilled out the nightmare that she'd lived through—that had changed her life for ever—she was still focused on the reason why she was there.

'Ask your question, Ruby,' he said and, unwilling to relinquish the intimacy that had grown between them, he added, 'Afterwards, if you need any help removing your foot from your mouth, I will do my best to help.'

She flushed. 'This is serious, Bram.'

Of course it was. She was always serious. Still punishing herself for something that was not her fault.

When, he wondered, was the last time she'd had any cap-over-the-windmill, let-your-hair-down fun? What would it be like to see her laugh out loud, let herself go without a care for what anyone else thought, without being afraid of being judged for enjoying herself?

When, for that matter, had he?

'I'm sorry, Ruby. Say what's on your mind.'

'Right…' She took a rather shaky breath. 'Are you absolutely one hundred per cent certain that Bibi has her heart set on a career in medicine?'

He frowned. 'Bibi?' That was the last thing he'd expected.

'How do you know that she has a place at Cambridge?' she pressed and this time it was her hand tightening around his. 'What I'm asking—' her eyes were velvet-soft, full of concern '—could it be that your brother invented her plea for help in order to get you to back off? Stay away.'

He'd been so sure that she was going to ask him to let her go so that she could slip out of sight, return to the hidden life she'd been leading until now. But she was still thinking of others. Thinking of him.

He was beginning to understand why a man like Jude Radcliffe had spoken so highly of her. She was not just clever, impressively cool—he couldn't think of another person who would have dared suggest such a thing to him—but totally selfless.

'So that he can hang onto the throne? Is that what you're suggesting?'

She nodded, almost as pale as when a chance encounter had exposed her true identity, and he lifted his free hand to her cheek. 'Have a care, Ruby Dance,' he warned. 'If you continue to demonstrate such acuity, such care for my well-being, I may not be able to let you go in the autumn.'

The heat of her blush seemed to flow through his hand, flood into his body and, without warning, the only thing on his mind was the kiss they'd shared, because she had been there with him in that lost moment and the memory of it was driving all his blood in one direction.

'Are you saying that I'm right?' she asked.

'No. But thank you for being brave enough to ask the question.'

'I think the word you're looking for is foolhardy.'

'I have the word perfectly,' he assured her and, fighting the urge to draw her close, sit quietly with her head against his shoulder, her dark curls soft against his cheek, he let his hand drop, stood up, turned away so that she should not see his arousal. She deserved better than that of him. 'It's been a long day and we have an early start tomorrow.' And before she could even think the question…

'I'll sleep in my dressing room.'

'Goodnight, Bram.'

'Goodnight, Ruby. Sleep well.'

He didn't move until he heard the bedroom door click quietly shut and then dragged a shaky hand over his face, waiting for the longing to subside. It was nothing. A reaction to the emotional minefield he was treading.

No man could spend so much time up close and personal with those eyes, that mouth, and fail to be affected.

Once tomorrow was over and they could get back to work everything would fall back into place. He turned away from the closed door and, needing a distraction, picked up his phone, checked for emails.

There were a dozen or so and he flicked down through them until, without warning, he was looking at the photograph that Violet had sent of the moment he'd kissed Ruby. Living the moment again—feeling the silkiness of her cheek beneath his fingers, the softness of her lips, hearing the smallest of sighs as what should have been the merest touch had become something deeper. Want, need, desire lighting a match in the darkness…

Violet had said, 'This one is just for you…' and she was right. It was not a photograph to put in a silver frame on top of the piano. It was a photograph that a man would keep close, look at when he was far from home and then he'd call to hear the voice of the woman he loved.

He tossed the phone aside. Dammit, he'd spent too long in his own company, been too long without a woman.

If they'd been at the fort he would have gone for a swim, slept in the stables on the pallet that Khal used when one of the horses was sick.

The welcome had been warm here in his cousin's palace but there was inescapable protocol, formality, the familiar suffocating confinement that had driven him to escape his father's palace when he was a boy, seeking the freedom of the souk. The freedom that he'd found flying headlong down the most treacherous ski-runs in the mountains of Europe and America.

None of that had changed but he would not lie to himself; if, at that moment, he'd been with Ruby, her arms around him, escape would have been the furthest thing from his mind.

He retrieved the phone and tapped the name 'Juliet Howard' into the search engine, searched 'images' and there she was, sixteen years old, astride some seriously impressive horseflesh, laughing for the camera as she held aloft a trophy, her eyes alight with the joy of triumph.

There were other photographs that had appeared in an article on promising young riders. Her dark hair, longer then, loose about her shoulders and her face, still with the softness of youth, brimming with optimism as she stood beside the horse that everyone believed would take her to a gold medal. And then he was looking at her five years older, leaving her office hand in hand with a man who she was looking up at with the glowing smile of a woman in love.

Jeff...

The name had slipped out. She'd quickly changed it to 'someone I worked with' but this was the man who'd phoned in the story. Set her up.

The man who was quoted as 'shocked', had no idea who she was and felt 'utterly betrayed' by her deceit. The man who had destroyed her life for the second time.

When Ruby slowly woke to a soft pink dawn she did not need to get out of bed and check Bram's dressing room to know that she was alone in the apartment. When he was near the air seemed to vibrate with the power he generated; her skin was sensitive to his presence.

She slipped on a silk wrap and checked the sitting room, expecting to see Noor. The room was empty but a table had been set up and on a snowy cloth was a jug of orange juice, a pot of steaming coffee and, under covers, an array of delicious breakfast treats. Fresh figs, olives, tomatoes, yogurt, soft goat's cheese, preserves. She had just lifted the lid on a dish containing warm unleavened bread when she sensed Bram's presence and looked up.

He'd been running, his face, throat, arms slicked with sharp, fresh sweat. The air was thrumming with pheromones and while she was still trying to think of something to say he reached out, took a fig and bit into it. The juice gleamed on his lips and she thought she was going to melt into a puddle right there at his feet.

'Did you manage to sleep?' he asked.

'Sleep?' With the scent from the jacket he'd worn all evening and then placed around her shoulders filling her head? When every touch of his hand had left a warm tingle on her skin that nothing short of a cold shower would remove?

'You were forced to confront a lot of unpleasant memories last night.'

Oh, that...

'It can be hard to switch off,' he said, regarding her with concern.

She called her brain to attention. 'The camomile tea helped,' she lied. The bed had been remade with fresh linen, but it would have taken a bucket of the stuff to float her past the image of Bram casually creating a damp patch as he'd added one last detail to her effort to fake the scene. 'When do we leave?' she asked in an attempt to get back into PA mode.

'As soon as you're ready.'

'Twenty minutes?' she offered.

'Noor is supervising the removal of your wardrobe to the boat,' he warned her.

'I've managed to dress myself since I was four years

old, Bram, but if I need help with a zip I know who to call,' she added, not bothering to hide her irritation.

His grin as he picked up another fig and backed into his dressing room caught her sideways.

'I could do it in fifteen,' Ruby muttered crossly when she could breathe again. 'Ten in an emergency.' She poured herself a cup of coffee, sliced a fig over some yogurt and carried them through to her dressing room.

Aware that she was still on show at the palace, she had been going to wear a simple—that would be designer simple—black suit with an ankle-length skirt that had been amongst the clothes sent up from the mall the day before, and her mother's pearls.

What Noor had laid out for her was a dramatic *salwar kameez* in a heavy dark blue silk, vividly decorated with the peacock tail appliqué and embroidery that was Princess Violet's trademark, and a fine silk chiffon scarf that had been embroidered in the same design. There was dark blue lace underwear, a pair of turquoise-blue suede flats and a featherweight silk *abbayah* to throw over everything to keep off the dust.

Her new make-up had been laid out on the dressing table, together with her brush and two jewellery boxes, one containing the diamond wedding ring that Bram had placed on her finger, the other a necklace and earrings of turquoises that exactly matched the appliqué on the outfit, the shoes.

It seemed very exotic for so early in the morning, but presumably princesses had to dress to a higher standard than the average PA. Not that she had any choice. The clothes that she had brought from England and the brand-new wardrobe that had arrived from the mall were all gone. It was the *salwar kameez* or nothing.

CHAPTER SEVEN

BRAM'S HEAVYWEIGHT EX-MILITARY patrol boat bypassed Umm al Basr's new marina with its sleek white yachts, expensive high-rise apartments, five-star hotels and shopping mall and edged into the old harbour.

They had left Ras al Kawi with Khal at the helm and Mina's sons on board as cook and crew.

The boat hadn't been fitted out in the luxury demanded by the average multimillionaire but Noor, doing her best to hide her disapproval at this form of transport when there was a perfectly good aircraft sitting on the tarmac, was hard at work turning the main cabin into a suitable bedroom for a princess.

The décor was functional rather than Hollywood but no expense had been spared when it came to communications.

There hadn't been so much as a wobble as Bram had video-conferenced with contacts in Hong Kong and Mumbai. This might be the day that Bram returned from exile, but his entire focus was on finalising deals, setting up meetings and she was still his temporary PA as well as his temporary bride.

The only distraction was the flash of the diamonds as she typed up notes. She had intended to remove her ring when she'd changed into a pair of lightweight trousers and a fine knitted top for the boat trip, but she'd felt self-conscious about removing it with Noor watching.

As the coastline of Umm al Basr appeared, Bram had gone up on deck. Certain that he would want to be on his own as he approached his home for the first time in five years, she made the excuse of calling Peter's mother to remain below.

Now, distracted by the shouting and clanging as they tied up, she gazed out of the porthole at a part of the city that didn't appear to have changed in a hundred years. There were dun-coloured walls, shops that were no more than rooms with wide double doors that opened onto the street, but where there would once have been camels and donkeys there were now luxury four-by-fours, huge American pickup trucks and sleek saloon cars with dark-tinted windows parked in every available bit of shade.

A port official waited while the gangway was lowered and then disappeared from view as he came aboard.

She reached for her bag, assuming that he would want to see her passport, but it was Bram who appeared in the doorway.

'Come,' he said. 'Walk with me.'

Ruby grabbed a couple of bottles of water from the fridge and stuffed them in her bag, threw on her *abbayah* and joined Bram on the quayside.

He'd changed into a grey robe, wrapped a red and white checked *shemagh* around his head, but if he thought it would make him less noticeable he was mistaken. He held himself in a way that commanded attention and he set off across the quay at a quiet, steady pace, ignoring the traffic that seemed to give way to him.

He seemed disinclined to talk and she took her cue from him as they passed through a dim, cool fish market that was being washed down now that the early morning catch had been sold.

They went on through the vegetable market and then out into narrow, dusty streets where dice rattled and counters clicked as old men sat outside street cafés, drinking tea and playing a board game at lightning speed.

There were traders selling spices from huge bins, pots and pans of all shapes and sizes, stalls with piles of jeans and bolts of cloth in every imaginable colour.

She lingered for a moment to admire a heavy dark red brocade that would make a gorgeous jacket. Bram did not stop and she shrugged apologetically at the man and hurried to catch up as he turned into an area where tradesmen were working.

There was the smell of freshly sawn wood, hot metal as a handle was welded to a pan and, in the dark recesses of his workshop, a blacksmith was sending showers of sparks into the hot gloom as he hammered on glowing iron.

Bram stopped at the entrance and the smith plunged the metal into cold water before looking up and calling out something in Arabic; she didn't understand the words but the mocking familiarity was unmistakable.

'He knows you,' she said.

'I used to escape from the palace and come here. No boring lessons, no one to shout if I got dirty, just the fun of pumping the forge bellows with Abdullah and, if his father was in a good mood, a chance to beat hot iron with a hammer we could hardly lift.'

'Boy heaven.' He turned and looked at her for the first time since they'd left the boat. 'What did he say to you?' she asked but, before he could answer, Abdullah, wiping his hands on a dirty rag, called out again.

'He said he heard that I was out of a job and he's looking for an apprentice. And he's offering tea.'

'Tea and a job offer. Go for it. I'll make myself scarce while you catch up on old times,' she said, thinking that she could go back and get some of that cloth. There were tailors working in little hole-in-the-wall shops that could run up a copy of a favourite jacket in hours and she wasn't going to be a princess for ever. Well, maybe for ever, but in a few months she'd be back in London, back on the temp roundabout where clothes had to be practical rather than exotic.

'Stay,' he said, catching her hand as she took a step back. 'We will stop to buy your cloth on the way back.'

'I wasn't…' She hadn't realised that he'd noticed. 'I don't want to embarrass your friend.'

'He will show his respect by acting as if you are not here.'

A boy fetched a chair, placed it in a quiet corner shielded from the street and wiped off the dust. She thanked him, sat down, sipped the sweet tea he brought her, asked his name, gave him the little box of mints she carried in her bag, let him take a selfie with her phone, took one of them both.

They were giggling at the result when Abdullah called him sharply and when she looked up she realised that Bram had been watching her. He turned back to his friend and they parted with a warm handshake.

True to his word, he retraced their steps, bargained with the stallholder for the brocade she had admired, then moved on without waiting for it to be cut, or paying for it.

'He will deliver it to the boat. Khal will deal with it,' he said without looking back. 'How is Peter?' he asked when she had caught up with him.

'He's flying home tomorrow. I've organised a care package. Books, his favourite sweets, home visits from a sports masseur. If there's anything else…?'

'You have it covered,' he said as they walked on through the old part of the town, past ornate mosques with exquisitely tiled domes, ancient arches, huge carved doors that occasionally opened to offer a glimpse into a shaded courtyard.

No longer silent, he shared memories of truant days

spent with the blacksmith, boat-builders and fishermen while his diligent brother stayed in the classroom and worked at his lessons.

'You were born to be a younger brother, Bram.'

'Feckless, irresponsible?' he suggested.

'Free.'

Free.

Bram stopped and looked down at this woman who knew when to be quiet but when she spoke went straight to the heart of what he was feeling.

She had swept down, unannounced, into his life, an angel on a rescue mission. Was capable of enchanting both princes and the small son of a blacksmith. Of enchanting him…

'How do you do that?' he asked.

Her forehead buckled in a frown. 'Do what?'

He shook his head and carried on walking, reverting to silence as he reconnected with his home.

Nothing had changed in this part of the city. There were children playing, stray dogs and skinny cats sloping in the shadows looking for scraps, a goat chewing on the remains of a cement bag and then, as they turned a corner, they were in a different world.

Before them lay the new city with its high-rise towers gleaming in the sun, the brilliant green of well-watered verges, trees and a square where a fountain cooled the air.

For a moment he paused, disorientated, then he headed for a bench in the centre of the square. 'I've walked you off your feet.'

'My feet are used to walking. I loved the chance to get a glimpse into your childhood, see the markets and the old part of the city.'

'Not this?' he asked, with a gesture that took in the concrete and glass surrounding them.

She glanced around, shrugged. 'It's very impressive,

but it could be anywhere.' She opened her bag and handed him a bottle of water.

He took it, drained half of it in a swallow. '*Shukran.*'

'*Afwan,*' she returned and he realised he'd spoken to her in Arabic without thinking. And that she'd replied.

'Not just for the water. For understanding that I did not wish to talk. For your kindness to Abdullah's son.'

'Again, welcome.' She took a sip of water from her own bottle. 'Has it changed much?'

'This—' he made a broad gesture taking into the square '—is unrecognisable.' He shrugged. 'Or maybe I wasn't looking. It was Hamad who saw the potential for tourism, trade, offshore banking. If he'd ever left his books to come to the smithy he would have been figuring out how it could be run more efficiently.'

'Is that what Abdullah told you?'

He turned and looked at her. 'He told me that there are new hospitals. That his daughters go to school.'

'Not his son?' she asked.

'Boys always had that privilege but it's a holiday today.'

'Because you are coming home?' she teased, her smile warming him in ways that the sun never could.

'The holiday is to celebrate my father's birthday.'

'Of course.' Her smile faded. 'I didn't mean to be flippant.'

'No.' Unable to retract the words, bring back the smile, he said, 'Abdullah told me that he has a new house built with the money flowing into the country. He said that people admire and respect Hamad for the changes he has pushed through.'

Ruby said nothing; she just put her hand over his, a silent gesture of understanding, compassion.

He'd told her that this was what he wanted and it was, but the reality had raised a confusion of emotions and, turning his hand around, he wrapped it around hers, glad that she was there.

For a moment neither of them moved, spoke, but simply sat there in the sun, their hands locked together. The temptation was to stay there all day, but it had been a long time since breakfast.

'Are you hungry, Ruby?'

She placed her free hand against her waist. 'You heard my stomach rumbling?' she asked, all mock shock horror. 'I hoped you'd think that was thunder.'

Bram, appreciating her attempt to lift his mood, played along. He glanced up at the clear blue sky, raised an eyebrow. 'You think it looks like rain?'

'I think,' she said, 'that I spotted a burger place over there.' And he discovered, as he looked back into silver-grey eyes that sparkled in the sunlight that it wasn't so hard to smile after all.

'One day married and you're fobbing me off with fast food?'

'When we get home I'll bake you a cake,' she promised.

Home? She was talking of the fort as home?

'What kind of cake?' he asked, as a world of possibilities opened up before him. The loss of one life but the possibility of another.

'Lemon drizzle, Victoria sandwich. Ginger? You choose.'

'All of the above,' he said, as the image of them alone in the kitchen as she made him some classic English cake gave him a warm rush of pleasure. 'And you beside me on Rigel riding along the beach.'

She hesitated and he knew why. Riding had been her passion and it had been taken from her. He was determined that, whatever happened, she would not lose it again.

'Ride with me and I won't make you slaughter a goat.'

She laughed. 'That's an offer I can't refuse but maybe

we should stick to something a little less messy for lunch? I don't know about you but I could do with some comfort food right now. I'll have mine with everything except the pickle, extra fries and a milkshake so cold that it will give me a headache.'

He shook his head, laughing despite the uncertainty of what lay ahead. 'Extra fries it is,' he said as he stood up and, her hand still fast in his, helped her to her feet.

For a moment it lay small and white against his calloused palm, the ring he'd placed on her finger flashing in the sunlight. Then the *abbayah* slipped from her hair and she lifted it away to tug it back into place.

She was so easy to be with. He'd lost count of the times he'd imagined his return to Umm al Basr, walking through the souk the way he had as a boy, reacquainting himself with the places he had loved, aware that much of it would be gone.

He had imagined himself alone but when the moment had come he had wanted Ruby at his side, walking with him. She had lost everything and he knew she would understand what he was feeling.

'What was here when you were a boy?' she asked as they walked towards the burger bar.

Bram looked up at the tall glass-fronted buildings skirting a square that had been laid out like an Italian piazza.

'The odd wandering goat,' he said. 'Scavenging cats. Sheep just off-loaded in the harbour and being driven along to the market. A camel or two. Donkeys.'

Umm al Basr had grown outwards and upwards, become greener, richer, glossier in his absence; it was a place where growing numbers of tourists came to shop in the designer boutiques in the mall, to camp in the desert and to soak up the winter sun on the unspoilt beaches.

He'd been aware it was happening—he'd followed the development of the city under his brother's guidance from a distance—but it had all happened without him and he felt like a stranger.

He pointed towards the mall. 'Over there were old go-downs used by the traders to store their goods. One had a pile of old track bought for a railway that was never constructed. Now Hamad is planning a tramline. Eco transport to cut down on pollution.' He looked around. 'The new marina was built on the site of a boatyard where for centuries craftsmen built dhows that crossed the Indian Ocean and sailed down the coast of Africa. That disappeared while I was away at school.'

'You were sent away?'

'My father understood that the future was global and he was keen that I had an international education. I went to schools in France, America, England, studied politics at Oxford.'

'Weren't you homesick?'

'I missed my family…' He looked at her. 'I missed my family but I made friends, was invited to their homes, skied with them, stayed at their cottages in France, their houses in the Hamptons, went shooting in Norfolk and Scotland…' There had come a time when he'd only come home for major holidays and even then it was under pressure from his mother to show his face. 'I loved Europe, America. The social life, the global culture. My friends were there. For a while I forgot who I was. My responsibilities.'

'What about your family, Bram? When did you see them?'

'After Oxford I bought a house in London and my mother, sisters, came to shop and see the latest shows so often that I saw more of them than I would have here in Umm al Basr.'

'And now?' she asked.

'I moved out of the house so that they could continue to use it but they always seem to find some reason to call me if I'm in London. A dripping tap. A door that sticks. Oddly, the problem has always resolved itself by the time I arrive.'

'That would be just in time for lunch or dinner?' she said, trying so hard not to laugh that he wanted to hug her, hold her, try a rerun of that kiss...

'What about your brother?' she asked.

'He did a business course at Harvard, but he hated every minute he was away from home. Even when he came to London it was for business—meetings with architects, engineers, bankers—and he never stayed a moment longer than he had to.' He made a broad gesture that took in the high-rise buildings around them. 'While I was playing,' he said, 'my brother was building the future. This is all his work.'

'So how does he feel about you coming back, Bram?'

'You still think he's trying to keep me away?'

She stopped. 'I think there's something you're not telling me.'

'It's complicated,' he said as the doors of the burger bar swished open, engulfing them in a rush of cold air.

'Life is complicated,' she said, letting it go. 'Carbs help.'

She helped, he thought. Straightforward, undemanding and, when she wasn't concentrating on keeping in place the mask she'd been wearing since her own world shattered, that hundred-watt smile slipped through and lit up his day.

Back on board, they settled in the big leather armchairs of the saloon, Bram's long legs stretched out in front of him, Ruby curled up with her feet tucked beneath her. Neither of them spoke until the burgers had been demolished and there were only a few fries left.

Ruby sucked the salty deliciousness from her right thumb, wiped her hands on a paper napkin and sighed. 'Eating healthy food is a very good thing,' she said, 'but there are days when only fat and salt will do.'

'I hope you brought your pretty tap shoes with you.'

He remembered? A ripple of pleasure warmed her. Not good... This might be a long run for a temp but it was a very short-term assignment for a wife. Forget the kiss...

'I'm afraid not,' she said, picking up the milkshake. 'I didn't think I'd be here for more than a few days.'

'You'll just have to come running with me.'

About to say running was very bad for the knees, she was assailed by the image of him that morning, his skin slicked with sweat...

'I... I...haven't got any shoes.'

'Not a problem. We can run barefoot on the beach. At the water's edge.'

'R-right.' She sucked hard on the straw and winced as the cold hit the middle of her forehead but it dealt with the assault of sensory images—his long feet, the muscles of his calves, thighs—that were scrambling all sensible thought. 'When are you going to the *majlis*, Bram?'

'We. You are coming with me.'

'Me?' Ruby stopped massaging the centre of her forehead. 'I thought those were men-only events.'

'As a rule they are, but there must be no doubt. I will have the falcon I've brought my father as a gift on my right arm and you on my left.'

Both of them scared spitless...

'You want your return to be as scandalous as your departure so that your father can never reinstate you as his heir?'

'Never say never, but Hamad has worked for this. Done all the right things. While I...' He shrugged.

'You are taking a risk, Bram.'

He shrugged. 'Taking risks is what I do. On horseback, on skis, in the market. Today I'm taking a risk that you are right and my father wants me home more than he wants me to succeed him.'

'No pressure, then.'

He smiled. 'You're not just a Garland Girl now, Ruby, you're a Garland Princess and you're going to have to live up to your billing.'

Her nerves hitched up a level. He was relying on her...

'Have you got a red dress?' he asked.

'Cut to the navel, slit up the side? Five-inch heels?' she asked. 'Do you really think that I'll need a scarlet woman dress to draw attention to myself?'

'No.' He looked at her for the longest moment before shaking his head. 'You'd cause a sensation if you were wearing a sack but I don't want you to look as if you're apologising for being there. Today is a triple celebration. My father's birthday, my return and my marriage. Wear something spectacular.'

The sun was setting as their limousine stopped at the entrance to the palace, where Noor and Khal were waiting. One or two people standing near the entrance to the palace glanced across as he got out but had already moved inside by the time he offered her his hand to help her from the car.

Noor immediately began fussing around her, rearranging the folds of her coat. It was heavy ruby-red silk, thickly embroidered and appliquéd in gold and worn over a floor-length full-skirted dress made from black silk chiffon that had a band of matching embroidery around the hem.

She straightened the ornate gold choker chosen from a chest containing tray after tray of jewels—Ruby didn't ask where they had come from, she didn't want to know. Finally, Noor draped a filmy red and gold scarf so that it covered her hair, carefully arranging the long tails that fell to the floor at her back.

'Eyes low, *sitti*,' she instructed, clearly not at all happy that her lady was being subjected to this shameful disregard for tradition. 'No smile.'

Bram, the falcon that was his gift to his father settled on his gloved hand, heard her and said something to her in Arabic. She shook her head but, after one last tweak of the scarf, she turned and walked away.

'What did you say to her?'

'To wait for you at the rear of the *majlis*. If things go well she will take you to my mother.'

'Right.' And that would be the good outcome. She didn't ask what would happen if things did not go well.

'And forget what Noor said to you. Keep your head up, eyes front and ignore everyone but my father.'

Her heart was pounding, her mouth dry. This was breaking all the rules, a gamble. She had nothing to lose but for Bram it was everything and she had to get it right.

'Head up, eyes front. Smile or no smile?'

Bram had waited, delaying his arrival until everyone was there. The vast entrance lobby, fifty metres long and nearly as wide, was now busy with men who'd paid their respects, drunk coffee with the ruler and overflowed from the *majlis,* where they were talking with friends, discussing business, catching up with the gossip.

'Be yourself, Ruby,' he said as she rested her hand on his so that the diamond ring on her finger flashed in the light from the chandeliers. She was trembling, he realised, and he turned his hand so that his fingers curled around hers. 'Just be yourself.'

She swallowed but lifted her head and looked straight ahead.

Despite its vast size, there was no room to simply walk through and he paused in the doorway until someone, noticing them out of the corner of his eye, took a step back to let them pass, then did a double take at the sight of a woman and another as he realised who was standing beside her and nudged his companion.

There was a ripple effect as men turned and the loud

burble of conversation gradually died away, leaving the room silent except for the rustle of shocked men stepping back, the pounding thud of his heartbeat…

'Bram?' Ruby murmured when, frozen to the spot, he could not move.

'This is like leaping out of the starting gate of the Lauberhorn,' he said softly. Two and a half heart-pounding minutes at over one hundred and fifty kilometres an hour on one of the most terrifying downhill ski runs in the world.

Ruby, who moments before had been shaking with nerves, gave his hand a reassuring squeeze and when he looked down at her she was smiling. 'Head up, eyes front,' she murmured. 'There is only one man here who matters.'

In that moment he knew that wasn't true; there was only one woman. Strong, brave, true…

Without a thought for where they were, the seriousness of the occasion, everything he was risking, he lifted her hand to his lips and the light from a dozen chandeliers caught the diamonds he'd placed on her finger and flashed a rainbow that lit up the room with colour. Or maybe it was just his life, he thought as he returned her smile, then looked to the front and took a step forward.

As they walked towards the *majlis,* the crowd closed in behind them, no one wanting to miss this. By the time they reached the great doors everyone was aware that something out of the ordinary was happening in the reception hall and the room was silent with expectation, all eyes turned towards them.

Another hundred metres, long seconds which gave his father, his open-mouthed brother and Ahmed Khadri all the time in the world to see the ring glittering on Ruby's finger, absorb the message he was sending, time to decide on their reaction.

At the foot of the dais he handed the falcon to a guard

who, at a nod from his father, stepped forward to take it. Then, his hand free, he placed it on his heart, making a low bow as he wished his father a long life, good health, many grandsons. Before the Emir could respond, he added, 'I have another gift for you on your birthday, my lord. May I present to you Rabi al-Dance? A daughter for your house, the mother of my sons.'

He was glad that he was speaking in Arabic so that Ruby did not know what he was saying.

His father, having been given plenty of time to consider his reaction, said, 'There is a contract between you?'

'Written and sealed by Sheikh Fayad al Kuwani, Emir of Ras al Kawi. Rabi has no living family but Fayad stood for her in the matter of a dowry.'

'He was demanding?' he asked.

'He protected her interests as diligently as any father, my lord, but there will be no call on you.'

Ahmed Khadri remained stony-faced, his brother's eyebrows were through the roof, but his father came very close to smiling.

'Where will she live?' he asked. 'Your mother and sisters enjoy your London house.'

His father was negotiating with him?

He smothered any notion of smiling. 'It is my gift to them. I have my own apartment and my wife, as is her right, will have a house of her own.'

His father nodded, rose to his feet and stepped down to embrace him. He was shockingly older, thinner than on the day he had disinherited him, but his grip was still strong. 'It is good to see you here, my son. It has been too long.' He looked at him for a long moment then nodded before turning to Ruby. 'You are welcome, Umm Tariq,' he said in English—mother of Tariq—a message to those present that he had accepted the wife his son had chosen and that her first son would bear his own name.

Ruby, head bowed, made a deep curtsey. '*Shukran*, Your Highness. I am honoured to be here.'

His father took her hand and, with a smile, urged her to her feet before turning to him. 'Take your bride to your mother, Ibrahim, and then come and sit with us.'

As he returned to his throne Hamad made a move to surrender his seat to his older brother but their father laid a hand on his arm, keeping him at his side, and Bram felt the tension slip from his shoulders. With that one gesture, his father had shown his people that while his oldest son had been welcomed back into the fold, Hamad remained his chosen successor—that the accord with the Khadri family would hold—and there was a shift in the air as a hundred men released the breath they had been holding.

Ahmed Khadri, meantime, had no choice but to surrender his own seat to make room for him but he took his time about it and, rather than move down the order of precedence, he sketched the merest nod at the throne, pausing beside him long enough to murmur, 'Take care not to turn the other cheek, Ibrahim al-Ansari. My knife will cut deeper.'

'It went well?' Ruby asked anxiously as he ushered her to a door at the rear of the *majlis* where Noor was waiting to escort her to his mother.

'It went well, thanks to you. My father not only signalled his acceptance of you but kept Hamad at his side, a clear indication to everyone present that he remains as heir.'

'And the man who left? That was Bibi's father?'

'Ahmed Khadri is no doubt on his way to inform her that I have disappointed another Khadri bride.'

She laid cool fingers against his cheek. 'That man hates you, Bram. Take care.'

He covered her hand with his, holding it against his face, resisting the urge to kiss her palm. 'It's in the past,

Ruby.' Reluctantly, he let go of her hand and took a small battered wooden box from his pocket. 'Give this to my mother. And if you see Safia, tell her that her prayers have been answered.'

'Prayers?'

'She will understand.'

Noor led the way towards the back of the palace, quickly running through the formalities of meeting the woman who was not only her mother-in-law but an Emira. Then, as a pair of wide double doors opened before them, she curtsied low and stepped aside, leaving Ruby on her own.

The news had clearly preceded her. The Emira was standing in the centre of a large room with her daughters, daughter-in-law and countless other female relatives gathered protectively around her, while children crawled and raced around them, oblivious to the drama.

This was not like the *majlis* where, at Bram's prompting, she had kept her head up, eyes forward, facing down the men who would be shocked by her presence. This was a moment for submission. As the door closed behind her, head bowed, she curtsied low, murmured, 'Emira…' as she offered her the box that Bram had given her on outstretched hands.

There was a moment of breath-holding silence and then the Emira put her hand beneath hers and, with the slightest pressure, invited her to stand before she took the box and held it, gently rubbing her hand over its battered surface as if it was something much cherished.

'This,' she said in clear, barely accented English, 'was the first gift that my son gave me when he was four years old.' She lifted the lid of the box and inside, on purple velvet, nestled a piece of turquoise-blue sea glass that she lifted out and held against her lips for a long moment before looking up. 'We were walking on the beach and he saw it being turned at the edge of the water. He thought it was a jewel and he gave it to me in this little box. I sent it to him when he was banished, a piece of home to keep with him,' she said. 'My promise that one day he would return.'

She replaced the glass in the box, looked up and, with a smile, extended a hand. 'Welcome, Rabi. Come and meet your sisters.'

His four older sisters each kissed her on both cheeks, and then there was Safia with her new baby. She was extraordinarily beautiful, with blue-green eyes that shone from her lovely face as she stepped forward to kiss her cheeks, and when Ruby, very quietly, gave her Bram's message those eyes filled with tears.

Before she could speak, Ruby found herself swept away into a comfortable inner sitting room strewn with toys for the little ones who were being entertained by the older children. Mint tea and small sticky cakes were pressed upon her, along with a dozen questions. All the women spoke good English but, to her relief, the Emira was not interested in how she had met Bram.

Inventing a world class romance for Violet was one thing, but Bram's mother had the kind of eyes that missed nothing. As she brushed aside her daughters' eager questions and asked about her family and their history, Ruby had the feeling that she knew exactly what Bram had done.

Fortunately, her family had plenty of history and she kept them entertained with stories—tales that had no doubt grown taller in the telling—of ancestors who had served kings and queens throughout the centuries until, at last, a stir beyond the doors announced the arrival of their husbands.

Bram, his hand upon his heart, bowed low to his mother then enfolded her in a heartfelt hug before turning to his sisters and embracing them each in turn. Finally he turned to Safia, acknowledging her with a formal bow.

'Your sister is not with you, *sitti?*' he asked, speaking in English, in deference to her presence. 'I had hoped to congratulate her on achieving her heart's desire.'

'We are very proud of her,' she replied. 'Sadly, she has been confined to her room with a chill.'

'I hope she will soon recover. Please give her my wife's very best wishes for the future.'

'Thank you, *sidi*. She will be desolate to have missed such a glad occasion.'

There had been nothing to suggest it had been anything but the most formal exchange and yet Ruby had been aware of an undercurrent, a deeper layer of meaning.

She glanced at Hamad, but he, like the other men, had been surrounded by the little ones as soon as he'd arrived and, bending to pick up the little girl clutching at his knees, had not witnessed the exchange. Or had he turned away rather than see his brother greet the woman who should have been his bride?

A birthday supper was served with three generations of the family together, a chaotic, happy, noisy mix of children and adults. Everyone wanted to talk to Bram, hug him, welcome him. And if Safia slipped away early looking pale, everyone understood that she had been unwell, needed rest.

Ruby, watching her leave, certain that there was more to her pallor than a difficult childbirth, jumped as Bram put his hand on her shoulder. He gave her a wry smile as she turned to him and bent to whisper in her ear, 'You're supposed to melt when I touch you, not jump.'

Which was all very well for him to say, but ever since that kiss it was as if she'd been wired up to jump leads— one touch and her feet left the ground—but, aware that they were the centre of attention, she whispered, 'So messy, melting…'

'Rabi—' Fathia and Nadiya converged on her, grinning as they shooed Bram away. 'Come and sit with us,' Fathia said, taking her hand and leading her towards a sofa. 'We want to hear exactly how you met Bram.'

'And how you got a man who swore he would never marry to put that gorgeous ring on your finger,' Nadiya added.

Swore never to marry? She turned, met his gaze and Bram shrugged.

'She's the best temporary PA in London,' he said. 'Hugely in demand. The only way I could ensure she stayed was to marry her.'

'You expect her to work for you?'

'Of course. In fact, I have a pile of emails that need attending to,' he said, disengaging her from his sisters. 'We have to go.'

Shocked, Nadiya said, 'But that's—'

'He's teasing,' Fathia said, grinning. 'Let them go.'

'Oh…' Nadiya blushed.

'Tomorrow,' Fathia said, smiling, 'we'll pick you up and take you shopping for honeymoon clothes while Bram spends the morning talking politics with Abbi and Hamad.' She leaned forward and in a loud mock whisper said, 'We'll have lunch and you can tell us *everything*.'

CHAPTER EIGHT

'THANK YOU FOR rescuing me from the third-degree back there.'

'A brief postponement, no more,' Bram said as, hidden within the dark-tinted windows of the limousine, they were driven back to the harbour. 'I thought you might welcome a break.'

After dinner there had been a seemingly endless round of visitors who wanted to welcome him home. Congratulate him on his marriage. Wonderful though it had been to see everyone, he was glad to escape to the peace and quiet of the boat.

To be alone with Ruby.

'I had a practice run with Violet and Leila,' she assured him. 'Your mother stepped in before your sisters could get started but if by "everything" they mean what I think they mean I'm going to need time to get my imagination in gear.'

'Just say if you need a refresher course.'

He anticipated one of her smart rejoinders but instead she caught her breath, lowered her lashes, turned to look out of the window and, without warning, he was the one struggling to breathe.

'Ruby...'

'I think I can remember the basics,' she said as she turned back to face him, breath almost back to normal, but her eyes, dark and deep as space, betrayed her. He was not alone… 'Your mother, I'm happy to say, was more interested in my antecedents than how we met.'

Melt… He'd told her she should melt but right now he was the one in meltdown, longing to hold her, kiss her, once more taste those lovely lips. Every cell in his body was responding to the look in her eyes. She was fighting it and he'd made her a promise but he was the one taking a slow, steadying breath before he said, 'My mother was ignoring the fact that we should not have met without her approval.'

'And family is far more important than romance. I understand that. Fortunately, although I'm short of the living variety, I do have centuries of ancestors to call on.'

She pulled at her lower lip with her teeth and he felt a more urgent tug of heat…

'I'm afraid I dropped names left, right and centre.'

'Names?' he repeated, hanging onto reality by a thread.

Her smile widened. 'You don't hang onto your estates through war and revolution for as long as our family did without making yourself useful to whoever wears the crown. My three times great-grandfather might have raised eyebrows with his chorus girl bride but his son was an aide to King George V.'

He tried to concentrate on what she was saying, but all he could think of was how her mouth had tasted. How it could become an addiction…

'Impressive. Safia—' *think of Safia* '—must have been praying very hard for you to have walked into my life at the exact moment I needed you, Ruby.'

'I gave her your message.' She frowned and he barely restrained himself from reaching out to smooth it away.

'What did she say?'

'Nothing. She was just shocked, I think, but she didn't have time to say anything before I was grabbed by your sisters.' She looked up. 'I won't be able to lie to your mother, Bram. If she asks me the direct question.'

'If she asks you the direct question do not hesitate to tell her the truth,' he said, reaching for her hand, meaning only to offer a reassuring touch, but somehow it was curled into his, a perfect fit.

'She'll be terribly shocked.'

'On the contrary. She will tell you that all great marriages are arranged for the good of the family and the state. The fact that we arranged it ourselves may be unconventional, but the result is the same.'

'Hardly great. It's going to be the shortest marriage in the history of Umm al Basr.' Was that regret? 'Perhaps I should have told her about my parents. Made myself a little less suitable so that she'll be relieved when you divorce me. But I wanted your homecoming to be a happy day.'

'Then you achieved your wish.'

He'd sat with his family, enjoying the teasing conversation that he could only have with those who'd known him from a baby, but his eyes had been constantly drawn to Ruby.

She'd fitted in so easily. He'd watched as one of his nieces clutched at her knees with sticky fingers. Totally unconcerned about her dress, Ruby had lifted her onto her lap for a cuddle, accepted a wet kiss, pretended to nibble on the half eaten biscuit the infant had thrust at her.

His mother, catching his eye, had smiled her approval and he had felt his wizened heart, so long deprived of all he loved, expand and fill with longing for this to be real.

Only Safia, unconvinced, had been quiet, distant, excusing herself early to see to her baby. She'd caught his eye once, a desperate, what-have-you-done? question blazing out of her eyes, but then only she and Hamad knew that he had been warned. Suspected that this marriage was a sham.

'Your mother showed me the sea glass,' Ruby said. 'She

told me how you put it in your treasures box and gave it to her when you were a little boy.'

'Did she tell you what she wrote when she sent it to me?' She nodded, her eyes suddenly liquid. 'Is that a tear?' he asked.

'Just a little one,' she said, blinking hard but failing to catch it. Touched by this evidence of her empathy, he took his hand from her and wiped the stray tear from her cheek with the pad of his thumb, before cradling her cheek as if it was the most natural thing in the world. Because it was.

For a moment she continued to look up at him, eyes glistening, her mouth temptingly soft, with only an anxious little frown to mar the smooth perfection of her skin. He wanted to kiss it away, reassure her, tell her that she'd been amazing. That he couldn't imagine a more suitable wife if his mother had lined up every single one of the well-born daughters of Umm al Basr for him to choose from.

The way she'd walked beside him through the *majlis,* had spoken to his father. She'd been like a rock at his side…

'You should have given it to her yourself but it was a clever move,' she said. 'It got us both over that first awkward moment.'

'That was my intention,' he said, lifting his arm and putting it around her, drawing her close. She didn't resist, but let her head rest against his shoulder. No doubt she was tired. She couldn't have slept much for the last two nights and it had been another long day.

'How was your father?' she asked.

'In very good spirits. He's brought me home without having to submit to the Khadris' demands—' in private the old man had scarcely been able to contain his delight at besting his old enemy '—and he's anticipating the swift arrival of a grandson to keep them out of the succession altogether.'

He saw the gentle ripple of her throat as she swallowed. 'I'm sure, given time for Safia to recover, your brother will do his best to ensure that doesn't happen.'

'That would be the diplomatic solution,' he agreed, 'and my brother is nothing if not a diplomat.'

'And he has a three-girl start on you.' She looked up at him, looked away again quickly but not before he saw the tinge of pink darken her cheeks. 'So today went as well as you could have wished,' she said quickly.

Not exactly, he thought, as her hair brushed against his cheek. His plan had been very simple. A paper marriage and a swift divorce. The marriage had succeeded beyond his wildest dreams but every minute he spent with Ruby made the divorce part of the deal less and less appealing.

'Everyone is happy,' he assured her.

'Except the Khadris.' She gave a little shiver and he drew her closer.

'They'll get over it.'

'What about you, Bram?' She turned her head to look up at him. 'Are you happy?'

'Happy… That's a very shallow word to describe the way I'm feeling at this moment.'

Sitting with his arm around this amazing woman… There was only one thing that would make him happier, but there was no rush. He had until the autumn to make their legend, all those stolen moments they had invented, a reality. To convince her to stay.

'I was happy when I escaped the palace as a boy, playing polo, risking my neck on ski runs.' Right now he felt as if he was on the verge of something new, life-changing. 'Maybe I was born too late. As a young man my grandfather was battling the Khadris for grazing and water, protecting our traditional fishing grounds and pearl beds from their raiding parties, stealing their daughters.'

'So you looked for other ways to risk your life. Will

you go back to the mountains now you've served your penance?' she asked.

'It's been too long. Downhill racing demands total dedication.'

'I don't understand why you gave it up.'

'Don't you? You gave up riding. It wasn't just the press, was it?'

She shook her head. 'I'd lost everything I cared about. I had no heart for it.'

'But you will ride Rigel?'

'Will you ski for fun?'

He'd never thought of skiing as anything other than a demanding sport but the idea of fooling around in the snow with Ruby was very appealing and she hadn't had any fun in a long time. 'It's getting a bit late in the season, but maybe we could spend the New Year in Switzerland?'

He held his breath, waiting for her answer.

'Skiing is just an expensive way to break a leg,' she said. 'Besides, you'd be bored to death teaching a falling-down beginner.'

'Picking you up will be a great deal more enjoyable than avoiding once-a-year skiers on crowded slopes.' She hadn't reminded him that the cut-off date for their marriage deal was September. She hadn't said no… 'However, for a woman expected to win equestrian gold at the Olympics, you appear to have a very high aversion to risk.'

'Or maybe a well-developed sense of self-preservation.'

'We can stick to making snowmen until you're begging to get out on the slopes.' He held his breath.

'Snowmen I can do.'

'In the meantime, how do you feel about scuba diving?'

'Scuba diving? That's not in the job description,' she said.

'Your job description, as I recall, is "whatever is necessary". Right now that's being my bride, and my sisters all wanted to know where I was taking you for our honeymoon.'

'And you told them you were going to dress me up in rubber and take me underwater?' she mocked, but he knew now why she did not like the sea. 'What did they have to say about that?'

'When I told them I was taking you to the Maldives they all just sighed. However, since there's nothing to do there but lie in the sun and make love, I thought perhaps we would need a distraction.'

'No…'

She struggled to sit up but his arm was about her waist and her weight against him was a pleasure gained that he was unwilling to relinquish.

'You would not be alone, Ruby, staring into the cold water of the North Sea, betrayed by the man you loved, your life in shreds. Your hand will be in mine as we swim in the warm blue waters of the Indian Ocean,' he said, 'and I will keep you safe.'

'Bram…' Her eyes were troubled, her lips trembling.

'I saw the picture of you outside your office with the man you could not bring yourself to tell me about. He was pointing at something so that you would be looking across the street, into the lens of the photographer who was lying in wait for you, but you were looking up at him. Had eyes only for him.'

'Jeff.' She swallowed. 'He'd been at a client site that day but someone called to warn him what was going around the office and he'd found the story on the Internet. He thought he knew me, Bram—'

'Don't make excuses for him, Ruby. No matter how angry he was, a man with any kind of a backbone—'

'Bram.' His name was so soft on her lips that it felt like a newly minted word and as she looked up at him, took her hand from his and laid it against his chest, the breath caught in his throat. 'I've seen how a man with backbone reacts when confronted with an unexpected revelation. How he stands by her. Protects her.'

'*Ya habibati*,' he murmured, completely undone. '*Ya rohi…*'

The kiss—so wrong, so right—was a breath away. A hand slipped to her neck, his fingers tangling in her hair. He could feel her breath on his lips…

'Workplace relationships are never a good idea,' she said, holding him off.

'I could fire you.'

'Or I could resign.'

'I accept,' he said, lowering his lips to hers, with the same nervous uncertainty of a boy kissing a girl for the first time. He was shaking with the hugeness of it, the knowledge that nothing would ever be the same again. That he would never be the same…

Her lips were soft, yielding sweetly until, catching her breath, she drew back a little to look at him, her eyes molten silver, black velvet, searching his face.

Trust me…

His head was booming with the words and he wanted to shout them to the skies, but they were hollow, meaningless in the heat of desire. They were spending so much time together, sharing secrets, growing closer but trust was something that had to be lived every day, every hour, every minute.

There had been moments when it would have taken no more than a look, a touch to ignite the tension that sizzled between them, set it ablaze. Always conscious of the deal they had made, he'd taken a step back and he would do it again and again for as long as Ruby needed to trust him, trust herself…

Ruby had been so certain that she could do this. She'd shied away from the possibility of any kind of entanglement for so long that, despite the undeniable attraction, she was sure she could play the part of Bram's wife for his family, for all the world, while keeping her distance in private.

She had been fooling herself.

The knee-melting heat of desire had been there in that first shocked moment when he'd appeared wearing nothing but a towel and, dry-mouthed, she'd watched water trickle down his broad golden chest. When she'd stumbled on the steps and breathed in the warm male scent of his body as he'd caught her, held her. In that moment when she'd been unable to stop herself from reaching up to touch the scar on his cheek.

He'd taken her hand then and it had felt like a perfect fit.

She knew it was the intimacy of co-conspirators that made the air thrum with tension when they were in the same room. That the only reason he caught her eye to share a private smile, touched her shoulder as he passed, was to convince the world that they were a couple. But the wedding had felt so real. His kiss had felt so real.

Now he was talking about a honeymoon, about keeping her safe. And he was kissing her, not like a man confident of his power but a man for whom this was the most important moment in his life. Giving her time to choose where this would go. Step out of the shadows and take the risk…

With no secrets between them, nothing hidden, she closed her hand over his robe, bunching it in her fist, closed her eyes and said, 'Ya habibi.'

His hand, cool, gentle, cradled her face. His lips brushed her eyelids, her cheek, and as they touched her mouth she felt herself melt against him, boneless, holding her breath, waiting for more, desperate for more. He took his time, cradling her head, his thumb against her jaw, his finger sliding through her hair, tilting her head back, brushing against her neck.

He paused to look down at her for a long moment before taking the kiss to another dimension; his tongue sliding over her lower lip before slowly, thoroughly, he took possession of her mouth, lighting up all the longing, need, that she'd suppressed for so long.

It was the impatient hooting of dozens of car horns that finally broke through the mist of desire and Bram drew back a little, kissed her again and then reached for the intercom switch. He exchanged a few words with the driver and then said, 'Someone's been rear-ended. It will be hours while they argue who's to blame.'

'Hours?'

'You're in a hurry to get somewhere, *ya habati*?'

He didn't wait for an answer but opened the door and they tumbled out, laughing, as they began to run, dodging around the cars until they reached the harbour.

The gangway bounced beneath their feet as they ran up it and then, as soon as they were aboard, he pulled her into the dark shadows of the bulkhead, took her in his arms. 'Are you sure about this, Ruby?'

'*Ya habibi*...'

'Ruby... My soul... My life...'

There was a slow, continuous beeping noise, the familiar hospital smell and wooziness as she surfaced from unconsciousness. Panic...

'Daisy,' she croaked. 'Is Daisy hurt?'

'Ruby...'

She opened her eyes, saw Bram, felt his hand, warm and strong, in hers and, certain that she would be safe, she let the darkness drag her back.

'Has she come round?'

Bram looked up as his mother reached his side, put her hand on his shoulder. 'She stirred a while ago.'

'She is strong. She will live to bear you many children.' She bent and kissed him. Kissed Ruby.

The beeping was back, insistent, annoying. Ruby wanted to tell someone to turn it off but when she opened her eyes the light was so bright that she closed them. Then opened them again. She had not been mistaken. Bram was on his knees beside her, his forehead resting against their joined hands, whispering words that she did not understand.

'Bram?' She made the words with her lips but there was no sound. 'Bram…' she repeated, trying harder. Her voice sounded rusty and it hurt her chest when she tried to catch a breath but he raised his head and she saw that his eyes were sunken, with dark shadows beneath them.

'Ruby.' Her name was layered with exhaustion, relief, emotions that she was too tired to unravel. 'Ruby, my soul, my life, how can you ever forgive me?'

Forgive him? What had he done?

'Could I have some water?'

He poured a little water into a glass, supporting her head as he touched it to her lips so that a little trickled into her mouth.

'Thank you.'

'Don't.' He looked as if he was the one in pain. Was he? Had he been hurt? 'Don't thank me.'

'I'm in hospital…' That beeping was a machine measuring out her vital signs. 'What happened to me? Was there an accident?' She tried to sort through the jumble of images in her brain. 'We were in the car.' She remembered a kiss. Or had she dreamed that?

'There was a hold-up. A collision at the entrance to the harbour.'

'Yes.' She remembered the blaring horns.

'You're smiling.'

'Yes.' The kiss had been real. But then… 'We were running.' Running, laughing as they'd run back to the boat, laughing as he'd drawn her into the shadows, unable to wait another moment to touch each other, hold each other. 'You asked me if I was sure.' She frowned. 'What did I say?'

'You don't remember?'

She remembered his arm about her waist, his fingers in her hair, the scent of steel and salt water and oil. The darkness of Bram's eyes, the anticipation of a kiss that would change her world and then something else. 'There was someone in the shadows. I saw a flash…'

'You saved my life, Ruby.' His hand tightened over hers. 'You cried out and, as I turned, Ahmed Khadri's knife missed me and hit you below the collarbone. You've lost a great deal of blood but there is no permanent damage, *insha'Allah*. If you had been taller…' He caught himself as if simply saying the words was to tempt fate. 'This is my fault. I should have stayed away.'

'There is only one person to blame.' She felt like lead, her shoulder was aching and the anaesthetic lingering in her bloodstream was dragging at her eyelids. 'The man with the knife.'

'You warned me. I did not listen.'

'Did he hurt you?' she asked.

He shook his head. 'When he saw what he had done he dropped the knife. I was yelling at him to call an ambulance while I tried to staunch the bleeding but he just stood there, useless for anything, but Khal heard me.'

'Where is he now? Ahmed Khadri?'

'He is at the *majlis*, waiting for the Ruler's justice. Waiting for my justice.'

'Your justice?' Woolly-headed, it took her a moment to realise what that meant. 'No!' She tried to sit up but she was hampered by wires hooking her up to the machinery and an IV tube in her hand. 'No, Bram…'

He caught her as she tried to pull them away, sending

the machine into a frenzy, held her against his chest for a moment before easing her back against the pillow. Brushing her hair back from her face, he said, 'Who is Daisy?'

'Daisy?' she repeated, distracted.

'You asked about her.'

'Daisy was the first pony I rode in competition. I was over-ambitious at a jump, she dumped me in it and I broke my collarbone.'

'Was she hurt?'

'No. Bram—'

'The nurse is here to sort you out,' he said but, aware that he had attempted to distract her, she hung onto his sleeve, coughing in an attempt to clear her lungs of the anaesthetic, pull herself up...

'Don't do it, Bram.'

He did not pretend not to know what she meant. 'It's what he would do in my place.'

'You are not like him.'

'You do not know me,' he said, his face expressionless as, with a formal little bow, he backed away.

'You will start a war. Undo everything you sacrificed yourself for.'

'Some things cannot be left unanswered. I'll send Noor to you.'

'I know you!' she shouted after him. 'Bram!' But it was a doctor who appeared, a starched white coat over her sari, a jangle of bracelets at her wrist.

'Please, Princess, calm yourself or you will undo all my good work.'

'I have to get out of here.'

'We'll have you out of bed this evening and see how you feel then. Maybe you can leave tomorrow. You will be well cared for at the palace.'

'Not tomorrow. Now.' Ruby began pulling off the pads connecting her to the machine, holding out her hand with the IV to the nurse who had been attempting to reattach them. 'Remove this, please.' The nurse looked at the doctor but Ruby didn't wait for them to gang up on her. 'You do it or I will.'

The doctor lifted her eyes to the ceiling but nodded to the nurse.

'Where are my clothes?'

'*Sitti?*' Noor appeared in the doorway, white-faced, shaken. 'I heard the alarms…'

'It's nothing. I need my clothes. And a car. I have to see the Emira.'

'She said she would come back later—'

'Now…' It didn't come out as the sharp command she'd intended but Noor was already rushing to her side to support her as she slid her feet over the side of the bed, holding her until the room stopped swimming.

'You should lie down, *sitti*.'

'Ruby. Call me Ruby…' Still hanging onto the night table, she pulled herself upright. 'Have I got any clothes or will I have to go to the palace with my backside hanging out?'

Noor helped her out of the hospital gown and into a nightdress and wrap she'd brought from the boat. Wrapped her in her own *abbayah*.

A wheelchair was summoned and by the time they were at the door a car was waiting with Khal at the wheel.

Ten minutes later they were at the entrance to the family quarters of the palace.

'Khal, find Bram and tell him I want to see him now. Immediately. Do you understand? Noor, take me to the Emira.'

'Rabi!' The Emira stood as Noor pushed her into the sitting room, filled with the same women who were there yesterday when they had been strangers. His sisters, Safia, all looking grave. No children.

'You have to stop him, my lady,' she said without ceremony. She had no strength to waste on unnecessary words.
'Please.'

The Emira rapped out words in Arabic, hands caught
her as she slipped sideways, lifted her gently onto a sofa.
A blanket was wrapped around her. The sharp, head-
clearing scent of smelling salts was waved beneath her
nose.

'Rabi...' Safia knelt beside her. 'Can you ever forgive
me?'

'You wanted to help your sister.'

'No. Before that. Long before that.' She looked across to
the Emira. 'The last time that Ibrahim came home, when
you sent for him to make the wedding arrangements he
saw...'

'Saw what?' she asked sharply.

'He saw that I loved Hamad.'

The Emira said something, sank into a chair.

'We were never alone, *sitti*,' she said quickly. 'We
never did anything that you would disapprove of, anything shameful, but I spent so much time at the palace with
you, learning how to be an Emira, that I knew him like a
brother. He cared for me like a brother. Never angry, always kind, always there. Ibrahim was a stranger.'

'What did he see?' the Emira demanded.

'Ibrahim saw me look at his brother, saw that there were
tears in Hamad's eyes. That was all.'

'And he left without a word, without signing the contract.'

'He gave Nadiya a note for me. She thought it was a
love letter but he said that when Hamad and I had looked
at one another it was as if we were the only two people in
the room. He said he would remember that look all his life.'

Unaware that behind her, in the doorway, Bram, Hamad

and the Emir were listening, she said, 'He said he would fix things so that I could marry Hamad.'

'Safia…' Hamad crossed to her, held her, then turned to his father. 'Ibrahim staged the incident in the fountain, arranged for someone to film it and put it on the Internet, to call the police and the press in full knowledge of the consequences.'

'When you're faking a scene you have to pay attention to detail,' Ruby murmured as Bram crossed to her, took her hand. 'You are so good at the details.'

'Hush, *ya rohi.*'

'I did not know what he'd done,' Hamad continued. 'I believed he had dishonoured the woman I loved. I was the one who cut his face.'

There was an audible gasp from the Emira and her daughters.

'I would have told you the truth years ago,' he said, 'but Bram forbade it.'

'And Ahmed Khadri let everyone believe that he was the hero who'd avenged his daughter's honour?' Hasna gave a snort of disgust. 'What a loser.'

'My son—' his father took Bram's hand '—if I'd known…'

'If you'd known you would have been in an impossible position. I knew what I was doing. I'd do it again.'

'What can I do?' he said.

'Give me a moment alone with my wife.'

The Emira cleared the room with a gesture. 'Just a moment, Ibrahim. Ruby is exhausted.'

He nodded, then, as the door closed, leaving them alone, he knelt beside her, took her hand. 'I left you safe in hospital.'

'You left before I had finished talking to you.'

'Shouting at me,' he said, but he was smiling. 'You sounded exactly like a wife.'

'I sounded like a woman who was afraid that you'd do something you would regret.'

'If I'd had a knife in my hand when he struck you, I would certainly have killed him where he stood, but in cold blood? He expected it but it seems, *ya habati,* that you do know me.'

'Yes, Bram. I know you.' The painkillers were wearing off and the dull ache in her shoulder had sharpened into something darker. 'What will happen to him?'

'The court will decide on his punishment.'

'Well, good.' She coughed, winced.

'Your hand is freezing,' he said, rubbing it between his to get some warmth into it. 'I have to get you back to the hospital.'

'No.' She shook her head, wished she hadn't. 'I want to go home, Bram.'

'You'll have to wait until you're strong enough to travel to the fort.'

'Not there.' She was feeling faint, knew that she wouldn't be able to talk for much longer, but this was important. 'Not there. I want to go home to London. To my flat. It's over, Bram. You are back with your family. You don't need me any more. Tell them the truth. Annul the marriage.'

'You must rest. We'll talk when you're stronger.'

'No!' She tried to tighten her grip on his hand, but the message wasn't getting through and he tucked it beneath the blanket. 'You don't have to explain, Bram. I understand.'

She'd wondered why Safia was so certain that he'd stay away from his father's birthday *majlis*, give up the chance to return home, give up everything that mattered to him for her sister. She knew because he'd done it for her and there was only one reason a man would do that for a woman— because he loved her more than life itself.

'I knew there was something off about that scene in the fountain.' She was struggling to keep her eyes open. 'It was out of character.'

'And last night?' His voice was barely audible above the thrumming in her ears. 'What was that?'

Last night. When he'd kissed her and all the barriers she had built around her had come crashing down.

'That was…'

A dream, a moment when she had thought her world had been turned the right way up. A fantasy.

'That was just…' She gave up the struggle to keep her eyes open—it was easier to lie when she wasn't looking at him. 'Just sex.'

'Just sex?' Bram thumbed away the tear that had spilled down her cheek, gently kissed her cheek and pulled the cover up to her chin as the door opened behind him.

The doctor rested the back of her hand against Ruby's forehead, checked her shoulder. 'The wound has reopened, Sheikh. We need to get her back to the hospital.'

'The doctor told me that you've been asking her when you can leave,' Bram said.

'They've been wonderful, Bram.' Ruby was standing at the window, looking out over the sparkling blue water of the Gulf, not trusting herself to look at him. 'You've all been wonderful, but I'm ready to go home.'

He joined her at the window and the sleeve of his robe brushed against her arm as he stood beside her. 'We will stay here until you are stronger.'

She had expected that, prepared herself. 'No—'

He turned to her. 'You are determined to return to London?'

His expression was unreadable. It had been unreadable since she'd lost consciousness on the sofa in his mother's drawing room. Since she'd denied that there had been anything between them but a rush of emotion-fuelled lust.

Just sex...

His close-cut beard had grown, there were shadows beneath his eyes and his cheeks were hollow. She'd told him that he looked a wreck, worse than she did, but he had been stubbornly deaf to her plea for him to go back to the palace and rest.

For two days she'd drifted in and out of consciousness but every time she'd opened her eyes he had been in the chair at her side or wrapped in a cloak lying on the floor beside her bed, waking the moment she stirred.

In the week that followed he'd had food specially prepared for her at the palace, brought little treats to tempt her to eat. He'd been attentive, endlessly caring, always there and yet as distant as a star.

He had not touched her, not even to hold her hand. Had not murmured soft Arabic endearments that she did not understand. Why would he?

There was no further need to pretend that this was anything but an arrangement that had run its course. It was guilt, duty, honour that was keeping him a prisoner at her side and if she had learned anything from him it was that when you loved someone you let them go.

She lifted the arm that had been pinned up in a sling. 'I'm not going to be much use to you as a PA, Bram.'

'As I recall,' he said, 'I fired you.'

'Rubbish. I resigned.'

For a moment she struggled to keep the mask in place, act as if that kiss had never happened, keep it strictly business. 'I'll ask Amanda to send you a replacement.'

'You think that anyone could replace you?' His face, voice, remained unreadable.

'Please...' There was a lump in her throat as big as a rock and she had to swallow hard before she could carry on. 'You are home. Reconciled with your father. You need to move on.'

'While you run back to your hiding place?' he asked, a flicker of annoyance breaking through.

'No. I've had a lot of time to think in the last few days, Bram. I've been looking at courses on the Internet.'

'Courses?'

'I'm going to train as a riding instructor.'

His face softened. 'Reclaiming a little of your past.'

'No. I'm not looking back, Bram. I'm building a new future and I have you to thank for the courage to do that.'

'I suppose it's pointless asking you to stay at my house, where there are people to take care of you until you are fully recovered?'

'That's very generous of you, but I want to be in my own home.' She needed to have her familiar things about her. Get back to normality.

'If that is what you wish, I have to honour it. My plane is at your command.' He turned back to the window, the distant horizon. 'I regret that if you insist on leaving today I will not be able to travel with you. The Emir has summoned his Council and has asked me to attend.'

'Then you must,' she said. 'This is why we went through this, Bram. So that you can be here to support him.'

'Yes.'

'Will you tell them the truth?' she said.

'About you?' He looked at her then and for the first time in days he was smiling. 'Yes, Ruby, I will tell them.'

'And you will arrange for the marriage to be dissolved?'

'Fayad sent a copy of the contract to your lawyer, with an English translation. My lawyers will deal directly with them. Being lawyers, they will no doubt take their time. You are not in any hurry?' he asked. 'Our agreement was until September.'

'September will be fine.' Pointless to regret the promised New Year in the snow.

He nodded. 'Noor will travel with you and there will be a car to meet you.'

She considered telling him that she would take a scheduled flight, that she did not need a companion, that she could arrange her own car, but since she'd be wasting her breath all that remained was to thank him.

'*Shukran*, Sheikh Ibrahim. *Ma'al-salaama*.'

There was the faintest hint of a smile as he lifted his hand to his heart and with the slightest of bows said, '*Afwen, sitti. Ila-liqaa*.'

Bram's sisters kissed her and said they would see her when they were in London.

Safia brought Bibi to meet her. She seemed unbelievably young but happy to be leaving for England and university within the next few weeks.

Ruby wished her luck but as they left Safia hugged her, said, '*Ma'al-salama*, Rabi. I am praying that your firstborn will be a son.'

'I...' Her breath caught in her throat and by the time she had recovered Safia was gone.

Her final visitor was the Emira.

'I had hoped that you would be staying with us for a while, Rabi,' she said. 'The Emir wanted to give you this himself but he has meetings all day.'

She opened the small leather-covered box she was holding to reveal a small falcon, wings spread, delicately modelled in fine gold and suspended from a dark red ribbon.

'It is the Order of the Golden Falcon,' she explained, taking it from the box and fastening it to the lapel of her jacket. 'It has never before been given to a woman but you saved the life of his firstborn son and when he announced

the award at the *majlis* this morning I am told that everyone stood and clapped.'

Ruby had known this day would be hard, but now, as
Bram's mother kissed both her cheeks, she was struggling
to blink back tears that she could not allow to fall.

'I am deeply honoured, my lady. Please thank the Emir
for me.' She forced a smile to her face. 'Will he restore
Ibrahim to the throne?'

'He offered it. His brother pressed him to accept.'

'But he refused.'

The Emira smiled. 'You understand him so well.'

Yes.

She understood him. Understood that the love he held
in his heart for the woman he had set free to marry his
brother was enduring, everlasting. Understood why marriage to her sister would have been unendurable.

'Bram told me that he was born for another age.'

'Maybe.' She sighed. 'He always found it hard to be inside. Was always escaping, looking for adventure.'

'He told me that too. He took me to the blacksmith's
shop where he used to play truant as a boy. His friend's
son brought me tea.' She picked up her phone to show her
the photograph she'd taken of the boy. Instead she found
herself looking at the kiss she and Bram had shared at their
wedding and reached blindly for the night table, afraid that
she was going to faint.

The Emira took the phone from her, looked at the photograph for a long moment, handing it back as Noor appeared in the doorway.

'The car is here, Ruby.'

'Yes.' She hugged the Emira. 'Thank you for your kindness. Please give the Emir my very best wishes.'

'You go with our hearts, Rabi.'

CHAPTER NINE

RUBY HAD EXPECTED her flat, unused for nearly two weeks in a reluctant spring, to be dusty and cold, but it was warm, aired and gleaming. The fridge had been stocked and, beside a pile of post, there was a basket of fruit on the sofa table.

She would have assumed it was Amanda's handiwork but for the fact that there were also half a dozen of the latest bestsellers in hardback, a florist's arrangement of spring flowers and a large box of liquorice allsorts on top of the bookshelf.

Amanda would have bought paperbacks, filled a jug with daffodils picked from her own garden and she didn't know about her love of liquorice allsorts.

A card listing appointments with a physiotherapist at the London Clinic was the clincher.

'You must go to bed now, Ruby,' Noor said. 'I will bring you tea, unpack your clothes, then I will go downstairs. If you need me just call.'

'Downstairs?'

'Bram said your flat is too small for me so I am staying in the one downstairs.'

'Downstairs?' She knew the tenants had been looking for something bigger. They must have moved out while she was away. 'Bram has rented the flat downstairs for you?'

'So that I can be close to look after you.' She took an envelope from her pocket. 'The driver gave me the keys.'

'Right.'

It did explain why Bram hadn't insisted she stay in his London house. This way he could be seen to be taking care of her while she was still, officially, his wife, while keeping her at a distance.

It was the solution she would have come up with if she'd still been his PA and he'd asked her to sort it out.

'Will you be all right on your own in a strange apartment?' she asked.

Noor grinned. 'It will be the first time I've ever had my own home,' she said. 'And I have family. My cousin works in London for the airline owned by Sheikh Zahir. He is Bram's cousin.'

'Yes.' She'd casually spouted that piece of information when she was attempting to impress him.

'We are going to have afternoon tea, visit Borough Market on Sunday morning and go for a ride on the London Eye. Not like you did with Bram when he booked a night-time ride just for the two of you, with all the lights of London at your feet.' She sighed. 'So romantic.'

'Oh.' Her sightseeing trips were culled from the legend she and Bram had invented, that she had shared with Violet and Leila while Noor had been ironing and stitching and fetching tea.

The Eye had been one of Bram's suggestions and yes, he had made it sound so romantic that she could have fallen in love with him just listening to him.

'I'm not sure about a picnic on the beach,' Noor said with a shiver. 'It's very cold to eat outside.'

'You have to wrap up warm, take a flask of hot soup…' That had been one of her ideas. She'd imagined a winter picnic on a deserted beach, a driftwood fire and the two of them cuddled up close under a tartan blanket sipping hot tomato soup.

She shivered.

'You are cold,' Noor said anxiously.

'I'll be fine once I'm in bed.'

'I will help you.'

'No.' She wanted to be on her own. 'I'll manage.' The sooner she got back to normal, got back to work, the better. 'And don't worry about tea. Just go and sort yourself out. Take anything you need from here.' Although, no doubt, her fridge had been stocked as well.

Her shoulder ached with the effort of getting out of her clothes but a bed had been made up for her on the plane and she'd slept most of the way.

She picked up the mail and curled against the pillows. Once she'd discarded the junk there wasn't much. Her bank statement, which she put to one side to check later, a bulky envelope from her lawyer and several letters from the bank used by the Queen and addressed to Princess Rabi al-Dance.

The first was from her personal account manager welcoming her to the bank, hoping to meet her when she called in at the branch and to call him for assistance at any time.

The second contained a bank card.

The third a pin number.

The fourth was a statement showing the six-figure balance in her account.

'No...'

She tore open the envelope from her lawyer. It contained a photocopy of the English translation of the contract that Bram had signed and documents requiring her signature regarding the purchase, in her name, of the house where she rented a flat. The accompanying letter congratulated her on her marriage and a suggestion that she make an appointment to discuss making a new will. There was also the contact details of a surveyor who had been engaged to look at the property and organise any necessary repairs. It also confirmed that the last restitution of funds stolen by her father had been made on the day of her wedding.

She quickly scanned the contract, her mouth drying as she read the terms of the dowry Bram had agreed with Fayad. A house of her own, the jewels, a car, clothes, a maid, driver, annual allowances for wardrobe, personal spending, maintenance of her property, all rising with inflation.

Not a problem. The marriage was over... Except that the divorce settlement terms were the same. A house of her own, maintained in good order, all the jewels she had been given during the marriage and, until she remarried, a maid, driver and all annual allowances.

It went on, laying out what would happen to any children of the marriage, even down to the dowries he would provide for their daughters.

A tear fell on the document. Not for the things she could never accept, but for the children they would never have. For the baby that, but for the deranged act of Ahmed Khadri, she might even now have been carrying.

Not just sex...

She curled her fingers into her palm, feeling the diamond ring that Bram had placed on her finger. She should take it off now, put it away.

Tomorrow. She'd do that tomorrow. And then she'd call Bram and tell him to stop all this nonsense.

Ruby was woken by her phone. She opened her eyes and for a moment had no idea where she was. Then she saw the discoloured patch in the corner of the ceiling, the one she had been all set to paint when she'd had an urgent summons from Amanda to fly to Ras al Kawi.

She was back in her little flat in Camden. The noise she

could hear was the swish of wet tyres as the traffic built up to the rush hour frenzy. If she opened her window she would smell wet pavements and diesel fumes instead of the salt tang of the sea.

The phone stopped ringing just as she reached for it. She checked the time, pulled a face but hauled herself out of bed and, having splashed her face with cold water and brushed her teeth, padded barefoot through to the kitchen. While the kettle boiled she checked her voicemail messages.

'Just checking to make sure you had a good flight...' Her hand shook as Bram's soft voice murmured in her ear, so close that she could almost touch him, almost smell him. Had he been waiting for her to ring? Reassure him? 'I'll talk to you later.'

'Yes.'

Realising that she had answered him as if he could hear, she quickly clicked onto the next message.

'Good morning, Ruby.' Amanda's voice, crisp and businesslike, was the dose of smelling salts that she needed. 'Have you seen this morning's paper?' Actually, forget smelling salts; that was more like brimstone. 'Under the circumstances, that seems unlikely,' she continued, 'but I suggest you check out the headlines online then give me a call and let me know what on earth is going on.'

Lori...

No. If it had been Lori, Amanda would have been concerned, sympathetic...

She fumbled with the phone, frantically keying her name into the search engine. The headline that came up was not the one she'd feared.

NEW RULER IN UMM AL BASR
Sheikh Hamad al-Ansari was today installed as the new Emir of Umm al Basr. His father, Sheikh Tariq,

*who underwent heart surgery last year, is stepping
down to allow a younger, more vigorous generation
to steer his country into the future.*

*His oldest son, former international ski cham-
pion Sheikh Ibrahim al-Ansari, was disinherited five
years ago after a drunken incident in a London fountain and although he and his new English wife, Princess Rabi al-Dance, were at Sheikh Tariq's birthday
celebrations earlier this month, a palace spokesman
confirmed that, while he will support his brother in
every way, he will continue to concentrate on his
private business interests.*

There was a small formal head-shot of the new Ruler
at the top of the piece, but beneath it were two more photographs. One was that horrible picture of Bram throwing
his heritage away in a London fountain so that the woman
he loved could marry his brother. The other was of herself
in a shimmering dress, diamonds and rubies at her throat,
her desert prince at her side.

She was still staring at it when there was a ring at the
doorbell. She opened it without looking up, assuming that
it was Noor, come to check up on her. Already hitting fast-
dial to call Amanda.

'I'll have to find you the spare key,' she said, stepping
back.

'That's a good start.'

In her ear Amanda was saying, 'That was quick, considering you're apparently on your honeymoon.'

'I'll call you back,' she said, disconnecting. 'Bram.'

She had been so sure that she'd never see him again
that she barely stopped herself from putting out a hand to
make sure that he was real. But an illusion had no scent
and his, so familiar, was overlaid with that of coffee and
warm pastry. 'What are you doing here?'

'Bringing my wife breakfast.' He was carrying a bag from an upmarket bakery. 'Coffee and warm *pain au chocolat*,' he said.

'How—?'

'The sitting room is on the right?' He removed a soft goatskin bomber jacket that was spotted with raindrops and then sat down on the sofa.

'What is this, Bram?' she demanded, although it was hard to stand on her dignity in a T-shirt nightie that was never going to pass the 'princess' test. She should go and put on a wrap, slippers...

'I am catching up, *ya habibati*.' He smiled up at her. 'Is that supposed to be a hedgehog?'

Beloved? He loved Safia...

'It is a hedgehog,' she said, perching on the edge of the sofa, leaving the maximum space between them, pulling the nightshirt over her knees. 'It's Mrs Tiggy-Winkle.' His grin was unnerving her. 'She's a very industrious hedgehog. And kind.'

'Then she is the perfect choice for you.' He took a carton from the bag and offered it to her.

'I'll pour them into mugs,' she said, putting it back in the bag and jumping up. 'And put the pastries on plates or they'll make a terrible mess.'

She hung on the counter for a long moment, wanting him so much but knowing that every moment he was with her Safia would be in his heart, his thoughts.

She jumped as he reached over her head to unhook a couple of mugs, poured the coffee into them.

'I don't understand why you're here,' she said, unwrapping the pastries, sliding them onto a plate, knowing that she could never eat them.

'Don't you?'

His breath was warm against the nape of her neck. All she had to do was lean back and he would have his arms around her. She picked up the coffee, turned and found herself confronted by his soft sweater. Wanting to lean into it, feel the softness against her cheek, feel his heartbeat.

She swallowed. 'No.'

'First we married, then we fell in love and now we are going to have the courtship. As I recall, this is how our story begins. I call on you at sunrise with coffee and *pain au chocolat*—'

'It's raining.'

He took the cups from her, put them on the counter, took her face between his hands.

'Beyond the clouds the sun is shining, Ruby, and this is just the beginning. Tomorrow the rain will stop and we might go to Kew Gardens, or take a boat down to Hampton Court, or have lunch in a little restaurant I know right on the bridge at Windsor.'

'Bram...' she protested.

'When you are stronger we will have our picnic on a beach, we will ride on the Downs, and in the winter we will go to Switzerland and make snowmen—'

'Stop!' He was offering her everything she wanted—a life with him—but she knew... 'I know,' she said. 'I know everything.'

'What do you know, Ruby?'

'That you love Safia. You gave up everything for her and would have done it again for Bibi. All she had to do was ask. A man would only do that for someone he loved, Bram. That's why you dropped out, became a recluse. She broke your heart.'

'Is that why you ran away?'

'I didn't run,' she said. Then, because she couldn't lie to him, 'I flew.'

He ran his fingers through her hair, pushing the curls back from her face as if to make her see him more clearly. 'My marriage to Safia was arranged when we were children, Ruby. I loved her because she was to be my wife, but not in the way you think of love. Not in the way I love you. It was duty, honour.'

'For family and state.'

'For family and state,' he agreed. 'If I'd loved her the way I love you, I would not have kept putting it off while I followed the ski circuit. I could not have waited…' He drew her close, put his arms around her. 'What haunted me, what I will never forget, my darling girl, is that if I had not seen the look that passed between them I would never have known that every time she lay with me there would have been a part of her heart that longed for another man. For his children.'

'But that's…' She stopped.

'That's what you thought it would be like if you stayed with me? That I would make love to you with another woman in my heart?'

'Are you saying that's why you would not marry Bibi?' she said. 'Because you knew her heart would be somewhere else?'

'That, and the fact that she was too young, a pawn to her father's ambitions, and I have to admit the thought that she would rather be cutting up cadavers in a laboratory than providing Umm al Basr with an heir did leave me a little underwhelmed.' He caught her chin, tilted her face so that she was looking up at him. 'Was that a smile?'

'Very nearly,' she admitted.

'Shall we sit down and have the coffee and pastries before they get cold?' he suggested. 'Then we can plan how this courtship will go.'

'If we stick to the script we should be in bed,' she pointed out.

'I have flown here overnight on a scheduled flight so bed does sound very attractive right now but if you only want me for my body… Oh, a smile and a blush.'

'You knew.'

'If "just sex" would do it for you, you wouldn't have spent the last few years alone, my love.'

'No.' He waited. 'What had Safia been praying for, Bram?'

'For me to find love, as she and Hamad found it.'

'You said her prayers had been answered.'

'I found you, Ruby.'

'And let me go.'

'Only so that we could start again. At the beginning. Make our legend real.'

'In my beginning,' she said, lifting her hands to his face, sliding her fingers through his hair, 'we forgot the coffee and began.'

* * * * *

*If you've enjoyed this book by Liz Fielding,
look out for*

*VETTORI'S DAMSEL IN DISTRESS
also by Liz Fielding*

*Or, if you enjoyed this
marriage of convenience story, look for*

*THE PRINCE'S CONVENIENT PROPOSAL
by Barbara Hannay*

Both available as eBooks!

"Maybe you just need a break from it all. There's been a lot to deal with."

"Maybe."

"No maybe about it," Wyatt said. "You were awfully clinical when you called me and told me you were in a mess."

She gazed into his face, reading his concern but more, his kindness. He'd always accepted her just as she was, and he was doing it right now.

He touched her cheek, and a pleasant shiver ran through her. Well, at least she could still feel that. It would have been so easy to just fall into his arms. Because she wanted to know what it would feel like to rest her head on his shoulder. To feel his lips on hers. To feel his skin against hers. To feel him filling the emptiness inside her.

She'd always wanted to know.

* * *

Conard County:
The Next Generation

HIS PREGNANT COURTHOUSE BRIDE

BY
RACHEL LEE

First Published in Great Britain 2017
By Mills & Boon, an imprint of HarperCollins*Publishers*
1 London Bridge Street, London, SE1 9GF

© 2016 Susan Civil Brown

ISBN: 978-0-263-92272-1

23-0217

Printed and bound in Spain
by CPI, Barcelona

Rachel Lee was hooked on writing by the age of twelve and practiced her craft as she moved from place to place all over the United States. This *New York Times* best-selling author now resides in Florida and has the joy of writing full-time.

Prologue

Circuit Judge Wyatt Carter had just finished a pleasant dinner at home, a too-rare occurrence, because he lived alone and was generally too busy to take the time to indulge in cooking. But this was a quiet Sunday evening after a comfortable day of catching up on his reading, and he'd made the effort to cook chicken Alfredo for himself and enjoyed it with a glass of pinot grigio. He felt somewhat self-indulgent, but considering how little time he had for indulgences, he didn't feel guilty.

When the phone rang, he assumed it was his father. Earl Carter ran the family law practice, although lately it had shrunk because Earl was getting older and didn't take as many cases. Earl seemed content enough to let the practice contract even though he'd once said it was his legacy to his son. Then Wyatt had become a

circuit court judge, and the plans of a father-son practice had melted away.

But it was not his father, much to his surprise. It
was a voice out of the past.

"Wyatt?"

He recognized Amber Towers's voice. They'd kept
in touch over the last decade, mostly by email and occasional phone calls. Amber had moved on from law
school to a large firm in St. Louis, then recently to a
much bigger firm in Chicago, headed for the heights.
Wyatt, who had graduated two years ahead of her, had
joined the military and spent three years in the judge
advocate general's office. Then he'd come back to out-
of-the-way Conard County to fulfill his father's dream
of a shared practice.

He and Amber had once been very close friends,
although nothing more than that, and since then they'd
maintained a long-distance friendship, except for dinner or lunch at a bar association conference.

Now he heard her voice with astonishment, since
she hadn't called in ages, and concern popped into his
mind. "Amber? What's wrong?"

"You're never going to believe it. I'm in a mess. Got
an hour or so?"

"Of course."

His mind dived down the byways of memory, re-
calling Amber as he had first seen her. She was young
for a first-year law student, having gone to college
two years early and finishing her bachelor's degree
in three years.

She had, in short, been barely nineteen. He'd been
twenty-seven, because he'd taken a couple of years
after college to try his hand at other things before

going to law school. She'd been very pretty, so pretty that every guy who wasn't already married—and some who were—chased her. He hadn't chased. It wasn't that he hadn't found her attractive, but facing his tour with the military in exchange for them paying his law school expenses, he felt it was the wrong time to get involved, especially since the direction she wanted to take was far from his path. He'd also felt that given the difference in their ages, it might be close to cradle robbing. Amber had seemed so young to him then.

So they'd become friends over textbooks and in oral arguments. He'd mentored her, having already taken the classes she was in, and she'd challenged him with her sharp mind.

A lovely woman barely emerging from adolescence, with dark hair, a pleasant figure and a face that had been pretty but painfully young. Of one thing he had been sure, though: Amber would rise to the top. He wouldn't have been surprised if she reached the Supreme Court.

But now she was in trouble?

He poured himself another glass of wine, carried it to his easy chair and prepared to listen.

It didn't take an hour, either. Amber was indeed in a mess.

Chapter One

"**I** think this is a bad idea," Earl Carter told his son, not for the first time in the last month.

"Amber needs a place to get her feet under her, Dad," Wyatt answered. The two men were sharing a beer at the kitchen table as they had so many times over the years.

"People will talk, a strange woman moving in with you."

"Dad, it's the twenty-first century."

Earl snorted. "Not in a lot of places in this county it isn't, Wyatt. Dang, you're a judge! Decorum and all that."

Wyatt hid a smile behind his beer bottle. Clearly Earl was one of those who hadn't quite come into the new century. But while he never would have admitted it to his father, he wasn't so sure about having Amber here, either.

First off, she was a city gal, and Conard City was barely a blip on the map. Secondly, they'd been friends in law school over ten years ago. A bunch of keeping-in-touch emails and an occasional phone call didn't mean he really knew the woman she had become. Nor could he know how all those years at huge law firms might have changed her.

"Maybe I should move back in," Earl said. He'd moved out after Wyatt had come back from his years with the judge advocate general's office, because—as he'd said at the time—he was tired of keeping up the huge old family house, and besides, what woman would want to marry a man who was living with his father?

"I don't need a chaperone," Wyatt said now.

"Maybe you need a headshrinker." Earl leaned back, his comfortable belly stretching his white shirt. He'd come directly from his law office, where he still wore a suit every single day. A Western-cut suit with a bolo tie, to be sure, but still a suit. He often evinced disapproval of his son's penchant for wearing jeans beneath his judicial robe. Of course, he voiced plenty of disapproval for Wyatt's motorcycle, too. "Look, son, it hasn't been that long since you broke it off with Ellie."

"What does Ellie have to do with it? That was over a year ago, and you know why I broke it off." Wyatt shifted irritably. "Any woman who expects me to dismiss charges against her cousin is a woman I don't want in my life."

"I get it. You were right, not saying you weren't. But that isn't the story she put around."

"So? What does that have to do with now?"

"Ellie's gonna make trouble, mark my words. Moving a big-city woman in with you?"

"Temporarily, Dad," Wyatt said with as much patience as he could muster. "It's nobody's business."

"You know better than that. You have an election coming up."

"Retention only. And if folks around here don't want me to be the judge anymore, you'll have a partner in that law practice again."

Earl sighed. "You never set your sights high enough."

Wyatt almost laughed. "I remember a time you thought that the practice of Carter and Carter was as high I needed to set my sights."

"But now you're a judge! You could become a district judge, maybe even go to the state supreme court."

Wyatt experienced a jolt of shock. He had never dreamed that his father envisioned that kind of future for him. It had been surprise enough when he'd been nominated to the bench as a circuit judge. Now this comment from a man whose highest ambition had once been to see his son's name on the shingle beneath his. "What got into you, Dad?"

Earl shrugged and took another swig of beer. "After you were nominated for the bench, I started wondering if I was holding you back." Then he winked. "Not that I want to see you taking off again. Hard enough when you were at school and in the military."

Holding the icy bottle in one hand, listening to the autumn wind picking up outside, Wyatt wondered if his dad was serious. He himself cherished no great ambitions that would carry him far away. He'd done that already, seen his share of the world with the JAG, and had decided things were just dandy here at home among people he'd known all his life. If he wanted adventure, that was what vacations were for. As it was, the daily parade of humanity that passed before his bench was entertaining and challenging enough, as was his work with youthful offenders.

"You should be thinking of these things," Earl said, returning to the whole point of his visit.

"I don't see a political future for myself, Dad. It's enough I can get away for a couple of weeks, that I can go hunting for a weekend or two in the fall…"

Earl snorted. "And when was the last time you brought home any meat?"

Wyatt stifled a grin. "Hunting is good for that image you're worried about. Someone from the city council or county commission asks me every year. I go to the dang lodge, drink with the boys, and I can't help it if I'm a lousy shot."

"You weren't always," Earl retorted, but a twinkle came to his eyes. Then his expression darkened again. "I know you're not going to listen to me. When's that woman arriving?"

"*Amber* is arriving some time this evening. Hang around and you'll meet her."

"And you're throwing a party for her, too?"

Wyatt smothered a sigh. He knew perfectly well his father wasn't this dense and that Earl was giving him a hard time. "Not a party, Dad. I'm having a few people over next weekend so she can meet some other women. I'm not around much, and maybe she can find some friends while she's here."

"Hmm." Earl drained the rest of his beer and tossed the bottle in the trash. "I think I'll head on back to my place. Maybe give Alma a call."

Alma was his father's latest interest, a woman in her midfifties with a warm smile and a nicely plump figure. Wyatt often thought that Earl hadn't moved out of the family house so that his son could date, but rather so Wyatt wouldn't cramp his father's style. Wyatt's mother had been gone for nearly thirty years, but Earl had never remarried. He had, however, enjoyed a series of relationships.

Apparently, he wasn't worried about appearances for himself. Wyatt just shook his head as his father grabbed his coat and left. Earl was no fool, obviously, but the way he'd been talking tonight? Wyatt wondered what was really behind it.

A short while later he stood at the front window, the large living room behind him, the lights out so he could see. Wind was ripping the last autumn leaves from the trees and sweeping them down the street.

No, Earl was no fool. So maybe he was right that having Amber here was a mistake. The thing was, Wyatt had never been one to turn away someone in need. Far from it. He always had an overwhelming desire to help.

Mistake or no mistake, Amber was going to have a place to stay while she sorted out her life and where she wanted to go from here. Because she was right: she was in a mess.

Amber Towers pulled into Conard City and wondered if she was about to drop off the map. It wasn't that the town was clearly small—she'd been in a lot of small towns in her life—but after driving so many miles with nothing on either side of the road except rangeland and mountains, it *felt* like the ends of the earth.

The streetlamps had come on, casting sharp shadows beyond the pools of light. From inside most of the houses came a golden glow that somehow seemed to beckon, promising warmth, shelter and friendliness.

Just an illusion, she told herself. Her GPS audibly guided her to Front Street and right up to Wyatt's door. She pulled up against the curb, not wanting to block him in his narrow driveway. Other cars scattered along the street told her that on-street parking wasn't forbidden here.

Then she sat, her engine running, wondering what exactly she was doing. But she'd been wondering that for a while now. The whole situation stank, starting with her own naive stupidity and ending with her here, at an old friend's house, unemployed and scared.

Yeah, she'd admitted she was scared. She'd never imagined that her rising boat and bright future could run aground. Certainly not this way. Not when everything had been going so well.

With both hands gripping the steering wheel, she continued to hesitate. Yes, she'd called someone who was totally outside her current circle, looking for objectivity and a true friend. Wyatt had sprung quickly to mind when she'd wanted a sounding board. Even back in law school, all those years ago, he'd been imbued with common sense, with a way of distancing himself that was excellent for a lawyer and something she'd had to learn. He could put feelings aside and see clearly.

So she had asked him to see clearly.

He had. He hadn't told her what to do, not even indirectly, but he'd managed to draw the situation for her in sharp lines and propose several options for dealing with it.

She had chosen this one, and as soon as she had he'd said, "Well, then, you'll need a place to stay while you make up your mind about what you want to do. I've got plenty of room."

That was Wyatt. Always ready to help, a quality she had always admired in him, a quality she'd seen him display repeatedly during that year they'd been in law school at the same time. She'd accepted, but now she wondered if she was taking advantage of him. Even as she had qualms, she knew why Wyatt had been the only person she had told about her situation. She could count on him. Always. Other friends in her life had been nowhere near as steadfast.

It remained, however, this was *her* problem, *her* mess, and moving in on him and his life, even by invitation, had probably been a selfish thing to do.

Finally she quit arguing with herself and switched off her ignition. If she felt she was disrupting his life, that she was in the way somehow, she could leave tomorrow or the next day. After all, she was traveling light, most of her belongings packed away in storage for some better future day.

At last she climbed out of the car. The wind felt a little like Chicago, although considerably drier. It nipped through her jacket and gray slacks like a familiar bite. Not that she'd had that long to get used to it.

She watched the leaves blowing down the street and wondered if her life were blowing away with them. Big mistake, big consequences, and in an instant everything was different. She'd been a fool. Maybe that was the thing hardest to forgive in herself.

The porch light flipped on. Wyatt had seen her. The house itself was mostly dark, but he must have caught sight of her from somewhere. A fan window over the front door spilled warm light, and stained-glass insets on the front door glowed with color. His home. Inviting her.

The front door opened. She recognized his figure immediately, tall and straight with broad shoulders and narrow hips.

"Amber?"

"Coming," she answered promptly, settling her purse over her shoulder. Her bags could wait. For later, for never—the next few hours would tell.

She strode up the walk, climbed three steps, crossed the wide covered porch and walked straight into his waiting arms.

She hadn't expected this hug, but it felt so good she simply accepted it and fought down unwanted tears of relief. He'd never hugged her like this before, warm and tight, and reality proved to be far better than her youthful imaginings. She wished she could stay there forever. All too soon, he let her go.

"Come inside," he said kindly. "It's getting cold out here."

The house was large, and the foyer bigger than she expected, designed in a very different age. A dark wooden staircase led to the upstairs, dark wood wainscoting lined the walls beneath walls painted Wedgwood blue and the floor itself was highly polished wood decorated with a few large oriental rugs.

But she was more interested in Wyatt himself. Time

had changed him some. His face had sharper lines and seemed squarer than she remembered from four years ago at that convention. She thought she saw flecks of silver in his nearly black hair. Age had filled him out a bit, but in all the right places. He wore a dark gray sweater and jeans and was walking around in his stocking feet.

He smiled. "Come get comfortable," he suggested, his dark eyes friendly. "You must be tired after all that driving."

He helped her out of her jacket and hung it and her purse on the wooden coat tree beside the door. Glancing around again, she felt as if she'd wandered into a museum.

"Somehow," she said, "I didn't imagine you living in a place like this."

"It's been in the family for nearly a hundred years. A white elephant, but one I can't let go of. Or should I say can't get rid of."

She laughed, feeling some of her tension ease. "I need to move around, if that's okay. I haven't been out from behind the wheel in five hours."

"Pushed it, huh?"

"Very definitely."

"Well, feel free to wander. Something to drink? Coffee, tea, cocoa or stronger?"

Stronger was out of the question now, although she would have loved a glass of wine. "Cocoa sounds great. Can I follow you around?"

"Be my guest."

How awkward, she thought. For both of them. All those years between, and a bunch of emails, a few phone calls and a couple of meetings didn't make up for it. And for all she'd recently bared her soul to him on the phone, being here still felt…like she didn't belong?

The kitchen had been modernized, a shock after the foyer. The appliances were all new, stainless steel, and there was even a dishwasher. What she guessed were the original wood cabinets had glass-paned doors outlined in fresh white. Countertops had been covered in light gray granite that matched a tile floor.

"This is beautiful," she said, taking it in. "Big." Big enough for a nice-size island and a matching table.

"I have a secret chef somewhere inside," Wyatt replied lightly. "He rarely gets the chance to come out and play, though. Too busy."

"I love to cook, too, but I hear you. Ninety-hour weeks and I usually wind up at some restaurant."

"Same here. Say, did anyone in law school ever warn you this profession wouldn't leave time for a life?"

She had to laugh because it was so true. "Powder room?"

"Under the staircase in the foyer. Can't miss it."

She walked back into that amazing area and found the half bath without any problem. It, too, had been modernized with pleasant wallpaper and fixtures of recent vintage. She paused in front of the mirror, however, and stared at her reflection, realizing she appeared gaunt.

God. This had taken a lot out of her, maybe more than she had realized. She finger combed her short dark hair and tucked the bob behind her ears, but of course that didn't hide the circles under her eyes, and she must have lost a few pounds. Desperate to look

less like a corpse, she pinched her cheeks to bring
some color into them. This couldn't be good for the
child she carried.

It was not the first time she'd thought about that,
but mostly she had skimmed over it. Now she faced
it, and felt her knees weakening. It was real, all of it
was real, and the cloak of numbness she'd been wearing much of the time since everything had blown up
simply vanished.

No longer an intellectual exercise, no longer a problem of humiliation, no longer a situation to be solved.
It was her and the child growing inside her and nobody
else. The reality was stark, the road ahead invisible.

A mess? It was more than a mess. She'd exploded
her entire life into little pieces.

Chapter Two

Amber had headed to bed right after the cocoa. Wyatt had brought her suitcases in and showed her to the best guest room, then returned to his work before going to bed himself.

Last night had been uncomfortable, he thought as he made coffee in the morning and scrambled some eggs. They hadn't talked at all, except superficially and briefly about her trip, about the room that was to be hers. Strangers. It felt like two strangers. He hadn't really anticipated that. In his mind their friendship had remained as fresh as yesterday. Emails and other contacts didn't quite bridge the years. Nor did it help his sense of awkwardness to discover that he still found her every bit as attractive as he ever had.

But he was worried about her, too. The stress of the past weeks had clearly worked on her. He'd expected her to look a bit older than she had when he'd run into her at that conference four years ago, but not this pinched and drained. Worn. Her situation was awful, so maybe he shouldn't have been surprised.

He paused, looking out the window over the sink, noting that the wind was still blowing and leaves were still flying. By now, he thought with mild amusement, all the leaves in town should have been gone. But as he watched some of them eddy between the houses, he guessed they would hang around to be raked.

He heard steps behind him and turned to greet Amber. She looked a bit better this morning and was already dressed as if she were going to work in a navy blue pantsuit and white blouse. A bit much for hanging around the house.

"Well, good morning," he said with a smile.

She smiled back. "Sorry I was so dead last night."

"Long trip," he said. "Eggs? Toast? Coffee?"

"All of the above, please." She settled onto a stool on the far side of the island. "You have to work today, of course."

"I cleared most of my schedule for the week," he answered, turning back to the counter and cracking two more eggs into a bowl to whisk. "A few hours each day, rather than all day. Some hearings I can't avoid, and a trial that'll probably be over in a couple of hours after we finish jury selection."

"Can I come watch?"

"Of course." If she were in the courtroom with him, at least he wouldn't be wondering if she were sitting here feeling like hell and unable to do a damn thing about it.

He gave her a cup of coffee and the eggs he'd already cooked. "Dig in."

He started making his own eggs and heard her say, "You didn't have to clear your schedule for me."

"No, but I did anyway. You could have gone anywhere if solitude and four walls were all you wanted."

He was pleased to hear a quiet laugh from her. "Sadly true," she answered.

A minute later he carried his own plate and mug to the island and stood on the far side from her. "It's okay, Amber," he said before he started eating. "You're welcome here and we'll get over the awkwardness soon."

"I didn't expect it," she admitted. "In some ways I felt as if all these years hadn't passed."

"In some ways they haven't." He sipped his coffee. "But even back then we didn't share quarters."

That drew another laugh from her, a small one.

"Look, this place is practically a hotel. Just do whatever you need to in order to feel comfortable. Spend as much time or as little as you want with me. Make your own ground rules. I'm pretty adaptable."

She raised her face to smile at him. "Generous, too. Most of the problem is me, Wyatt. Everything is all messed up. Blown up. I feel as if I'm in a million pieces right now."

"Hardly surprising. You want to talk some more?"

"Maybe after court. You must need to go soon."

He glanced at the clock. Seven thirty. "Fifteen minutes. Can you be ready?"

"I *am* ready. But don't you need time to change?"

Wyatt looked down at his jeans and polo shirt. "No."

"Wow," Amber breathed. "I might like this place."

"Well, I do wear a robe. Most of the time."

The sound of the laughter that pealed out of her warmed his heart. If she could still laugh like that, then everything would be okay. For her.

Because suddenly, for him, he wasn't so sure. An attractive damsel in distress. Always his weak point, and more so for Amber.

The day was chilly and the wind whipped with ferocity. Amber almost felt like ducking as they left the house and walked to his car in the driveway. "Is this wind usual?" she asked once they were in the car.

"No. Usually we have a breeze, nothing bad, although it can get to be pretty constant if you get out onto the prairie. But here…" He shook his head as he turned over the ignition. "Some kind of front must be in the area, but I haven't looked at the weather."

"I was getting used to the wind in Chicago. I don't think it ever stops. But this is pretty with the leaves tossing in the wind."

"Until it comes time to rake," he answered.

"Will there be anything left?" she wondered as he wove their way down the street toward where she presumed they'd find the courthouse.

It was only a few blocks away, and she was instantly charmed. She'd half expected some functional building that had been erected recently, but instead saw a gorgeous older redbrick building with impressive columns sitting in a square filled with concrete benches and tables and the remains of summer flowers. And the statue of a soldier, watching over it all.

"Did they transplant this from New England?" she asked, amazed.

"The folks who built it wanted something to remind them of home, I guess. We have a church that looks like it was snatched out of the jaws of Vermont, too."

Amber was charmed. It might not be a large town, but what she had seen of it so far was gracious and inviting. Wyatt pulled around to the back of the courthouse and into a parking space labeled with his name: *Hon. Wyatt Carter.* Some of the other spaces had filled up, but they were all reserved—county attorney, court reporter and others.

"We finally emerged into the new century," he remarked after they climbed out and headed for the back door.

"Meaning?"

"We had to build a new jail outside town. It wasn't so long ago prisoners were kept in cells over the sheriff's office, but six cells is just about enough to dry out the drunks overnight. So…big jail. And I do a lot of my hearings over closed-circuit TV. No big deal to you, I'm sure, but it was a very big deal when we transitioned here."

She could almost imagine it. In a very short space of time he'd given her the feeling that this was an old Western town stepping very slowly into the modern era. She looked around just before he opened the door for her and saw that the entire square was surrounded by stores. She liked it.

She followed him into a narrow hallway painted institutional green with wood floors that creaked beneath their feet. They passed restrooms, the rear side of the county clerk's office, then climbed some equally creaky stairs to the second floor, where they entered his chambers.

The walls in the outer office were lined with books of statutes, something that must be left over from earlier days, she decided. Everyone relied on online research these days, and law libraries were available at the touch of a key if you had a subscription. They'd certainly done that in law school. But she looked around the walls, admiring the books, their solid look and feel. Two desks sat in the middle of all this magnificence.

"My reporter and clerk work there," he said.

Then they passed through to a chamber that was all dark wood, a massive desk and a few chairs. She thought she could detect old aromas of cigar smoke embedded in the walls. The only modernity was a multiple line phone and a computer.

"My home away from home," he said, glancing at his watch. "I've got a few minutes. Do you want to stay here or go into the courtroom?"

She'd been in a judge's chambers before, of course. It was inevitable for a lawyer. It didn't look like a place to browse, and she'd come to see him in court anyway.

"Courtroom," she answered decisively. A kind of tickled excitement awoke in her. She was going to see her old friend in the role of a judge. It was just cool enough to make her forget her other problems.

She walked through the door he pointed out and emerged in the courtroom, walking past the raised bench and past the attorney's tables, which were already occupied, ignoring the curious looks as she took a seat in the front row. She had no idea what was on his docket for today or whether the people waiting in the gallery with her were here to deal with legal problems or just to watch, but the place was filling rapidly.

The clock slipped past eight, almost as a courtesy to late arrivals, then a bailiff, in what appeared to be a deputy's uniform, called the court to order and announced Wyatt. "All rise. The Tenth District Circuit Court of the state of Wyoming is now in session, the Honorable Wyatt Carter presiding."

He came striding in, wearing a black robe, his jeans and boots flashing beneath it. She had to cover her mouth with her hand. She hadn't expected to enjoy this so much.

Wyatt tapped the microphone in front of him, and the thump came across the speakers. "All right," he said, looking out over the room. "Traffic court. Really, folks, don't you know better?"

And thus it began.

Amber was soon amazed. Wyatt didn't treat most of these people as if he just wanted them to pass out of his sight as soon as possible. He actually talked to them, and when he deemed it appropriate, he asked questions. He even postponed a few cases when the charges were serious and the accused claimed to be unable to afford an attorney. He promptly assigned them to the public defender on the spot.

"This is the second time you've come before this court for not having a driver's license," he said to a thirtysomething man in work clothes. "Didn't I order you to get a license last time?"

"Yes, sir."

"So why are you still driving without one?"

The man shuffled his feet. "I need to go to work."

Wyatt leaned back a little and studied the notes on his desk. "It says here you can't read. The state has an application for people who can't read. Why didn't you get one?"

"I tried."

At that Wyatt leaned forward. "What kind of work do you do?"

"I work at the ranches. Hired hand."

"No reading required for that, I suppose."

"No, sir."

"So why didn't you get a license?"

"I keep calling but they're busy. I can't even talk to someone. Always busy."

Wyatt turned to the clerk. "You get me the license people and you get this man an appointment with them before this day is over."

"Yes, Your Honor."

Wyatt turned back to the man in front of him. "Will you go to the test when my clerk tells you the time?"

"Yes, sir."

"You'd better. And I'm suspending your case pending your getting that license. Crap, can't get through?" He turned to the clerk again. "Let 'em know I'm not happy about this."

The clerk almost grinned. "Absolutely."

He looked at the man. "You stay here until she gets your appointment. And you'd better find somebody to drive you home, because you cannot drive without a license and I don't want to see you here again. Understood?"

Amber was amazed. Wyatt took a lot of personal interest, sometimes waiving fines when people simply couldn't pay them. But again and again, when something caught his attention, he zoomed in.

Then came the guy who was in front of him for the second time for driving on a suspended license.

"I told you to stop driving," Wyatt said. "What makes you think you can ignore the law like this? Your license was suspended for DUI. Now you're in front of me again for driving when you're not allowed to?"

The amusing part came after Wyatt ruled, telling the guy that the next time he was going to jail and was being spared this time only because he had small children to support. Then he added, "I'm leaving here in another few minutes, so you'd better find someone to drive you home. Because I'll recognize your face now and I'll chase you down and arrest you myself. Got it?"

Amber had never guessed that traffic court could be so fascinating and even moving. And Wyatt broke the mold.

Amber waited in the court after everyone had departed. She didn't feel free to just walk back into Wyatt's chambers. He might be dealing with something that was none of her business, or he might just be busy. She only waited about twenty minutes, though, before he entered the courtroom again, this time wearing his jacket and no robe and carrying a briefcase. "Free for the rest of the day," he said with a smile. "Do you want to go home or would you rather go down the block to the diner with excellent food and service that never comes with a smile?"

That surprised a little laugh from her. "Really?"

"Maude and her daughter are the local gorgons, but the food more than makes up for it."

"Then by all means the diner."

"Let's walk," he suggested, and this time they exited the courthouse by the grand front entrance. "I think these places were built to impress and intimidate," he said as they walked down the wide marble steps.

"I think you're right. It's a beautiful building."

"That it is. And you see the stone benches and tables scattered in the little park? When the weather allows we have people at nearly every one of them playing chess or checkers." He pointed. "Over there is the sheriff's office."

It looked like a regular storefront, which surprised her. "No Corinthian columns for him?"

Wyatt laughed. "None. They used to be in the courthouse basement a couple of generations ago, but then they needed more room and were getting squeezed out by the records and clerks. So they took up one side of the street there, and their offices run back inside behind the storefronts. Bigger than it looks from out here."

They crossed Main, which was right in front of the courthouse, to a side street where he pointed out other shops to her, one of them a craft shop in a house a little way past the diner, a dentist's office, a dress store, a bail bondsman and a couple of lawyers, one of them with the name Carter painted in gold letters on the window.

"Your father?" she asked.

"The same."

"So you practiced there for a while?"

"Yup." Then into the diner, which was quite busy. She couldn't miss the silence that fell suddenly as she walked in with Wyatt and felt like a bug under a microscope.

"Ignore it," he said under his breath. "They're just curious. Something new to talk about."

She hadn't considered that possibility. Being the subject of talk wasn't something she wanted, but then she reminded herself that she was only visiting. A week, two weeks, whatever, but eventually she was going to have to figure out the next path she needed to walk. And after what had happened in Chicago, she figured large law firms were off her list for some time. People gossiped there, too, and that gossip spread. For her it would be the kind of gossip that would make another firm leery of hiring her.

All of a sudden a man in a sheriff's uniform stood before them. He had a burn-scarred face and a gravelly voice. "Hey, Wyatt, we were just leaving. Take our booth."

Wyatt smiled and held out his hand to shake the other man's. "Amber, this is Gage Dalton, our sheriff. Gage, a lawyer friend of mine from Chicago, Amber Towers."

Gage's crooked smile was friendly as he shook Amber's hand. "Welcome to Conard City, Ms. Towers. If you decide you want to get out of town and visit a ranch, let me know. I've got several deputies who'd be glad to oblige. Or you can take a trail ride." He laughed. "Whole bunches of things to do, if you know where to look."

She met three more deputies as they departed, one of them a woman who had the same last name as a much older man with a Native American face. They didn't at all resemble each other, which raised her curiosity.

"The two named Parish," she began after they sat and the table had been cleared by a scowling woman.

"Micah Parish and his daughter-in-law, Connie."

Well, that explained a lot. "Family business, law enforcement?"

Wyatt flashed a grin. "Not exactly. Micah has a ranch, too, and his son, Ethan, left the sheriff's department to help out there. Unfortunately, I think we're going to see Micah retire before long. It'll be the end of an era."

"Meaning?"

Coffee cups slammed down in front of them and were filled by an older version of the woman who had cleared the table. Looking up at that face, Amber almost hesitated. But then she plunged in. "I can't drink much coffee. Could I please have milk instead?"

She was answered with a grunt as the menus slapped onto the table.

"Was that a yes?" Amber asked Wyatt quietly as the woman stomped away.

"Mavis or Maude will bring your milk." He winked. "I warned you about the service. Okay, end of an era. Micah's been a deputy here ever since he mustered out of the army. Nearly a quarter century now. He started working for the old sheriff, Nate Tate, who retired a while back, which was another end-of-an-era event around here. Anyway, at first Micah wasn't very well accepted."

"Why? Because he's Native American?"

"Bingo. A lot of those prejudices still exist. He's become kind of iconic over the years, like the old sheriff. And folks still call Gage the new sheriff, even though it's been years."

"I'm beginning to get the picture."

He nodded. "Things do change here, they just change slowly."

She was also adding together her impressions and began to feel very uncomfortable. "Wyatt? Will my staying with you cause problems? Because people are bound to talk and you're a judge…"

"God, you sound like my father," he said with a hint of exasperation. "I don't care what they say. If I did, I wouldn't have invited you."

But her stomach sank even more as she realized his father had objected to her visit. Wyatt had often struck her as the knight-errant type, willing to fight for what he thought was right, despite the consequences to himself. That could be an admirable thing at times, but sometimes not. Like possibly now.

She had to force herself to look at the menu and find something she thought she could eat. As self-absorbed as her problems had made her for the last six weeks, she hadn't lost her ability to care. She didn't want to cause this man any trouble, so she'd need to figure out something quickly.

At last she chose a grilled cheese sandwich with a side salad. Despite the lack of service, their orders were placed in front of them quickly, and Wyatt dug into what looked like a really juicy steak sandwich.

"You're rather unconventional in your approach to being a judge," she remarked. "I'm used to judges who don't take an interest beyond the law."

"I don't know that I'm unconventional. I just know these are real people with real problems, and a lot of them are my neighbors. Some come from the next county over and I may never see them again, but they're still human beings."

She looked up from her sandwich with a smile. "You were always like that. I remember how much you wanted to be a defense attorney. And why. Still tilting at windmills, I see."

He half smiled. "I don't know if they're windmills, but while there are some things justice should never see, I think she needs to take off that blindfold once in a while."

"Mercy."

"Maybe. Certainly everyone's entitled to a fair shake, and by the time some of them come in front of me, they've hardly had a fair shake in their lives."

She nodded and reached for the second half of her sandwich, glad her appetite had returned. "I worked in a different world at those big firms."

"I'm sure you did."

"Most of my clients had gotten more than their share of fair shakes in life. They were just looking for another one. Or maybe for a better-than-fair outcome." She shrugged one shoulder. "Well-heeled, successful, mostly men who thought they had the world by a string. It came as a real shock when they found out they didn't."

Distasteful, she thought. Yes, it was the way up the ladder to maybe becoming a judge herself one day, but a lot of her clients…just because they had money didn't mean she respected them.

But she did like the pro bono work she did when she could at the free legal clinic. She was going to miss that.

"Do you like chili?" Wyatt asked, drawing her out of her maunderings.

"Sure. Not the beans so much, though."

"I make it without beans. How about we have that for dinner tonight?"

"You cooking?"

He laughed. "Absolutely. The chef is going to love having an excuse."

Chapter Three

On the way home, he took a detour to the grocery. Despite having just driven all the way from Chicago, she opted to stay in the car. Instead she pulled her jacket snugly around her to wait, then decided to climb out and stroll around the parking lot.

The wind seemed to be dying a bit. To the west she saw brilliant blue sky right over the mountains, although it remained overcast overhead. The ends of the earth, she thought again, but this time with amusement. The town had some appeal to it, though, and she suspected if you lived your whole life here, you might get to know almost everyone. They wouldn't necessarily be friends, but you'd recognize them.

Having been anonymous on crowded streets for so long, she wondered how that would feel. Good? Bad? Or maybe people here were so used to it they never even thought about it.

But she thought about it now.

He didn't keep her waiting long, and as they drove back to his house, she leaned her head back and watched the passing houses. Some better kept than others, a whole mishmash of different designs, but lots of trees lining the streets. Pretty. A grace of its own.

But then they were home, and after he'd put his purchases in the refrigerator, he invited her to join him at the kitchen table.

Now, she thought edgily, he was going to want to talk. He had every right to bring up her mess. Every right to understand better. Hadn't she basically thrown herself on his mercy by coming out here, by calling him in the first place? Of course she had, and she owed him the whole sordid story. And maybe the story of everything else she'd done since starting her career. It wasn't like it was all bad.

But he surprised her with the direction he took. "What's off-limits because of the baby?"

"Off-limits?" she asked, not following.

"Foods, beverages, that kind of thing."

The question startled her a bit, because she hadn't been thinking much about that aspect. She knew to avoid alcohol and over-the-counter meds, but other than that…

He frowned faintly. "Have you seen a doctor yet, Amber?"

"Well, my regular doctor. He said to make an appointment with an obstetrician, and he gave me some vitamins to take. He also advised me to limit myself to a couple of cups of coffee but…well, I think he was expecting the obstetrician to give me all the details."

"But you haven't gone."

"Not yet." She looked down, feeling inexplicably stupid. "I'm not an idiot," she protested. "But with all that's been going on… I was going to get to it. I'm not that far along…"

"Okay." He brought her a glass of milk instead of coffee, which he made for himself. "I'm not criticizing you. You've been through a rough time. But maybe it wouldn't hurt to see the obstetrician here. Just to be on the safe side."

She didn't answer. Instead of looking at him, she turned her head and stared out through the window at the gray day. Okay, she hadn't really been dealing with the reality of this pregnancy. She'd hardly been thinking about it except in the vaguest of ways. Yes, she'd followed the directions she'd been given, but beyond that…beyond that, she didn't want to face the fact that she was becoming a mother and that her whole life and all her dreams had changed. She might tell herself she wasn't stupid, but stupidity had gotten her here, and now stupidity was keeping her from facing reality.

Too much, she thought. *Too much.* She didn't know how she was going to deal with it all. No idea where to go, how to handle it. All she knew was that she'd had to get away from that law firm. Everyone knew she'd been seeing Tom. Everyone knew he'd lied about his divorce, because he'd done it before. But so far none of them knew she'd managed to get pregnant. The one humiliation in the whole affair that hadn't become public.

But if she had stayed, it would have become very public. She suspected she wouldn't be welcome there once everyone knew about the baby. Tom was a junior partner. She was no one. Time to get out before she felt as if she were in the public stocks.

Wyatt had agreed with her once she told him what had happened. Staying at the firm would have been very uncomfortable, and while she could have lied and said the baby was someone else's…well, most people wouldn't have believed it, and she'd have had Tom trying to make her life enough of a hell that she'd quit anyway.

At least that was her read, and Wyatt had agreed that she might not be able to convince everyone that the father was someone else. How much that would affect her future at the firm was anyone's guess. Wyatt said he'd like to believe no one would give her trouble, but… He'd let that dangle.

It was her suspicion that the moment she became a potential embarrassment to Tom, her career would be in jeopardy. Maybe they'd have given her time to find another position, but she didn't want the humiliation. There was already enough of that, knowing she'd had an affair with a married man, and that others knew it as well.

She sighed and returned her attention to Wyatt. "I guess I've been trying to ignore it. To deal with the nitty-gritty of quitting my job, packing up my life and heading into the unknown. But I couldn't have stayed. I couldn't."

He nodded slowly. "You could have tried. It certainly would have been miserable, but if you said nothing, maybe they would have gotten past it."

"You said that. I wasn't buying it. If I hadn't just joined the firm last spring, maybe. But my track record was so short…" She wrapped her hands around the glass of milk and stared into the liquid. "See if I ever trust a man again."

His dark eyes turned suddenly inscrutable. "Ouch," he said quietly.

She flushed. "I don't mean you. You're different."

He merely gave her a half smile. "Of course, we all know who should be paying for this mess, but unfortunately life isn't always fair. Kicking up a fuss would probably have bought you more trouble than you'd ever want. You think this guy Tom would have retaliated in some way?"

"Probably," she said glumly. "Even if I never said a word, I'd have worried him. I'd be hanging there like a threat. I saw how he handled his cases. He's not a man you want to cross swords with if he feels threatened."

Wyatt nodded. "I accept your judgment. Never having met the guy, I have no idea what he's capable of." He paused. "Did I ever tell you about Ellie?"

She shook her head slowly, grateful for the change of subject. "Who's she?"

"I dated her for a while about a year ago. Along about the time we started to get serious, she asked me to dismiss a bunch of charges against her cousin."

Amber gasped, totally diverted from her problems. "No!"

"Oh, yes. That relationship ended instantly. So to get even, she told everyone she knows that I'm gay."

"Oh! That must have made you angry."

He grinned suddenly. "Why? I don't care. That's my business and nobody else's. Anyway, it's old news. I'm just saying, life throws curveballs. It's what we do about them that matters. I chose the high road and she tried to get even. The point is, I understand why you worried about what Tom might do. He had a job and a marriage to protect. A reputation, even. He'd probably have done everything he could to submarine you. I'm not saying he would have succeeded, but it could have made you miserable for a long time. You decided how you wanted to handle it, and here we are."

For the first time, she drank some of the milk he'd offered her. "Yes, here we are," she said after she'd dabbed her mouth with a paper napkin. "Where is that?"

He laughed. "Just take some time to figure out whatever you need to. The only thing I ask is that you get to a proper doctor. Wherever you may be in seven or eight months, you don't want to be with a baby that could have been healthier if you'd taken care of yourself."

Right now, Wyatt thought as he studied her and listened to her, the pregnancy was a major concern whether she was ready to face it or not. While he was no expert and had no personal experience, he seemed to remember hearing that the first few months could be absolutely critical to a fetus. Were vitamins and avoiding coffee enough? He had no idea.

That was the point of doctors, and he had great respect for professionals. Amber needed one, and he was determined she see one before long.

She was a beautiful woman, a very smart woman, and it troubled him to see her in this situation. From all he'd heard from her over the years, he got the feeling that she'd been one of those people for whom everything went right. No major problems, a skyrocketing career, the world on a string.

But of course, nobody got through life without their share of troubles. She'd apparently lumped many of hers into one enormous mistake. And she was dev-astated. Everything she'd worked for had been taken from her by a lying jackass. He had plenty of questions to ask, basic ones like, hadn't she been using protec-tion? But it was none of his business.

His only business was to be supportive until she could figure out what she wanted to do. In the mean-time, quashing his attraction to her would probably be very wise. She'd been through the wringer; she'd said she wouldn't trust men again. Having her place him in a separate category meant she didn't see him as an eligible man. Which was fine by him. Neither of them needed any complications, and she'd probably be moving on in a month or two.

Given Amber's dreams, he couldn't see her hang-ing around here for long.

But still, there was an errant part of him that had belonged to Amber ever since the first day they had talked. Friendship? Of course. Something more? No point in thinking about it, even though over the years he'd occasionally daydreamed about what life would have been like with her. Pointless fantasy, reawakened by phone calls and running into her at the convention. Fantasies he'd put aside again every time they rose.

She finished her milk and rose to rinse the glass at the sink. Standing there with her back to him, she began to speak. "I need to wake up," she said.

"Wake up?" Curious, he twisted in his chair to bet-ter see her, even if it was only her back.

"Wake up," she repeated. "This has been like a nightmare. Do you know how it started?"

"Which part?"

She shook her head, and a heavy sigh escaped her.

"Which part? Good question. You know working for a firm like that doesn't leave any room for a social life."

"I've heard." Not that being a judge was a whole lot better, unless he put his foot down as he had this week.

"Two thousand billable hours a year is forty hours a week for fifty weeks. Which doesn't sound all that awful until you add all the hours that aren't billable. I didn't get a day off and I didn't expect one. Not for many years to come. Your friends, such as they are, are people you work with. If you have a family, you might see them for a few minutes as you're falling into bed or running out the door in the morning. I loved most of it."

"Okay," he said to show he was listening, but unsure if she was looking for a particular response from him.

"In a few more years, if I'd been lucky and continued to rise, I'd have reached the level where I could get out of the office to go golfing with clients. I might even have been able to take an occasional weekend. The point is, though, that your whole life revolves around the firm. They even arrange the social occasions. Dinner with the partner, a party at a partner's house, where in theory you'd win some new clients. All business."

For those who wanted to get ahead in that game, he thought. Plenty of others chose an easier path, but Amber had always been driven. Law school at nineteen?

"Human nature will have its way eventually," she said. "Tom started to express interest. He was attractive, and considering we were pretty much working all the time, he was what was available. Office romances are dangerous. I knew it, but I took the chance anyway. He was in the middle of a messy divorce, he said. And I believed him."

"Why wouldn't you?"

She turned slowly to face him and folded her arms tightly. "I think that from working all the time I let parts of my development become stunted. The practice of law gave me a view of a lot of ugliness in life, but that ugliness didn't include a coworker deliberately lying to me to get me into his bed. Regardless, in the last ten years I haven't had time for a boyfriend. I only dated a couple of times, but my schedule blew everything up. So there I was, missing a massive part of life, and this coworker was suddenly pursuing me. I was flattered. I was stupid."

"You're not stupid. Some very smart people get conned, Amber."

She smiled crookedly, without humor. "Well, I got conned. Funny, it never seemed odd to me that the only time we got together was in a hotel over our lunch hour. When we had a lunch hour. It's not like I couldn't have escaped the office sometimes just for dinner. There should have been red flags all over it."

He couldn't disagree. "I imagine you really liked him."

"Of course. I thought I was falling in love. Maybe I was. But then I found out. God, that was awful. I caught one of the clerks drinking in the bathroom, and when I started to tell her she couldn't do that, she stopped me dead in my tracks. It seems I wasn't the first newbie Tom had taken advantage of, and if she hadn't been drunk she probably wouldn't have told me. Everyone kept quiet about it because they didn't want to get fired."

She shook her head, then held out one arm, almost a pleading gesture. "I broke it off immediately, of course. He started giving me a hard time, but there wasn't a whole lot he could do except make me uncomfortable. I was uncomfortable enough that all my coworkers probably knew what had been happening. I felt so numiliated!"

"I'm sure your coworkers knew you had been used," he offered quietly.

"I'm sure. At least that's what I kept telling myself. Until I found out I was pregnant." A bitter laugh escaped her. "Birth control fails sometimes. I was one of the minuscule percentage of failures. Ironic, huh?"

"I think it stinks. I don't find it ironic at all." He wished he could hug her, but he wasn't sure that would help. If she needed to talk, the best thing he could do was listen.

"Anyway, that's when I called you. I could stick out the knowing looks. I figured the whispers would go away. But a pregnancy? Everyone would know. And I have no doubt Tom would have used every bit of influence he had to get rid of me if he knew, because he could deny everything except a paternity test."

As a lawyer and then a judge, Wyatt had learned to separate his emotions from his thinking. He had to. He was the one who had to remain objective as much as possible. He'd be no good to a client if feelings clouded his judgment, and that hadn't changed much on the bench. He might dispense mercy when he could, but he still had to have an unemotional, clear grasp of the situation, the facts and the law.

He was finding that objectivity very difficult to achieve right now. In fact, damn near impossible. He looked at the young woman, his friend, nearly curled up on herself as she relived her nightmare, and he would have dearly loved to get his hands on this guy Tom. His fists had clenched, and he had to make an effort to relax them. He didn't want to frighten Amber with the impulse to violence that was building in him now.

"Anyway," she said presently, "it's been a nightmare, especially since I found out I was pregnant. I couldn't believe that on top of everything else. Maybe I still can't believe it. It's almost like if I close my eyes and pull the blankets over my head, the bad things will go away." She shook her head. "I know better than that. And you're right, whether I'm ready to accept it or not, I need to take care of the child growing inside me. That's one thing I can still do right."

His chest felt as if a steel band wrapped around it, and it tightened at those words. One thing she could do right?

"Amber..." Maybe he was wrong, but he remembered the woman he used to know. Had she entirely given up because of this? He wouldn't have expected it.

Maybe she just needed time and space to get used to so much. It sure as hell had been a huge, shocking change.

It had been a month since she first phoned him. Back then the emotionless delivery he'd heard from her had been understandable. He'd believed she'd been merely discussing her options, ways to deal with an untenable situation. But now she seemed to be in some kind of shock. Maybe she had been when she first called, and her clinical attitude had been some kind of an emotional withdrawal. Did this mean it was now becoming emotionally real to her?

He'd thought he'd been offering refuge to a friend, a safe place where she could rest and decide what to do. Now he was wondering just exactly what she needed, and if he could even begin to help her deal with what was clearly a bigger trauma than he'd imagined.

A friend quitting her job because a relationship failed and she was pregnant hadn't sounded so bad. Now that he was getting the dimensions of all this, he didn't think *nightmare* was too strong a description.

"Anyway," she said after a minute or so, "sorry for the dump."

"Don't be sorry. You needed to dump on someone. And maybe your friends weren't listening."

"Friends?" She shook her head and at last returned to sit at the table with him. "I had coworkers, colleagues. People I knew, but no one I was able to get intimate with. I was always on guard. You have to be careful what you tell a coworker."

There was no arguing that. He went to pour himself some fresh coffee, asking her if she wanted anything.

"I'm full from lunch. Thanks."

When he faced her across the table again, he was still trying to find something to say to her. She'd been unsparingly honest with him, telling him far more than she had on the phone, and in the process giving him a better view of the dimensions of all she faced. Come here for a few weeks to catch her breath and make a plan?

That's what he'd thought, but now he wasn't so sure it was going to work that easily. She was still having trouble believing she was pregnant. Maybe she still hadn't really started to believe any of this.

If so, it would take more than a few weeks.

"Wyatt? Remember when we first met in law school? We were in the first week and I was already overwhelmed."

"I remember." He'd never forget it. He'd seen not only a pretty young woman, but someone who didn't look old enough to be facing the fire of law school. He'd thought he'd detected a bit of panic in her gaze, so he'd wandered over to the bench where she was sitting beside a pile of books, handouts and notebooks, and introduced himself.

"L-1 is a hard year," he'd offered. "I'm in my last year."

Her head had swiveled then, and she'd truly seen him. "I'm scared to death."

From that moment, they'd become friends. "I remember," he said again.

"You seemed so calm," she said. "And friendly. You told me things to pay attention to…oh, you gave me a load of good advice for doing well and getting through it. But I never told you something."

He waited the way he waited in a courtroom, knowing that important information was coming his way.

"I didn't want to be there," she said. "And I don't just mean the first weeks, or the overwhelmed feeling. I didn't want to be in law school at all."

That shocked him. He'd never imagined that law school hadn't been her choice. He'd spent three years surrounded by people who wanted to be no place else. "Then why did you apply?"

"Because of my parents. I didn't graduate early because I wanted to. I didn't go to college at sixteen because I wanted to. And I sure as hell didn't go to law school because I wanted to. Although I have to admit, I started to like the law. I still enjoy the practice of it. Parts of it, anyway."

But he saw her in an entirely different way now. So much suddenly became clear: her push for success, her moving up the ladder in firms that could tear the soul out of a person simply through overwork, client demands and the constant threat of losing your job if an important client grew unhappy. And he also understood something else. "So your parents don't know anything about this...situation?"

"Not a thing. Mom passed away five years ago, but no, my father doesn't know. I guess he's going to have to know eventually, but not right now. He'll be furious."

Wyatt would have liked to argue with her, but how could he? He'd never met Amber's father.

She sighed and reached for the napkin she had used to wipe her mouth and smoothed it out with her fingers. "I've been a wuss," she said finally.

"That's one thing I'd never call you."

She lifted her head with a smile that didn't reach her eyes. "I let myself be used to fulfill their dreams for me. It only got worse when Dad told me after Mom's funeral that she'd be so proud of all I'd accomplished."

"More pressure."

"Exactly. Evidently somewhere along the way I failed to grow a spine." .

He doubted that was a fair assessment, but he could understand where it came from. "Well," he said finally, "you're here now, you can stay as long as you like and

the only thing I'm going to pressure you about is seeing a doctor."

She nodded. "Fair enough." After a moment she
asked tentatively, "Did you feel pressured because your
dad was a lawyer?"

"He didn't pressure me," Wyatt said truthfully.
"Yeah, we talked about me going into the practice
with him, but he didn't offer a single objection when
I took two years after I finished my undergrad degree
to see if I liked something else."

She shook her head a little. "I can't imagine it."

"Evidently not. It sounds to me like you never had
a chance to take a deep breath."

She closed her eyes briefly but didn't answer. "I
guess you're saving my life again."

Two things struck him in that. Offering her a place
to stay was hardly saving her life. Over-the-top. But
then… "Again? What do you mean?"

"You saved me that first year in law school. I was
totally at sea, totally unprepared to be so much on my
own. For the first time in my life, my parents weren't
watching my every move and helping me make every
decision. I could have made some really big mistakes.
But you were always there to remind me."

"In short," he said almost irritably, "I was another
parent."

"No!" That caused her eyes to widen. "No, that isn't
what I meant. I didn't want to fail. I dreaded failing.
I needed every bit of help you gave me. That's all I
meant."

He wasn't sure he was buying it. He had thought
they were friends, that he was simply helping another
student when she ran into trouble with her studies. The

idea that he might have been in loco parentis for her didn't sit well at all with him. He'd helped her with law issues. The most advice he'd given her apart from that was to never let herself fall behind. He'd hashed out legal arguments with her. But never, not once, could he remember giving her advice on how to live her life. Hell, he hadn't even paid attention to who she was dating, if she dated anyone.

"I guess I said that wrong," she offered. "I didn't mean it the way you took it. I liked you as a friend. I admired a lot of things about you. I tried to be a little like you. But I never saw you as a parent figure. Ever."

He hoped she wasn't lying, because here they were in his house, her pregnant and unemployed, and if she was looking for a father figure, he wasn't prepared to apply for the role. No way.

Finally he spoke again, seeking different ground. "In the midst of all this upset, have you had any chance at all to think about what you want to do next? I realize you're probably still feeling sideswiped, but you must have had some impulses."

"I have. But can I trust them when I'm so emotionally messed up? I've pretty much concluded I'm done with silk-stocking law firms, though. Even if gossip doesn't get around, I'm not sure that I want to keep living that way. And then there's this baby. Much as I seem to be in denial, it keeps popping into my head. How could I continue a job like that with a child? Turn it over to someone else to raise?" Her mouth drew down at the corners. "I don't think I can do that, Wyatt."

That statement eased some of the tension inside him. Why, he couldn't say. Her life, her baby, her decision, but somehow he felt better about her knowing that she wasn't going to dump the child on a full-time nanny.

"A lot of people might put it up for adoption," he said, hating the words even as he spoke them. But it was his place to be logical, not emotional. Life had drilled that into him.

"No," she said without hesitation. "I can't do that. There's like… I don't know exactly how to explain it. But there was a moment, absolutely etched into my mind and heart, when I knew there wasn't going to be an abortion and there wasn't going to be an adoption. Everything in me clamped into a tight ball of resistance as soon as I thought of those things."

He nodded and released a breath he hadn't known he'd been holding. Why her decision should matter so much to him, he couldn't begin to guess. "Then it appears you have a whole new life to build."

"To put it mildly," she agreed. Placing her chin in her hand, she smiled at him. "It's been awful, Wyatt. Just awful. Everything blowing up around me, finding out I'd been lied to and used by someone I trusted, leaving my new job…it's been terrible. But I feel the most ridiculous sense of freedom for the first time in my life."

He nodded in understanding, but wondered how much of that was real and how much was a reaction to all the stress. He hoped it was real, because she sure as hell had blown up her bridges behind her.

Chapter Four

The room Wyatt had given her was lovely, Amber thought. She hadn't really seen much last night because she'd been so tired, but when she came upstairs to change into more comfortable clothes for the afternoon and evening, and maybe to grab a short nap, she took it all in.

A wide four-poster bed with its head against a wall covered in floral wallpaper. A rocking chair with comfortable pillows, a small writing desk, an armoire that looked like it was as old as the house and a surprisingly large walk-in closet.

A person could almost live in a room like this. Heavy rugs were scattered across the wood floor, their pastel colors matching the roses on the wall. It felt fresh and new, yet it retained the charm of an older age. When was the last time she'd seen wallpaper like that?

She changed into jeans. Her pregnancy hadn't yet started expanding her middle, or at least not enough to affect what she wore. Over that, she pulled an off-white cotton sweater. Autumn was here and there was a slight chill in the house, but she couldn't stand wool. She had occasionally thought with amusement that a lawyer without a wool suit was doomed to failure. So far she'd managed, though. There were enough cotton blends that she'd been able to look properly well-to-do. Once she'd found a tailor who got it, anyway.

She still felt tired from all the traveling, packing and stress, but lying down only sent her mind roaming anxious pathways. No good. Finally she rose, put on some ballet slippers and returned downstairs. She found Wyatt in the kitchen, doing something with beef in a frying pan that smelled absolutely delicious.

"Hi," she said.

He glanced over his shoulder and smiled. "No nap?"

"Couldn't quiet my mind. Is that for chili?"

"Yup. There must be a million recipes for it. I've tried a lot of them."

She managed a small laugh. "Fond of it, are you?"

"My fondness for chili is so famous that I've been asked to judge the chili cook-off the last few years."

"Seriously?"

"Seriously. Grab a seat. If you want a cold drink there's a choice in the fridge. If you want hot, I can make some more cocoa."

She chose a soft drink and passed close to the stove to see what looked like cubes of high-quality meat browning, already aromatic with seasonings. "I always use hamburger."

"Hamburger and beans. You can do a lot with those."

"So how did your chili become famous?"

He laughed as she sat at the table. "My chili isn't famous. My love of it is. When I have friends over, it's chili. When I throw a bigger bash, it's a bigger pot of chili. When I'm invited to a backyard barbecue, I bring some chili. Not always the same recipe, but it's a great way to feed a crowd easily. And I *do* enjoy it."

"So no fancy canapés?"

"No. Just hearty, stomach-filling food." He chuckled quietly and pulled the frying pan off the burner. "How hot and spicy do you prefer? I don't want to burn a hole in your tongue or stomach."

"Medium."

"Good enough." He went back to adding ingredients to the pan—tomato sauce, some floury substance he said was masa and more seasonings. Then he put the chili on to simmer and joined her at the table.

"So, too anxious to nap?"

"That'll wear off," she said. "I guess I need to just settle things inside me. Get used to it. And you couldn't possibly want to hear me talk endlessly about myself, Wyatt." She shook her head a little. "I've got one topic and one topic only lately. As for everything before... well, most of that wasn't very interesting, either."

She watched him smile and remembered how much she had always liked his smile. Something about it seemed to radiate warmth and charm. "I think you're very interesting," he answered. "But...what else would you like to talk about?"

An answering smile was born on her own face. Despite everything, he could make her smile. After the last month, she appreciated what a wonder that was.

All her smiles had been forced, required, and none of them had been real. Until she saw Wyatt again.

"Well," she began, "how did you become a judge?"

He gave a bark of laughter. "Not even an interesting story. For some reason known only to them, some members of the Wyoming bar gave my name to the judicial commission and I was selected. Now I'm up for a retention vote in November."

Amber felt her heart lurch. "Wyatt…that's only a few weeks away. Me staying with you, could it cause you problems?"

He shrugged one shoulder. "Fact is, Amber, I don't care. I like being a judge just fine. I also liked practicing law with my dad. If folks around here don't want me on the bench, well, it's not as if I'd be out of work. Hell, I can't even campaign, so they either like what I've been doing or not."

She shook her head a little. "Most of them probably have no idea what you've been doing on the bench. But gossip about you having a woman staying with you, that could get around, couldn't it?"

"Maybe it already has. Gossip around here has wings."

Her stomach sank for a whole new reason. "You never should have invited me here. I'll never forgive myself if you aren't retained."

"You probably would be the least of it. As I was telling my dad the other day, this *is* the twenty-first century."

Amber's head snapped up, and her heart pounded uncomfortably. "So he thought it was a bad idea, too?"

"It was more a case of the pot calling the kettle black. He has a thirty-year history of sharing his home with a variety of women, but he still gets clients. Nothing to worry about."

"I hope not." But now she felt a little sick. "Maybe I could move to a hotel."

"I wouldn't put my worst enemy in that fleabag. No, you're staying here, and I don't want you to worry about it. If people choose to boot me because I have a friend visiting…well, let 'em."

Of all the things she had considered when she decided to accept his invitation to stay here, she had never once thought that she might be putting him in an untenable position as a judge. So very selfish of her not to have given that a thought.

In fact, now that she faced it, she realized she had pretty much become a selfish person all the way around. When was the last time she'd seriously given consideration to anyone's needs but her own? So totally focused on her career…had she ever really thought about anyone else?

Mad that Tom had betrayed her, yes, but as she was busy considering what that meant to her, had she given a single thought to Tom's wife? Of course not. When Wyatt had told her she was welcome to stay with him while she figured things out, had she ever once asked if it might cause him any problems?

Of course not. Filled with self-disgust, she pushed back from the table and ran up the stairs to her room.

For the first time it struck her that not only had her parents constantly pushed her, but they had raised her to believe she was the only one who mattered. Everything was about Amber.

No wonder she'd hardly given a thought to the baby inside her. Pure selfishness.

* * *

Wyatt guessed he shouldn't have mentioned the upcoming retention vote. He certainly hadn't expected her response to it, or that the first thing she would consider was that her mere presence in his home might cost him the election.

Amber was turning into more of a puzzle than he'd anticipated. But then, he'd only really known her well when she was nineteen. A whole lot of years lay between then and now, and life changed people.

She surely couldn't believe that she and she alone could make people vote not to retain him. He didn't think there were that many uptight, judgmental people in this county. Everyone had their peccadilloes, and as he'd discovered as a judge, some of them had major ones. Who was staying with whom seemed the least of it.

No, if he wasn't retained it would be for other reasons, but the likelihood of that happening was slim to none. Generally speaking, it would take a truly major scandal to get him thrown off the bench, the kind of scandal that would make headlines outside this county.

Anything could happen, of course. Regardless of what Earl thought about Amber staying here, Earl himself could be a major liability in the upcoming election. Thirty years of affairs, and who could guess how many clients he might have angered over the decades. That would have far more of an impact than Amber's presence.

Although he was sure Earl would view it very differently.

He sighed, wishing he hadn't mentioned the election, although she'd probably have heard about it one way or another. He was planning to introduce her to people in the hopes she wouldn't have to spend too much time alone when he was working. One of them would have mentioned it, even if he hadn't.

But there was absolutely no reason for her to take blame for the outcome.

She had changed, he thought. The years had changed her. Well, they'd probably changed him, too, but it remained there was little of the girl he'd known left, and yet perhaps too much of that nineteen-year-old.

Or maybe she was overreacting because of her pregnancy. How would he know? It was easy to assume that such a massive physical change would have emotional effects, but that skated too close to the edge of sexism for him to be comfortable with the thought.

Just leave it, he told himself. She'd been through so much she was a bit rocky. Give her a few days of stability, and she might begin to feel better.

He really felt for her. No question that she'd been through a lot, more than most people would handle well. He needed to give her space to deal with the emotional toll. She'd been sailing along fairly well and then this.

It would be a test of her spirit, all right.

But then, he thought about what she'd said about her parents pushing her. Had she ever had time to figure out what *she* wanted from life? Apparently now she was going to get it, wanted or not.

Because Amber was right: except for her baby, she was utterly free for the first time in her life. No parental pressure and a whopping big mess to push away any internal drive she'd been feeling to reach the heights.

A crash for sure. But if that drive had all been the

result of the way she'd been raised, she was sure going to be at sea now.

Everything she had been taught to consider important had just blown up on her. Transitioning would involve a lot more than just finding a new job. It was going to involve a whole new way of thinking about herself and her future.

He was glad he wasn't facing that. He'd sprung out on his own for a couple of years after college, tested his wings, decided what he wanted was to be here. He'd been his own decision maker.

Aside from leaving a job and keeping a baby, had Amber ever decided anything for herself?

This mess appeared to be growing bigger by the moment.

Amber cried for the first time since everything had blown up on her. She seldom cried, mostly because her parents had taught her that tears were useless and that instead of indulging in them, she ought to be fixing the problem.

But she cried now, and she didn't give a darn whether it was a waste of energy, or that it was useless. She needed to cry more than she ever had in her life. Everything was a mess, and she seemed to be creating a new mess just by coming here and…

Her self-image had blown up. Like getting slapped in the head by a two-by-four, her entire view had just shifted so much that she felt like a stranger in her own skin.

Selfish. She had never thought of herself that way before, but as she tested the word, the truth of it settled harshly in her heart. Oh, she donated her time and money to charity, she never passed a homeless person without giving them something and she thought about the ills of the world and bemoaned them. But when it came to Amber, only Amber mattered.

At an early age her parents had set her feet on a path and hadn't let her divert from it. They had told her she would do great things for the world and she had believed them. But their idea of doing great things had meant climbing to the top rung of financial and career success.

Was that really so great? She'd watched Wyatt in his courtroom that morning and had been touched. He'd been unsparing when people deserved it, but what had reached her most was how often he tried to help one of the miscreants get things sorted out. It hadn't just been the man who couldn't read. There had been others, like the woman who had no auto insurance because she couldn't afford it. He'd talked to her about her situation in depth and had suspended sentence, giving her two weeks and a reference to a charity that would help her get the insurance. If she came to the clerk of the court with an insurance card, the charge would be dropped.

How many judges would bother with that? Of course, when she was in court she was trying very different cases. Cases that involved money, mostly civil litigation between parties in contract disputes. Those people were able to hire the best law firms and really didn't need the kind of mercy Wyatt got to show in his courtroom.

So maybe there were plenty of judges like him. How would she know? But the difference was striking, and she suspected that had had something to do with this abrupt internal shift.

Wyatt was a good judge. Why had she never once thought of him and the problems she might cause him? That question hung in her mind while her tears dried.

She hadn't thought of him. She hadn't thought much about her baby. She certainly hadn't spared a thought for the wife of the man who had betrayed her.

No, it was all about Amber's humiliation, Amber's pain, Amber's feeling that she had been stupid. Amber's messed-up life.

And the desire to get away from her humiliation had led her here. To an old friend she could perhaps now add to her list of mistakes. She'd never forgive herself if he lost this election. Retention elections were rarely lost unless something happened to make an awful lot of people think you weren't fit to be a judge.

In a big city her presence here wouldn't even be discussed. But this was a small town, and she had some experience of small towns. Her parents had left one when she was young because her father had been accused of having an affair with an important man's wife. He claimed he hadn't, and she didn't know what the truth was, but life in the little town had become untenable for them.

Sure, this was the twenty-first century. But how much had attitudes really changed about some behaviors?

Then there was the baby. *Her* baby. Wyatt had expressed more concern about it than she had yet. She hadn't gone to the doctor for prenatal care, she'd gone to have her pregnancy confirmed. So far, she hadn't followed the most important order of all: get to an obstetrician.

So what did that say about her? Was she wishing the child away? Unable to cope with what it would mean to her future? Hoping something went awry if she just ignored it long enough?

A fresh wave of tears hit her, and she buried her face in a damp pillow so the sounds couldn't escape the room.

It would be very easy to hate herself.

She just hoped Wyatt didn't come to hate her, too.

Wyatt finished making the chili and wondered if he should heat the tortillas now or wait for her. Or if he should go up and see if she was all right.

He wasn't sure what he had expected from Amber's visit, but matters were taking some unexpected turns. He hadn't been prepared for what appeared to have the makings of an epic self-reevaluation on her part.

Yet why should that be surprising, in light of all that had happened to her? Maybe she'd been running on automatic until she got here. That wouldn't be surprising, either, especially given what she'd said about her parents.

So they had pushed her all the way. Early college, then law school at too young an age. Had Amber ever had a real chance to find *herself*? He knew how those large law firms worked. They pretty much owned you. If life had been all work and no play, how could she ever find Amber?

And if that's what she was doing right now, maybe he ought to prepare himself for some major fireworks, because it wasn't going to be easy. Whoever she thought she was had just been blown up. As always, he wished he could help, but he had absolutely no idea what kind of help he might be able to offer. Just that he still had a place in his heart for her after all these years, so he gave a damn about her. That wasn't likely to fix much.

Sighing, he gave the chili one more stir, deciding that the spices must have blended well enough by now and the pepper had grown as hot as it would. Then he heard light steps approaching, solving one of his problems: he wouldn't have to go disturb her in her room.

She smiled as he turned, but he could see her eyes were swollen. She'd been crying. Oh, hell. "You okay?" he asked immediately.

"Fine. A little self-knowledge can be overwhelming. I've never had this much time to just think about myself and my life. Difficult but informative."

"I hope you're not thinking bad things," he said carefully.

"I'm thinking there's a lot I don't like about myself. Man, that chili smells wonderful!"

He accepted the change of subject and got the dishes out, deciding that eating in the kitchen would be cozier than that mausoleum of a dining room. Some of his forebears had had grandiose notions of themselves.

Amber immediately started helping, placing the bowls, spoons and napkins so that they would sit across from each other.

"To drink?" she asked.

He usually enjoyed a beer with this meal, but out of deference to her pregnant state, he opted for water. She found glasses and filled them with water.

"Do you want tortillas with this?" he asked. "I can heat them in a jiffy. Or we can just have crackers."

"Crackers, please," she answered.

He pulled out the box of soda crackers and placed it on the table. "Be careful of my mother's silver serving box. It's been in the family for generations."

To his relief, she laughed. "You mentioned your father but not your mother."

"Ah." He ladled chili into each bowl, then put the pan back on the stove. "My mother died when I was almost eight. She slipped and fell on the ice and cracked the back of her head pretty badly."

"I am so sorry!"

"Me, too. But that was thirty years ago, and while I still miss her at times, I'm used to it." They sat facing each other. "Are you going to call home, Amber? Your father will wonder where you've gone if you haven't told him."

"He's used to me not calling for long periods because of work. I'll get around to it. Not that I want to hear what he has to say."

He hesitated, a spoonful of chili on the way to his mouth, watching her pull out a few crackers and place them in her bowl. "You're thirty. Why would you be worried about what they might say?"

Stupid question, and he knew it. Earl was always kibitzing about Wyatt's life. But it bothered him that she didn't want to tell her father. He'd have thought a woman in her situation would want to talk to family. Instead she had chosen him.

When it came to issues like this, he was about as inexperienced as it was possible to be. Looking firmly down at his bowl, he began to eat.

Amber was quiet for a while, except to tell him how delicious the chili was. Then she asked, "So you have a variety of recipes?"

"I collect them. Some are better than others, of course, but I find it a whole lot easier to entertain a group of people with a meal like this."

"Do you entertain often?"

"I have friends. Some will be coming over Saturday night. Then there are the others."

"Others?"

He winked at her. "Yeah, the people I have to be polite to because of my job. County commissioners, city councilmen, a couple of local magistrates who help handle my caseload, other important people."

"You don't like them?" She didn't seem shocked by the idea.

"It's not that I don't like them. They're just not my closest friends. I have more friends in the sheriff's department, for some reason. Then there's a couple of schoolteachers, some ranchers, oh, a whole assortment. You'll get to meet some of them."

He couldn't interpret her reaction. Her face revealed nothing, but finally she said, "That'll be nice."

"It's not a work thing," he said, then regretted the tone of his voice. He didn't want to add any more discomfort to her plate. "You don't have to come if you don't want to."

"I'll come," she said quietly. "It'd probably be good for people to learn who I am. Just an old friend visiting."

What was going on here? He had begun to think they were getting past the awkwardness, then she had run upstairs for a couple of hours and come back with swollen eyes, which meant she must have been crying. Why couldn't she share that with him? Why go hide away when she might most need some kind of understanding and comfort?

He didn't think he was particularly special, but he *could* listen. He'd expected to do a lot of it when she arrived here. He had figured she'd want to rant about how everything had gone to hell, maybe cry a bit, maybe start thinking about options and talking about them.

Instead… It struck him as odd, but he didn't remember her being so remote when they were in law school. But maybe he just didn't remember correctly. He wondered what had built those cold walls around her. What had made her feel she needed to hide herself.

Hell, he was mostly an open book. Of course, he lived in a town where he could hardly have been anything else. But what had shut Amber down like this?

He made up his mind then and there that he was going to find out.

She helped him clean up after dinner, then he announced he had some work to do.

"Decisions from last week," he said. "I picked them up this morning, so I need to read them over then sign them. You can come into my office with me down the hall if you want, or I can show you the entertainment room."

She blinked. She'd dealt with a lot of rich muckety-mucks in her career, but she would never have expected Wyatt to be in the class who could afford that. "You have an entertainment room?"

He laughed. "A spare room. I kinda rattle around

in here by myself, if you haven't noticed. So I just put the TV, DVDs and sound system in there and left the living room for when I have people over. And...you'll find a lot of books in there, too. We've always been a family for buying books."

She eyed him, feeling inexplicably amused. "No e-reader?"

"Of course I have one. I even have both a computer and a tablet for working on. Modern in every way."

His wink drew a laugh from her. He made her feel good, she realized. But he always had, she thought, looking back over the years. Even in law school when she'd been so overwhelmed, he'd had a way of getting her to relax and keep things in proportion. She could definitely use some proportion now.

But gazing at him, she also found her mind wandering a different path. How could she ever have been attracted to Tom? Because he flattered her? Because he was the only guy around that she could manage to have a relationship with, and the only one willing to risk the difficulties of a romantic relationship with a colleague?

Because he was her only choice?

But so soon after some of the biggest shocks and disappointment of her life, she was feeling a strong attraction to Wyatt. Was she crazy? A stupid question to ask herself when she thought back to their law school days and the huge, secret crush she had had on him. Wyatt was the only guy in school she'd wanted to date, and as a result she didn't date at all.

He was an attractive man with a fine physique of broad shoulders and narrow hips. His face was strong, almost patrician, but one of the things she liked most was the way the corners of his eyes crinkled when he smiled. Everything about him physically would draw the female eye, but nothing about his behavior invited it. She wondered if it was Ellie, his past interest, who had caused him to put up the off-limits signs she sensed, or if they'd always been there. Or if it was just her. He'd definitely been off-limits to her back in law school.

It did seem odd that he hadn't been snatched up at his age, though. She doubted this place was crawling with so many eligible bachelors that he would have been overlooked. Yet here he was, unattached.

And gorgeous.

She looked down, hoping she hadn't revealed her sexual response to him. Now *that* could make things very uncomfortable for them both. He'd offered her a place out of the storm to collect herself. That wouldn't last long if she made him feel uncomfortable in his own house.

So she opted for the entertainment room and some reality TV show that she hardly saw. She was sure that if she'd followed him to his office, she would have sat staring at him like a starstruck kid.

Because for the first time since law school, Amber looked past the end of her own nose and saw once again the man she had wanted years ago. Attraction had slipped past the edges of the nightmare and awakened her to never-fulfilled possibilities.

Possibilities that weren't for her. And certainly not when she was pregnant with another man's child.

Chapter Five

Amber awoke in the morning to realize she'd slept all night in front of the TV. Some morning show was on, murmuring quietly, but she wasn't interested.

Sitting up slowly, she felt a little stiff, even though the recliner had been comfortable. Not moving at all while she slept wasn't a good thing. Events and the long trip must have taken more out of her than she realized.

The clock on the box beneath the TV told her it was past nine. She must have slept close to twelve hours.

The minute she stood up, however, she felt sick, so sick that she ran for the hall bath and had dry heaves for a few minutes. Sweating and shaking, she sat on the bathroom floor and waited for the nausea to pass.

It didn't pass, but it settled a bit. Morning sickness? She couldn't remember what her doctor had said about it if anything, but she had the impression it should have started earlier. Or maybe not. She was still in her first trimester. Wyatt was right, she had to get to an obstetrician, because suddenly she was staring straight at the reality of her condition and accepting the fact that she didn't know a damn thing about it. Not one thing.

If she'd needed another wakeup call, she'd just gotten it.

Eventually, she dared to stand, waiting a couple of minutes to be sure things had settled a bit. She finally took a shower and changed into fresh clothes, all the while wondering if the nausea would ever quit.

Downstairs she found a note from Wyatt in the kitchen.

I'll be in court for a trial, don't know exactly when I'll be done. The fridge and cupboards are full, so help yourself to anything. P.S. Asked a friend to stop by and look in on you.

Oh, great. She didn't know if she was ready for that, especially the way she felt now.

Eating seemed impossible. Searching the refrigerator, she found some apple juice that looked possible. She poured a small glass and tested herself with a single sip. It stayed down.

Obstetrician, she reminded herself, except she didn't see a phone book anywhere. Of course not. Who used phone books anymore?

After she finished about four ounces of apple juice, she decided to go look for Wyatt's office. He had a computer in there, and maybe even that old-fashioned notion called a phone book. She had her laptop in her car, but she'd have no idea where or how to hook it up here.

Pulling her cardigan closer about her, she noticed for the first time that some sun was showing outside and leaves were no longer whirling around. Inside, however, she felt chilly. She wondered if it was warmer out there.

She also knew the weather was the last thing that should be preoccupying her. There were serious matters on her plate, and she was evading them.

Six weeks ago, she'd learned the truth about Tom. Two weeks after that she'd taken a home pregnancy test and found out the worst. A month ago, after talking to Wyatt, she'd given her notice at the firm, accepted a generous severance package even though she didn't deserve it—she was pretty sure she knew why it had been offered, however—and the firm had sent her on her way without letting her finish out her notice. They apparently wanted her gone as much as she wanted to be gone.

All very civilized, but a whole lot of butt covering for everyone, including her. Bad enough she'd had an affair with a married junior partner. How much worse if they'd learned of the pregnancy.

So she'd skedaddled, packed up, escaped her lease and headed straight for one of the only people on earth she felt she could trust.

And during all this, she'd been nursing some painful emotional wounds, trying to adjust to a different self-image and failing, and not considering what she was going to do next.

She'd been overwhelmed again, like the first week of law school. And once again there was Wyatt. She hoped he didn't feel used, because she feared that was exactly what she was doing.

Before she could look for Wyatt's office, the doorbell rang and she froze. This must be the friend he'd sent. A wave of rebellion rose in her and she considered not answering. Then she felt like an idiot for not wanting to.

"Stop dithering," she said aloud. This wasn't like her.

Marching to the front door, she opened it and found a lovely woman standing there. "Hi," the woman said, tossing her blond hair back from her face. "I'm Hope Cashford, a friend of Wyatt's. He asked me to stop by and look in on you when I dropped my daughter off at preschool."

Amber blinked, surprised. When Wyatt had written *friend* on his note, she'd expected a guy. Or an older woman. Certainly not a beauty.

"Hi, I'm Amber Towers. Would you like to come in?"

"Love to," Hope said.

Amber didn't quite know whether to take her to the living room or kitchen, but shouldn't she make coffee or something?

"It's hard being a new guest in someone else's house," Hope said. She slipped her arm through Amber's and led the way straight to the kitchen. "I'll make coffee even though I guess you don't want any. Do you mind?"

"How could I mind and why wouldn't I want any?"

Hope paused midstep to look at her. "Morning sickness?" she asked gently.

Amber gasped. "Does it show?"

"No," Hope said cheerfully. "Wyatt told me you're

pregnant. And trust me, I have a similar story, so we've got a lot to talk about."

Astonished, all Amber could do was sit at the table while Hope made coffee as if she knew her way around the kitchen. "How are we similar?" she asked.

"To the extent that we were both done wrong by men and got pregnant, I think we've got something in common."

"Maybe," Amber agreed, waiting to hear more. This was so frank that it surprised her. This woman didn't know her at all.

Hope came to the table as the coffee started brewing, reached into her jacket pocket and took out a business card. "This is a great obstetrical practice. I use them, and now there's a woman doctor there as well, if that matters to you. I was further along when Cash took me in, but this guy didn't even scold me. His new partner seems every bit as nice. Anyway, you keep that card."

Amber put her fingers on it and smiled weakly. "I was just thinking about this before you arrived. Thank you."

"Wyatt said you needed a doc. So…" She grinned and pulled a mug out of the cupboard. "You can have a cup if you haven't already, or should I make you something else?"

"My stomach's upset. Thank you, but I don't feel like eating or drinking anything right now."

"Ah, so it *is* the dreaded morning sickness. Have you met the soda cracker?"

"Cracker?"

Hope grinned and slipped her jacket off, hanging

it over the back of a chair. "Let me get you a few. Try them slowly. They might settle your tummy."

Soon Hope had placed a half dozen crackers on a plate in front of her, along with a glass of water. "I kept the dang things beside my bed the first three months. I couldn't even get up until I'd eaten a few. You don't seem as bad."

Amber had to smile back. "If you don't count my time in the bathroom this morning."

"Then you definitely need to see the doc soon. Anyway." She finally sat with her mug of coffee, still smiling at Amber. "You may not want to tell me much about what happened to you, but I'll gladly share my story. It kind of made the rounds thanks to my husband's teenage daughter. Not that I'm surprised. I was raised in Dallas and there were few secrets in my circle there, I can tell you."

Amber nibbled a cracker slowly, feeling her curiosity growing. "How'd you get here?"

"I went on the run." Hope's face shadowed. "My fiancé, who had been tapped to become a candidate for the US Senate, raped me."

Amber gasped, feeling her heart squeeze. "Oh, my God."

Hope shrugged. "I'm over it, thanks to Cash. But long story short, my family had a lot of money, my fiancé Scott was the perfect choice for them, I was apparently the perfect choice to be his wife and none of them were going to let a little rape and a pregnancy get in the way. I was a prisoner in my own home with two choices—have an abortion or marry Scott quickly. You can imagine how I felt about that. So I ran as soon as I had the opportunity. I wound up here with only a hundred dollars left to my name, and Cash hired me to be a nanny to his daughter." She smiled. "I am so glad about how it all turned out."

"And Wyatt became your friend?" Certainly a good enough friend that Wyatt had felt free to tell her about Amber and her pregnancy, and her need for a doctor.

"Yeah, actually. Cash has known him most of his life, and when we decided I should adopt Cash's daughter, Wyatt helped. But I had the chance to meet him before then. He's a nice man. He mentioned that you became friends in law school?"

Amber nodded and nibbled another cracker. It was staying down, and the nausea eased a bit. She hoped it kept easing. "I was in my first year, he was in his last, and he was a great help. I'm not sure I would have survived without his advice."

Hope laughed quietly. "I can imagine that man being a great help, but don't put yourself down. You'd probably have made it, even if it was harder. So...what happened to you?"

Amber hesitated. Hope hadn't given her many details, so she supposed she could skim over the most humiliating stuff and just give an outline. "Bad office romance. I had to leave and he doesn't know I'm pregnant."

Hope held her mug to her face with both hands and regarded Amber over it. "Did he lie to you?"

"Hell, yes. I didn't know he was married." And it felt so surprisingly good to just say it. There it was, the ugly thing, out there in plain view. She hadn't been reluctant to tell Wyatt, but she had no desire to tell anyone else—yet she just had.

"What a creep," Hope remarked. "And don't worry,

I won't tell anyone. Certainly not my mouthy eldest daughter, who spread my own story far and wide. But how awful for you!"

"Not as bad as a rape," Amber said weakly, fighting the all-too-familiar urge to just slip into a hole and pull the ground in over her. Her chest had begun to tighten again, making it harder to breathe. But it had felt good to say it. Why did she want to run from it again?

"Oh, I don't know," Hope said. "You were violated in a different way. Used. I know what that feels like. You come away feeling dirty and humiliated even when it wasn't your own fault."

Amber lifted her gaze, the hard knot that had been growing in her chest easing some. "That's true," she admitted. This woman *did* understand, and she wasn't judging Amber. She drew a long, shaky breath.

"It gets better," Hope said gently. "What's more, there's life for us after the bad men. Even some good men around. So hang on, Amber. Eventually you get past the shock, then you get past the anger, and then life begins again. I hope yours turns out as well as mine has."

"I hope so, too."

"Well," Hope continued, "when I arrived here I was at the end of my rope, emotionally and financially. All I knew was I had to figure out a way to take care of my baby. That was all I had left to hang on to. You hang on to that, Amber." Then she rose.

"Cash insists our younger daughter go to preschool because he doesn't want her to miss the social interaction like she would out on the ranch. But this is also my free time to catch up with errands, and I only have a few hours." She turned and pulled a piece of paper off the memo pad on the refrigerator door and scribbled down her number. "Here's my number. Don't be afraid to call for any reason at all."

Then she grabbed her jacket, patted Amber's shoulder and headed out the door.

Feeling almost as if a whirlwind had blown through, Amber sat eating crackers, and as her stomach settled, she even felt the return of some appetite.

She liked Hope and she could understand why Wyatt had confided in her. She looked at the business card on the table and reached for the phone hanging on the wall. She needed to do this. Playing ostrich wasn't good for her or the baby who was finally becoming real to her.

After ten minutes she had an appointment later in the week with the doctor, Joy Castor. She wrote it on the back of the card and then went out to the foyer to tuck it in her purse. That would make Wyatt happy, she thought. In the meantime, she needed to shake herself out of the mental stasis that seemed to be enveloping her again. She'd quit a job, packed up her life and come running to a friend, but everything else seemed to have shut down. No thoughts for the future, no plans in the works, and for the first time the denial about her pregnancy seemed to be waning.

So what next? She wished she could think of something. Anything. God, she needed a plan. Right now the future looked empty and threatening, and it didn't seem to be getting any better.

Midafternoon, just as she was deciding she couldn't hibernate in this house and at least needed to get out for a walk, the doorbell rang again. Now who had Wyatt sent?

She opened to the door and faced a young woman somewhere near her age with upswept hair wearing a dress and heels. She was used to seeing that in the city, but she already had the sense it wasn't that common around here. She thought of Wyatt wearing jeans under his robe, and most of the people he'd talked to in the courtroom yesterday. They hadn't even dressed up for that.

"May I help you?" she asked.

"So you're the new girlfriend."

Shock rammed Amber. She wasn't usually thrown off balance easily with the law. This was a side of the world she had only minimal acquaintance with. "I'm sorry?"

"Wyatt's new girlfriend," the woman said. "I heard about you."

Already? "Um…we're just old friends."

"Sure. Well, I'm Ellie Rich, his former fiancée. I just wanted to see who was stupid enough to fall for that guy. Big mistake, lady. He's all nice on the outside and ugly on the inside. Or maybe you're his new cover story."

Then the woman turned and walked away, leaving Amber standing there with the door open and hardly aware of the chilly air. Ellie climbed into her car and drove away fast enough to leave a little rubber behind. The instant she disappeared around the corner, Wyatt's car appeared from the opposite direction and pulled into the driveway.

Abruptly aware that she was getting cold, Amber pivoted and reached for her jacket but didn't close the door. Wyatt climbed out, clad in jeans and a blue sweater, paused to look at her standing in the open doorway, concern creasing his brow, then loped up the sidewalk and onto the porch.

"Something wrong?" he asked.

"Ellie. At least she said she was."

His face darkened. "Damn that woman. You're shivering. Let's get inside."

He urged her into the foyer and closed the door. "You look like you need a hot drink." A gentle hand on the small of her back urged her into the kitchen.

"I'm fine. There's coffee. Your friend Hope made it earlier. I think it's still good." In some crazy way, it was as if she were pulling out of her body, standing at a distance from everything. How strange. How very weird.

"I'm not worried about coffee," he said, an edge to his voice. "I'm worried about *you*." Without another word, he pulled out ingredients. "Cocoa coming up."

Amber sat at the table again, trying to figure out what was wrong with her. It was as if she was removed from everything, but she was sure she hadn't felt that way until just recently. Maybe since she got here. It was weird, as if nearly everything inside her had shut down. Before, she'd put a few matters on hold to deal with later. But all of a sudden she felt as if everything was on hold. She felt numb, almost disinterested, after her teary meltdown just yesterday.

As soon as Wyatt had the cocoa simmering, he got himself some coffee and joined her at the table. "Ellie didn't say anything to upset you, did she?"

"I think I'm past getting upset about anything." A blessing perhaps, but not normal. "She basically told me she was your ex, accused me of being your new girlfriend, or alternatively your new cover story, then she left."

"I'm sorry," he said. Reaching across the table, he clasped her hand briefly. His touch felt surprisingly warm and pleasant.

"Don't be sorry. I'm quite sure you didn't ask her to stop by. That's all on her."

"Regardless, you didn't need it. I don't believe that woman." Rising, he went to stir the simmering cocoa. "It's been over a year. You'd think she would have moved on."

"I don't know. I seem to be having trouble moving at all."

In a flash he was squatting beside her. "What's wrong, Amber? Are you sick?"

She shook her head a little. "I'm fine. Some morning sickness, but Hope helped with that. No, it's like... it's like everything has shut down. I'm numb. I can't think. I've got to plan a future, and it feels as if my brain went on vacation. My emotions, too." As busy as she'd been in the last month, maybe this had been happening all along and she just hadn't noticed it. Was she losing her mind?

He nodded and touched her shoulder lightly. "Maybe you've been through all the emotional turmoil you can stand for a while. Your mind and emotions might just be forcing a holiday on you."

"Holiday?" Despite her oddly removed state, she almost laughed. "Some holiday."

"A rest, then. Maybe you just need a break from it all. Or maybe you can't deal with it all at once. There's been an awful lot to deal with."

"Maybe."

"No maybe about it," he said. "You were awfully clinical when you called me and told me you were in trouble. It's a bit of self-protection going on here. I hope it doesn't all just crash in at once."

She gazed into his face, reading his concern but more, his kindness. He'd always accepted her just as she was, and he was doing it right now. Some part of her acknowledged that she ought to feel a whole lot more messed up than she did, but except for that crying fit yesterday, she felt as if her mind and heart were wrapped in cotton. So maybe he was right. Yesterday she had wept and hurt for quite a long time. Then everything had been steadily and slowly stilling inside her. Enough for now.

He touched her cheek, and a pleasant shiver ran through her. Well, at least she could still feel that. It would have been so easy to just fall into his arms. Because she wanted to know what it would feel like to rest her head on his shoulder. To feel his lips on hers. To feel his skin against hers. To feel him filling the emptiness inside her. She'd always wanted to know.

"You did cry yesterday," he reminded her. "Privately, but it was there on your face when you came down for dinner. Take it a step at a time. Now I need to check that cocoa before I scorch it."

He stirred it a few more times while she watched and tried to think of a safe place to go with their conversation. It would be almost impossible to feel any more disconnected than she did right now. Except for one connection, that was. Her desire for him was probably the only part of her that was still awake and responding.

"How was court?" she asked.

"A very interesting bigamy case."

That caught her attention and drove her preoccupation into the background. He filled two mugs with frothy cocoa and put one in front of her. "How could you commit bigamy in a town this size?"

He laughed and sat across from her. "Believe it or not, you can. But not the way you'd expect."

"So what happened?"

"This couple split maybe thirteen years ago. She threw him out and told him she was filing for divorce. So he moved to California, where he got a job and, believe it or not, sent regular child support checks."

"Why believe it or not?"

His smile widened. "It was never ordered by a court. He was just doing what he thought was right."

"I already like him. Then?"

"Then, all these years later he comes back to town. Stops by to see his kids, meets a new woman, they date and after a few months they got married. Supposedly ex-wife hears about the marriage and immediately calls the cops to press bigamy charges. She had never divorced him."

"But…" Her mind boggled. "How did he not know?"

"You're a lawyer, you understand how this works. This guy was poorly educated, never had anything to do with the law until this. My guess is it never occurred to him that he was supposed to get divorce papers to sign, or a decree. Anyway, after listening to all of this, the jury apparently decided that after thirteen years he probably believed he was divorced and therefore didn't intend to commit bigamy."

"And it's an intent crime?"

"That's one of the elements."

"I love it. He must have had a good lawyer, though."

"Public defender," he answered. "And she was good. She kept hammering on the intent part of the crime and how you have to *knowingly* be married to two women at the same time." He laughed quietly. "I enjoyed that trial. I think I enjoyed the outcome even more. That guy was no more intentionally guilty of bigamy than I am. And all those years he paid child support without a court order. I know a lot of men who begrudge it even when a court orders it."

"I've heard plenty of them gripe about it," she agreed. "Honestly, I don't get it. When you dump a spouse you don't dump your kids. Or at least you shouldn't."

"I absolutely agree. I do family court as well, and failure to pay child support is the most frequent type of case to come before me."

She arched a brow, surprised. "You're a jack-of-all-trades."

"Within my jurisdiction, yeah. Look at this place, Amber. I have a couple of magistrates who help deal with the really minor things, but they aren't even lawyers. So I get everything in the area that doesn't need to go to the district court."

"This is so very different," she murmured, even as she realized he had successfully pulled her away from her spiraling concern about being so numb. Maybe he was right. Maybe she just needed a break from it all. God knew, she was weary of feeling overwhelmed, rudderless. Her old life was over. She needed to move on. And apparently she needed some time to do just that. Time that Wyatt was giving her.

Then he asked, "Did you make an appointment?"

"Yeah. For Thursday. You can relax."

"I wasn't uptight," he answered. "So you had morning sickness?"

"I guess that's what it was." She looked down at herself, trying to imagine the child growing inside her. It still seemed so far away, so removed. At two months she could barely see any changes in her body.

"You'll probably find out tomorrow morning." He winked, but this time she didn't even smile back. She had found a safe, quiet place in the middle of the maelstrom her life had become, and right now she didn't want one damn thing to disturb it.

Wyatt was more concerned about her withdrawal than he let on. After yesterday's crying jag upstairs—and yeah, he'd known from the puffiness of her face when she came back downstairs—now this? Like a switch had flipped?

He'd tried to be reassuring about it, but he wasn't at all convinced it was a normal reaction. When he thought about all that had happened to her in the last month or so, he supposed she was entitled to withdraw for a while. It was enough to devastate anyone, and she hadn't allowed herself much time to just sit, cry and brood.

She'd made two incredibly tough decisions, the first to quit the firm, the second to keep her child. Life altering, life shattering.

Yeah, she was entitled to shut down for a while. He just wondered at what point he should start to really worry.

At least she was drinking her cocoa. "I was thinking about roasting a chicken for dinner tonight. Does that sound good to you?"

She nodded. "Very good, actually." Then, just as he started to rise to get the chicken out of the refrigerator, she said, "Ellie."

He sat again. "What about her?"

"She's very pretty."

"Only on the outside," he said, a slight edge in his voice. "I told you."

"I know."

He put his elbows on the table and studied her. "What does it matter what she looks like?"

"It doesn't. It's only that I can't imagine why she came over here. It was pointless. You broke up with her a long time ago. It's just weird that she evidently wanted to say something nasty to me about you."

Ellie was at least outside the circle of Amber's problems, and therefore safe. He got it. Well, if she wanted to talk about that woman, he supposed he could as well. He'd left Ellie in his distant emotional past.

Amber spoke again. "Did she hurt you very badly?"

He hesitated. "At first I was so angry I learned what it means to see red. Asking me to intervene on the charges against her cousin…she should have known me better by then. But no, she thought she could manipulate me into doing something that violated all my principles. That's when I knew what she really thought of me. So later, when I stopped being so angry, yeah, I was hurt. I'd thought I was in love. I'd almost asked that woman to marry me. It took a while for me to just feel grateful she'd pulled that stunt *before* we were married. Or had kids."

"I bet," she said quietly.

"So I escaped by the skin of my teeth." He shook his head and gave her a lopsided smile. "Live and learn. Trite but true. A wise man, namely my dad, once told me that we learn more from our mistakes than we do from getting it right. I'm here to testify that it may not feel like it at the time, but he was right. I learned a lot from that experience."

"Any of it good?"

He reached across the table and took her hand again. Her fingers felt cold. "A lot of it. Give yourself time, Amber. Do you want mittens or another cup of cocoa?"

That at least broke through her frozen state enough to make her smile faintly. "Cocoa, please. I don't know why I feel so cold. I'm sure it's warm enough in here, and it's not like I just came from some southern climate."

He had no answer for that. Maybe she was just run-down. Regardless, he was glad she would see the doc in two days. "It'll warm up in the kitchen soon, because I'm going to turn on the oven. In the meantime, do you want me to get you a wrap? A blanket? A shawl?"

At that she looked up. "You have a *shawl*?"

He laughed. "They used to be quite common, and you have to remember a lot of generations have lived here. Yes, I have a shawl. I have a few of them. Lucky I didn't give them to the church rummage sale, but I can still remember my great-grandmother wearing them. I loved that woman."

"I'd like to hear about her."

"Let me get that shawl and I'll bore you to tears."

Responsive at least, he thought as he dashed upstairs to a storage closet. Distant, but not gone.

There was a cedar closet off the wide hallway. Over the years it had probably stored many things, especially when woolens were so popular and moths a big problem, but now it was down to mostly keepsakes, carefully wrapped in plastic by his mother before she died. Earl and Wyatt had never used it for much, although Earl did have one good wool coat hanging in there from many years ago. Wyatt doubted he'd be able to squeeze into it now.

Most of what was left were items he and his father hadn't been able to part with. It was easy to find one of his great-grandmother's shawls, and he paused a few minutes, lost in memories of her. More than anyone else, she had helped him get through the weeks after his mother's shocking death.

He stroked the shawl with his hand, remembering her wearing it. Suddenly remembering that a long time ago Amber had told him about her aversion to wool. Well, all the rest were wool shawls, with the exception of this one, his favorite. His grandmother had tatted it herself, he was told, and she liked peacocks. This had been tatted out of colorful embroidery silks.

Anyway, it was pretty, and while he cherished it more than the others, it was the only one Amber could wear.

Downstairs, he draped it around Amber's shoulders. "Not wool, but warm anyway, I imagine."

"I seem to be allergic to wool," she replied. "Thank you. It's beautiful."

He didn't tell her that he'd recalled that errant remark from so long ago. He didn't know why, but he felt it might make her uneasy to know she'd made such an impression on him. "My great-grandma tatted it out of some embroidery silk. Every time I look at it I think about time, patience and talent. And I remember she wore it only on Sundays."

He paused to switch the oven on and pulled out a roasting pan, which he oiled. Then he stood at the sink washing the chicken under a stream of cold water. "You just want it plain?"

"That might be safest right now."

He glanced over his shoulder and saw her looking down at the shawl, stroking it with her hand.

"It's so lovely," she said quietly. "Was it fashionable?"

"Now that I can't tell you. I remember her from when she was in her seventies and eighties and I was just a kid. She made me feel special, though. Every time I was with her, I felt wrapped in love."

"You were very fortunate."

From what she had said yesterday, he wondered if she had, even once in her life, felt wrapped in love.

"I was," he agreed. "She used to take me on walks in the summertime for a picnic. She mixed her home-made preserves with powdered sugar to make icing and spread it on graham crackers. Then we'd hike out to the railroad tracks and back. It always seemed like an adventure, even though I could see the town in the distance. I was small, though, so those distances seemed huge."

He buttered the chicken on the outside, then washed his hands. It was a nuisance, getting the butter off, but he'd never found a better way to oil the chicken, and he liked the way the butter tasted. He skipped his usual preference for some paprika and just lightly salted it. Then into the oven. When he turned around, drying his hands on a towel, he saw Amber sitting with her chin in her hand looking quite pensive.

"Something the matter?" he asked.

"Just thinking about how nice those picnics must have been for you. I'd have liked to do something like that."

"What kinds of things did you do as a child?" He hoped it hadn't all been as bleak as she'd sounded yesterday, pushed every step of the way by ambitious parents.

"Normal stuff, I guess. My grandparents were gone by the time I was five, and I don't remember them well. Except they never seemed like grandparents."

"How so?" He moved closer to the table.

"I don't know. It was like visiting people I didn't know very well, and I always had to be on my best behavior. Not one of them made cookies." She gave a mirthless laugh. "I see that stuff on TV and wonder where those grandparents are. Your great-grandmother sounds like she might have fit the bill."

"She did. Of them all, she was my favorite. But maybe she'd reached a time in life where other things didn't preoccupy her. I guess she spoiled me in a lot of ways."

She moved her head a little. "Maybe every child deserves someone to spoil them. I get that parents can't afford to, but other people can."

"How much of a monster do you want to raise?"

At that he finally drew a laugh from her. Was she coming back? He hoped so. "So nobody spoiled you?"

She twisted her hands. "I guess that depends on what you mean by spoiling. I was luckier than a lot of kids. A stable home, concerned parents, never hungry, always well dressed. Yeah, I was spoiled in a different way."

"By helicopter parents?"

Her eyes widened. "What is that?"

"Parents who get involved in every aspect in a child's life, always there to dive in and straighten a crooked path, to defend a kid against any kind of trouble at all. Overly involved, I guess."

She appeared to think about that. "I don't know," she said finally. "I wouldn't say they were overprotective. On the other hand…" She shook her head. "I didn't have a whole lot of opportunity to get in trouble. Guess I just made up for that."

"Big-time," he said with a wink. "Seriously, Amber, we all make mistakes, some big, some small, but we all make them."

"This is a humdinger."

He hesitated. While he wasn't much for Pollyannas, he could sometimes be one. "Maybe someday it'll look like the best thing that could have happened. No guarantees, of course, but you might find that life with a child makes you very happy, and you might find another position that doesn't consume your entire life. Just spitballing here. I don't expect you to believe it."

She looked down at her twisting fingers. "I don't make mistakes. The first thing I have to learn to live with is that apparently I do make them. Then maybe I can move on."

He felt truly bad for her. There hadn't been a whole lot of time for her to adjust to anything and being used that way by the jackass at her firm was something that might leave bruises, if not scars, for a long time to come.

"And no talking to your father?"

"Not yet," she said, her head snapping up. "I can already write the lecture in my head. I don't need to hear it."

God, that was a statement, he thought. And it sure explained why she'd called him rather than her father. "I'm not saying you have to call."

He wished he had some clue how to help her with all this. He'd split up families in court, usually for damn good reasons, but it was usually painful for all involved, no matter how valid the reasons.

"I'm selfish," she blurted.

Surprised, he didn't answer, just waited. What in the world?

"I realized yesterday that I've been the center of the universe my entire life. My parents put me there, and I believed it. Anyway, yesterday it struck me that I had no business calling you, without a thought for what you might have going on in your life, and running straight to you for help. Then you mentioned your election coming up... I never thought of you, Wyatt."

"Yes, you did. You called me. Couldn't have paid me a higher compliment. So relax."

"How can I relax when your ex shows up at the door ready to start an old battle, one that doesn't affect me but could certainly hurt you? What happens if someone notices me going to the obstetrician? Someone will undoubtedly start speculating that you got me pregnant. None of this is going to help with your election!"

Well, the withdrawal was gone temporarily, but he didn't like this turn of events at all. "I don't care what people think."

"You have to," she said hotly. "You're a freaking judge!"

Wow. He tried to remember if he'd ever seen this much fire in Amber. No, he was sure he hadn't. Fear, nerves, humor...but never fiery. Always the good girl. Now this? He hated to admit it, but he rather liked it.

"It's okay, Amber."

"No, it's not okay. Most especially it's not okay that I dropped myself on you without a thought to the consequences to you. I need to leave as soon as possible."

"And go where?" he asked quietly.

She averted her face. Clearly she had no answer. And apparently he hadn't convinced her that she was truly welcome here. He wasn't worried about the election. However that went, he wasn't that involved. He liked being a judge, but he'd liked working as a lawyer, too. His whole life didn't hang on one thing.

But hers did now. She'd just given up everything, lost everything she had worked for. Maybe she thought a career change would be as troubling for him as hers was for her.

He was still trying to think of ways to reassure her when the doorbell rang. The sound struck him as poorly timed in the worst way. Amber needed something right now, and that wouldn't come from answering the door.

But before he could stir to go see who it was, he heard the door open. In an instant he knew who had arrived.

Just what they needed right now: his dad.

Chapter Six

"Do I smell chicken roasting?" Earl asked cheerfully as he entered the kitchen. At once his sharp dark eyes measured the situation.

Wyatt figured he and Amber looked pretty tense, and Earl wouldn't miss it. He tried to divert his father. "Are you inviting yourself to dinner?" It had happened a hundred times before, but not at a time like this. Earl knew he had company.

"Wouldn't miss it. Alma's gone to visit her sister. This must be your friend Amber."

Amber stared at him, clearly wondering who Earl was and why he had just walked in and invited himself to dinner.

"Amber, this is my father, Earl. Dad, my friend Amber."

"From law school, right?" Earl said, offering his hand. Amber shook it without speaking, merely offering a faint smile.

Earl pulled out a chair and sat, eyeing Amber. "You look a lot younger than I would have expected."

Wyatt wondered how to handle this. His dad was probing, and like a good lawyer he probably wouldn't stop his cross-examination until he was satisfied. "Amber started law school young, Dad. And I don't think she appreciates your inquisitor's tactics."

Earl twisted his head to look at his son. "She can stand it. She's a lawyer, too."

At that Amber made a muffled sound, but her face revealed nothing. Earl studied her for a few more seconds as he shrugged his jacket off and let it drape over the back of the chair. He paused a moment to smooth his gray hair, then he charged in again. "I'm surprised I didn't meet you before. For friends of long standing, you two sure haven't spent any time together."

Wyatt wanted to groan. He shouldn't have to explain anything, nor should Amber. "We kept in touch, Dad. Now drop it, please."

Amber spoke at last, surprising him by the firmness of her tone. Earl must have awakened the lawyer in her. "I was two years behind your son, Mr. Carter. He went his way when he graduated and I went mine, to St. Louis and then Chicago. Unfortunately, my work didn't leave me any time for visiting old friends or taking holidays."

"A good reason to avoid those big firms," Earl remarked. "But you'll probably be bored to death here." He twisted again to look at Wyatt. "What are you serving with the chicken?"

"I haven't fleshed out the menu yet."

"I like that boxed stuffing mix. Or how about yel-

low rice? I realize you won't get to show off by opening a box for your friend here, but it's good stuff."

That elicited a welcome laugh from Amber. Earl's
gaze settled on her again. "I heard you met Ellie today."

Amber's eyes widened. "You heard about that? She
was only here for a minute."

"Word gets around. Did Wyatt tell you about their
breakup? He should have told more people."

"Dad…" Wyatt was ready to throw up his hands.
He wished he could ask his father to leave before he
managed to upset Amber, but…well, it was his dad's
house, too.

"Only a bit," Amber said.

Wyatt spoke. "Don't encourage him, Amber."

"Why not?" she asked. "The woman came by, obviously with an agenda. Maybe I should know more
about it."

Earl fixed her with his gaze. "I could like you. Of
course she had an agenda. She's always had an agenda.
First it was to marry one of the most powerful men in
the county, one who owned one of the biggest houses
and had a social life with the movers and shakers…
if you can call them that around here. Big dreams,
that girl."

Wyatt sighed and gave up. He poured his father
some coffee and joined them at the table. "I'm a
slightly large frog in a very small pond, Dad. No more
important than anyone else."

"I'm glad your ego didn't grow," Earl said, "but the
simple fact is you're a judge. That's important, however small the pond." He turned back to Amber. "So
did he tell you Ellie wanted him to dismiss charges
against her cousin?"

Amber nodded.

"Well, of course he wouldn't do it. Not that he couldn't have, but Wyatt, I'm proud to say, has very strong principles and ethics. So of course he said no. And of course he realized that he'd almost gotten engaged to exactly the wrong kind of woman. Although she certainly claimed to have been his fiancée. The woman couldn't tell the truth if her life depended on it. Now while Wyatt probably wouldn't tell a soul this, *I* know how deeply hurt he was."

"Dad…"

"Let me continue. So Ellie sets about trying to sabotage him by telling everyone they broke up because he's gay. Wyatt doesn't care about that. But some folks do. Only time will tell how much damage that woman managed to do to him in some quarters. Now he's coming up for retention."

"I know," Amber said quietly. "I was saying just a little while ago that I need to leave so I don't cause any problems with that."

"Well, I was thinking the same thing," Earl said. "Before. But with Ellie in the mix…do Wyatt a favor, Amber. Stay."

Wyatt shook his head, wondering what kind of machination his father was up to. "My election prospects aren't Amber's problem, Dad."

"Maybe not, but if she's a friend, she'll care anyway. She can put any rumors to rest even if Ellie tries to wind it up again."

Wyatt clenched his teeth. His dad wouldn't let go of that, couldn't get it through his head that if people were going to choose a judge based on something as irrelevant as his social life, then he wasn't sure he wanted to be a judge any longer.

Amber spoke slowly. "I'm aware of the concern. But I don't want to be a new one."

Earl sighed. "How could a woman staying with my son be as big a problem as…"

Amber interrupted. "I'm pregnant. And not by Wyatt."

"Well, no one needs to know…"

"From what I gather about this town, some will when I see the obstetrician on Thursday."

Wyatt had the rare pleasure of seeing his father shut up.

"Anyway," Amber said, "just before you arrived, I was telling Wyatt that I should leave soon so I don't somehow become an issue in this election. Ellie said something about me being a cover story. Do you really think my mere presence here could change that perception in those who believe what Ellie said originally? And if people start to believe that he got me pregnant and we're not married, how does that help?"

"Damn it," said Wyatt, "this is the twenty-first century and I'm not going to be guided by Victorian rules. Period. What's more, Amber, you have no place to go from here yet. No plan. You were blindsided and I offered to help. To hell with everything else."

"That's my son," said Earl, smiling faintly. "Full steam ahead and damn the torpedoes."

"I wouldn't have imagined that," Amber replied. "He's so very thoughtful, contained, even tempered. He's full of good sense."

"Usually," Earl said with a significant look at his son. Wyatt was losing his usually even temper. "Dad, just stay out of this. Amber needs a friend. I'm her friend. I told you before that I'm not worried about the election. Period. So just leave it alone."

Amber looked at Earl. "From what I saw yesterday in court, he's a very good judge."

"Most folks seem to think so."

"Then what's the problem," Wyatt demanded.

"There's just so much you can thumb your nose at people."

"The people I'm thumbing my nose at will probably wind up in my courtroom sooner or later charged with something!"

"Ha," said Earl. "I was beginning to wonder if being a judge had deprived you of your passion." He turned back to Amber. "He hasn't been told yet, but he's getting the endorsement of the police association and the chamber hereabouts. And a few others. It's going to come out in the local paper and news in about ten days. Plenty of endorsements. But endorsements alone don't win an election. Then there's that group of religious fringe types run by old Loftis. They don't like you at all."

"A whole thirty of them," Wyatt said. "Can we change the subject, please? This is nothing for Amber to worry about."

"I'd like that yellow rice with the chicken," Earl said, then looked at Amber. "If you don't mind."

"It sounds good to me."

Wyatt seldom felt off balance, but his father and Amber had succeeded in making him feel that way. He was used to making his own decisions, choosing his own path, and now it seemed these two were conspiring. He supposed they thought they were helping, he certainly didn't think either of them wished him ill, but... Damn, it was *his* election. A lot about Conard County still resided in an earlier time, but that was part of the place's charm. He would rise or fall by it, and he accepted that.

The chicken began sizzling in the oven, adding more of its delicious aroma to the air. He glanced at the clock and decided it was going to be an early dinner. Which meant his father would be out of here soon after, before he did something to upset Amber.

He was very much afraid his father would, too. It wasn't that he was a hurtful man, but all these years of practicing law had taught him how to guard his tongue, as well as how to speak out when he believed it necessary. In protective father mode, he could be quite harsh.

"So," Earl said as Wyatt pulled out the rice cooker, "Wyatt says you were blindsided?"

Wyatt stiffened. *Why don't you poke a little harder, Dad? Maybe you can make her cry again.*

"Sort of," Amber said. "A married partner who said he was getting a divorce but wasn't. And an unexpected contraceptive failure."

Earl nodded. "Relax, son, I'm not here to hurt your friend."

Maybe not, Wyatt thought, placing the cooker on the island near an electrical outlet. Then again...

"Old story," Earl said. "If history were a record of men lying to women, it would be a thousand times as long."

Relief washed through Wyatt as he heard Amber laugh quietly. "You might be right, Earl."

"Course I am. Now, Wyatt, he's often right. I'm *always* right."

Another laugh. Then quietly, "Earl, I really don't want to cause him any trouble."

"You won't," Earl said decisively. "Made up my mind. You stay put and I'll get out ahead of the gossip. It can be done."

"I'm still here," Wyatt reminded his father acidly. Cripes, a person would have thought he was running for the presidency, not circuit judge.

Earl turned his head. "My gosh, you still are. Cook away, boy. I got a lady to get to know." Then he leaned toward Amber and said the last thing Wyatt wanted her to hear. "Never could figure out why Wyatt didn't date you in law school. He called me every weekend and we talked more about you than we did about his studies."

Wyatt wanted to sink as his dad turned to him. "Think I didn't remember, son? Of course I did. You were sweet on this lady." Then he looked at Amber. "Didn't you want to date him?"

Wyatt wanted to strangle his father. But Amber smiled faintly. "Very much, Earl," she answered. "But he thought I was too young for him."

"Funny," said Earl, "how that matters less as we get older. How much longer until dinner?"

Amber really liked Earl. She could easily see how he might annoy Wyatt no end sometimes, but he obviously loved his son. Coming from that place, he could be forgiven a great deal, not that he'd really done anything wrong yet. And she could see where Wyatt had gotten much of his remarkable personality. Not all of it, of course, but quite a bit of it.

She wished she'd had a father like Earl, so involved in protecting his child. Her own father had been rather distant and had measured her by her achievements. Earl, while pushing about this election, seemed to want only what was truly best for Wyatt.

Nor had she minded hearing that Earl thought Wyatt had been sweet on her all those years ago. Wyatt probably had, but it made Amber feel good.

During dinner, which was delicious, she asked, "Did you always want Wyatt to be a judge?"

"I wouldn't have cared if he wanted to do something besides the law, though I have to admit I often talked to him about joining my practice. But if that was my dream and not his, that was okay by me."

Wyatt spoke. "Then why are you so wound up about this election?"

"Because you enjoy it, son. You enjoy being a judge even more than you enjoyed practicing law. I see it in you. Hell, you might become a district judge eventually, if that's what you want. The point here is I'm not going to let that nasty woman ruin something you love. Period."

Then Earl surprised Wyatt by turning the conversation to the practice of law, comparing notes with Amber. Just two lawyers talking about their work, about the differences between small-town solo practice and working for large firms.

As they ate, Wyatt kept fairly quiet, watching something grow between Amber and Earl. Some kind of connection, although he wasn't sure what type. But Earl had always been good with people, Wyatt a little less so. As Earl had pointed out more than once, Wyatt could get stubborn when he shouldn't.

Wyatt acknowledged his own stubborn streak and tried to rein it in, but he was well aware that opposition stiffened him, even if he was wrong. Every time his dad tried to tell him he needed to worry about the election, he got his back up.

Idiot, he told himself. His dad was right—he did love being a judge. Losing the position wouldn't kill him, but it would disappoint him. Yet here he was, holding the line because he refused to bend about his personal life, because he honestly thought his personal life shouldn't decide how people voted for him as a judge.

Yet what could he do about it? He couldn't stop rumors if people wanted to believe them. But he also didn't want Amber being used in some way. Certainly not as the cover story that Ellie had suggested and which Earl now seemed to be seconding.

He couldn't say much about it right now, because Earl and Amber were deeply involved in their conversation about being lawyers. Amber appeared to be cheering up a bit, returning from wherever she had been when he came home. Irritated as he might be with his father's butting in, he was grateful that it helped Amber.

At last Earl seemed to have gotten what he wanted, and as usual skedaddled before the cleanup. That had always amused Wyatt. From the time his mother had passed, Earl had hired someone to do all the cooking and cleaning for him. Earl might do repairs around the house, but he had apparently maintained a very old-fashioned notion of gender roles.

Wyatt didn't mind, however. He enjoyed cooking, and cleaning was no bother. He had a crew in twice a month to do this monstrosity of a house from top to bottom simply because of the time involved, but he had no objection to doing any of the work himself. Least of all cleaning up after a meal.

Amber offered to help, and rather than make her feel like some kind of burden, he welcomed her. The job was a little more confusing because she didn't yet know her way around the kitchen, but it gave them an opportunity to talk about the most innocuous things, like how to put the remaining chicken away and did he want to save that little bit of yellow rice. Boring, safe stuff.

But then they were done and the long evening stretched ahead. Instead of leaving her to her own devices, he asked her if she wanted to join him in the office. He had some more work to do, prep for up-coming cases, motions to review. She accepted with alacrity, then asked if there was some way she could hook up her laptop.

Well, of course there was. He soon had her wired in and settled in a deep armchair with an ottoman. Ten minutes after he started reading the motions in front of him, he looked up to see that she had fallen asleep.

He was glad to see her resting, but it made him a bit uncomfortable, too. In the lamplight, he couldn't fail to notice that as attractive as she had been a decade ago, she had grown even more so.

She was a woman who would have caught his eye if she'd been a stranger. But she was no stranger. She was living under his roof, and he'd better submerge the impulses she was waking in him.

Sitting there while she slept, he could admit that he wanted her. Hell, he'd wanted her all those years ago but felt it would be taking advantage of her. Maybe at some level he'd never stopped wanting her.

So while his body responded, his mind put on the brakes. If he'd thought he would be taking advantage of her all those years ago, the current situation hadn't improved things. Not while she was so wounded and so dependent on him. It wouldn't be right.

He forced his attention back to the papers on his desk, but instead of seeing the motions, he could only see Amber.

In two short days, she seemed to have filled his life.

Amber awoke slowly, gradually becoming aware of her surroundings. She was still in Wyatt's office at the rear of the house. Lined in floor-to-ceiling bookshelves that held a lot of beautifully bound books, it was warmly lit. A heavy burgundy curtain covered the only window. His desk was large, made of mahogany, the computer on it looking out of place in a room that appeared to have come from a different era. A welcoming room.

Wyatt's face was illuminated by the glow of his computer screen. Her own computer had been removed from her lap and set on a table beside her, its screen black as it slept.

Wyatt, she thought sleepily, must be verifying the legal references in the motions he was reviewing. The light on his face flickered a bit as he changed pages.

She was curled up in the wing-back chair, quite comfortable, and staring at Wyatt felt pleasant. All those years ago, she'd had a crush on him, hardly admitted it even to herself. Then he'd left and they'd kept in touch only loosely as life had taken her down paths far from his. But she remembered those feelings now and felt their rebirth.

Her eyelids at half-mast, she watched him and wondered. What would it be like to rest her head on his shoulder and inhale his scents? What would it be like to feel his lips on hers, his hands exploring her secrets? A trickle of barely tamped desire began to grow into a river inside her.

Was she losing it? If so, she didn't care. He'd done not one thing to make her feel she was any more than a lost kitten he'd taken in, a stray. Kind, friendly, allowing her to make claims on a friendship from ages ago as if it had been only yesterday. Despite what Earl had said about Wyatt being sweet on her all those years ago, that didn't seem to be true now.

Earl's concerns floated back to her, and she decided that Wyatt might not be making the best decisions for himself. Yes, he'd come riding to her rescue. He'd always been a bit of a white knight in her experience, but he was putting an awful lot at risk. His ex-girlfriend apparently still harbored enough of a grudge that she wanted to hurt him, and what better way than by costing him an election?

Wyatt could dismiss those concerns, but Amber discovered she couldn't. She had dealt with enough clients to know that taking the high road wasn't always the best solution. In fact, those who were willing to sink to the lowest level often took advantage of those who refused to.

Was he really that unconcerned?

She stirred and discovered that he'd draped a dark blue throw over her legs to keep her warm. He looked up.

"Sleep well?" he asked.

The words popped out without warning. "We should get engaged."

Under other circumstances she might have enjoyed seeing Wyatt flummoxed. After all, he was always so controlled and in charge of himself. But she heard her own words on the silent air, took in his expression and wondered what devil had possessed her.

"Sheesh," she said.

The stunned expression on his face began to slip into amusement. "I hope it was a nice dream."

For some reason that irritated her. "I wasn't dreaming about you," she said sharply. Or had she been? Any dream had vanished like a wisp of smoke, whatever it had been. But certainly those words had popped out of her as if they had begun somewhere earlier.

They *had* begun earlier. With his father. With the feeling she might cost him something very important by staying with him as a friend, especially if people saw her going to the obstetrician. Maybe Earl *could* get out in front of it, explain that she had left a broken relationship in Chicago and was indeed just visiting for a short while. But how would that help stop the viciousness that Ellie was spreading? While she agreed with Wyatt that it shouldn't matter to people, she knew that in the real world such things *did* matter.

"Did Earl get to you?" he asked finally.

"I guess he did."

"Don't let him."

"Actually," she said, stiffening her spine, "I thought your father made some good points. I saw you in the courtroom. You're a good judge, Wyatt. Very good. People here are lucky to have a judge like you, and you love it. So it just seemed to me that since I'm going to be here awhile, we could get engaged, turn the gossip around and then break up eventually. It's not a big deal for me."

He was silent for a while, steepling his fingers and sitting back in his chair. "I don't like pretense," he said finally. "I appreciate your generosity, but..." He shook his head.

All of a sudden she felt scalded by shame. Maybe she was, in a different way, no better than Ellie. Proposing to live a lie? Of course he would object. "I'm sorry. I know you better than that."

"I'm sure you do," he said quietly. "You weren't fully awake, and my father is probably responsible for your thoughts running in that direction. He was sure trying."

She wished she could hide her face, but she had more backbone than that. "Was he?"

"In an indirect way, yes. It's okay, Amber. You're just trying to help, and he was busy planting ideas that you could. He can be subtle, sometimes, but never say he doesn't understand the human psyche. With a different upbringing he'd probably have been a great con man."

She gasped. "That's how you see your father?"

He laughed quietly. "No, but I've had a lot of years to get to know him. He'd never con anyone. But he does know how to, um, get people moving in a direction he wants. Not exactly manipulative. Sometimes I think he doesn't even know he's doing it. It just comes naturally."

"It'd be a useful skill with a jury," she admitted.

"Well, that's what we lawyers try to do in a trial. Make a jury see the case favorably for our clients.

Nothing wrong with that. The other side is working just as hard to make everything look bad for us. So Earl is good at what he does."

"Well, I'm still sorry. I hope I didn't offend you."

He smiled. "I was more worried about trying to find a way to say no that wouldn't offend *you*. I know you well enough to be reasonably certain you weren't thinking of your offer in the way I took it."

"No," she admitted, looking down and picking at the blanket over her legs. "Not for a second did I see it as a lie, though obviously it would have been. So I guess you were right when you said I wasn't fully awake."

"How *did* you see it?"

Her blush returned. "Well, the part about being engaged to you sounded pretty good. The part about breaking it off didn't sound good at all."

A hearty laugh escaped him. "Thanks for the honesty. I wouldn't mind being engaged to you, either. If it were real. So there we are."

Yes, there they were, Amber thought. He turned back to his work, and she reached for her laptop to find something to get her mind to a safe harbor.

Because it was true she wouldn't mind being engaged to him. She thought she'd like it a whole lot. But there was just one little obstacle to that kind of happiness: another man's baby.

After that little scene, Wyatt could no longer concentrate on the legal motions in front of him. He'd had trouble earlier because he was responding to her as a man, and that kind of sexual response was always distracting. People distracted by those urges got themselves into a pickle sometimes, as he saw so often in family court.

But they were still distracting, he still kept feeling a desire to make love with her, and...her suggestion of an engagement had acted like a match in tinder. The man who sat on a bench wearing an impressive robe and looking down at a courtroom full of people while dispensing justice was still just an ordinary man with ordinary needs.

From the moment he had welcomed her to his home with a hug, he'd been uneasily aware that this situation was going to be difficult. In some ways they didn't know each other very well even after all these years. In others...well, the passion he'd never allowed to blossom with her was still there, like a seedling that had just poked its head up to the sun. It wanted to grow and spread.

He didn't believe in pretense, but the idea of trying out an engagement with her didn't repel him. The trying out was different and could be accomplished by that famous old ritual called dating.

Amused by the direction of his thoughts and the constant background hum of desire in his body, he glanced up to see Amber studiously staring at her computer. He'd made her uncomfortable, and while he'd tried to smooth it over for her, he was sure she was still wondering what had possessed her. Experienced lawyers rarely just blurted things.

And while he'd blamed it on his dad in order to make her less embarrassed, the truth was Earl hadn't in even the slightest way suggested a pretend engagement. He thought Amber should hang around, not leave, said he was going to get out in front of the gos-

sip, but Wyatt knew his dad well enough to be sure
the man wouldn't lie. As for mentioning to Amber that
Wyatt had been sweet on her all those years ago…
Well, Wyatt honestly believed Earl hadn't had an ulterior motive. It was probably his father's attempt to
make Amber feel comfortable about staying.

Which was the other thing about Earl. Wyatt didn't
really see him as capable of conning anyone, but he
had a good instinct for saying things in a way that
would lead others in the direction he wanted.

Still, he hadn't tried to manipulate anyone today.
In fact, it was kind of interesting to see where Amber's mind had taken their before-dinner discussion.
Evidently she felt a need to act, not just sit back and
let matters take their own course.

He forced his gaze back to the motions in front of
him. He wasn't going to take advantage of Amber. She
was down on her luck and in an awful situation. Nor
was he going to let anyone else use her.

He believed his father truly understood that. And
if Ellie tried to drag Amber into her gossip war, she
was going to be one sorry woman.

Chapter Seven

Amber's appointment with the obstetrician was at four in the afternoon that Thursday. To her surprise, Wyatt wanted to go with her.

"But…that might cause even more talk!"

He arched a brow at her. "So? You're staying with me. And if she has any special directions about diet and so on, maybe I need to hear it."

She threw up a hand, feeling at once frustrated and touched. "You'll drive me mad, Wyatt. Women do this on their own all the time."

"I know, and I'm quite sure you can do it all by yourself. But you don't need to while you're staying with me, and I'd really appreciate it if you'd let me in."

"Let you in?" Confused, she stared at him. They were standing by the front door, ready to go out, and things had just taken a strange turn.

"You're going to have a baby. I get that single mothers succeed all the time. Women are strong. I've seen it, I've heard the arguments and... I'm still feeling a responsibility toward you and this child."

She felt her jaw drop. "To the child? This baby isn't even yours!"

"I know. But that doesn't mean I can't take an interest its father won't take. Or that I don't feel a responsibility toward it."

"God, do you feel responsible for everything?"

One corner of his mouth lifted. "Only for those things I can do something about."

Realizing that if she climbed into her own car and drove off by herself he'd probably just follow her—this wasn't the first time she'd seen signs that he could be stubborn—she gave in. As he drove her to the office, she even had to admit there was a tiny bit of comfort in his caring enough to do this.

Her future yawned in front of her like a huge gulf that held nothing. She was having trouble imagining that in about seven months there'd be a baby in her life. She was getting closer to it, but it still seemed...like someone else's dream. Maybe this visit today would make it feel more real.

Regardless, she decided as they wound along the autumn streets of Conard City, it was nice to have Wyatt with her. She wasn't alone. He'd made it clear that she didn't *have* to be alone, even though this mess was mostly her responsibility.

And in his usual way he was going right ahead and involving himself. The way he had when they'd first met at the law school. He'd only talked to her for a few minutes before he was volunteering to help her with her studies in any way she needed. And far better than the other guys who'd approached her trying to wangle her phone number or suggest they meet, Wyatt had simply given her his own name and phone number. No pressure. *You need some help, call me.*

He'd meant it, too. The first time they'd met for a study session had been in the library. After that they'd sometimes met at other places, growing from tutor and student to friends until it finally hadn't seemed at all out of place to occasionally do something else together.

She'd always felt safe with him, certain that he didn't have some ulterior motive. And then he'd graduated and left for the navy. Only in his absence did she realize how much care he'd taken of her.

Now he was doing it again. She smiled faintly as she looked out the car window, forgetting all her troubles for a few minutes. Wyatt. He'd always been remarkable.

Too bad he'd never acted on his interest in her back then. Too bad he wasn't acting now.

Or maybe she was sending all the wrong signals to him. Maybe she always had.

Then she drew herself up short. How many more problems did she need to add to her life? She'd already done a pretty effective job of hashing it up. Why ruin a perfectly good relationship?

The doctors' office was in a small medical center right near the community hospital.

"This is it," Wyatt said. "Pretty good care from such a small institution."

She hesitated before getting out of the car. "I want to see the doctor by myself."

"You don't think I'd follow you into the exam room, do you? But if there are any instructions…"

She interrupted, giving in. "I get it. You can talk to her after."

"Thank you."

She glanced at him, wondering if he was being sarcastic, but his expression appeared sincere. Well, he *had* pushed himself into the middle of this, and Wyatt wasn't an insensitive dolt. She'd protested, he'd pressed, and he was surely aware that the doctor didn't have to tell him one thing…and wouldn't without her permission.

She had to admit, however, it felt a whole lot better to walk into that office with him at her side. She was nervous about this, although she couldn't exactly say why. She'd had pelvic exams before. This wouldn't be much different.

And yet it was, but she couldn't put her finger on why.

Apparently he sensed her discomfort, because he surprised her by taking her hand and giving it a gentle squeeze before she walked up to the counter to check in. Then he sat in one of the waiting room chairs, and by the time she finished at the counter, he was in conversation with a young woman near her age.

"Amber, this is Julie Archer. She's having her first, too."

Julie had a warm smile and beautiful auburn hair. "Nice to meet you, Amber. Wyatt says you're an old friend of his. I thought I'd meet you Saturday night, but this is a pleasant surprise. How long will you be in town?"

"I'm not sure," Amber answered honestly. "I'm between jobs, and Wyatt's being very generous."

At that moment, a door to the side of reception opened. "Julie? Doctor's ready for you."

Julie smiled warmly at Amber. "I'm sure we'll talk more."

"I hope so." Then someone else in scrubs appeared to give Amber a clipboard full of questions to fill out. Medical history. But as she stared at it, she remembered what Julie had said. "Why would I meet her Saturday night?" she asked.

"I'm having a few friends over, remember? You don't have to attend."

But clearly he'd mentioned Amber. Dang, she thought as she tried to focus on the questionnaire. Was she going to be a bug under a microscope?

"Just a few friends," he said again. "I think you'll like them, and if you stay awhile you won't feel as much like the stranger in a strange land."

She doubted that. Since Tom, there wasn't a day when she didn't feel like a stranger to everything she'd known.

Except Wyatt. After the first brief awkwardness caused by such limited communication over the years, she felt the decade had just slipped away, that she knew him at least as well as she had way back in law school.

Weird. Then she turned her attention to answering all the questions.

The wait for Amber wasn't terribly long, maybe forty-five minutes, but Wyatt had to admit he was a little impatient. Racing around the edges of his thoughts was concern for this child of Amber's. To never know its father? And what about Amber? Sure, women could do this alone. They did all the time, but wouldn't it be easier to have a helpmate, someone to share the burdens? And better yet, the joys.

He'd been looking forward to starting a family as he'd grown more serious with Ellie. Now he'd had one dumped on his doorstep, an old friend he cared about. He hoped he could find a way to persuade Amber to let him be a continuing part of her life and the baby's.

Odd feelings to be having, but it was as if Amber's situation had opened up a surprising place in him. He'd been telling himself he was content and fortunate, and when Ellie had hurt him so deeply, he'd decided it was better to forge ahead alone than to take that risk again. Especially since he could be a bad judge of a woman's character.

Amber's situation should have convinced him he was right. Trusting another person so much, letting them inside so far, only to have them rip out your heart, seemed like a stupid risk to take.

Yet here he was, forming an attachment that could be equally risky. He felt as if the years were slipping away, but he was well aware that Amber couldn't be the young girl he remembered any longer. The years and experience changed people. That should be warning enough, but there was more.

She would be here only temporarily. She had a thirst to do the bigger things in life, hence her decision to go with a large law firm. She clearly wouldn't find enough to stimulate her in a one-horse town like this.

But, damn, he wanted her. The need was growing

with each passing day, and the fact that she was pregnant wasn't stopping it. He supposed he should feel
guilty, considering what she was going through and
what she still faced. She needed his support and his
understanding, not his desire. Hell, she probably felt
worse about romantic relationships than he did.

Another woman he vaguely knew arrived for her
appointment. He was acutely aware that she did a double take at seeing him here, then smiled and nodded.

And thus began the gossip. He wondered what
they'd be saying by tomorrow. Then the receptionist
called him. "Judge? You can go back now. First door
on the right."

He didn't have to look at the woman—what was her
name? He ought to know it—to realize that had sealed
the deal. Rockets would be going up in a town where
gossip was the only free entertainment. He hoped they
enjoyed it.

Setting a smile on his face, he marched through the
door and into the office as directed. Dr. Joy Castor sat
on the far side of the desk and Amber was seated in
one of the two chairs in front of it.

Joy smiled at him. "Hey, Wyatt. Amber tells me
you're a buttinsky friend."

"I just want to make sure I do everything right
while she's visiting me."

"There speaks a man who's never experienced this
before." Joy winked. "Okay, as I told Amber, pregnancy is usually a very healthy, uncomplicated process.
A few dos, a few don'ts, unless problems develop, and
at this point I don't see anything to worry about. Early
days yet, so she should be coming in once a month
for the next few months unless she notices a problem

of some kind. I gave her a list, so I'm not going to re-cite it."

"Fair enough," Wyatt agreed as relief swept through him.

"Your job," Joy continued, "will be to make sure she takes a walk every day for at least a half hour. Other than that, pamper her all you want." Joy gave a little laugh. "Pampering is a great thing."

When they walked out of the office, the woman who had been there earlier had vanished and no one else was waiting. Wyatt stood by while Amber paid the bill, even though he would have liked to pay it himself.

However, he had a feeling he might have encroached enough for one day. She hadn't even wanted him to come this far.

He stopped by the diner on the way home. "I didn't start dinner," he said. "Want to dine in or should I get takeout?"

She leaned her head back and he saw that she looked tired. "Amber? Are you all right?"

She turned her head, smiling faintly. "I guess I was more uptight about this visit than I realized. I feel drained."

"So eat at home?"

"Please."

It was only Thursday, such a short time since her arrival on Sunday, but she already felt as if she were coming home as she entered Wyatt's house. The min-ute the door closed behind her, she felt cocooned in warmth and safety. Wyatt had always made her feel safe, and she guessed that sense extended to his home.

She *was* tired, though. Hanging her jacket on the coat tree, she followed Wyatt into the kitchen.

"We can eat in here," he said as he began to empty items onto the island, "or I can make you comfy on the living room sofa with a tray table. Your choice."

"The couch might put me to sleep right now, and frankly, I'm more hungry than tired." Barely. She hoped the food would increase her energy level. When he waved her into a chair, she took it and let herself sag a bit. God, she must really have been on pins and needles about this doctor visit. Usually only a trial or a truly difficult client left her feeling this drained. And she'd hardly done a thing today.

Wyatt didn't leave the food in the containers. Instead he scooped just about everything into serving bowls and plates, then invited her to help herself to anything that appealed.

She eyed the amount of food. "You expecting an army?"

He laughed. "No, but leftovers are good, usually, and I didn't bother to ask what you'd like. So a little of everything."

"That sandwich doesn't look *little*," she said.

"No, it's pretty big, but I cut it in half." He poured her a glass of milk and a water for himself, then sat facing her.

"So, okay, what didn't the doc tell me?" he asked as he took half of that huge sandwich. She reached for the salad. Those greens and tomatoes were calling to her like a siren's song.

"Nothing, really," she said. "Life will continue pretty much as normal for a while. Don't wear anything that binds my waist, no more than two cups of coffee a day, take my prenatal vitamins."

"And the morning sickness?"

"I should just avoid any foods that don't appeal to me and otherwise keep crackers beside the bed."

He nodded. "I'll see to it."

She smiled. "It's nothing to worry about unless it gets really bad. So here I am, extremely healthy, and maybe I should try to focus on what I need to do next."

Holding the sandwich in his hand, he raised his gaze to her. "There's no rush, Amber. Let me be perfectly clear about that. You're not putting me out in the least, and I'm actually enjoying getting to know you again. So please, don't feel like you have to rush for any reason. Take your time."

Amber nodded, suddenly unable to speak as her throat tightened. Oh, no, was she going to weep again? Moving between utter numbness and tears was hard to take, swinging back and forth as if she had no control of her emotions. Maybe she didn't. Maybe she was out of control. Maybe it was the pregnancy. Damn, why hadn't she thought to ask the doctor about that?

But Wyatt's generosity had touched her to her very core. She tried to remember the last time anyone had wanted to take care of her without asking anything in return, and she couldn't. Her life had been too work driven, but even her one folly with a man had never made her feel as cared for as Wyatt just had.

"Amber?"

She hardly dared look at him, for fear that he would read her. A lawyer learned to be inscrutable in a courtroom, but she couldn't seem to manage that with Wyatt.

"Do you need to cry?"

"I don't want to," she said thickly.

"Let it out. I'm not scared of it, and if it helps, do it. You've been to hell and back, and all in a short time."

Her voice remained thick. "I haven't been to hell. People have worse than this happen to them." She speared a cherry tomato and popped it into her mouth, forcing herself to chew.

"Hell is relative," he said. "I like to say people have troubles, and it's kind of pointless to argue which is heavier, fifty pounds of rocks or fifty pounds of sand. Sure we could find someone who has it worse, but you've been lied to and betrayed, you had to give up your job and with it a chunk of the future you had planned, and you're unexpectedly on your way to becoming a mother. If none of that feels particularly good right now, I sure won't blame you. Big, little, who's to say. Fact is, your plate is full."

"I should be happy about the baby."

"Eventually."

She dared to look at him finally. "You don't think I'm awful?"

"No. Give yourself time. You've had a lot of shocks."

"You're kind," she murmured.

"Just honest."

She shook her head. "I'm so used to being in control, Wyatt. And I'm ashamed that when things went out of my control I couldn't handle it. I'm still not handling it. I seem to be on some kind of emotional roller coaster with no idea where I'm going, no idea why this is happening, no idea what to do about it. I don't like being helpless!"

He pushed a plate her way. "Hummus and crackers.

Unless I'm mistaken, carbs are good for your stomach right now. Don't just rely on salad. You might feel sick again. And you're far from helpless."

She swallowed hard, then decided he was right. Inviting as the salad had looked to her, the tomato didn't seem to be settling well. She reached for a cracker and spread some hummus on it. "How can you say I'm far from helpless? I've landed here and I'm taking advantage of your generosity. That's a long way from independent."

"You're not taking advantage of me at all. As for independence… Amber, none of us is truly independent. Sooner or later we need someone's help. How very nice it is to have friends. Life would be awful without them."

After dinner, he told her to go take a nap, anywhere she felt comfortable. She didn't argue. Weariness was weighing her down the way numbness had before. It *was* a roller coaster.

She went upstairs and changed into comfortable yoga pants and an oversize sweatshirt. She thought about stretching out on the bed, but it felt so far away. From what she didn't know, but she didn't want the privacy of this room right now.

Heading back downstairs, she heard Wyatt cleaning up in the kitchen. Part of her wanted to join him, but she was just too tired. She wandered into the living room, outfitted with overstuffed furniture in burgundies and blues, a large room that looked like it might have emerged from the set of a period piece. Smiling faintly, she guessed no one had changed this room in a very long time. It was probably almost ready to be roped off like a display in a museum.

How odd, she thought as she curled up on the sofa beneath a knitted afghan. She never would have imagined Wyatt living in a place like this.

A throw pillow cradled her head and she closed her eyes. Set free, her mind started to wander. What if she hadn't become pregnant?

Well, she wouldn't be here, that was for sure. She'd still be at the firm, ignoring the occasional stares until everyone else became bored.

But as sleep crept up on her, she decided she was very glad she was here. She felt comfortable with Wyatt. Felt as if she mattered.

And she wished he were holding her right now.

When she awoke, the only light in the room trickled in from the foyer beyond. Wyatt must have turned off the lamp in here.

She felt ever so much better, she realized as she sat up. As the throw tumbled from her shoulders, she discovered the room was a bit cool, despite what she was wearing. Wrapping the afghan around her, she rose and went to discover if it was the middle of the night or if Wyatt was still up.

Standing in the foyer, she at last picked out the sound of tapping keys from his office. From the kitchen, the refrigerator suddenly kicked on, humming. At night, in this big house, sounds seemed louder, more noticeable.

Well, she could head up to bed, but she wanted to be with Wyatt. She made her way down the hall to his office and found the door wide-open. He was intensely absorbed in reading on his computer, and as she looked she recognized the distinctive layout of an online law library.

After a moment's hesitation—because she didn't know if she should disturb him—she knocked lightly on the door frame.

Immediately he swung his chair around and smiled. "Feel better?"

"Much. Am I bothering you?"

He shook his head and motioned her to the arm-chair. "I was just catching up on my reading. Current federal Supreme Court filings. Some recent cases in this state."

"Trying to keep up can be almost a full-time job."

"Not unless you want to read every word. Mostly I just want to know what's out there so I can look it up when I need to." He gave a quiet laugh. "Then there are the times when I get intrigued and become too deeply involved in reading the facts of the cases."

"Some of them are fascinating."

"Some of them are head-scratchers. How many times have you asked yourself, *How in the heck did they manage to fall into this tangle?*"

"Truthfully? Rarely. Because I was mostly dealing with corporate clients, and their motivations were as clear as the contracts they weren't written in."

He laughed again, more heartily. "Remember Professor Jagger?" He lifted his voice to a higher tone. "'Most lawyers would be out of work if people were just honest.'"

Amber laughed with him. "So true. I certainly would have been, since I mostly dealt with contract disputes."

"Did you enjoy it?"

She thought about it. "I'm not sure," she said finally. "I didn't think about it, I just did my job. But sometimes…well, sometimes I'd get annoyed when I looked at deliberately fuzzy language and wondered how someone had gotten away with it. I mean, it's the job of people like me to make contracts clear, to avoid leaving wiggle room."

"So you came in on cases once the wiggle had showed up?"

"Sometimes. Then there were the contracts where the language was totally clear but expectations weren't." She shrugged. "Sometimes I had to remind myself that misunderstandings happen, and not all of them are malicious."

"Did you ever do estate law?"

"No. I hear when there's money involved, people can get really nasty, though."

He nodded. "So now you could move on to a different kind of law. Would you? You're as free as a bird to make a big change."

"Not quite free," she answered, her hand drifting toward her tummy. A baby. Little by little the child within her was becoming real, part of more and more of her thoughts. "Wyatt? Did you ever want kids?"

"I sure did. And do. I happen to like them. Especially before the world erases the wonder from them." His eyes crinkled at the corners. "Especially before they wind up explaining to me why they thought boosting a car for a joyride was a good idea, or why they couldn't resist drag racing down a public street."

She laughed again.

"You didn't eat much at dinner," he said, rising. "Let's get something in your tummy while you're feeling good."

Surprising her, he crossed to stand in front of her

and held out his hand. Gripping the throw with one hand, she reached out with her other and slipped it into his. At once she was overwhelmed by his warmth, the feeling of his skin against hers.

As they walked toward the kitchen, she realized she felt happy. Excited. Walking down the hall holding hands with this man made her feel good in a way she had seldom felt. Like her law school graduation day. Like when she got her first job with a big firm. Like the few times in her life when she'd felt her dreams were coming true.

"You seem to be feeling a whole lot better," he remarked.

"*Giddy* might be a better word." It was true, she thought as she entered the kitchen with him. Roller coaster indeed. Let the giddiness reign. It was like being on a first date with a guy she'd been crazy about forever, and she didn't want to quell the emotion.

"Why?" he asked.

She glanced at him in the bright overhead light, and all of a sudden the air went out of the room. He had a smile on his face, but his dark eyes seemed to reflect fire. Her heart skipped beats, and longing poured through her, happiness giving way to an almost painful hope and anticipation.

His voice became quiet. "Don't look at me like that. I might not be able to resist. Anyway, you need to eat something."

She fought to draw a breath. "No," she whispered. "Not now."

"What not now?"

"No food. Just you."

"God, Amber," he muttered. Then he lifted his hand

to cup her cheek, to run his thumb over her cheekbone. "You're driving me crazy. I'm not supposed to feel like this."

"Why not?" she murmured, her whole body coming alive.

"Because you're in my care."

"To heck with that. Wyatt... I always wanted..."

He didn't let her speak another word. Bending his head, he brushed his lips lightly against hers, as if testing. At first she felt as if she were melting, a calm warmth flooding her. Then a quiver ran through her, and flames leaped along her nerve endings. All from that simple, tentative touch. She let the throw slide to the floor as her body heated.

Then his mouth brushed hers again. A soft moan escaped her and he returned for a deeper kiss, one that took possession of her mouth the way she wanted him to take possession of her entire body.

Yes, she'd wanted this all the way back when she'd been fresh to law school and he'd decided to help her along. All the time he'd avoided becoming more than her friend. All the time she had never dated the men closer to her age because Wyatt was all she wanted.

Time had passed, they were both different people, but the hunger in her had apparently never died. She had to know. Even if only once, she needed Wyatt's loving. It was a question that had been begging for an answer for more than a decade.

Her limbs began to turn syrupy. As if he sensed it, he slid an arm around her waist, but even as she reached up for more of his embrace, he broke the kiss gently and stepped back, holding her loosely.

"Wyatt?" she breathed.

"Not now," he answered. "Not now."

She opened her eyes and could have sworn she saw her desire reflected on his face, in his now heavily lidded eyes.

"You're vulnerable," he said simply. "Too vulnerable. So…"

So. She got it. She understood it, even. But that didn't mean she liked it. Somehow she was seated at the table and he was placing food in front of her, as if that would answer any of her cravings.

"It would be nice," she said eventually, "if you would tell me what just happened."

"You know," he answered. "We kissed. It's early days and you aren't in any way settled. I don't want you to ever feel I took advantage of you."

He was right and she knew it. She had admitted that she was riding a roller coaster right now. But understanding didn't diminish her huge disappointment. Saddened, she picked up the throw and draped it over the back of a chair.

Wyatt laid out leftovers that he thought might appeal to her, judging by her choices at other meals. She didn't seem inclined toward anything spicy, so he put out the potato salad, a couple of rolls that hadn't had time to go stale and some jelly and butter.

She reached immediately for a roll and spread it lightly with butter.

He could read the disappointment on her face, and he definitely shared it. He'd known a powerful moment when he'd kissed her, a need that had roared to life with an intensity that had taken him by surprise. Yeah, he knew he was attracted to her, knew he had to keep pushing aside sexual thoughts about her, but he'd kissed other women without responding that fast and hard.

Wow.

So yes, he was disappointed, too. But she wasn't through the worst of her reaction to all that had happened, as had been evidenced by the way her moods were swinging. He didn't want to make love to her in a moment of weakness only to add to her problems. Nor would he like himself very much if he did.

She ate half the roll and drank some milk. Pushing her plate aside, she said, "I'll settle down."

"I know you will," he answered.

She looked up and gave him an impish smile he hadn't seen since law school. "Then?"

"Then we'll see if we both still feel the same way."

"Good. Because I realized it hasn't changed in a decade."

His brows lifted.

"Really, Wyatt, did you think I was immune to you all those years ago? But despite what your father said about you being sweet on me back then, the off-limits signs were easy to read, even for me."

He studied her a moment, then laughed. "They were up to protect you."

"You've got to stop feeling like you have to protect everyone," she said. "Maybe I was too young ten years ago, I don't know. But I'm not too young now. Did you *really* want me back then?"

"Do you think I was a robot? Of course I wanted you. But you seemed like such a lost lamb at first, and I was so much older. I would have been a cradle robber."

"Not quite." She drew a long breath. "Just grant me one thing."

"What's that?"

"Admit that messed up or not, I'm an adult now. I'm entitled to my mistakes. God knows, I've made enough of them. Sheltering me doesn't protect me, it only leaves me more vulnerable because I lack experience."

"Meaning?"

"Meaning I might have had the sense to realize that Tom could have been lying. It's such an old lie, a man saying he's in the process of a divorce. Meaning that I should have had the experience to know that someone who could only meet me at lunch hour was probably leading me on and hiding me. There should have been red flags waving over that entire situation. Now that it's happened, I won't be so trusting in future. I've learned a painful but necessary lesson."

He leaned back in his chair, studying her thoughtfully. "You're right. But I can't take credit for sheltering you except that year in law school. And frankly, Amber, you were wide-open to every wolf who sniffed around, but you were totally focused on your studies. I may have been posted off-limits in your view, but you were pretty much swamped in a desire to succeed."

Her gaze wavered, then dropped. "You're right," she admitted. "I noticed you, but I didn't notice anyone else. And with the way I'd been raised, and my parents practically breathing over my shoulder with their expectations, I didn't leave much room to learn about life. It wasn't much better once I started practicing. Those big firms consume your life, especially at the lower levels."

"Don't take all the blame on yourself, though. Plenty of women have been misled by unscrupulous men like Tom. However, I would never advise you to stop trusting people, because most people are trustworthy. Unfortunately, that leaves you open to the creeps."

She nodded. "But…well…as a lawyer you often get to see the darker side of human nature. I failed to extrapolate."

He couldn't argue with that, but given that she'd been mostly involved in contracts law, she'd gotten a different view than if she'd handled divorces, trusts and estates.

On the other hand, his experience with family law and all its ugliness hadn't kept him from falling into Ellie's clutches.

He snorted, drawing her attention back to him.

"What?" she asked.

"I don't think there's any armor or knowledge that can prevent any of us from being fools at times. I almost married Ellie. I look back and wonder how I could have been so blind. Or she so deceptive." He shrugged. "Life is one big, long lesson. All I want for you is to get your feet under you again."

She'd been in his house for four days. During that time he'd seen her moods swing wildly. Hardly surprising with all that she had to absorb. He didn't remember her emotions bouncing around like this, so he didn't think it was her usual state. No, this resulted from too many shocks too quickly.

"I'm very attracted to you," he told her. "I want to get to know you a whole lot better. But I also want to see you comfortable in your own skin again. Fair enough?"

She nodded slowly. "I'm trying to get there."

"Just a bit at a time," he said. "You've got a lot to deal with, and it's not all going away overnight."

Chapter Eight

Morning sickness kept Amber at home the next morning. Wyatt had family court, and she'd wanted to see him in action, but not even crackers would settle her stomach enough to make her feel safe about going out.

Regretfully, she watched him drive off, then ran to the bathroom again, fearing the crackers were about to be lost. She sat on the stool in the powder room while cold sweat beaded her brow and her stomach churned, but she held her food down and eventually felt well enough to head for the kitchen and think about eating a few more crackers.

By lunchtime, just before she expected to see Wyatt's return, the doorbell rang. He hadn't said anyone might be stopping by, but she hesitated only a moment before going to answer it. He might be expecting a delivery.

She opened the heavy door with its stained-glass inset to see two very drab-looking women standing there. She blinked, wondering if they'd stepped out of a black-and-white movie—there wasn't a hint of color about them, their hair drawn severely back under old-fashioned hats with net that covered the tops of their faces. Their coats were just as drab, gray wool, fully buttoned up. Their dresses reached well below their knees and their feet were shod in sensible black oxfords. They might have come from another era.

"May I help you?" she asked.

"We're here to help *you*," said the older of the two women, her face stern.

"I'm sorry, but I don't need help."

"You do," said the older woman, stabbing her finger at Amber. "Living in sin with Judge Carter, not even married and carrying his child!"

"It's not his..." Amber began, her first impulse to protect Wyatt, even as a sense of unreality began to overtake her. Surely she had become unmoored in time.

"Lying, too," remarked the younger woman. "But it's not too late. Come with us. We'll help you find your way again."

Amber didn't care if she was rude. She closed the door in their faces.

What in the world?

Heavens, that had left her shaking. Unreal. Not like her to be so slow to react, but she soon forgot her nausea and trembling as anger replaced her initial reaction. Was that what they were saying about Wyatt around here?

She needed to leave. Now. He had that election com-

ing up and if people were talking this way... The urge
to run was almost overwhelming. She didn't want to
harm Wyatt, no matter how unconcerned he'd seemed
about it. Living in sin? She supposed some people still
thought that way, but how many of them were around
here, and how could that affect Wyatt?

He'd been kind enough to take her in, now she had
to be kind enough to leave. It didn't matter where she
went. The only thing that mattered was that she not
mess up his life as well.

She had her foot on the bottom stair, prepared to
pack and leave quickly, when she heard another knock
on the door. If it was those women again, she was
going to give them a piece of her mind. Her chin set
with determination, the surprise that had kept her from
responding before now gone, she marched back to the
door and flung it open, ready to do battle.

It was Earl. "I see Wyatt's not home yet," he said
cheerfully. "Mind if I come in, Amber?"

Her anger deflated instantly, and she felt her stomach roll over again. "Not at all." She tried to smile.

After he crossed the threshold and closed the door,
he peered at her. "What's wrong?"

Like his son, he seemed to miss little.

"I had some visitors. They weren't very pleasant."
She could talk to Earl, she realized. She knew he
would be concerned about Wyatt's position as judge.
He'd already offered to get out in front of rumors. Yes,
she had to tell him.

"I didn't make coffee," she said frankly. "Too nauseated."

"I'm not surprised. My Beth had the morning sickness something bad. Well, come on, I can do with a beer as well as coffee."

He urged her into the kitchen and made her sit at the table. "Maybe not beer," he said, eyeing her face. "Might not smell good to you right now. Can you eat anything?"

"I was considering more crackers."

So Earl brought her the box of crackers and a plate and started a pot of coffee going. She liked him, just as she liked his son.

"So tell me about it," he said as he joined her at the table. "It must have upset you."

"Mostly for Wyatt's sake. These two women in very drab clothes…"

"Say no more," Earl interrupted. "I know them. I know the whole lot of them. Followers of Fred Loftis, who unfortunately owns our only pharmacy or I suspect he and his would have been ridden out of town a long while ago. Anyway, you don't need to worry about them. I'll see that they don't bother you again."

"I'm not worried about *me*," she said vehemently. "It was what they implied. I don't want to cost Wyatt his retention."

Earl sighed, rose and went to get a cup of coffee for himself. "Are you thirsty?"

"Water, please."

He brought both drinks to the table. "Wyatt told you he's not worried, right?"

"Of course. But should he be?"

Earl smiled. "Not about that lot. Judgmental bunch, and hardly anyone can stand them. You might give old Loftis an excuse to spout fire and brimstone for a few Sundays. And if you need anything from the pharmacy, send me to get it, because old Fred's not famous for keeping his yap shut. But put them out of your mind."

Wyatt walked in just then. As usual, he'd worn jeans and a gray sweater to court. Amber was surprised she hadn't heard him enter the house. "Put who out of her mind?" he asked.

"A couple of Loftis's women showed up here and upset Amber. I'll deal with them. They won't come round again."

Wyatt's face darkened. "They'd better not, or they'll be dealing with me."

"Trespass," Earl said. "I'll warn 'em. Then I might even enjoy watching you have them arrested."

At that the cloud passed from Wyatt's face and he laughed. "That would be a pleasure." He joined them at the table with a mug of coffee and reached out to lay his hand over Amber's. "I'm sorry I wasn't here to take care of them for you."

"I'm not worried about me," she said again. "But if people are talking about you like that…"

He shook his head. "People might be curious, but most of them won't take that tack about you visiting me."

Earl sniffed.

Amber looked at him.

Wyatt said, "Let's not do that again, Dad."

"Do what again?" Amber demanded.

Earl looked a little sheepish. "Well, before you got here I was telling Wyatt it wasn't a great idea right before the election. People *will* talk."

"See," said Amber, jumping in before Wyatt could

respond, "I've got to leave. If I'd known you had this election coming up I'd have gone somewhere else."

Both men spoke simultaneously. "No."

She blinked. "No what?"

"You're not leaving." Again they both spoke, sounding like a chorus.

She wrapped her hands around the glass of water she'd barely tasted and looked from one to the other, trying to figure this out. "Okay," she said finally. "I get that this never concerned Wyatt, but why did you change *your* mind, Earl?"

"Because I was wrong to be concerned. I told you when we had dinner, I think it's better if you stay. And I'm right. I've been poking my nose around since you arrived, and most people think it's nice that Wyatt has a friend visiting. Almost nobody seems inclined to criticize him for it."

"But if those women…"

"Those women won't be listened to by anyone outside their poisonous little group." Earl shrugged. "And, as usual, most people just don't give a damn one way or the other. Might make a nice topic of conversation for a few minutes, but… Wyatt was right. It's just not a big deal."

"Told you," Wyatt said.

After all the tension she'd been feeling, she almost giggled at the smug way Wyatt said that to his father. Earl grinned at him.

"In fact," Earl said, "the whole seven-day-wonder aspect of this may already be wearing off. Ellie, though…" Earl shook his head. "She can't make up her mind which story to try to spread. After what she said a year ago when she and Wyatt broke up, there's not a whole lot she can say about you being pregnant by him. This is fun to watch."

"Just as long as those women don't come back to bother Amber, I'm fine with it."

Glancing at him, Amber thought she wouldn't want to have to deal with an angry Judge Wyatt Carter.

"Bah," said Earl. "Now look, Amber, I know you don't have a license in this state, but I sure could use a little help at my office. You can practice under my license, help with motions, research and so on. Say, Monday afternoon?"

Wyatt snorted. "I should have known you had an ulterior motive."

"What ulterior motive? I can use help, and this lovely lady is hardly going to be happy rattling around in this big old house all by herself while you're in court."

Amber didn't even have to think about it. "I'd enjoy that, Earl."

Wyatt smiled. At first she couldn't imagine why, then she realized—she had just committed to staying. At least for a while.

Oh, boy. She hoped she hadn't made a bad decision.

That evening after a dinner of Wyatt's homemade chicken soup, he suggested they take that walk the doctor had recommended. Amber liked the idea. Now that her stomach had settled, she wanted some activity. She'd been here for five days now, and all she'd seen were a couple of pretty streets, the courthouse and a diner.

Donning jackets, they stepped out into the cooling night. The last signs of twilight were fading over the western mountains and the streetlights cast golden puddles of light on the sidewalks and streets. The air smelled amazingly fresh. She could even detect sage on the gentle breeze.

"I should really show you around my town," Wyatt remarked, tucking her arm through his. "You haven't seen much of the good that keeps me here. A morning in court, a visit to a doctor and two women hell-bent on salvation…"

She giggled. "Do you realize how that sounds? 'Hell-bent on salvation'?"

He laughed quietly. "I meant it exactly the way it sounds. Most of the time that group is just a minor irritant around the fringes. People hardly pay them any mind. We may like our gossip around here, but few people are cruel about it. Anyway, our city police chief, Jake Madison, is married to Loftis's daughter, Nora. That got a little attention. And then one of Loftis's followers tried to poison some of the chief's cattle as an expression of his displeasure, so for a while they had everyone's attention. Then things settled down again."

The streets were quiet, inviting. Lights glowed from the houses, giving Amber a few twinges of loneliness. So much life behind those windows, maybe a whole lot of love, and she'd never felt more on the outside in her life, not even as a too-young student in college and law school.

"There's the library," he said, pointing to the instantly recognizable facade of a Carnegie library. "Emmaline Dalton, the sheriff's wife, has been the librarian there since she left college. Her dad was a judge, too. Anyway, if you hear anyone mention Miss

Emma, they're talking about her. No one knows when it started, but that's what everyone always calls her."

"Miss Emma. I like the sound of it."

"You'd like her, too. And the sheriff, Gage Dalton. Now there was an interesting story."

"Yes?" Her curiosity piqued.

"Back when he first arrived here, Gage was a loner, a complete unknown. All anyone knew was his face was scarred from burns, he had a wicked limp and he lived above Mahoney's Bar. Every night he'd walk into the bar, have a shot, then take a long, painful walk. People started calling him Hell's Own Archangel."

"Really? Wow. He must have looked awful."

"A little scary, too. Anyway, he eventually took a room with Miss Emma…she was running a boarding-house mostly for women. I never heard the details of why she rented a room to Gage. Anyway, it was just after I left for college, so I don't know much about it, but I heard he wound up saving her life. Then marriage followed."

"And Gage? What had happened to him?"

"He used to work for the DEA. A car bomb killed his family and he barely survived."

Amber thought about that as they continued to stroll. "I guess he would have looked like Hell's Archangel after that."

"That would be my guess. Things have changed for him since Emma, though. Anyway, he went to work for our old sheriff Nate Tate… I hope you get to meet him. An icon in this town. When Nate retired, Gage was elected to replace him."

Amber could almost feel the threads that knit this town together. She envied the people who lived here.

They had something she'd never had—a community and lifelong friends. All the while she'd been pursuing her parents' goals and then her own, it seemed she had missed a huge chunk of life.

"You're lucky," she blurted.

"Me? Why?"

"Because you live in a place like this. Oh, I get it isn't perfect. I met some of the imperfection this afternoon, but…you must know so many people, have so many friends, it's… Well, I've never known anything like this."

"It's not Currier and Ives," he warned her. "Plenty of warts to share around."

"I'm sure." She sighed. "I guess I'm feeling…adrift. And like I missed something important."

He didn't answer as they continued down the block and rounded a corner onto another tree-lined street. Here the wind had ripped most of the autumn leaves from the branches. Bare fingers stretching upward and outward. She refused to consider them skeletal.

"Must be awfully pretty in the spring when the trees leaf out," she remarked.

"You're welcome to stay and see."

"Wyatt! I can't put you out like that."

"Who says you'd be putting me out?" he answered quietly. "I like coming home to see you. I hated how empty that house was before. Anyway, where will you go? To your father?"

"Oh, God, no."

"A friend?"

She fell silent. When she'd needed a friend, whom had she called?

"I thought so. You can stay with me. I'm not being

a male chauvinist when I say a woman shouldn't have
to face pregnancy, birth and a newborn without some
emotional support."

Actually, the thought of facing all that alone had
terrified her when she allowed herself to think about
it. She was a strong woman, able to take care of herself in the man's world of the law, but this?

"Women all over the world have a community of
support," he continued. "You could have one here."

She glanced at the lamp-lit houses again and wondered if he could be right. If just a piece of that could
be hers.

"Amber?"

She turned her head toward him, trying to drag
herself out of the wisps of dreams that were probably
unattainable for her. "Yes?"

"Remember what you said about having a pretend
engagement?"

She almost flushed. "And you went all moral on
me."

"Well, I'm not much fond of pretense. But it just
occurred to me...you're about to have a baby without
a father. Don't kids need fathers? If you married me,
we could get you through this and I could help take
care of the child in any way you think best."

She froze in her tracks and faced him. "What about
pretense?" she demanded even as shock flooded her
all the way to her toes. She was going hot and cold
faster than she could believe.

"You suggested an engagement to end after the
election." He faced her, too. "Amber, there's no pretense in a marriage. It's real."

Her jaw dropped. Words almost deserted her. Her

heart hammered wildly. She had no idea how long it was before she could speak. "Have you lost your mind?"

"Maybe," he answered. "It just popped into my head. Not like it's something I've been thinking about. But now that it popped out…well, I could take care of you and the child. So think about it."

Think about it? With difficulty she turned and started walking again, but this was no gentle stroll. She strode quickly, and when he took her arm again, he kept pace with her. A marriage? All because she was having a baby?

God help her, it sounded like a solution to all her fears and worries. Which, she supposed, made her despicable.

Wyatt deserved better. Much better.

They didn't speak again until they were back inside the house. Wyatt was still trying to figure out what had caused him to blurt that without thinking it through beforehand. He wasn't usually the type. He was also worried about the apparent shock he'd given Amber. Damn, what had he been thinking? Even if he wanted to ride to the rescue, there ought to be some easing into a question like that. But no matter how badly he had brought the subject up, it was out there and he wasn't backing down. He'd be lying if he told himself the possibility hadn't crossed his mind more than once over the years. A fantasy, just a fantasy, but now it somehow felt *right*.

He urged her into the kitchen for a warm drink and suggested a few cookies. She merely nodded. Apparently she was still stunned. Maybe even working up to a good rage. She'd have every right. She'd offered a pretend engagement, he'd gotten on his high horse and embarrassed her, and now he was offering marriage out of the blue.

She must wonder if he'd gone mad. He was certainly wondering.

He settled her at the kitchen table with chocolate chip cookies and asked if she wanted her milk warmed. She simply shook her head.

Oh, man, next thing she'd be packing up to escape this insane asylum. First those women this afternoon, and now him. Really?

She drank half her milk while he downed a beer and waited for whatever was to come. Weirdly enough, he had no desire to withdraw his proposal, even though her reaction told him the thought had never entered *her* mind, unlike his. But the attraction he felt was strong enough that he was sure it could grow. Whether it became love, who could tell right now? He just knew he needed to protect this woman and her child in any way he could.

"You know," she said finally, "the other day you didn't want us to make love because I needed time to settle."

He almost winced, because it was true.

"Now all of a sudden I'm settled enough to decide whether to marry you?"

She had a point. When she started drumming her fingers on the tabletop, he braced himself.

"Wyatt, you're not a knight-errant. You can't go around acting like Don Quixote and expect any better outcome than he had. Maybe this seems like a perfect solution for my problems to you. I admit, it's attractive to me. But marriage? That's a hell of a commitment for both of us when I'm just in a spot of trouble. A temporary spot of trouble."

One thing he had to say. "A child isn't temporary, Amber."

"You think I don't know that?" Her voice rose a little. "I've been spending the last month trying not to think about how *un*temporary this is. How to deal with it. How to change my entire future to accommodate it. I've spent more time denying my pregnancy than planning for it."

He nodded, not wanting to interrupt her.

"You've already hinted that I'm not of sound mind right now. Well, what about you? What the hell are you thinking?"

He took a moment, closing his eyes and searching deep within himself. He rarely blurted things. Being a lawyer and a judge had taught him to be very considered in all he did and said.

But thinking back to when he'd first known Amber, he faced something else, something she needed to know, even if it was uncomfortable for him. He opened his eyes and looked at her, glad to see her color was returning. For a little while there she had appeared pale.

"Wyatt?" she asked.

"You know, back when we were in law school, I was really attracted to you. My dad and I both told you that. But I was eight years older, and you seemed like a lost lamb. No way was I going to take advantage of you. But if you'd been older, I'd have asked you out. And if we hadn't been headed in different directions—me to the navy and you to the big law firms—we might be married right now."

Her eyes had widened, and she drew several quick breaths. "What are you saying?"

"I'm just saying that we've been friends for a long time. That if things had been different back then, we might have become more than friends. Honestly, I've even thought about it more than once. But now we're here."

"And once again you want to protect me," she said sharply.

"No," he said levelly. "I want to take care of you and this child. There's a difference. Anyway, marriage would guarantee that you'd be cared for even if something happened to me. You and the child. Who else am I going to take care of, Amber?"

Her face changed and he wished he could read what had suddenly made it so soft and sad all at once. "Just think about it," he said. "Like I said, marriage is real. This would be no pretense. You can tell me in the morning. If you say no, I'll never mention it again. And now you know the last of my secrets. I've always hankered after you."

Then he rose. "I need to go do some work. Come get me if you need anything."

The walk to his office, his ears straining to hear her call his name, seemed a lot longer than usual.

But she never called his name.

Amber ate a cookie absently, hardly tasting it, sipping some milk to wash it down. What in the world had possessed Wyatt? He said he wasn't concerned about the election. Maybe those women earlier today? Maybe he felt he needed to protect her from any more of that kind of attention? But wasn't marriage an extreme solution?

Then she remembered what he'd said: marriage was real, not a pretense. That he wanted to care for her and her child. That he'd sometimes thought about it in the past. So he meant it. But why?

Sure, she'd been attracted to him in law school. She'd had no idea back then that he reciprocated. None. He was always a perfect gentleman with her. Of all the men in law school, he was the last one she would have thought felt any sexual interest in her.

Had it lingered over the years? Apparently. When he'd kissed her, he'd said he'd wanted her all those years ago. So maybe having her back in his life—and not just at the other end of a phone call or email—had awakened those feelings again. They'd certainly preserved their friendship. Why not the rest of it, especially since it had never been expressed?

But marriage. That was such a huge commitment. He said he liked finding her here when he came home. He'd said something else, too, and it had tugged at her heartstrings: *Who else am I going to take care of?*

There was such loneliness in those words. Reaching for another cookie, she bit off a small piece, trying to focus on just that one thing. Wyatt was thirty-seven, maybe thirty-eight now. That was young in this day and age. But maybe he was longing for a family to fill this house, and maybe after Ellie he'd felt too burned to start over again with another woman. Or maybe there weren't a lot of prospects around here.

Regardless, the loneliness of those words reached through all her preoccupation and touched a part of her she'd thought would remain frozen forever. After

Tom, she'd told herself she wanted nothing to do with a man ever again. They were liars and cheats.

And then there was Wyatt, in a class by himself. He'd *always* been in a class by himself. Unfailingly honest and upright. If Wyatt said he'd do something, you could count on it. If he made a promise, he kept it. All these years he'd been a sort of touchstone for her, keeping her straight when the twisting paths of the law might have led her to take some turns that, while not illegal, would have made her ashamed later. And how many cases had he helped her think through over the years?

A good sounding board, a good friend and now... while he said he wanted to do something for her, she felt he needed something *from* her.

Rising, she walked down the hall to his office. The door was open. He turned at once from the papers in front of him. "Yes?"

"Tell me all about Ellie, Wyatt." Picking up the beautiful shawl he'd lent her, she seated herself on the comfortable chair and wrapped the delicate tatting around herself.

His brow furrowed. "Why? She's in the past."

But Amber thought she was very much in the present. That woman had wounded him deeply. Maybe as deeply or more deeply than Tom had wounded her. Certainly deeply enough that he was considering marriage to her. It wasn't the same as asking a total stranger to marry him, but the years had still flowed down the stream with the two of them apart, and did emails and phone calls make up for face time?

"I loved her," he finally said. "Or at least I loved

the woman I thought she was. Who can tell the difference? But it's over."

"Except that she's evidently still mad at you, according to your friend Hope. Maybe it's not over."

"It is for me," he said flatly. A spark appeared in his eye. It seemed he didn't like being questioned as if he were on the stand. What judge would?

She could have laughed if she hadn't been so concerned about him. And herself, too, but right now he was at the center of her worries.

Then he said something that struck her deeply. "I can honestly say that I think I know you better than I ever knew Ellie. All the conversations over the years… I know your moral compass. I know a lot about what drives you. I think you know me as well. Marriage is always a risk, Amber. Nobody can honestly promise that the vows will last forever, that the love will last forever. I see it in my courtroom all the time. So love isn't the only reason to get married. In fact, there may be better reasons."

She had to admit that was a novel idea to her. At least he wasn't trying to persuade her that he was in love with her. She wouldn't have believed it. In lust? Oh, yeah, they both were. But that was a long way from love.

"Anyway," he said, "I'm not withdrawing my offer. It might benefit us both…or not. Think about it. I could have us married by noon tomorrow, we could have a long engagement or we could just continue as we are for as long as you need and want. Your decision."

Which did nothing at all to help her parse through what had happened. What had propelled him to this offer? She looked at him and realized he was studying her, almost drinking her in. She could see the hint of passion in his expression, and her own body responded to it. Maybe if they just answered that need, everything else would become clearer.

But she knew one thing for certain—she didn't want him to take her under his wing the way he had during law school. If they were to move forward in any direction, she had to be an equal.

Oh, God, this was all a mess. He was a natural caretaker. A natural knight on a white horse. She'd seen it before. But she wasn't some helpless miss who needed rescuing. Yes, she needed help at the moment, and he was providing it. But that wouldn't be forever.

But right now...hell, it sounded so good to her. And she knew it would help protect him from the ugly gossip. Oddly enough, she wanted to take up her lance in his cause as well. She wondered if he even guessed that.

She almost smiled. Two knights-errant, charging forward. Each wanting to help the other.

Maybe he was right. Maybe there were better reasons for marriage than love.

"Sorry," he said finally. "I told you just to think about it. I'm not trying to pressure you one way or the other."

"Assuming *arguendo*," she said, using a lawyer's familiar Latin term to indicate a hypothetical, "that we marry. You've told me what you'd like to give me in terms of security. But what exactly would you expect from the arrangement?" She hoped she sounded clinical, because she was feeling anything but. Marriage. While it terrified her, it also meant that they'd share a bed, something she'd wanted to do with him for a long time. An old desire that had been growing larger since her arrival, despite everything else.

He steepled his fingers beneath his chin and regarded her steadily. "I'm going on thirty-eight years old. I live in a small town where there aren't any marital prospects that have caught my attention. Ellie's been the only one, and that was a helluva mistake. Then there's you. I think we'd have a chance to build something that would last. And frankly, Amber, I'd really like to have a family. The older I get, the more I seem to want it. Not that I'm trying to pin you here. I mean, I get that you might want to go to a practice elsewhere, but that doesn't mean we couldn't still have time together, here or wherever. The point, I guess, is that I'm sick of a solitary existence, and you and I have been friends for such a long time…well, I'd like to keep you rather than lose you. Like I said, I've always wanted you. That hasn't changed. I'd like to give it a try."

She thought over what he was saying. Wyatt, ever logical and truthful. He'd admitted he was lonely. Her trip here had awakened feelings long left behind for both of them. Whether they were enough…

She knew one thing for certain, though. Desire was muddying these waters. They'd both think more clearly once they'd satisfied it.

Without another thought, she rose from the chair, dropped the shawl and went to sit in his lap, twining her arms around his neck.

"So, Wyatt," she said quietly, "make love to me now."

He didn't reject her, but wrapped his arms around

her, holding her close. Then, gazing into her eyes, he said, "Why? Why now?"

"Because the smoldering between us is getting in the way of rational thought. I want to be sure neither of us is considering this for the sake of sex."

He continued to study her face, as if he were looking deeply into her being. She felt her heart racing, her breaths coming rapidly, her body turning into warm honey. And through it all an almost painful hope and expectation. Like teetering on a cliff edge, not knowing if she'd fall or find solid ground, but ready to fly.

He leaned in, taking her mouth in the gentlest of kisses. She let her head tip back, begging for more as her heartbeat seemed to strengthen in every part of her. Her thighs instinctively clamped, trying to find the answers she didn't yet have.

Then, slowly, gently, he eased her off his lap. Disappointment crashed through her, and her eyes began to burn with unshed tears.

"I'm going to lock up the house," he said quietly. "My bedroom is at the far end of the hall from yours. If you still want this, meet me there."

Crashing disappointment transfigured into amazing exhilaration and nervous hope. Yes. Oh, yes. She turned and headed for her room, filled with anticipation.

Chapter Nine

Wyatt didn't move for several minutes. He closed his eyes and considered what he had done and what he was about to do. It had seemed like such a logical solution for both of them: both of them lonely, her in trouble, him lacking things he wanted, a marriage that could give them both what they needed, at least right now.

Love didn't guarantee a successful marriage. Nothing could. So marrying for other reasons wasn't necessarily any riskier.

He had feelings for her, he just didn't know what kind. Protective, yes. Friendship, yes. Love? Who knew? It seemed too soon.

Oh, hell, he thought, rising. She was right. Once they'd made love, things should become clearer one way or another. The smoke would turn into fire, then die down.

Maybe then they could both really decide what they needed, and not just what they wanted.

It was crazy, all right, but even Wyatt Carter sometimes did crazy things, like racing a motorcycle around windy mountain roads, like off-roading in his ATV a little too fast. Like going to Afghanistan with the JAG as an investigator, a task for which he'd been required to take quite a bit of field training. He'd volunteered for that one.

So for all he presented a staid facade, there was a bit of wildness in his nature, and he guessed it was exerting itself now.

Shaking his head, he checked the few doors and windows that might have been opened at some point, then headed up to his room, half hoping that Amber would be there, half dreading that she wouldn't.

It was as if a puzzle from long ago was about to be completed. Maybe all these years part of him had been waiting for this woman. Who the hell could tell now? But he also knew from experience how rarely reality lived up to the dream.

This could destroy everything they'd managed to keep over the years. One way or another, it was certainly going to answer a question they'd both apparently had for a very long time.

Amber wasn't in his room. He looked down the long hallway and saw her closed door. His insides squeezed with disappointment. He seemed to remember that *she* had been the one who had sat in his lap and asked for lovemaking.

Sighing, telling himself he was overreacting to what was probably a good bit of common sense on her part, he stripped and stepped into his large private shower, washing the day away with hot water.

Oh, hell. He'd been ham-fisted about everything. Where were the hearts and flowers? The dating? The romantic interludes that were supposed to lead up to this? God, his offer had been so *logical*. What woman wanted a marriage proposal that sounded more like a merger?

Then, when he should have swept her into his arms and made passionate love to her on the rug, on the sofa…he'd coolly collected himself, mentioned locking up and told her to come to him if she still wanted this.

Cold-blooded. Stupid. Trying to give her space to change her mind, but he doubted she wanted that space or she wouldn't have so boldly sat on his lap.

As he toweled off, he wished he could kick himself. Wyatt Carter hadn't always had the temperament of a judge. Yeah, he'd never been one to leap easily into the deep end about anything, but this? These were the actions of a cold fish. Was that what he'd become? Hiding behind walls of restraint and logic? Because he seemed to be hiding.

He hadn't been like this with Ellie. Had she really scarred him so deeply that he'd locked his heart away?

Damn, he needed to apologize to Amber. If she hadn't felt offended before, she was probably rapidly getting there.

With a towel wrapped around his waist, he stepped out of his bath into his bedroom, and the first thing he saw was Amber. She stood there in a yellow terry-cloth robe, her hands fisted in the pockets.

"Amber…"

"Wyatt…"

They both spoke at once.

She immediately fell silent. Her chin was up, but this woman who had spent years wending her way through tough law firms and tough cases looked very uncertain right now.

He cussed.

"Wyatt?" She blinked. Well, of course, he didn't swear often, and never *that* word.

"I'm sorry," he said. Then he crossed to her, tugged one of her hands out of her pocket and drew her to the edge of his bed. "Please sit."

She did, then he sat beside her, reclaiming her one available hand.

She waited, looking at him.

"I just realized I handled this all poorly," he told her. "I offered marriage like a contract, and when you wanted to make love I sent you on your way while talking about locking up the house. In the romance department I get a great big goose egg."

She shook her head a little. "I didn't ask for romance. At least I don't think I did."

"Well, you deserve it."

She astonished him then, her expression becoming almost ferocious. "I had enough romance for four months, even if it was only over lunch hour. Flowers, candies, fancy foods, the finest hotel and promises of a future. I was dazzled, all right. Look where it got me. All of that can be faked. I don't trust it. You were honest. You gave me an option and you didn't conceal it in roses. If you had, I wouldn't have believed you."

Surprise rocked him again.

"I'll bet," she said more quietly, "that Ellie made you feel the same way. I know you're capable of the romantic part. You could do it if you wanted. But it's all… I don't know. Not as real as what you said to me today, at any rate. You were honest. That allows me to be honest. Thank you."

He certainly hadn't expected this, but he admired it. "Somehow I should have handled this better," he said, repeating his earlier thought.

"But how?" she asked. "We're friends. We're honest. You don't need to woo me, and I don't need it. God, Wyatt, I have a crying need for honesty. Just honesty."

He could understand that. He rather needed it himself after Ellie. But still…

She went on. "Maybe our courtship has been happening over ten years. I don't know. But you did absolutely nothing wrong today, and I want you to understand that. Believe it. You offered me what seemed like a perfectly logical solution to the problems I'm facing, to the things you want in your life. What the devil could be wrong with that?"

Plenty, he thought. "You asked if I'd gone mad and called me Don Quixote," he reminded her.

She flushed a bit. "Well, if you were dashing to my rescue alone…yes. But if there's something you need in a marriage…well, then it might be mutually beneficial."

Again he had the feeling that this was too damn clinical. They were both being cold about something that shouldn't be cold. Except treating this as a problem to be solved seemed to be the only place either of them could go comfortably.

Sighing, feeling as if they needed to find a way to break through to real emotions, the places they had both locked away, he drew her down on the bed beside him and wrapped his arms around her. He felt good when she hugged him back. Raising his hand, he stroked her dark hair.

"You're beautiful. You always have been."

"I'm older, and sometimes it shows."

He smiled faintly. "Not to me. You've grown into a marvelous woman. Maybe I'm glad I waited all these years."

She caught her breath then smiled. "There's that romance."

"It's true," he said. "Some things are well worth waiting for. I've been waiting for you forever."

She wiggled a bit and brought her mouth to his, giving him a butterfly kiss. "Let go, Wyatt," she breathed, closing her eyes. "Let the passion out."

Now it felt right, he thought, then utterly gave up thinking as he loosened the belt of her robe and tossed his towel aside. As he pushed the terry cloth back from her body, he found she exceeded his dreams. One would never have guessed from the clothes she chose to wear just how perfect and generous her figure was. She concealed it well, and probably deliberately, for professional reasons.

But she proved to be a cornucopia of delights to explore. Bending over her to kiss her again, plunging his tongue into her mouth, he began to run his hand over her, from behind her ear, which made her shiver, then down over her smooth throat.

"Oh, Wyatt," she breathed, and to his delight he felt her hands begin to caress him.

Yes, the time was right. Then long-denied passion swamped him.

* * *

Amber felt a wild, demanding urge to strip away all the restraints from this man. She wanted to see the raw side of Wyatt Carter, not the judge, not the lawyer, not the mentor. She wanted the part of him he had cloaked so carefully over the years.

She never doubted it was there. She had occasionally caught flashes of it, quickly tamped. She ran her hands over his shoulders, reveling in his smooth skin and the surprising strength she felt there. This was not a man who spent all his time at a desk or on the bench. She could feel his muscles bunching as he leaned over her, pillaging her mouth with a hunger that amazed her and then swamped her.

So good, she thought hazily. No kiss had ever felt like this, no tongue had ever been so welcome inside her mouth. Then he pulled his mouth away, and a mewl of protest escaped her, only to be silenced as his lips and tongue trailed downward, following the line of her throat as shivers ran through her, then trailing lower toward her breast.

She caught her breath, but he held her suspended in anticipation as his tongue trailed slowly, deliciously over the mound, avoiding her nipples. Just when she thought she could bear no more, he found one engorged nipple. The brush of his tongue over it felt like a lash of fire, and the flames ran straight to her center, deepening the hungry ache there. She needed…had she ever felt such need?

Surprising her, he moved suddenly, turning her one way then the other as he yanked the robe from her. No gentleness there, and she wanted none. When she reached for him, he caught her hands and pinned them to her sides.

"You're mine tonight," he muttered.

His. Oh, yes…

His mouth trailed lower, running over each rib and lower to just above the thatch between her thighs. Then back up it trailed until it found her other breast. This time it was no lash of the tongue. He drew her deeply into his mouth, sucking on her with a power that was almost painful, a power that seemed to want to draw her all the way inside him. Helplessly, her hips rolled, but he ignored the silent plea.

Just when she thought she could bear no more, he moved his mouth again, brushing a kiss on her lips, then slipping slowly downward. He never released her hands, holding her prisoner to his wishes, holding her prisoner to his desires and her own needs.

In taking control from her, he left her feeling strangely free, like a soaring bird. All she could do was experience whatever he chose to give her.

She gasped when he flipped her over. He caught her hands over her head and began to sprinkle kisses over her back until he reached her bottom and kissed her there. The sensation was so exquisite, so new, so exciting that moans began to escape her.

He took liberties with her, teaching her new things about her body, and she loved every sensation. Then he released her hands, and just as she thought she was about to become an active participant, he lifted her hips and slid into her from behind. She cried out with pleasure as his erection stretched her, filled her, answered the need that seemed to have always been there. Then his hand slipped around in front and cupped her, his fingers spreading her and teasing that hypersensitive nub of nerves.

She felt utterly possessed, utterly beautiful, utterly wild as he pumped into her from behind and lifted her higher and higher until her entire body felt as taut as a bowstring.

She hardly heard her own moans, in thrall to the roaring waterfall of feelings that was sweeping her away into unknown territory.

And then, in an instant, she arched, almost hurting as the orgasm ripped through her from head to toe.

He didn't give her long. Didn't allow her to collapse. Before she felt the descent to peace, he'd rolled over, bringing her with him, lifting her until she straddled his hips.

"Ride me," he said hoarsely.

His hands gripped her hips, guiding her until he once again filled her. She threw her head back, thrilled, feeling the tension building in her all over again. His hands urged her on until the rhythm became perfect. The ache in her rose impossibly until she shattered in satisfaction.

And this time she felt him join her, felt the sheer delight of him jetting into her, pumping more strongly, then finally easing until he drew her down on his chest.

Amber couldn't move a muscle. She rested on Wyatt feeling as if the last strength had been drained from her, but also feeling more content than she ever had in her life.

She never wanted to move again. Never before had she felt what Wyatt had just made her feel. Never. She wished it never had to end.

But finally, as the perspiration on her body began to dry, she felt chilled. Almost as if he sensed it, Wyatt lifted her easily to the side of the bed. Then he sat up and tugged her gently until she followed him to the bathroom.

Once there, he turned on the water in the shower then held her close, saying nothing, his face in her hair while she buried hers in his shoulder. After a few minutes, he reached out to test the water, then drew her into the large cubicle with him, putting her right under the comfortably hot spray.

She opened her eyes and saw him smiling at her, an almost wistful smile. Without a word, he began to soap her from her shoulders to her feet. She spared a moment to be grateful the enclosure was so big, because she wouldn't have wanted to miss a single sensation.

Each silky sweep of his hands and the bar of soap seemed to refresh her and excite her anew. When he had done both sides of her, taking his time, he turned her to face him, and now his smile was wider. "Feel good?"

She took the bar of soap from him. "Let's see."

He was a magnificent man, she thought as she ran her hands all over him, admiring the strength of his arms and shoulders, the power of his chest, the narrowness of his hips. Feeling a bit wicked, she spent some extra time on his privates until finally his hands reached for her head.

"Witch," he said. "Stop."

She laughed and did as he asked. After all, there were still his perfectly formed legs. When he turned around to let her soap his back, she paused.

"Wyatt? This scar…"

"I was in Afghanistan for a while," he answered. "It wasn't the safest place on earth."

"You never said!"

"I wasn't allowed to."

The thought disturbed her, driving away the growing net that desire had been casting over her. He faced her immediately. "It's okay," he said, then pulled their slick bodies together for a deep kiss.

It was over. He rinsed them both and then stood her on the large mat while he briskly toweled her dry. He gave her an extra towel to wrap around her wet head and grabbed one to tuck at his waist.

"I'm sorry," she said.

"For what?"

"For breaking the mood. I shouldn't have said…"

He laid a finger over her lips. "You didn't do anything wrong. No apologies, please. We just spent some time in heaven. Unfortunately our feet have to hit the ground again."

She nodded, knowing he was right but hating it anyway. She wanted that heaven again, wanted to never let go of it, no matter how unreasonable she was being. Summoning a smile, she decided to keep that to herself.

She didn't want him to feel bad, not after what he had given her.

She wrapped herself in her bathrobe, and Wyatt donned his own, a rich burgundy color that suited him. Together they went downstairs.

"I have a theory we need to try," he said.

"Which is?"

"That maybe if you eat something before you go to bed the morning sickness won't be so bad."

"I'm willing." She balanced the towel that was still wrapped around her hair.

"That's going to make it hard to sleep tonight," he remarked as he saw the gesture.

"I *do* have a blow dryer," she said wryly.

"Then let me do it for you after we eat."

He pulled out the toaster, suggesting they stick with toast and jam. "Who knows when morning sickness starts, but we're getting close."

She looked toward the digital clock on the microwave, and surprise jolted her. "Where did the time go?"

"I think we were having a good time." He winked, enjoying it when she blushed faintly.

"A very good time," she agreed huskily. "The best time ever."

Man, did that make him feel good. He could identify with a conqueror of old. He busied himself making the toast, hating the interruption but hoping she'd feel better in the morning if she didn't wake with a completely empty stomach.

At last he was able to put a stack of toast and a selection of jams on the table, along with a glass of milk for her. Instead of sitting across from her, however, he sat right beside her.

Much as he'd wanted her all those years ago, he wanted her more now. He hoped to God he hadn't just made a big mistake that would hurt both of them.

Conversation had died away. Far from wanting to talk, it was as if the haze of desire was growing around them again, making speech difficult as thoughts ran along racier paths.

After he got a couple of pieces of toast into her, he guided her back upstairs. "Get your blow dryer," he said. "You'll sleep with me tonight?"

The expression on her face made his heart skip a couple of beats. "Of course," she answered softly.

Yeehaw, he thought. Better than racing around mountain curves at high speeds on his motorcycle. Better than anything.

She brought her crackers, too, and soon he had her sitting in the rocker near the bed, running her brush through her hair as he used the dryer. She'd never worn her hair long, so the job was easy. Soon her bob was sleek and smooth again.

"That was a treat," she said when he switched off the blow dryer. "Do you do this often?"

"I've never done it before for anyone."

He came around to stand in front of her, smiling and holding out both hands. "Sleep," he said. "You need it."

"If we can," she retorted, making him laugh.

Naked, they crawled under the covers together, and soon Wyatt was spooning Amber from behind. He would have made love to her again, as passion rebuilt in him throughout every cell, humming until he felt he was connected to an electrical circuit.

But it was late. The digital alarm clock warned him in red numbers, and the doctor had said she needed her rest. So he kissed her hair and the nape of her neck, murmuring, "Sleep, Amber. There's always tomorrow."

It was a promise he wondered if he would be able to keep.

* * *

Curled up with her back against Wyatt, Amber allowed the good feelings to flow. It seemed like almost forever since she had last felt anything approaching this happiness and contentment. Even during the first heady days with Tom, she was quite sure she had never felt like this.

Wyatt had satisfied her at levels Tom had never even tried to reach, and then afterward, instead of bundling her on her way, he had taken care of her needs, from a shower to food.

The years collapsed, and she remembered Wyatt as he had been in law school, extremely attractive, wonderfully confident and always helpful and kind. He'd been remarkable then, and from what she'd seen, the years had only made him more so.

He was blessed with a judicial temperament, and she wondered if the people here had any idea how fortunate they were to have him on the bench. She'd seen enough judges in her day to tell a good one from a bad one.

But as he'd shown her, he was also full of passion. Wyatt cutting loose was magnificent.

She smiled into the dark and wiggled backward a little to get closer to him.

"Keep that up and there won't be any sleep," he mumbled.

She smiled into the dark, but a heaviness began to fill her, too. She couldn't remain Wyatt's dependent forever, and while he had offered marriage, she was sure he hadn't thought it through. To be father to another man's child? Maybe he could. But it remained, she had to build a future for herself, and there didn't seem to be a whole lot of opportunity for law-yers around here.

She pushed the sad thoughts aside, however. There was always tomorrow, as he'd said. For now she just wanted to cherish the glow.

Chapter Ten

The instant she sat up in the morning, nausea washed over Amber.

"Oh, God," she said and flopped back down.

Wyatt was still beside her. He raised himself immediately on an elbow, looking down at her with concern. "I take it the toast last night didn't help."

She swallowed hard. "'Fraid not."

"Crackers?"

"Give me a minute."

It had been lying in wait for the moment she moved, she thought irritably. She'd opened her eyes, seen sunlight flooding through a crack in the curtains and she had smiled as memories of last night flooded her. Then, because she needed to answer the call of nature, she had sat up.

Morning sickness had pounced on her like a cat

on a mouse. Now she was afraid to move, but she still needed to get to the bathroom.

"Crap," she muttered.

"Conflicting needs?" he asked, as if he could read her mind.

"Yeah."

He rolled out of the other side of the bed and came to perch right beside her, reaching for the box of crackers. He passed her a single cracker. "Try this while I get you some water to wash it down."

It felt so wrong to be eating a cracker in bed. Crumbs. But Wyatt hurried into the bathroom to get water, and she obediently nibbled the dryness, hoping it would help. She didn't want to get sick all over his bedroom rug, but there was something even more embarrassing likely to happen if she didn't move soon.

He was back with the water before she had finished half the cracker and perched beside her again. "When you're ready, raise your head as far as you dare."

She shoved the remainder of the cracker into her mouth and chewed. It seemed to stick in her throat, so she lifted her head to sip water and immediately regretted it.

Her head flopped back on the pillow.

"Wyatt…"

"I get it. Hold on a sec."

He grabbed a wastebasket from the bathroom and returned waving it. "In case," he said cheerfully enough. "Now let's get you on your feet. Don't worry about a thing."

He helped her out of bed. Her stomach roiled so much that she hardly cared they were both naked as jaybirds. With his arm around her waist, the wastebasket in front of her, he guided her into the bathroom and helped her sit. He put the basket in front of her feet.

"I suppose," he said, "you'd like privacy for this."

"Yup," she said, forcing the word out.

He closed the door, leaving her alone with her misery. God, this was awful. Was it this bad for most women? How many more weeks...

But eventually she got the cracker all the way down, with the help of the water Wyatt had left on the edge of the sink. Even just that little bit helped enough to make it possible for her to stand.

Embarrassed by her own weakness, she eased back into the bedroom. Wyatt was waiting patiently, still standing. "Okay?" he asked.

"A little better."

"Then how about we get you wrapped up and downstairs for some dry toast or fresher crackers."

He helped her into her robe and slippers, then pulled on his own. This time he didn't hold her hand as they went downstairs but kept her arm tucked firmly through his as if he was afraid she might fall.

"I know I can't help it," she said, "but this is embarrassing anyway."

"Why? Apparently it's perfectly normal. I've even heard that it's a good sign. Regardless, this is the last thing that should embarrass you."

In the kitchen—which had a tile floor, thank goodness—she reviewed her own situation with something between irritation and amusement. It was bad only at the very first, she admitted. Once she got a little something in her stomach, it eased, not totally going away, but it eased enough for her to carry on. She supposed she should be grateful for that.

But the idea that she might feel like she had a borderline case of stomach virus for weeks didn't appeal to her.

"God," she said finally.

"What?" He was brewing coffee and making toast.

"This is disabling."

He turned to study her. "How so?"

"Well, while this is going on, I can hardly pop into my car and move on. I'm not sure I'd interview very well, as ill as I feel most of the day. I mean, it's not intolerable except for first thing, but I can't ignore it. I feel sick."

He brought some of the toast and coffee to the table. "Milk?"

"Not yet," she answered.

"Okay." He sat across from her. "First of all, you don't have to hit the road. I thought I'd made that clear. You'll get past this. Maybe it won't be this bad after a while. Regardless, just take it easy until you feel completely fit again. Then you can make your decisions."

Not that she was in a hurry to go anywhere. She looked at the dry toast and wondered if she could handle it. Especially since last night. But being dependent rankled. She'd never been dependent before.

She also noticed that Wyatt hadn't mentioned his proposal again. Was he just giving her space or regretting it? After last night, she'd hate to think he wished he'd never offered marriage. As shocking as it had originally seemed, after the lovemaking they'd shared, it didn't feel shocking at all. She wanted to play with the idea, think about it, imagine a future being married to him before she made up her mind.

But if he was no longer interested…

She sighed.

"Penny?" he said.

She put her chin in her hand, arguing with herself. If she brought up the proposal, he might feel stuck. If she didn't mention it, she might never know. Was it so important that she know? He could always bring it up again.

"Oh, heck," she said finally. "Your proposal. Would you like to withdraw it?"

"I thought I'd made it very clear last night. I don't leap into the sack with just anyone. The proposal stands. Why? Are you thinking about it?"

"Of course I'm thinking about it," she snapped. "How could I not think about it? It's like telling me to ignore the elephant in the room."

"Hmm," he said, then a twinkle came to his eyes. "The elephant? I like elephants, but I'd also like my proposal to be a bit more attractive than that."

"Oh, hush," she said.

"Besides, you're feeling pretty bad this morning. Not a time for thinking about much except getting through this."

Except she *was* thinking about more than her morning sickness. Last night still flooded her senses and her mind. This morning his proposal sounded almost irresistible. At the same time, she had to decide from a position of strength, not weakness. It wouldn't be fair to Wyatt to use him as a life preserver when she felt she was drowning.

"Amber? Just put it aside for now. My offer isn't going away, so take your time, decide what's best for you, okay?"

She nodded, but she was honestly beginning to

wonder what was best for her. She'd been pursuing one goal for so long, and last month when she'd resigned from the firm, she'd felt her life had been totally upended, her prospects now limited. Partly because she'd have a child, but partly because leaving a firm after six months, no matter how good a recommendation they'd give to make sure she didn't cause any trouble, still looked bad. Large law firms didn't want to hire someone who might leave so quickly. There was just too much to learn about clients, and most such firms expected a lawyer to remain for many years, if not for the rest of their lives.

She had made herself look flighty, and everyone she sent a résumé to would wonder what was wrong with her.

She'd been wrecked the whole time she'd packed up to leave. But always at the back of her mind, little as she'd wanted to think about it, was the child growing inside her. Ninety-hour weeks were now out of the question. Even if she could afford a nanny for all those hours, at some level it struck her as wrong. If she brought a child into this world, she owed it more than material support. Much more.

And some wistful little corner of her mind had been pressing her more and more with a desire to see the first steps, hear the first word, enjoy the first smile. Yes, working women had to turn to day care. She got it. But not for ninety or a hundred hours a week.

She bit into some dry toast and washed it down with water. It stayed down, although it didn't cure the remaining nausea. "So we're having a party tonight?"

"Not exactly. Just a few friends I thought you'd like to meet. I can cancel it if you want."

"Let me think about it. I'm not antisocial, it's just..." Just that she didn't want to sink any roots in this place. Not when she was at least half-sure she'd have to leave.

But she *had* enjoyed meeting Hope and Julie. It would be nice, if she were here a few more months, to know some people she might be able to pal around with occasionally. She certainly wasn't used to long, empty days, and Wyatt still needed to work.

"I'm not used to having nothing to do," she remarked.

"Me, either," he agreed. "Well, Dad has said you can work with him if you want. And you're welcome to come to court with me when you feel well enough. I'm sure there's more than enough work to go around. Too bad you don't have your Wyoming bar license. We could sure use a pro bono public defender around here."

It was a fact that while the Supreme Court had said all accused persons were entitled to a legal defense, most places underfunded public defenders compared to prosecutors.

"I don't know criminal law," she remarked.

"You could learn fast. Or you could get into family law. Regardless, you'd have to see about licensing. If you're still licensed in Missouri..."

"I am."

"Then Wyoming offers reciprocity."

She nodded. That would make things easier. Far easier. No miserable bar exam to repeat. "I'll think about it."

And she would. She hadn't been in Conard City for long, nor seen much of it, but she already liked it here. It struck her as a friendly place to live, a good environment to raise a child.

There she was again, thinking about her child. She guessed it was sinking in at last, perhaps made real by her morning sickness. About time, too. She wasn't an ostrich by nature, although recent events with Tom might leave that an open question.

She realized she'd eaten half a piece of toast and was feeling somewhat better. "Thanks for the toast. It's working."

Wyatt smiled. "Good news then."

"Do you need to work today?"

"No. I've still got some papers to review before Monday, but that won't take long. As for tonight, I ordered up a bunch of deadly sins from the bakery, so all I'll need to do is make coffee and tea. In short, I'm all yours for the day. Is there something you want to do?"

"Walk around town," she said. "I'd like to get to know this place better."

Wyatt was agreeable, but he figured once she looked around and saw how little there really was here, she'd probably be checking out cities again. After all, her whole life had aimed that way. Now she was in a tiny town, which showed movies only on weekends and where the biggest entertainment was plays at the college or the county fair. Or dancing at one of the roadhouses, which could get a bit risky when the cowboys got frisky.

Yet, it was better she know exactly what she was looking at if she thought about staying here. He was sure the PD's office would keep her really busy, as would working part-time for his dad…or even getting her license and joining the Carter practice. But however accustomed Amber was to working around the clock seven days a week, a person needed more in her life. Here she'd have enough free time to look for other things, for herself and her child.

He hoped she wasn't horrified, because after last night he'd have offered her marriage all over again.

He'd have liked to offer her love as well, but he didn't think it was there. Not yet. And he was far too old to mistake passion for love.

"We can walk around this end of town when you're ready," he said. "Later I'll drive you a bit. It may be tiny, but if you want to see everything, we'll need wheels. Too bad I won't put you on my motorcycle in your condition."

He enjoyed watching her jaw drop and her eyes widen. "You have a motorcycle?"

"A big black hog. I'm dangerous on mountain roads."

Laughter escaped her, and finally she had to wipe her eyes. "Wyatt, you'll never cease to surprise me. I never would have imagined you with a motorcycle."

He wiggled his eyebrows. "I am not what I seem."

"Apparently not."

He enjoyed her laughter and the smiles that followed. It wasn't long before she felt well enough to go upstairs to shower and dress.

A good morning, he thought. He just hoped the town didn't disappoint her.

The midmorning air was a bit chilly, whispering of winter's approach. The trees were mostly bare, although here and there patches of autumn color remained. Only a block over from his house was a park, and since it was Saturday it was full of young children and their parents. Amber paused, smiling as she watched them. The parents knotted together on various benches, keeping one eye on their children while they chatted. She loved it.

New urges were stirring in her. She wanted to be one of those parents on the bench watching a small child and talking with friends.

Man, she'd never seen herself that way before, but she was seeing it now. When at last they turned away and walked down another pleasant street, she wondered at herself. Was this the result of changing hormones, or was she just facing that a lot had been missing from her life, and now she wanted it? How could she know?

Their talk was desultory. He told her stories about the town, about its past, about things he remembered and things he'd heard about. There was a time when someone had been dumping toxic chemicals in an arroyo on a ranch. The time a devil-worshipping cult had tried to make a sacrifice of Miss Emma. Other stories, each of them almost a warning that as peaceful as the place appeared, it wasn't always so. They'd had a serial killer, an arsonist…all the bad types of people who existed everywhere.

Yet still the town felt quietly and contentedly settled. Not even the economic hard times that came and went could break up families and friendships.

Amazing.

People nodded and smiled as they passed, some waving from their front porches. Front porches. She'd almost forgotten they existed. A few others out walking paused briefly to chat with Wyatt and to be introduced to Amber. Then they hurried on because it was

Saturday and they had errands. Catch-up day, Amber thought with amusement. True everywhere.

When they got back to the house, Wyatt insisted she eat something. It was easy now; the nausea had died down to almost nothing, so she joined him in a liverwurst sandwich.

After lunch he drove her out to the community college campus, a hive of activity, much of it occurring on sports fields. Then back through town with its small businesses, and a stop at the bakery to pick up the goodies for tonight.

"Next weekend," he said, "I'll take you up into the mountains, and maybe to a friend's ranch."

"I'd love that." Another week. The urge to move on was rapidly vanishing.

"When we get home," he said, "maybe you should consider a nap. I was warned to make sure you get your rest. You certainly got your walk."

Since Amber seemed strangely reluctant to go off by herself to nap, Wyatt took her upstairs with him. In a minute he'd smoothed the sheets and coverlet still rumpled from the night and encouraged her to lie down on top of the covers with him.

She'd be asleep soon, he thought, but in the meantime he was only too happy to hold her close, stroke her hair and back, and listen to her breathing slow and deep. She *was* tired, more tired than she had probably thought, but she didn't want to be by herself. Didn't want to leave him behind.

That tugged at his heart. This woman was essentially all alone in the world. He got it. It was probably meaningless that she was clinging to an old friend, but he liked it anyway. Liked knowing that the lovemaking they'd shared last night had only made her feel closer to him. There was no more reluctance on her part to reach out and touch him. She'd done it dozens of times today, just casual touches, but they hadn't been there before.

Inevitably, he wondered if he'd be able to keep her. And inevitably he realized he couldn't. As far as he knew, this was not the kind of life that Amber had ever wanted for herself. The baby, leaving her job... those were temporary hitches he was certain she was smart enough to deal with in a way that pleased her.

He didn't fit into that equation, although he was still surprised that she'd brought up his proposal. He'd expected her to act like it had never happened.

It had sounded so cold-blooded, so calculating. *Here's what you need, here's what I want, so let's make a deal.*

Damn, that got uglier the more he thought about it. Forget his intentions. He wasn't even sure he remembered what had moved him to make the offer. But what he knew now was that it hadn't been pretty.

It had been a moment of wildness on his part. He was prone to them from time to time and had spent a lot of his life learning to temper the impulse or direct those moments safely.

Now he'd done the wildest thing of all, and he disliked himself for it. Amber had enough on her plate without him leaping on to join the load.

But last night... He sighed and snuggled her closer, drawing a murmur from her even as she slept. All unconsciously she wound her arm around his waist. It felt so good he closed his eyes.

Maybe it was time to give some serious thought to

exactly what he was doing here. He'd been winging it since the moment she'd told him she was in trouble. His only thought had been to give her a place to stay while she sorted her life out.

Any friend would do that. But not just any friend would offer marriage, and certainly not the way he had. Not just any friend would take her into his bed and unleash a new craving, stronger than any he had ever felt before for her. Stronger than any he had ever felt in his life.

He'd messed up. Earl would be delighted if he knew. On the surface, at any rate, he thought Wyatt was too sedate and straitlaced. Needed to kick up his heels more. A funny attitude from a dad who was equally worried about his "judicial decorum." What did he expect Wyatt to do? Travel to another state and have a fling?

Which, thought Wyatt wryly, was probably what at least part of this town was already thinking he'd done.

A couple of hours later, noises from outside woke him from his doze. Wyatt eased carefully away from Amber, trying not to wake her, and went to look out the window with the street view.

Hell, it looked like Loftis's ladies were out in force. He was being picketed, by God. They waved handmade signs with words like *Sinner* and *Abomination* on them. He decided that was enough.

He straightened himself quickly, running a brush through his hair, tucking his flannel shirt into his jeans and jamming his feet into his boots.

Time to deal with these jerks. He didn't want them

bothering Amber, and he had guests coming in a few hours.

On the way downstairs, he called the dispatcher for the sheriff's office and police department. In this town they were one and the same.

He got Velma, old as the hills, and her ragged smoker's voice. "Velma, Wyatt Carter. I'm being pick-eted by some of Loftis's people."

Velma snorted. "Probably no law against it, but Jake and Gage will find a way."

"Or I will," Wyatt said. He was, after all, a judge. And while sidewalks were public property, his lawn wasn't. However, being a judge, he knew the limits of what he could do, and as much as he'd like to erupt at these women, he figured he'd only make it worse. Time for some of that damn judicial restraint, despite his annoyance.

"You hang on, honey," Velma said. "I'm rousing the troops."

He wondered what troops she meant. A deputy or two?

As soon as he stepped out on the front porch, the picket line of maybe ten women grew louder, shouting various ugly condemnations his way. He was a sinner, an abomination and some other things he didn't bother to really hear. He went to the edge of his porch and stood, folding his arms, simply staring at them.

Presently, their shouts began to trail off as his continued silence and inaction began to make them uneasy. When they became quieter—although not completely quiet—he raised his voice to be heard.

"Ladies, while you're free to protest on the public sidewalk, it's incumbent on me to warn you that you are disturbing the peace. You can be arrested for that. I suggest you protest quietly, especially since this is a residential neighborhood."

Well, that didn't work. Now he heard shouts of how he was violating their constitutional rights. It was all he could do not to grin. Most people didn't realize that there were time, place and manner restrictions on the First Amendment, allowed by the Supreme Court. They'd have done better to protest in the courthouse square.

Some of his neighbors had come out on their porches and waved to him. He didn't wave back. He wasn't going to do a thing to encourage these women. All he could see was that this might convince Amber to move on, and he didn't want that.

So he stood, keeping his arms folded, and simply stared. He didn't want to provoke trouble, but he was going to make it absolutely clear that they didn't intimidate him in the least.

Then the sound of approaching engines and flashing lights caught his attention. He looked to his left and saw a sheriff's cruiser, flanked by a city police car, coming down the street. Between them they blocked all traffic.

Then, to his utter amazement, he saw a small crowd behind them. *What the...?* When Velma had said she was going to call out the troops, he hadn't expected a counterdemonstration. Now he almost wanted to laugh.

The two police cars came to a halt just before they reached the line of women on his sidewalk, and Sheriff Gage Dalton and Police Chief Jake Madison climbed out.

"Howdy, Judge," Gage called. "Just here to ensure everything remains peaceable."

"Thanks, Sheriff."

Then from the other direction came two more cars, county and city. A whole section of street was now effectively blocked.

And into that section of street poured the crowd that had followed Jake and Gage in. Oh, this was priceless, Wyatt thought, trying not to grin. Outnumbered by the dozens of people on the street, the women on the sidewalk began to look uncertain.

Wyatt came down from the porch while a few voices from the street told the women to go home. One elderly man, leaning on a cane, spoke angrily. "You women go home and mind your own business, not everybody else's!"

Smothering a laugh, Wyatt ignored him and walked up to the women on the sidewalk.

"Ladies," he said, "you really should go home. Even though the sheriff and the chief are here to keep you safe, with this many people around, there could be a slip, which might cause trouble. Consider your message received."

"What are you going to do about it?" demanded one of the women, her gaze fiery.

"The right thing," he said, then stared her down.

"You'd better watch your step," she spat.

Gage Dalton, only a few feet away, asked mildly, "Was that a threat?" The woman clamped her mouth tightly shut.

"I don't feel threatened," Wyatt said easily. "These ladies are just doing what they think is right. But let me make something perfectly clear," he said, raising his voice a bit. "Do not trespass on my property or harass my guests. I *will* file charges. You've been warned."

Looking at once afraid and furious, the women stormed off down the sidewalk and around the corner to wherever they'd come from.

The crowd in the middle of the street clapped and whistled, and Wyatt walked out among them to thank them. He knew all of them to one degree or another, and he shook a lot of hands and received a lot of claps to his shoulders.

God, it felt good. Dozens of people had dropped everything to come help him out. His love for his community nearly overwhelmed him.

Wanting to thank them, he invited them in and broke out the treats he'd picked up at the bakery. So much for his small gathering tonight, but he knew his friends would understand.

Then, after he started the coffee and teakettle, he ran upstairs to check on Amber. She was standing at the window in his bedroom, and when she turned there was a smile on her face.

"Quite some show, Judge."

"I had a lot of help from my friends."

"I saw. I heard you, too. You were quite restrained under the circumstances."

He shook his head. "I didn't want to be. I don't want those biddies bugging you at all. But I couldn't see any point in making it any worse."

She walked toward him, right into his arms. Their lips met in a kiss he never wanted to end, but after a minute she pulled back a bit. "I hear a party downstairs, and as much as I want to tumble in bed with you..."

"It would be rude of me." He gave her a squeeze, cupping her rump to lift her up against him briefly, and dropped another kiss on her lips. "Come down if you want to. They're great people."

"I actually saw that." Her smile was wide.

God, he hated to leave her, but there was no escaping the fact that he'd just opened his house and he had no doubt the crowd was going to grow. His neighbors, then others who heard about it. Dang, he should have made a ton of chili anyway.

As it happened, a potluck was soon taking place. It filled his front porch and yard and spilled into the backyard, where there were tables and chairs. Soon there was even music.

He paused by Gage, who was eating a sandwich someone had brought. "And to think I warned those women about disturbing the peace."

Gage laughed. "This is a different kind of disturbance. All your neighbors are here."

And then some, Wyatt thought, looking around. It was beginning to look like a super-size block party. Kids were running around having a good time, their elders were knotted together in chatting groups and some folks had gotten folding tables from his garage and set them up as a buffet.

He held gatherings like this from time to time, but he'd never before had one create itself. Thank goodness he had a large house and yard. And out front, Gage and Jake had left the street blocked off, making it safe for everyone to cross and kids to run heedlessly back and forth.

"Don't you mind them biddies," the old man with

the cane said as he passed by with a plate full of sweets. "They don't influence anyone but themselves."

With a nod, he moved on.

"That was Harry Jenks, wasn't it?" Wyatt asked. While he knew almost everyone by sight after all these years, there were an awful lot of them, and apart from his friends he was mostly inclined to remember people who came before his bench.

"Believe so," Gage answered. "He was in town for some reason when he decided to join the party. You know his son, though. Keith Jenks, the rancher."

"Indeed I do. But I don't see Harry often."

"Doesn't come into town much anymore. I think he's glad he was here today."

Wyatt laughed. "I get that impression."

Gage faced him. "I know you have an election coming. I hope you're not worrying about it. It's in the bag, Wyatt. Folks think you're a good judge."

"Thanks, Gage, but I haven't been worrying about it, which seems to be driving my dad crazy."

Gage snorted. "Earl's good at that when it comes to you, I've noticed. Good thing he moved out of the house. You'd never have been able to breathe."

It was true, Wyatt thought. Earl had become a lot more enjoyable when they weren't sharing a roof, and while he still poked his nose into Wyatt's affairs, it wasn't nearly as bad as a few years ago.

Just as he was beginning to wonder if Amber had decided to sit this one out, she appeared on the back porch dressed in fresh jeans and a blue sweater. Before she could come to him, she got swallowed by a group of women he knew well: Hope Cashford, with a child on her hip, Julie Archer, swelling with her first pregnancy, and Ashley Granger, the fourth-grade school-teacher. The only ones missing from their little coterie were Connie Parish and Marisa Tremaine. A group of inseparable friends, they drew Amber in among them.

"Gage?"

"Yo?"

"Where's Connie? Is she on duty?"

"She got off forty minutes ago. Should be here soon. Why?"

Wyatt shrugged. "She and Ethan were on my guest list for tonight. Just a small gathering. She accepted, so I expected to see them."

"Small gathering?" Gage repeated. "That got all blown to hell." Then he gave his crooked half smile. "Now I gotta find out where my wife went." He limped away to look for Emma.

Wyatt circulated, pausing to chat briefly with everyone but working his way slowly around to Amber. At least she appeared to be enjoying herself. But that was a good group of ladies, and he'd hoped she might find some friendship with them. For however long she was here, she needed people besides him. That was just natural.

The cause of the party was nearly forgotten as everyone turned their attention to having a good time. Wyatt figured that was probably a good thing. Those women might have been a nuisance, but he didn't want anything stirred up against them. Sure, nobody much cared for that group, but most people were willing to live and let live.

He almost froze when he saw Ellie. What the devil? Why in the world would she have come here? He started to change directions, but she called out his name loudly enough that it carried over the conversations around him.

In an instant the cacophony quieted a bit, and he suspected people were waiting to see what happened. Slowly he turned.

"Ellie," he said quietly. Conversations in the immediate vicinity died even more. This was the downside of small-town life. There probably wasn't a person here who didn't remember him dating this woman.

He hoped she didn't make a scene, because he'd had quite enough. Her lies, those women out front, Amber being troubled by both Loftis's women and Ellie…yeah, he'd had enough. If she said the wrong thing, there were going to be words. Words he didn't want to say, because they were nobody else's business.

Just then, he felt an arm slip through his. Looking to the side, he realized that Amber had joined him and was smiling. "Hi, Ellie," she said. "It was nice of you to drop by the other day."

Oh, boy, Wyatt thought. *Here we go.* He saw the spark in Amber's gaze and understood that she was ready to go to battle on his behalf. Funny, he'd always seen himself in the role of protector, and now here she was assuming the mantle.

Reaching across his body, he laid his hand over Amber's, where it rested on his arm.

"Yeah, thanks for welcoming Amber to town, Ellie," he said. "I don't know if I ever told you, but we've been friends since law school. I've been looking forward to sharing my town with her."

Whatever Ellie had intended, he'd apparently defused it, because while her eyes narrowed, she said only, "Nice to meet you, Amber," then quickly moved away.

"Good job, buddy," said a familiar voice, and he turned his head to see Connie Parish. Quickly he introduced her to Amber, only to learn that Connie's other friends had already done so. "So, Wyatt, the gals and I want to take Amber out tomorrow afternoon, show her around a bit. After she feels better, of course. That okay?"

"Why wouldn't it be okay?" he asked, smiling. "I barely started introducing her to Conard City. I'm sure you gals can do a whole lot better."

"And enjoy some time away from family demands," Connie added wryly. She winked at Amber. "Pick you up around one?"

Amber smiled back. "That would be great."

As they resumed strolling through the crowd, stopping to pick up some finger foods, Amber said, "I feel like I'm surrounded by a squad of protection."

"You are," he answered. "You definitely are." And if he had anything to say about it, she was going to stay that way.

"This is a great party, Wyatt."

"Not exactly what I'd planned," he admitted.

"So I heard. But any place that can rustle up a potluck and party this fast…well, I'm impressed."

He caught her smile and saw that for the first time since she'd arrived, it didn't hold even a hint of shadows. For just this little while, Amber was free of everything and happy.

He just wanted her to stay that way.

Chapter Eleven

They made gentle love that night, very gentle, but Amber was tired and didn't take it amiss when Wyatt encouraged her to sleep.

It had been quite a day, she thought. She'd seen a lot of the city, she'd watched Wyatt defuse what could have turned into an ugly situation and there'd been a big party and even an encounter with Ellie.

As she drifted off to sleep, she appreciated just how interesting this town could be. And how full of surprises.

In the morning she was nauseated again, but it didn't seem quite so bad. She didn't have to go racing to the bathroom; just took her time eating crackers and sipping water until she felt she could rise.

Wyatt remained with her in case she needed anything, but when she felt over the worst, he headed downstairs to make breakfast and leave her to dress.

She thought over the day before again and actually smiled while she washed and donned fresh clothes. She wondered how much of a mess might be left downstairs. Everyone at the party had helped with cleanup, but she was sure at least some of the mess had been overlooked.

It had been fun. Much better than the formal parties she was used to attending, and she'd met loads of nice people who talked about things besides the law and business. This town was definitely growing on her, even the warts like Ellie and those women who had picketed Wyatt.

She almost giggled remembering it. Picketing him? Seriously? It seemed so extreme and so pointless. Truly over-the-top. And while she had at first been concerned for Wyatt, it had been no big deal for a lot of other people who had stayed to party. Just one of the quirks of this place.

Keeping in mind that she was going out with her new girlfriends that afternoon, she put on a good sweater and slacks. Truth to tell, she'd have loved to just stay here with Wyatt, but it would have been rude to turn down the invitation from the gals, as they called themselves. Besides, she shouldn't become too reliant on Wyatt. At some point she was going to need to go her own way.

Then she plopped on the bed as she remembered his proposal. He hadn't withdrawn it. But sitting there, she felt the urge to accept it growing stronger. That didn't seem fair to him. Didn't he deserve something better that a woman who was taking advantage of his protection? A woman whose career goals...

Oh, heck, what career goals? The last month or so

had given her plenty of reason to reconsider her entire future. She didn't want to go back to working for a big firm. Not anymore. So what did she want?

Maybe she owed it to herself and Wyatt to figure it out. Only when she was clear about that could she fairly decide such a momentous question for both of them. Or even just for herself.

She'd felt run over, smashed, by all that had happened. Then she'd turned her attention to just getting the hell out and away. Now she'd been here for a week, settling in, discovering that making love to Wyatt was even better than she had dreamed, but she still hadn't faced up to what lay ahead. She could either let life happen to her again, or she could make it happen.

Well, partly anyway. She knew that chance affected everyone in life, like the extremely remote chance that she would get pregnant while using birth control. But when you could take charge, you should. Not doing anything was a decision all by itself.

Wyatt had made some scrambled eggs with cheese for breakfast, and there was a stack of the inevitable dry toast if that was all she wanted. Given that her queasiness didn't seem quite as bad, she took a tablespoon of the eggs and tried them cautiously, aware that Wyatt watched her.

After she swallowed he asked, "Okay?"

"I think so."

He grinned. "Then dig in. I made plenty."

"So do we have much to clean up after last night?"

"Not a thing. My friends were especially nice, but the trash collectors are going to wonder at all the bags in the alley. Well, actually they won't, because they'll have heard if they weren't here." His dark eyes seemed to twinkle.

"People are going to hear a lot about yesterday, I bet." She glanced at him. "What in the world do you think Ellie intended to do?"

"I haven't any idea. Maybe nothing. Or maybe she decided that wouldn't be the best place to make a scene. It's even possible she's giving up her vendetta. It's probably hard to get anyone to listen after all this time."

She smiled, remembering. "You sure handled that smoothly. Your old friend from law school. Hard to come back with a stinger on that one." She looked at him again. "You handled all of yesterday wonderfully."

"I kind of had to, given that I'm a judge. It wouldn't have looked good if I'd erupted at those women and chased them down the street."

She bit her lip, holding in a smile. "Did you want to?"

"Hell, yes. Judicial temperament goes just so far. Underneath that robe is a mortal man, and I was angry. I don't care what they think of me, but I don't want them bothering you. Not at all."

She let the smile slip past her guard. "It was so over-the-top, Wyatt. Honestly, they didn't worry *me*. I was thinking about you but finding it so ludicrous. Who pickets for those reasons?"

"The Loftis gang. Gage got some of it two years ago when he was up for reelection."

"What in the world for?"

Wyatt shrugged. "They resurrected his old nickname. I told you. Hell's Own Archangel. That went away nearly a quarter century ago, but for some reason… I don't know what motivates them, Amber. Sometimes I think Loftis just stirs these things up to keep the group cohesive."

"Your dad advised me not to go to the pharmacy. He said he'd go for me if I needed anything."

Wyatt nodded slowly. "Or I will. Sometimes I'd like to put a gag on that man."

"Now that definitely wasn't judicial." She let laughter escape her and soon he joined her.

"The man behind the robe," he said in a deep voice, like an announcer. "His secrets, his failings, his…"

"Wonderfulness," she interrupted. "Of course you're human. I've seen some judges get pretty human on the bench. My favorite, though, was the one who snored his way through my closing argument."

"No!" He broke out laughing.

"Kid you not. I just kept going because I was talking to the jury anyway, and the bailiff looked almost frantic. He couldn't decide whether to wake the man or let him sleep. He probably figured he'd be in trouble either way."

"I hope not. Did you ever get an apology from the judge?"

"No, but he didn't need to apologize to me. I think the jury deserved that. Well, it *was* a boring case. The jury probably wished they could nap, too."

"Did it last long?"

"Weeks."

He nodded. "Even my longest-running cases rarely last more than a day or two. It's one of the reasons I like being a circuit judge. Always something fresh, even if I've seen it a hundred times before."

"Now that's a contradictory statement," she teased.

"But true. Different people make each case different, even if the applicable laws are the same."

"Unending soap opera?"

"Sometimes. Almost. I hope I never get so bored or burned out that I don't see the individuals, just the cases."

Then he paused and looked straight at her. "What about you? Are you settling? Feeling any better emotionally?"

After two nights in his arms, of course she felt better. But that wasn't what he was looking for, so she poked around inside herself, testing for the sore places.

"I'm not numb or furious anymore," she said slowly. "I'm not even sure I'm embarrassed that I was such a fool."

"Hard to be embarrassed by being conned when you look at what people were doing out in front of my house yesterday." He winked.

She laughed a little. "Point taken. I'm glad I came here. I spent a month stewing in my own juices, running around inside my own head and feelings. No room for anything else, and no room to start letting go. But since I came here... Thank you, Wyatt. It's all starting to feel different. I screwed up, but it's not the end of the world. Sometimes now I can even think about the baby and actually look forward to it. That's a big change in a week."

"I'm glad to hear it. Take as long as you need." He reached across the table and squeezed her hand. "The most important thing to me is that you find yourself again and decide what you want from life."

"Marriage?" she said lightly. At least she meant it to be light. Instead the one word seemed to suck all the air from the room.

His gaze grew intense, his hold on her hand tightened. "Are you proposing now?"

She pressed her lips together, suddenly in the midst of a whirlwind of uncertainty. Was that what she really wanted? He couldn't possibly be in love with her. He'd never even hinted at such a thing.

But as he'd said, there were other good reasons to marry, and love was no guarantee of success.

He didn't seem to expect an immediate answer, though. He released her hand and leaned back in his chair holding his mug of coffee. "I'm not pressing you. Take your time. But I'm also not withdrawing the offer."

How weird, she thought. Not bad weird, but still weird. He'd offered her marriage to take care of her and the baby, come what may, but the part that stuck in her mind was that he wanted a family. And from that she had understood that despite knowing hundreds of people around here, despite having an important and satisfying job, he felt lonely. What was missing? The intimacy of a live-in companion? A child?

She hesitated. "Your mother died when you were very young."

"Yeah." He tilted his head a little. "Are you going to psychoanalyze me? I'm sure it affected me, but it's not driving me. I made peace with it a long time ago."

He did seem awfully well balanced. Shaking her head a little, she sighed. She'd been too sheltered, she guessed. When life had decided to pull her shelters, it had done so in a big way all at once.

Now she was going to be a mother. Day by day, as she finally allowed herself to get used to the idea, that seemed to be the most important thing in her future. A mother.

What would have happened to Wyatt if he hadn't had a father to look after him? Gazing at him, she almost felt her heart stop. He was such a contained man. He had once referred to himself as staid, but she didn't see him that way at all. As he had said, he was human like everyone else, and she'd tasted some of his wildness when they made love the first time. She had also, over the years, seen flashes of anger in him, usually about an injustice. He felt, and felt deeply, but he didn't wear his heart on his sleeve.

So what had happened to make him so controlled? Certainly not simply the practice of law. No, he'd probably developed that a long time ago…maybe after his mother had died. He'd had to soldier on somehow.

She didn't want to pick at those scabs or demand he drop his guard. That wouldn't be kind. But she didn't think she was reading him wrong. Life had made him a rock. A rock she had leaned on before. A rock she was leaning on right now.

But a lonely rock. Did she make him feel less lonely? He'd said how nice it was to come home and find her there. Maybe it was the simple things he most lacked. Maybe that had prompted the proposal. Concern for her, certainly, but also a need of his own.

For the first time in a while, she was considering someone else's needs before her own, and she acknowledged once again that she had become quite selfish. Her parents had made her the center of their universe, and maybe in the process she'd started to think of herself that way. At least until she'd been scalded by life. The thought had entered her mind before, but now it was burrowing home painfully.

"Wyatt?" She spoke before she could stop herself. "I may be the most selfish person you know."

His eyes widened. "What do you mean?"

"My whole life has been about me until just recently. You couldn't possibly find that attractive." Not after what Ellie had done to him.

"I think you underestimate yourself."

"Really?" She waved a hand. "I've spent most of my life thinking about me."

He shook his head a little. "I think you've spent most of your life thinking about your parents. What they wanted. Anyway, that doesn't make you selfish."

"Sure it does. I moved myself and all my problems into the center of your life, upsetting everything, maybe risking your election. Did I ever once ask if this was convenient for you? I should have been able to take care of myself."

"Whoa," he said, a long, drawn-out breath. "Easy. Since you got here you've been worrying about me, even though it's not necessary. And if you remember, *I* was the one who suggested you come here. You never asked."

"No, I dumped. I didn't have to ask. I knew you'd come riding to the rescue if you could. That was unfair of me."

"So? You needed help. What are friends for? And I rather like the idea that you felt you could trust me to help. What kind of man would I be if I didn't?"

Well, she'd had experience of the other kind of man and didn't think that was a fair question. Maybe better to ask what kind of person he'd be. Silly quibble, though. As a lawyer with a love of very precise language, she had lately found herself in a place where that precision had little meaning.

She spoke, taking a risk, but needing to know. "What did you do in Afghanistan? I thought you were with the JAG?"

"I was, but not all cases happen here. I volunteered to investigate a mess involving some SEALs. They gave me some basic combat training before I went, but nobody expected things to blow up. Unfortunately they did." He made a gesture, as if pushing the subject away. "It's over and I'm fine."

Fine. "Kind of a wild thing to volunteer for."

"Someone had to do it." He shook his head. "It's a long time in the past."

Maybe so, but it told her more about him. Motorcycles and trips to dangerous places that he didn't want to talk about. He had his moments, too. That made her feel better. He wasn't perfect. But maybe most of his perfection had been created in her mind.

Thinking back she could remember his occasional impatience with people who made illogical legal arguments. He despised liars. It wasn't as if he hadn't shared frustrations of his own when they talked over the years. And some of his comments about one of the speakers at the last bar convention had been downright cutting.

So, okay, he was indeed human like everyone else. Somehow that eased her mind. What had she been doing? Turning him into some kind of superhero? Sheesh.

She could have laughed at herself. She looked across the table at him, feeling truly comfortable with him now, not inadequate in the way she had when she first arrived.

If she had been put through a blender in the last six weeks, she seemed to be coming out of it now. She was, indeed, settling down. Her mistakes didn't seem so big, and she no longer felt that surely Wyatt was way above her.

Obviously he didn't think so, but it was a little surprising to understand that she'd been harboring that feeling without recognizing it. He'd probably laugh if he knew, because she had learned that Wyatt didn't take himself that seriously. If he did, he wouldn't be wearing jeans and sweatshirts under his judicial robes. Ha!

She was so glad they had renewed their friendship, even if the circumstances weren't the best. Phone calls, emails, the rare meeting at a convention…none of those had served to cross the bridge of the years the way this week had. She finally felt as if they were meeting as equals, all the detritus from the law school years swept away. She no longer needed to see him as someone awesome and unattainable.

But she still thought he was pretty awesome. She smothered a giggle, because she didn't want to have to explain it to him. Didn't matter, anyway. When she'd needed a safe harbor, he'd welcomed her.

And now…now they could move forward, possibly together, possibly not, but he'd given her the space to become ready to take her first few steps in that direction.

Pretty amazing guy.

When the women came by to pick up Amber a while later, Wyatt waved goodbye from the porch then went back inside to his office. He had some work to do, but his thoughts kept straying to Amber.

He hadn't been fair to her by offering her marriage. He would have kicked his own butt if he could have. She needed to regain her strength and independence, not become reliant on him. Sure, it had seemed to make sense, and he wasn't going to withdraw the offer, but he'd feel better about it if she didn't decide it would be just an easy escape. He knew she'd thought of that. For one brief moment it had showed on her face. But only that once.

Thank God she hadn't leaped. This was one case where his help might have been harmful. He certainly ought to know better.

But by the same token he was a man of his word. He'd made an offer and said he wouldn't take it back. He just didn't want it to become a way to cripple Amber.

Sitting there, he had an urge to take his bike up into the mountains while Amber was out. Ride fast and ride hard to clear the cobwebs from his head.

Without another thought, he called Connie's cell and told her he was going to be out for a few hours. He'd leave the house unlocked for Amber.

After he disconnected, he thought he should give Amber a key. He should have done that when she first arrived. Shaking his head at himself, he ran upstairs to don his leathers and biker boots. Ten minutes later he and his bike were in the driveway. He put on his helmet and revved the motor.

The deep thrumming of that magnificent engine always satisfied him at some deep level. Moments later he was motoring carefully down the streets. Soon he was on a back road headed for the mountains, feeling free and happy, throwing caution to the winds.

As speed and dangerous curves forced him to concentrate on exactly what he was doing, his subconscious went to work. And out of nowhere he realized he might be making a mountain out of a molehill.

There was no reason that a proposal to Amber needed to be this complicated. He'd asked. She was an adult who could reach her own answer.

What he needed to do was stop worrying about all of it. He'd given Amber a haven, hers to do with as she pleased. He needed to drop his guard with her, and he just needed to settle back and enjoy whatever life brought his way.

Because it had brought something pretty amazing his way the past week.

"Just be grateful, jerk," he said, his voice bouncing back at him from his faceplate. *Just be grateful and let life flow.*

The girls introduced Amber to yet another member of their group, Marisa Tremaine, while they sat at tables that had been pushed together for them at the diner. Maude, the owner, was her usual grumpy self, but she didn't seem to mind the space the women took up, or the fact they were drinking bottomless coffee and tea. A different kind of friendliness, Amber realized. Maude's diner was evidently also a hangout.

Mostly she listened to the other women talk. They seemed so happy, laughing often and smiling constantly. They shared bits of their lives with complete comfort.

"Trace is back in DC," Julie Archer said at one point. "I wonder if he's ever going to be done with the hearings and investigation." She turned to Amber. "My husband still works at one of those alphabet soup agencies. He's trying to retire."

Marisa spoke. "Mine did, too, same agency. He managed to get away, though." She laughed quietly. "He's called Ryker, Amber. You'll like him."

As much as she liked all these women, she suspected she would like their husbands as well.

Ashley gave an exaggerated sigh. "I'm the only spinster among us now."

Julie grinned. "Maybe some alphabet soup guy will land on your doorstep, too."

"I can wish," Ashley said. She turned to Amber. "When you live in this place all your life, you know everyone. Or at least every eligible guy. I've tried most of them. Now I want a big surprise."

Amber had to laugh, because it was obvious Ashley wasn't really feeling sorry for herself. In fact, she said quite enough to convince Amber that she was happy with her life as it was.

"Tied up in a big bow," suggested Julie.

A peal of laughter escaped Connie. "Just make sure I don't have to arrest him for nudity."

Ashley giggled. "Actually, tied up with a bow sounds more like getting a dog. I'd like a dog."

"So get one," said Marisa, and soon they were discussing the relative merits of breeds and the possible complications of trying to work with no one at home to look after a pet.

"My kids want a dog," Connie said. "Begging constantly. But with Ethan and me both working? I don't know if that would be fair."

"A cat," suggested Marisa.

Amber listened, smiling, enjoying the free flow of conversation among these women. But all too soon they grew aware of the time and the need to get home.

"Next week?" they asked Amber.

"I'd love it."

Soon enough she was dropped off at the front door. Connie had told her that Wyatt had gone out but left the door unlocked for her. She climbed the steps, hoping he was home. His car was there, after all.

Just as she put her hand on the knob, however, she heard the distinctive rumble of a motorcycle coming down the street. She turned and saw a man in black leather riding a black Harley, his head totally concealed by a black helmet.

Oh, be still my beating heart, she thought when the bike turned into the driveway. Wyatt? She hoped so.

He brought the bike to a halt near the end of the porch and pushed his visor back. That was definitely Wyatt smiling at her. Her heart sped up immediately.

"Hey, Amber," he said easily. "Go on inside. It'll take me a few to park the hog."

She waited briefly, however, enjoying the sight of him until he maneuvered the bike into the garage. Only then did she go inside to await him. She even started coffee for him, figuring that if he'd been out riding for a while he might be a bit cold.

It was high time, too, she told herself, that she started helping with some of the chores around here. He cooked every breakfast, and she couldn't take that over as nauseated as she felt in the mornings, but maybe she could prepare a dinner or two when he was working the entire day?

Then Wyatt entered by way of a side door off the mudroom behind the kitchen, still in his leathers but without his helmet.

Her heart once again slammed into high gear as she spoke. "Do you have any idea how scrumptious you look right now?"

He grinned. "I like the sound of that. So leather turns you on?"

"When you're in it," she admitted.

His smiled widened and his eyes sparkled. "Then I'll wear it a little while longer."

Crossing the room and rounding the island, he said, "Do I smell coffee?"

"I'm making it…" Then before she could say more, he caught her beneath her bottom and lifted her. She reached for his shoulders for support, and the two of them met in a sudden explosion of fire.

He kissed her until she was breathless, then lifted his mouth from hers. "Our problem," he said huskily, "both of us, is that we put walls around ourselves and our feelings. Much safer that way."

Still partly dazed, she blinked, clinging to his shoulders, loving the feel of his hard body against hers. "What…when…"

"We need to talk," he said, slowly lowering her to

her feet. She hated it when he let her go. "Things just suddenly got very clear when I was riding. Coffee?"

She shook her head, waiting while he poured. Then she made her way to a chair, certain she wasn't going to like this at all.

Because when did *we need to talk* ever precede anything pleasant?

Chapter Twelve

He brought her a glass of milk, then asked if she wanted to stay in the kitchen or move to his office.

"Office," she said immediately. He'd made it a cozy, welcoming room, and for some reason she felt that whatever he wanted to say to her would be easier to take surrounded by books, old wood and comfortable chairs. Not here in the harsh edges of his modern kitchen.

He let her lead the way down the hall. She took the armchair she always used, set her milk on the side table and picked up his great-grandmother's shawl, spreading it over her lap, staring at its brilliant colors as if that beauty would save her somehow.

Instead of sitting behind his mahogany desk, however, he pulled the other armchair closer and sat facing her, cradling his coffee in his hands. She waited nervously, wondering what he had to say.

"I've been slowly realizing," he said, "that since Ellie I've been in a kind of emotional stasis. Hiding out so nothing like that will happen again. I think you started doing the same thing since Tom. What we feel…well, we'll never really share it unless we pull those walls down, Amber. In fact, I think both of us have been building those walls for a very long time. I'm honestly not sure Ellie ever got behind them, even though I considered proposing to her."

She nodded and swallowed hard. She couldn't deny it. All her life a big part of her had been locked away for whatever reason. Because she was so on task trying to please her parents. Because her need for success wouldn't let anything else get in the way. Until Tom.

"In my case," he said, "I closed up after Afghanistan. Mostly. There are parts of me I absolutely won't share. It's a self-protective shell. I need to stay objective, levelheaded…and not just because I'm a judge. I need it for myself."

She nodded again. Oh, did that sound familiar. "I let Tom get through and look where it got me."

He looked at her with a half smile. "Yeah, we both picked wonderful people to lower our barriers with. So as I was riding today I realized that I'm hunkered down in my fortress when what I really want to do is live. Not saying I don't want to stay here or be a judge, but I'm not letting anything else into my life. I'm not living a rounded life. And my proposal to you was like a business offer because I can't get around these walls, and yet I was reaching out for something I need. So I offered a merger, which must have offended the hell out of you."

"I wasn't offended," she said. "Did I say I was? But I *was* shocked."

"Of course you were. I've been kicking myself ever since I did it."

Her heart slammed. Here came the bad news.

"I didn't handle it well, and I'm not proud of myself. Not at all. My dad told you I was sweet on you back in law school."

"Yes." And she'd felt the same way. She looked down, running her fingers over the shawl. "I felt the same way, Wyatt. So don't be embarrassed."

"I'm not embarrassed. I just look back at those days and think I was a fool."

That jerked her head up, her heart racing. "A fool? You were never a fool."

"Yes, I was. Because I had all sorts of good reasons for keeping our relationship purely friendly, but I ignored the most important reason in the world not to."

She caught her breath. "Which was?"

"That I was in love with you. Instead of coming up with reasons why it couldn't work, I should have been fighting to find ways to make it work. But I didn't. I gave you up simply because I thought it was right for you."

"You never asked," she whispered, her heart climbing into her throat.

"No, I never asked you what you wanted or how you felt. Which makes me a complete ass, I guess. But I didn't. I went my way, you went yours and I tucked away a whole lot of what was in my heart because I had myself convinced it couldn't be."

"Oh, Wyatt…"

"When I think of that wasted decade, I feel like

a double fool. And maybe I'm wrong. Maybe you wouldn't have wanted me enough back then to risk your plans and future. I don't know and you can't possibly know. It's just that after this last week I got that you've always occupied a huge place in my heart. You're already inside my walls. I might as well open the gates and let you the rest of the way in. Unless you don't want it."

He stood up, walking around the room, amazingly handsome and attractive in his leathers. She wanted that image always seared into her mind, whatever happened.

And she wished she knew what to say. She was amazed that he was saying he'd always loved her. Had she always loved him? She knew she'd wanted him, that the desire for him had never faded entirely away. That phone calls and emails had never been quite enough to content her.

During this week, she'd seen the Wyatt she had grown to care about in law school, but she'd also seen the man he'd become. Impressive in every way.

"Anyway," he said, standing still and facing her, "you're free to do whatever you think is best for you. I just wanted you to know that my offer of marriage was nowhere near as loveless as I made it sound. I've always loved you, Amber. But I don't want an answer now. Marrying me would upend everything you've ever wanted."

Like she hadn't already done that? But she knew what he was saying. He wasn't going to leave this town nor would she want him to. She had to decide if she was prepared to make a life here with him, if she'd be content with it simply because she had his love.

Her heart was already swelling with her answer, but she withheld it, closing her eyes and trying to think rationally about something that in the end was going to be very irrational. But she owed it to both of them to be sure she wouldn't become discontented.

"I can work with your father?" she asked.

"Didn't he say so? He'd probably love a partner since I failed him in that respect."

A small-town law practice, the exact opposite of all her dreams. But those dreams seemed so fruitless now, so dry and pointless. A small-town law practice would never make her a federal judge, but from the way Wyatt talked it would also rarely be boring.

"And my baby?" she asked, her heart squeezing. Now that the child had become real to her, she had to think about it, too.

"Would be mine. It's yours. How could I not love it? Biology isn't everything."

She felt the last of her own walls beginning to crumble, and only in feeling them fall away did she realize how much of herself she'd been denying all these years.

Then she asked the question that burst the tension in the room and made him laugh. "Are you going to explain this to my father?"

It felt so good to watch him laugh like that, the sound rising deep from within him. "Yes," he answered when he caught his breath. "Pistols at dawn if necessary."

Then she laughed, too, and certainty began to settle into her own heart. She put the shawl aside and rose, walking over to him. When she reached for him, he welcomed her, wrapping her in his arms.

She gazed into his dark eyes and felt as if a load had lifted and only joy remained. "I love you, too, Wyatt. I think I always have. Who would have ever thought that I'd be grateful I met a cad like Tom?"

He laughed again, but not for long. This day had changed him. He looked young and exuberant again… just as she was feeling for the first time in forever.

Then he brushed his lips against hers. "Is that a yes?"

"Yes," she said firmly. "It's yes, and yes, and yes. How soon can we do it? Because now that my dreams are coming true, I don't want to wait."

"Your dreams?" he repeated. "Are you sure?"

"These are the real ones, not the ones I was given."

He smiled, then swept her away with his kiss, his touch, his loving.

They were married the following Saturday. Wyatt had planned to hold the ceremony in the clerk's office with the magistrate, a good friend of his, presiding. But in no time at all their small party of friends grew, and finally they had to move into the courtroom to actually take their vows.

"Like the potluck party," Amber whispered to Wyatt.

She was beaming, he noticed. Just glowing. She'd wanted nothing fancy or special, had reluctantly accepted the loan of a white dress from Julie Archer, over which she wore his grandmother's shawl, and she swore all she wanted was him. He couldn't have been happier and gazed at his lovely bride with amazement. God, she was beautiful inside and out.

The courtroom was filled to overflowing, but Wyatt forgot everything as he stared into Amber's eyes.

When he said his vows to her, his heart lifted until it felt like a balloon.

Over fifty of Wyatt's—and now Amber's—friends stood up to applaud when the marriage was completed, and they stepped out into a sunny, pleasantly cool late-October day to find that while they'd been inside the entire square had been festooned in white balloons and crepe paper streamers, and that another potluck had been marshaled by folks who had waited outside.

The number of people amazed Amber. She looked at him with a smile. "I'm touched. And I think you're pretty much a shoo-in for retention."

He smiled out at all the people as they came down the steps. "It kinda feels that way." He squeezed her hand where it lay on his arm. For once the judge was wearing a suit. "I'm sorry the honeymoon has to wait."

"I'm not. I've got a whole new life to discover."

So did he, he realized, watching her adjust his great-grandmother's shawl with her free hand. A whole new side of life, anyway. Marriage. Fatherhood. But mostly love.

The circle of their friendship had completed, and it was wonderful.

* * * * *

Come back to Conard County
for Ashley Granger and Zane McLaren's story
in Rachel Lee's next book in the
CONARD COUNTY: THE NEXT GENERATION
series from Mills & Boon Cherish!

And catch up on previous installments:
AN UNLIKELY DADDY
A COWBOY FOR CHRISTMAS
THE LAWMAN LASSOES A FAMILY
A CONARD COUNTY BABY
REUNITING WITH THE RANCHER

Available now wherever Mills & Boon
books and ebooks are sold!

MILLS & BOON®

EXCLUSIVE EXTRACT

Pastry chef Gemma Rizzo never expected
to see Vincenzo Gagliardi again. And now
he's not just the duke who left her
broken-hearted… he's her boss!

Read on for a sneak preview of
RETURN OF HER ITALIAN DUKE

Since he'd returned to Italy, thoughts of Gemma had
come back full force. At times he'd been so preoccupied,
the guys were probably ready to give up on him. To
think that after all this time and searching for her, she
was right here. Bracing himself, he took the few steps
necessary to reach Takis's office.

With the door ajar he could see a polished-looking
woman in a blue-and-white suit with dark honey-blond
hair falling to her shoulders. She stood near the desk
with her head bowed, so he couldn't yet see her profile.

Vincenzo swallowed hard to realize Gemma was no
longer the teenager with short hair he used to spot when
she came bounding up the stone steps of the *castello*
from school wearing her uniform. She'd grown into a
curvaceous woman.

"Gemma." He said her name, but it came out gravelly.

A sharp intake of breath reverberated in the office.
She wheeled around. Those unforgettable brilliant green
eyes with the darker green rims fastened on him. A

stillness seemed to surround her. She grabbed hold of the desk.

"Vincenzo—I—I think I must be hallucinating."

"I'm in the same condition." His gaze fell on the lips he'd kissed that unforgettable night. Their shape hadn't changed, nor the lovely mold of her facial features.

She appeared to have trouble catching her breath. "What's going on? I don't understand."

"Please sit down and I'll tell you."

He could see she was trembling. When she didn't do his bidding, he said, "I have a better idea. Let's go for a ride in my car. It's parked out front. We'll drive to the lake at the back of the estate, where no one will bother us. Maybe by the time we reach it, your shock will have worn off enough to talk to me."

Hectic color spilled into her cheeks. "Surely you're joking. After ten years of silence, you suddenly show up here this morning, honestly thinking I would go anywhere with you?"

Don't miss
RETURN OF HER ITALIAN DUKE
by Rebecca Winters

Available March 2017
www.millsandboon.co.uk

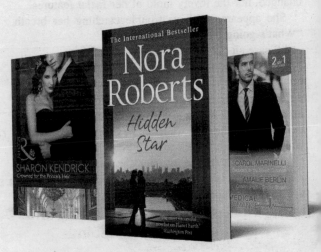